THE
HUNTED

Books by Charlie Higson

YOUNG BOND SERIES
SilverFin
Blood Fever
Double or Die
Hurricane Gold
By Royal Command

SilverFin: The Graphic Novel

THE ENEMY SERIES
The Enemy
The Dead
The Fear
The Sacrifice
The Fallen

THE
HUNTED

CHARLIE HIGSON

Hyperion
Los Angeles • New York

Printed in the United States of America

First U.S. Edition, June 2015

10 9 8 7 6 5 4 3 2 1

G475-5664-5-15074

Library of Congress Cataloging-in-Publication Data
Higson, Charles, 1958–
The hunted/Charlie Higson.—First U.S. edition.
pages cm—([The enemy; book 6])
"First published in Great Britain in 2014 by the Penguin Group."
Summary: Ella is out in the country, alone now except for her silent rescuer,
Scarface, about whom she knows nothing, while Ed leaves London on
a dangerous quest, determined to find Ella and keep his promise to
Small Sam that he will reunite sister and brother.
ISBN 978-1-4231-6567-5
[1. Horror stories. 2. Disfigured persons—Fiction. 3. Mutism—Fiction.
4. Zombies—Fiction. 5. Survival—Fiction. 6. London (England)—Fiction.
7. England—Fiction.] I. Title.
PZ7.H5446Hs 2015
[Fic]—dc23   2014036074

Reinforced binding

Visit www.hyperionteens.com

SUSTAINABLE FORESTRY INITIATIVE   Certified Sourcing
www.sfiprogram.org
SFI-00993

THIS LABEL APPLIES TO TEXT STOCK

For my brothers, Andrew, Barney, and Dan

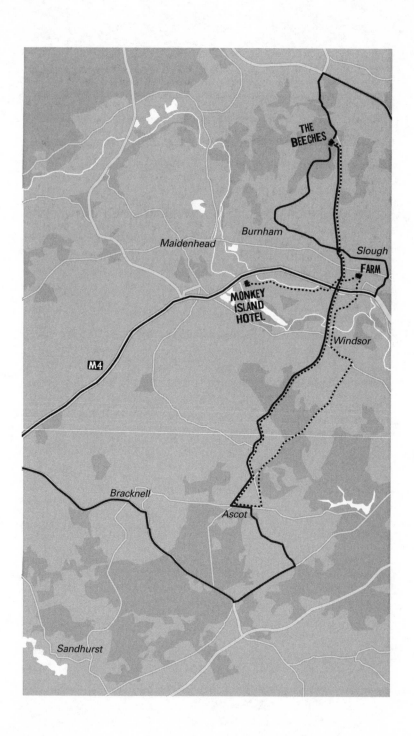

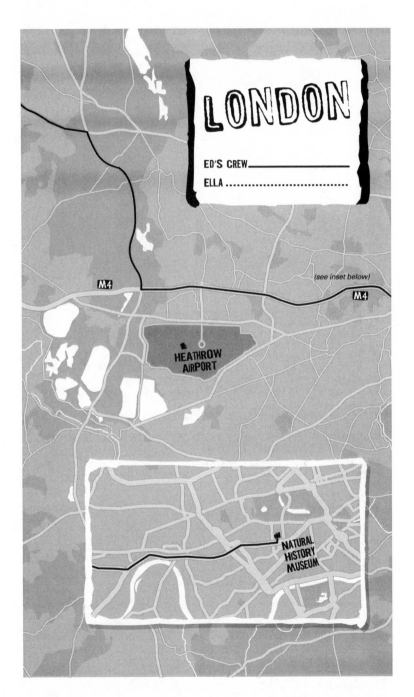

SAINT GEORGE

His teeth sank into the boy's neck and he felt a warm spurt of blood fill his mouth. A deep calm came over him. The chattering in his head fell silent. The fidgeting and twitching in his arms and legs stopped. The deep itch dulled. He felt like he was plugged into the universe, or as if the universe was plugged into him. As he drank, he looked up at the stars. They seemed to spell out a message for him, if only he could read it. He squinted and strained, his brain throbbing in his hot head. What were they trying to tell him? No good. No good. He closed his eyes and concentrated on the blood. It tasted like life, clearing out all the poison inside him, cleaning his tubes and guts, lighting up a million stars within his brain. He shuddered with pleasure.

The boy was still moving, feebly trying to break away from his grip, but Saint George was holding him tight. When he'd drunk his fill, he'd give him to the others. They were sitting in a circle around him, waiting. The closest were the ones who'd been with him from the start. His lieutenants.

And behind them, in circle after circle, the others, spreading out, filling the park. Sitting there, quietly waiting, their faces lit by moonlight. And out past them, all around, working their way through the city streets . . . his army was hunting. Maybe that's what the stars were showing him. The sky was a map and each star was one of his people. He was at the center, the brightest star of all. And they were all connected, in a circle of light, so that he was out there hunting with his people, and they were feeding with him now.

They'd only found this one child so far tonight, but there would be more. Each night it took longer as they emptied the nearby streets and had to search farther and wider.

He was always the first to feed. Sometimes only drinking the blood; sometimes tearing off the flesh. The blood was the best part. The blood was electricity, driving his brain and body, blowing away the darkness and the fog. And with the blood came the memories. Flooding into his thoughts. His life up there in the stars, and in the jungle, traveling across the sea, searching for a new home and finding it inside this body.

This body.

This man.

Greg . . . Greg Thorne. Of Greg's Organic Gaff.

Meat is life.

He was Greg. He had to hold on to the memory. It was like waking from a beautiful dream and feeling it slip away from you. He'd been a butcher. With a son. A boy. His own boy. *What was his name . . . ?*

His boy?

No good. Not coming.

He was Greg, though. He remembered that. He'd worked with animals. Cutting them up, chopping through the fat and the muscle, the tendons, skinning and deboning. *Eviscerating*. Yes, he remembered it well. Pictured the carcasses hanging from the hooks in the freezer at the back of his shop. Cows, sheep, pigs, chickens, children. Animals and children . . . Was that right? Had he always butchered children? Or had life been different then? That was the problem with the blood. For a few brief moments everything would be clear, lit up, written in the stars. He could read the messages. And then the clouds would come down, the mist and fog and shadows, and he would be so bloody hungry and the rage would take him. There could never be enough children to feed his hunger.

Already the images were fading. He'd known his name. He'd remembered a place. Knives and hooks and skin . . .

Cold. A cold place.

His head ached with the thinking. What was he to do?

He loosened his bite and looked down at the boy in his arms. The boy looked back at him. His eyes were sad. Blinking. His body trembled. Like a little bird. A chicken before you break its neck.

"Liam?" Greg smiled at him. "We should get home," he said. "Or we'll miss the game. The Arsenal are playing."

He closed his eyes. He could hear the cheering. The hard, tight thud of boot on ball. The halftime whistle . . .

His team was going to win. It was an away game next. They would have to travel. Meet the opposition. He was captain. He was general. He was king. He was a saint. Saint George, and he would slay the dragon.

First he needed his army. He had to wait. There were more of them coming, more of the others, more glinting stars, a universe of them, all moving toward him. He could hear them out there, calling to him, telling him to wait. From everywhere they came, and when they'd all arrived, when he was strong enough, when he was unstoppable, he would move on.

Move on to where *they* were. The enemy. The fast ones. The young ones. They had to be herded up like sheep, penned in like chickens. And when they were ready they would take his sickness from him; the host would move on and live inside them.

He felt the boy struggle and he opened his eyes.

Until the time was right, they were just like this boy. Just meat.

He snapped his neck and threw the boy to the others, who leapt up and tore into him.

This boy was nothing, but there were others who were dangerous, and those they had to kill. The shining ones. The ones who wouldn't take the sickness, the ones whose blood was strong. And, strongest of all, the bright little one, the little twinkling star. Twinkle, twinkle . . .

He had the power of light, that one did. He was made of light. He had to be destroyed. And all the others like him. Not as powerful as him, but dangerous all the same.

The stars had told Saint George this.

That was their true message.

He knew what he had to do.

To make the ripest children ready to take the host.

To kill the rest.

To kill the bright little star.

He'd seen him that time. At the Arsenal. The stars hadn't given him his orders then, though. He'd let him slip away. If only he'd known the small boy was a nasty little dragon.

It wouldn't happen again. He was Saint George and he would slay the dragon. That was how it worked, wasn't it? He knew the story. He was a hero, a patron saint. He was England. This country was his. His people were marching toward him from all corners. He would take his throne.

But first he had to destroy the dragon.

He would butcher him like a piece of meat; a long pig, that's all he was: cutlets, chops, ribs, and chitterlings. He would make sausages out of him, ham, because in the end he was nothing more than a side of pork. . . .

No, smaller than that.

He was just a lamb.

A leg of lamb.

Yes.

He would slaughter the lamb.

1

Everyone at the Natural History Museum was gathered in the Hall of Gods, an area that had big white statues lining both sides and an escalator at the back rising up through a weird, rusted metal globe. Ed had hoped that the meeting would be somewhere quiet and he could have talked to just one or two key people. Instead he had to face rows and rows of them, all sitting there, staring up at him and picking their noses like he was giving a talk at a school assembly.

That was how it was with Justin, though. He was in charge here and had his way of doing things, and you couldn't argue him out of it. Ed supposed there was a reason behind it all. These kids, like all kids, were bored most of the time. There was work to be done growing food, or scavenging for it; you could read books, or talk to your mates, but that was about it. No football, no computer games, no TV or music. Meetings like this gave the kids something to occupy their minds and fill up their conversations.

Ed had known Justin at school. A few of the boys from

Rowhurst had ended up at the museum. Chris Marker and Kwanele, Wiki and Jibber-Jabber. And it was Justin who had gotten them all safely there. He'd been pretty unmemorable before, a nerdy wimp, not the type of boy Ed used to hang out with. Ed had been into sports, mostly. But it turned out there was a lot more to Justin than Ed had ever imagined. He'd learned a hell of a lot since the disease had hit. Like how you needed all sorts of skills to survive. Brains being a very important one.

Justin was still fussy and nerdy, but he had authority. The kids respected him and he seemed to be able to control them. Something that Ed was utterly failing to do. Even the more streetwise kids from Holloway had sat there obediently through Justin's bit. He'd gone through some tedious stuff about tasks for the next day and menus and cleaning duties, and there'd been hardly a squeak out of them.

Even a scarred troublemaker named Achilleus had stayed fairly quiet, only occasionally whispering something to the two boys who sat giggling on either side of him. One younger kid and one of the Twisted Kids, as they called themselves. Ed had thought that Wormwood, the intelligent adult he'd brought here with him, was strange, but the Twisted Kids were off the scale. This one's name was Skinner, which was appropriate, as he had folds of loose skin all over his body.

As soon as Ed had opened his mouth, though, everything had fallen apart. Achilleus kept making snarky comments, and he was now lounging in his seat, yawning theatrically. The other kids had just started talking to each other, not loudly, but they were making enough noise to set up a steady, distracting buzz, so that Ed had lost all confidence in his speech—if you could call it a speech, which, unfortunately, Justin did when he'd introduced him.

Ed hadn't been ready for this and had stumbled along, talking about how Sam was searching for his sister, Ella. How Ella had left that morning and Sam had missed her by only a few hours and how Ed needed to go after her. He'd rambled on for about five minutes before he'd run out of things to say. What was there to say? He needed their help on a dangerous and probably pointless expedition. He hardly believed in it himself, so how could he make anyone else buy into it? If he'd been in the audience, he would have ignored his stupid speech as well.

It was time to finish up. He'd done his best.

"So anyway . . ." he said, gazing out across the rows of kids, some looking at him, some chatting with their friends, some bored, some staring at the ceiling. "That's it, really. I'm going off to find Ella—you know, tell her that Sam's alive, and, hopefully, bring her back. And if anyone wants to come along and help me, then, er, I guess, see me afterward. . . ."

See me afterward . . . ? Had he really said *see me afterward*? That's what teachers used to say. "If you want to come on the school trip to the theater, *see me afterward. . . .*"

"What if she don't wanna come back?" said a hefty black girl. Ed thought she was one of the kids who had recently arrived from Holloway with Ella.

"She'll want to see Sam," Ed replied. "I mean, wasn't that the main reason she left? Because there was nothing here for her except bad memories?"

"Whitney's right," said another of the Holloway crew. "What if Ella's got a better thing going on out there?"

Ed noticed a commotion near the front and then saw Sam jumping out of his chair.

He didn't need this now.

"What do you mean, 'bring her back' here to me?" Sam shouted. "I'm going with you."

"I'll talk to you afterward, Sam. Not now, okay?"

"There's nothing to talk about. I'm going with you."

"No, you're not." Ed tried to sound firm, like there was no argument. "Too dangerous," he added. "What if we got attacked on the way and you got killed? What then? This whole thing would have been a big waste of time."

"You're totally selling this, Two-Face," said Achilleus. "Sounds like a real picnic. I'll bring the cupcakes."

"Yeah, and maybe some macaroons," said the small boy next to him, who had a strong Irish accent.

"I never said it was going to be easy," Ed protested, holding Achilleus's stare. "That's why I need fighters, and only fighters. If we're a small but solid team we'll be fine. I mean, I'm told you're the best fighter here."

"Yeah." Achilleus nodded. "You heard right. No one can touch me."

"You'd be really useful, mate."

"I ain't your mate."

"No."

"I saved this place," said Achilleus. "I saved everyone's ass. Is what I do. Only I don't never seem to get no reward for it. So I'm sitting tight, thanks all the same."

"We been out there once already," said the little Irish kid.

"Yeah," said Achilleus. "And I ain't going again, *mate*. Not on a suicide mission. I mean, you don't even know where she's gone, do you?"

"I'll find her."

"You'll probably find her body, yeah. It's sicko central out there. They probably already eating her."

"Achilleus!" A girl in a leather jacket had stood up and was yelling at him. This was Maxie, one of the leaders of the Holloway crew.

"Ella's one of us," she said. Achilleus just smirked. "*Sam* is one of us. You keep your thoughts to yourself from now on. Have some respect."

"Whatever."

"What about you?" Ed said to Maxie.

"What about me?"

"As you say, Ella was one of yours. You gonna come with me?"

"No way," said the hard-looking black kid next to her. He was the other leader of the Holloway kids, Blue. "I done my bit out that way, and me and Max is sticking together from now on. We need to be here with our people."

"I don't get it." Ed put out his hands in a hopeless gesture. "Is anybody going to help me, or what?"

"Why should we listen to you?" called out a girl Ed didn't recognize. "You're the one who brought a sicko here. Brought a grown-up into our home. Made him a nice comfy room. When we'd just spent ages clearing them all out. Why should we trust you?"

There were shouts of agreement from around the room.

And then someone stood up. Ed was pleased to see a familiar face. A friend's face. It was Finn, a big lad from the Tower, the only survivor from DogNut's expedition.

"Ed's all right," he said. "I'd trust him more than any other kid I know."

"You going with him, then?" said Achilleus, and he snickered.

"You know I'm not," said Finn, and he raised his right arm, which had a bandage around it. "I can't do anything until my arm's properly healed."

"Yeah, good excuse."

"It's not an excuse."

"It's all right!" Ed shouted. "Leave it."

Finn had already come to see him and explained that the wound in his arm was still causing him problems. A shame. Finn had been one of the best fighters at the Tower.

"As I say," Ed went on limply, "anyone who wants to help, come and find me. It's gonna take me a few days to get everything ready."

He stepped down from the speaking platform, glad it was over. As he tried to get away, Sam came running over and tugged at his sleeve.

"I *am* coming, Ed," he said, almost shouting. "She's my sister."

"You are not," Ed snapped. "And if you say one more thing about it to me, I'm not going either. Okay?" He had lost it and come across much heavier than he'd intended, but it did the trick. Sam let go of him. Shut his mouth and looked at the floor. His weird little friend, the Kid, came over to him.

"I told you," the Kid said to Sam. "Don't push your luck

up a hill. It might roll down the other side. We made it here against the odds and ends. Let's count our blessings and our blisters. Leave the hard stuff to the experts now, eh?"

Sam looked at Ed, tears in his eyes.

"She's not dead, is she?"

"No."

"And you *will* find her?"

"I will."

Ed hoped he sounded more certain to Sam than he actually felt.

2

Ella wasn't dead. That was the first thing she thought when she woke up.

Not dead. Alive. Not dead.

And the second thing she thought was, *Why not?*

Why aren't I dead?

She was lying on her back, in long grass, looking up at the stars. They were a mess. She'd never been able to make out any constellations. She couldn't see any pictures there, just a lot of random dots.

So why wasn't she dead?

She closed her eyes. Felt for any pain. There was none. Only a slight tiny soreness in one wrist. It was more like the memory of pain than an actual feeling. Someone must have held on to her by the wrist, pulled her. She couldn't remember that. The last thing was . . .

Ella opened her eyes in panic.

The grown-up. The ugly one with the chewed face. Where was he? She was too scared to move anything except her eyes. She rolled them around, trying to see where she was.

"It's all right."

She turned toward the voice without thinking. There was someone next to her. Lying on the ground. She recognized the voice. It was Monkey-Boy.

"Are you alive?" Ella asked.

"Yes . . . but it hurts." Monkey-Boy said this very quietly, and he sounded sad. "Are you hurt?" he added.

"I don't think so." Ella thought of mentioning her wrist, but decided not to. It really wasn't important.

Monkey-Boy was just a dark shape on the ground. There was a faint line of starlight across his cheek. The last time she'd seen him, the grown-up had been holding him and they were still inside the hotel. Nothing made any sense to her. How had they gotten out here? Ella wasn't sure she wanted to know. She was quite enjoying just lying there not hurting. Not knowing. In the dark.

"He saved us," said Monkey-Boy.

"Who?"

"The grown-up."

"What? You mean the one with the mashed-up face?"

"Yes. He wasn't with the other ones." Monkey-Boy's voice sounded croaky, wobbly, weak. "He attacked them. He saved us."

"Why?" Ella asked and immediately wished she hadn't. The grown-up had probably captured her and Monkey-Boy to keep them both for himself. Like a lone wolf fighting off other wolves to get to a killed deer or something.

And now she heard herself asking the question she never wanted answered.

"What happened?"

"I woke up," said Monkey-Boy, and now Ella could hear that his voice was all wheezy and bubbly as well, like he needed to clear his throat. All full of phlegm.

"And then what?"

"I needed a wee. I was desperate. I didn't want to make any noise. Maeve and Robbie had told us to keep quiet, and stay hidden."

"You needed a wee?"

"Yes, I was bursting. It was horrible. I didn't want to wet the bed, because you and Maeve were sleeping in it. I was embarrassed."

Ella wished yesterday had never happened. She wished she'd never left London and all her other friends. Maeve had promised her, though. She'd been so sure. That she'd take them to a better place, in the countryside, with fresh air and fresh food and no grown-ups. A new life. They'd only gotten as far as a hotel on an island in the river. Monkey Island. That had felt right, a place for the boy who loved to climb, for the Monkey-Boy.

They'd found a room and settled down for the night. Just the four of them. Her and Monkey-Boy and Maeve and Robbie. Robbie, who couldn't even walk properly because of his wounded leg. What chance did they have? Stupid. Stupid. You needed an army.

Ella fought to stop herself from crying.

"I thought I was going to explode," Monkey-Boy went on. "Lying there in the bed for hour after hour. I couldn't sleep. In the end I got up and tried to find the door for the bathroom. It's what you call an ensuite. It means that—"

"I know what 'ensuite' means," Ella snapped. "It means

you have a bathroom right next to your bedroom. I'm not dumb."

"Sure. Okay. Sorry. I thought I had the right door. Maybe I did and they were hiding in the bathroom, or maybe I opened the door to the corridor by accident and they were waiting out there."

"Who?"

"The grown-ups. They were waiting. Quiet in the dark. They came in quickly. I don't know how many. Quickly and quietly. I couldn't make a sound, or shout for help. They were real clever; one of them smothered my face in his stomach. It really stank. I thought I'd be sick. I did wee myself then. And he dragged me away. Up the corridor. He hurt me. He bit me. And two more grown-ups came out with Maeve. She was already dead. I couldn't watch what they did to her. I went all unconscious. I don't know how long for, but he did worse things to me when I was asleep.

"And then the other grown-up arrived. The one whose face is all scarred. There was a fight and he easily beat the one who hurt me. He killed him. I saw him. He was ferocious. With knives and everything. He cut him to pieces and then he picked me up, and he was carrying me away when you came running down the corridor with more grown-ups behind you. Scarface tried to help you, but you fainted and you banged your head. And then he had to fight the new grown-ups. He didn't waste any time. No way. He killed them quicker than you can imagine, and he brought us here. I don't know what he's going to do. He comes and goes."

"Where is he now?"

"He went back inside the hotel, I think. For more killing."

"And where are we?"

"Just on the grass, near some trees, by the river. You can see the hotel over there."

Ella looked over and saw the big square black shape of the building against the stars. Her eyes were getting used to the light and she was seeing more and more. All the time wishing she was still asleep, where she was safe. Eyes closed. In the dark.

"What will he do when he comes back?" she said.

"I don't know. He just sits there. Like he's keeping watch."

"He's going to do something bad to us," said Ella. "We have to get away from here. We have to run away."

"I can't," said Monkey-Boy, and now Ella could see that his face was all shiny and wet. He was crying.

"What's the matter?" she asked.

"I can't move," said Monkey-Boy. "It hurts too much."

"Where does it hurt?"

"All over. I'm bleeding a lot."

"Badly?"

"I don't know. It feels bad. I feel bad. All hot and cold and shivery. I've got pins and needles in my fingers and my feet."

Well, that doesn't sound too bad, thought Ella, and she shuffled closer to him. It was cold out here. That was why he was shivering. She was shivering too, her teeth clacking together. Her body shaking. Or maybe she was just scared.

"Let me see," she said, squinting in the dark, kneeling over him, her shoulders hunched, as if she were expecting something to swoop down out of the sky and attack her.

"I can't hardly see," she said and touched Monkey-Boy's

sweater. It was soaking wet. Sticky. She held her hand to her face. It looked like it was covered in black ink. Ella knew, though, that if there was more light it would look red, not black.

And then she remembered the flashlight she kept in her backpack. She quickly felt her shoulders. The straps were there. Robbie had told them all to sleep with their packs on in case they needed to make a quick getaway. She slipped the pack off her back and rummaged around inside it until she felt the familiar hard plastic. It was a windup flashlight and she always kept it wound. She pressed the button and the light shone right into Monkey-Boy's face. He winced and shrank away from it, blinking.

He was breathing very fast. Panting like a dog. His face very white and splashed with blood. She moved the beam down his body. He was absolutely soaked and there was more blood puddling in the grass around him. How much blood was there in a human being? Her teacher had once told her it was eight pints. She wasn't quite sure how much a pint was, let alone eight, and surely children would have less blood than adults? How much of his blood had he spilled, though? It looked like a lot.

He was holding his hands over his stomach. His fore-arms were all scraped and scratched, the skin raggedy and torn, and there was more blood oozing up between his hands and fingers. It was steaming in the chilly night air.

There was a smell coming off him, like the smell of a grown-up. Like bad toilets and old garbage. This was worse than pins and needles. He was being very brave. If it were her, she would have been just screaming and screaming.

"It's all right," she said, using the same words he'd said to her earlier. Had he been lying too?

"I don't want to move my hands," he said. And she saw that there were bubbles coming from inside the blood. Inside his body.

"If you move them a little I can see how bad it is," said Ella.

"It's very bad," said Monkey-Boy, and she could hear the crying in his voice. "He bit me. He was trying to eat me, Ella. Trying to eat me alive."

"Well, he didn't!" said Ella angrily. "We were saved, remember? You were saved—you're going to be all right. Just move your hands a little and I'll see . . ."

Then he did and she wished he hadn't, because she saw stuff. Awful stuff. Coming out of him. Like a nest of fat worms, gray and blue and brown and white. And then she screamed as something knocked into her hard and the flashlight was grabbed from her and shut off. She felt a hot hand pressing over her mouth so that her scream was strangled into silence. She was crushed to the ground, the smell of grass and mud filling her nose, and she knew that soon she would be like Monkey-Boy. She waited for it. The teeth in her skin, her bones snapping . . .

Eaten alive . . .

But the body on top of her didn't move. Just lay there all hot and still, the hand holding her mouth closed. She could hear his breathing, harsh and raspy through his nose. . . . She remembered the nose, how it had looked all mangled, the nostrils open like in a skull. She felt a calm come over her. If this was the end, then she would never be scared again.

She waited, the man breathing in her ear.

And nothing happened.

She was still alive. In the dark. A little disappointed that she would have to keep on being scared, keep on struggling. At last, slowly, slowly, the thing rolled off her, still holding her in one strong arm. She could see Monkey-Boy. He hadn't moved. He was very still. And, beyond him, moving figures. Three people, adults, coming toward them. The grown-up who had ahold of her turned her head so that she was facing him—he had his fingers to his lips, shushing her.

She swallowed and nodded. He let go of her. Moved his hands and the next thing she knew he was holding two knives, their blades glinting.

Were they for her?

She didn't think so. There had been something in his face. Something almost friendly.

Ella heard a noise and turned back to see that the three grown-ups had almost gotten to Monkey-Boy, and he still hadn't moved. Was he playing dead to fool them?

One of them, a father—she could see now—stooped over Monkey-Boy. And then, in a flappy rustle of clothing, Scarface was up and running, crouching low. He punched out at the father, who dropped to the ground. One of the other two grown-ups, another father, hissed and swung his arms wildly, but Scarface dodged them, went under, then up, stabbing at his face. The father fell over backward. The last of the three was a mother. She was holding her hands up to protect herself, fingers like claws. Scarface easily darted around her, and stabbed twice at her side. She squealed, holding her stomach, and ran in circles. Finally Scarface did something to her that Ella couldn't see, and she went down with a thump.

It was very quiet and still now. Scarface waited there, as if listening, raised his face, sniffing the air, then moved among the three dead bodies. Finally he came back over and looked at Monkey-Boy. His shoulders drooped. He touched Monkey-Boy's face. Knelt there in silence, and then came over to Ella. He gave back her flashlight, then jerked his head as if to say, *Come along.*

"What about my friend?" said Ella, nodding toward Monkey-Boy. Scarface shook his head.

Ella felt a great weight of sadness crash down on her, forcing tears out of her eyes and down her cheeks.

It wasn't fair. Monkey-Boy had never wanted to hurt anyone, he just loved to climb things. Now Ella was all alone in the world.

Except for this creature. This Scarface. And she had no idea what he wanted from her.

But she got up and followed him as he walked away.

3

Ella didn't know how far they walked that night, but it felt like miles. Sometimes they walked on the road, sometimes across fields, and for a little way, through woods. Scarface obviously knew where he was going. Ella followed just behind him. Watching his back. Staring at the logo on the bag he carried. *Nike.* A grown-up with a Nike bag. She soon got tired. Her legs ached, her feet were sore, she wanted to sleep, and her throat was painful from holding in tears.

When she couldn't stand it anymore, she flopped to the ground.

"I can't go on," she said. "I'm tired and I don't know where we're going and what you want from me. I'm not moving."

Scarface stopped and turned to her, walked back to where she was sitting, squatted down, peered into her face.

She didn't like to look at him and was glad that it was too dark to see him very well. His face was horrible, like he'd put it in a crocodile's mouth for a bet. She wasn't scared of him anymore, though. Surely if he wanted to kill her he would have done it by now. . . .

Unless . . .

"Why are you doing this?" she asked. "Are you just leading me to your den, or something? So that you don't have to carry my dead body all the way?"

Scarface tilted his head to one side, thinking.

"Are you going to eat me?" said Ella, and the creature's face twisted a little, exposing his teeth, as if he was trying to smile. He shook his head, then pulled something out of his pocket and offered it to her.

It was a cold potato in its skin. She sniffed it, then bit into it greedily, only now realizing how hungry she was. She gobbled it down and swallowed it, feeling it nudge its way slowly down her dry throat. Afterward Scarface offered her some water from a plastic bottle. She drank half of it and immediately felt a million times better. Scarface then took off his Nike bag and turned around, still squatting in front of her, and indicated with a jerk of his chin that she should climb onto his back. She hesitated a moment, then thought, *What the hell,* and clambered on. He gripped her legs with his elbows and straightened up, carrying his Nike bag in front of him. His body felt warm but didn't smell as bad as most grown-ups'. Ella rested her head on his shoulder, and as they jogged along, she gradually drifted off to sleep.

She was jolted awake a little while later and found that Scarface had stopped. He was standing among some trees in a wood, watching something—Ella couldn't see what—and after a while he relaxed and started walking again. As he did so, Ella spotted movement around them. Animals were approaching, like ghosts in the dark. Ella felt a moment's fear and panic, but was calmed when she saw that Scarface wasn't bothered. He just walked on. Ella could see now that the animals were dogs. They didn't growl or anything, just sniffed around Scarface. Sniffed at his legs and bag, then trotted off back into the darkness under the trees.

Scarface moved a bit faster now, and soon they were out of the woods and in a wide-open space. There was another smaller clump of trees ahead and a cluster of buildings half hidden among them. As they got nearer, Ella saw that it was a farm of some sort. Scarface stopped to let her down. Her legs felt stiff and weak and she had to stamp her feet to get everything working properly. She was just about to walk to the farm entrance when Scarface grabbed her and held her back, then indicated with his open palms that she should go carefully and stay behind him.

He walked on very cautiously now. There was a road going through the trees to a gate, and beyond it was a farm-yard with large, mostly modern-looking buildings and an older farmhouse in the middle, the sort you saw in picture books, except the windows were all dark and the top half was black from fire. Ella noticed that part of the roof had collapsed as well. As they neared the gate, Scarface pointed to a low wire that was stretched out across the road. He stepped over it carefully and Ella did the same. A few paces farther on there was another wire, this one higher up, that they had to duck under. When they got to the gate, Scarface didn't open it, but climbed over it instead. Ella could smell animals and animal poo. It wasn't a bad smell. Not like the rotten stink of grown-ups. Still Scarface was going carefully, pointing out to Ella all sorts of traps and obstacles. He then skirted around the farmyard into some bushes at the side.

Ella held back, not sure what he was doing, and that was when she noticed the things hanging in the trees and bushes all around. Skulls and bones, and weird bits of animals, birds' wings, foxes' tails, claws and teeth and ribs, all sort of tied together with wires into weird shapes. Like warnings. Ella didn't like it. She went to find Scarface and discovered him huddled over an animal trap. There was a dead rabbit stuck in it and he freed it, then held it up and waved it at her triumphantly, his face pulled into its horrible, tooth-bared grin.

Ella wasn't quite sure what she thought about the dead rabbit. It had been a long time since she'd tasted fresh meat, but she supposed it would make a good breakfast. Better than a cold potato.

Scarface stuffed the rabbit into one of the pockets in his big loose coat. It was made of some sort of waxy material that had felt uncomfortable when she'd rested her head on it. She realized now that all his clothes were good; he had on boots and black cargo pants with more bulging pockets. Two knives hung at his belt, plus a longer weapon, like a sword with a wide, hooked blade. He was a little bit muddy, but, if it wasn't for his mutilated, deformed features, he would have looked like an ordinary farmer out to trim his hedges, or maybe a gamekeeper or a poacher, like the ones Ella used to read about in her Roald Dahl books. She certainly hadn't seen a grown-up dressed in normal clothes for months. They mostly wore rags and filthy bits and pieces that they never changed.

Scarface checked some more traps around the edge of the farm and then led her, not over to the main farmhouse, but to the side door of a big barn built out of metal. There was a complicated series of locks and traps around the door that he patiently worked his way through, which gave Ella a chance to look at his hands. They were as mangled as his face, and he had at least one finger missing. Eventually he got the door open and they went inside.

The first thing that Ella noticed was that half of the roof was missing; she could see the open sky and stars far above. The next thing she noticed was that Scarface had made a camp down at the covered end, with a bed up on a platform. It was quite neat and tidy, with various other bits of furniture, and even pictures hanging on the walls.

Scarface took the rabbit out of his pocket and hung it up next to a couple more dead animals, another rabbit and a squirrel. Ella wondered if he ate squirrels and whether she'd be able to if he offered her one.

All she wanted to do now was sleep, though. He took her over to the platform and pointed at the bed. She was too tired to do anything but curl up in it under a pile of sleeping bags.

She slept well, untroubled by any nightmares, but woke up in the early morning, screaming at the light.

For the next few days Ella felt like she'd gone mad, as if a demon or something had taken over her body and she was like a tiny pilot sitting inside her head, watching what was happening. Her body was acting without her telling it to. First there was the screaming. It felt like there was a massive weight pressing down on her chest, suffocating her; she was gasping for breath, and as she tried to breathe she screamed, her body shaking in the bed, soaking wet from sweat. Mad. Hours spent just screaming. It reminded her of an episode of *The Simpsons* where Homer can't stop screaming and he doesn't know why. Turns out it has to do with a dead body.

Just one.

What did he *have to worry about?*

There were nasty dark thoughts hiding at the edges of her brain. She was making herself not think about them, but a part of her, a hidden part, must be looking. . . .

And screaming.

In the end she was too exhausted to scream anymore and fell into a feverish half-world, not awake and not asleep, only dimly aware of what was happening around her, the coming and going of Scarface as he brought food and water. She didn't always know what it was she was eating, but most of it was warm, and it always made her feel a little better.

Except when she was sick. How many times did that happen? She wasn't sure. Wasn't sure of anything. Her body was carrying on without her. Nights came and went; days came and went. Some days it rained; other days it was sunny. Eventually a numbness came over her, and at last, one morning she was able to sit up. Weak, a little fuzzy in the head, a little shaky.

Scarface was sitting on the edge of the platform with his back to her. There was a light drizzle hanging in the air and the day felt gray and misty, not all there.

She needed a wee and she thought of Monkey-Boy, back at the hotel, too scared to get out of bed. He was just a memory now. She couldn't let him be real.

"I need the toilet," she said, and Scarface turned. It was a shock to see his face in the light. His skin was sort of ripped and folded over, shiny in places, rough and chopped up in others. His lips were fat on one side, like sausages, but missing on the other, so that they didn't close properly and she could see his teeth. He had an ear missing, but hadn't lost any hair. One of his eyes was cloudy and red, weeping, the other stared at her, clear and brown and perfect.

He nodded, standing up, and Ella got out of bed, walking stiffly on wobbly legs. She followed him across the barn to where there was a bright blue chemical toilet sitting in the corner. It was plastic and had a door in the front, a bit like a Porta-John. She opened the door and went inside, and she remembered it now. The harsh smell. She'd been here before. She must have come when she was crazy. She sat down and tried not to think about anything.

She couldn't help thinking about the creature's face, though. It was so horrible. She wondered if it hurt. *Face-ache.* That's what her dad used to call her when he was teasing her. "Come on, Face-Ache, finish your breakfast. . . ."

When she came out, Scarface was ready with some food for her. A bowl of porridge. He'd gone to the trouble of setting a place for her at a table with three unmatched wooden chairs. As she ate, she looked over to where the dead animals had been hanging; the rabbits and the squirrel were gone, but a duck was strung up there now, its neck broken.

When she'd eaten the porridge, Scarface gave her a hard-boiled egg in its shell, which Ella cracked and peeled off in one try. He watched her as she ate, like her mom used to.

"Don't look at me like that," she said. "It's embarrassing."

Scarface shrugged and wandered off, made himself busy cleaning some animal traps. Ella properly looked at the barn for the first time. Scarface had collected lots of stuff, odd bits of furniture, garden ornaments and statues, a mannequin dressed in camouflage gear, some bicycles, parts of engines and machinery, garden tools and weapons. There were pictures and mirrors, and even a stuffed boar's head, attached to the wall, and stacks of wood, boxes filled with junk. She noticed that there were even some shelves of books.

She didn't understand it. Grown-ups weren't supposed to read books and ride bikes. They were no better than dumb animals. Maybe this one had somehow avoided the disease, in which case, why was he so chewed up and rotten-looking?

When she'd finished eating, she went over to the shelves and looked at the books. They were a mixed bunch; most of them she'd never heard of, but there was one she did recognize. *The Twits* by Roald Dahl. She took it off the shelf and flicked through the pages. It was so familiar, like meeting an old friend. She wondered what had happened to all her old books back there in her house in Holloway. Were they all still where she'd left them? She hadn't thought to take any with her when she'd moved into Waitrose with the other kids. And there wasn't a day when she wished she hadn't left them behind. It had been so boring living there with nothing to do all day.

No. Best not to remember any of that. Best not to picture her old room that she'd shared with Sam. Poor Sam. Her big brother—even if he was only little. Taken by the grown-ups. Gone forever. She mustn't think about him.

Ella put the book back on the shelf and looked up at the gray sky, the fine rain falling through the roof. Why did Scarface live in here and not in the house? It must get very cold. And damp. She remembered how the bricks of the farmhouse were black from fire. Maybe it wasn't safe in there?

And here? Was this going to be her life now? Stuck here with this—what did the kids back at the museum call them?—*sicko*. Stuck here with this sicko. Nothing had been right since Sam had been taken and they'd left Holloway. She still thought of it as home.

"What are we going to do today?" she asked, then saw that he'd picked up a short pole with a clubbed end studded with nails and jagged bits of metal. For a second she thought he meant to attack her with it, but instead he walked over and gave it to her, then went to the door they'd come in by. It was well protected, with bars and bolts and a steel post jammed at an angle, the bottom end wedged against a concrete block set into the floor.

"What do you expect me to do with this?" Ella asked as he started to remove everything so that they could get out. "I'm too small to fight, and it's really heavy."

Scarface ignored her, but when she propped it against the wall he patiently picked it up and gave it back to her.

Ella thought it best not to argue anymore.

Eventually Scarface was able to open the door and they went outside. Ella looked around the farmyard. There were three more barns of different sizes, and in the middle was the half-burned farmhouse, looking dark and miserable.

Scarface took Ella over to one of the other barns. The door here also had all sorts of locks and things on it, and she had to wait while he straightened them out. She looked at the club he'd given her. Didn't think she could ever hit anyone with it, but had to admit she felt a bit better holding on to it.

Once Scarface got the door open, they went inside. There was a strong smell that clawed at the back of her throat, like old stale wee, and there was a dry, dusty feel to the air, and the sound of something humming and buzzing, as if there were a huge crowd of people inside the barn. They went through a small entrance area and into a much larger space. Ella was amazed to see a great pen full of hundreds of chickens all running around clucking. She laughed. This was crazy.

Scarface went over to a big bin and scooped out a shovelful of grain that he threw at the chickens, who squawked and clucked even louder and started pecking at it like mad things. She was amazed that he would use food to feed chickens. That meant there must be lots of it here. A whole farm full of stored-up food. No wonder he had so many locks and traps around the place. He handed the shovel to Ella and she copied him, hurling more grain at the chickens and still laughing. There was a line of henhouses down one side, and Scarface showed Ella the warm eggs sitting in straw under lift-up wooden flaps. She helped him collect them and carefully put the eggs into a bucket.

It was just like Maeve had said the countryside would be—farms and animals and food and lots of friendly kids to play with.

Except it wasn't really, was it? Because Maeve had left out the part about having your head chewed off by a grown-up. And Ella wasn't skipping around a sunny farm with a jolly farmer. She was trudging about the place with a nasty spiked club in the rain with this weird sicko, old Face-Ache.

Life was never like the stories in books, was it?

They took the eggs back to the main barn and Scarface let Ella carry them. They were putting them away in a tin box when Scarface suddenly stopped and straightened up, listening, sniffing the air. Ella listened too. She could just hear the faint tinkling of a bell in the distance. Scarface let out his breath and scratched his armpit. He looked at Ella, as if deciding something, then passed her the club that she had put down to stack the eggs. He walked to the door and started unlocking it.

What was going on now?

Ella pulled her gold necklace out of her sweater and rolled

the gold beads between her fingers. She'd gotten the necklace in the Victoria and Albert Museum, next door to the Natural History Museum. Chose it out of all the ones in the display cases. It had gold beads and a man's head with a beard dangling off the bottom. It was the head of Achelous, apparently. Some sort of Greek god. The name had reminded her of Achilleus, who was a great fighter.

If only Achilleus had come with them when they'd left the museum. He would have protected her and Monkey-Boy. He was their champion. If he knew she was here, he'd come charging out of London with his spear and kill everyone.

But he didn't know, did he? And all she had was Face-Ache and this necklace.

Ella prayed to Achelous to look after her.

5

When they went back outside, Ella saw that there was something tangled in the wires on the other side of the farm gate. Some large animal. The wires must be connected to a bell, as a warning. She could hear it ringing, off in the bushes. As they walked closer, though, she saw that it wasn't an animal; it was a grown-up, a mother. And she was still alive. Struggling feebly. Ringing the bell. *Ting-a-ling-a-ling.*

They climbed over the gate, ducked under the high wire, and Scarface went to inspect his prey.

Ella held back. Shaking slightly.

The mother was quite a large woman and most of her hair was missing, apart from a few long, trailing, greasy strands. She was wearing what looked like a filthy nightie and had bare legs and feet. Her skin looked all white with purple blotches and lumpy yellow growths.

She was hanging off a long pole with spikes running down it, some of which were stuck in her back.

The wire must be a *trip wire.*

Sam used to have one he'd gotten from the Science

Museum. It made an alarm go off if you stepped on it. He sometimes used to put it in the bedroom doorway.

This trip wire was different. It obviously made this long, bendy pole fly out from the bushes. Ella remembered arriving here the other night. Stepping over the wire, not knowing what would happen if she touched it . . .

She imagined that pole springing out, whacking into her, those spikes going into her skin, her body.

The mother was impaled on it. She was wriggling, trying to get free, not understanding what was holding her there. Blood was dripping into a pool beneath her. Her mouth and eyes were twisting and going narrow then wide, like she was trying to make faces, chewing the air, bending her neck. Scarface sighed through his nose, took a knife from his belt, and lifted her chin.

Ella turned away as he put the blade to her throat.

Why was it always like this? You had something nice like the chickens, then something horrid like this trapped mother. Nice then horrid. Nice then horrid. And always the horrid thing was a hundred times worse than the nice thing.

Ella sat on a tree stump and waited for Scarface to finish what he was doing. Finally she heard the thud of the mother's body hitting the ground and the sound of her being dragged away. Ella couldn't help turning back to watch. Scarface had the mother by the ankles and was pulling her along through the field next to the road. Ella followed them at a distance.

There was a harsh croak from above and she looked up to see a whole flock of crows circling above them, black marks against the gray sky.

Scarface got to the middle of the overgrown field and

stopped, let go of the mother's puffy legs. Ella stopped too, not wanting to go any closer. She could see a clump of white sticks. Scarface left the mother there, rubbed his hands together, wiped them on his cargo pants, and then came back over to Ella.

He waved to her to come with him and went over to a tall tree growing high above the other trees and bushes that surrounded the farm. He showed her some wooden boards that had been nailed to the trunk, making a sort of ladder, and she saw that there was a platform up in the branches, like a tree house. He started to climb and she went up after him, trying not to slip on the steps that were wet and slippery from the rain. It was drier at the top as there was a canvas sheet tied to the branches above the platform to make a roof.

Ella noticed that there were other platforms in the trees, half hidden among the branches and leaves, with ropes joining them. Scarface sat on the edge of the platform and Ella joined him, dangling her legs over the edge, trying not to look straight down. The platform was much higher than it had looked from the ground and you could see for miles. The area they were in was mostly fields and woods, but not far away were other buildings, and here and there she could see the gray streak of a road.

She felt safe up there in the treetops and began to sing. "Ella and Face-Ache sitting in a tree, K-I-S-S-I-N-G." She stopped and turned to Scarface, who was staring at her with his one good eye.

"No offense," she went on, "but that's you . . . *Face-Ache* . . . because you've got that face on you. I bet it hurts.

And I don't mean to be rude, but . . . you're very ugly. And we're not kissing. That's just the words of the song. And I'm sorry if you don't like the song, but really you're just an ugly old sicko, so why should I care what you think? I expect you can't understand anything I'm saying. You're just like the other grown-ups. Dumb. Dumb old Dumbo Face-Ache."

Scarface turned away.

Ella could see the mother's body in the middle of the field and realized that what she had thought were white sticks were actually bones. Scarface must have dragged lots of dead bodies there and left them to rot away. She had to admit he did seem to be a good hunter. She could see the crows landing around the body, pecking at it.

And then, in the woods on the far side of the field, she saw something else moving. Moments later it came charging out into the field, then another came, then more and more. She could see now that they were dogs. Of all shapes and sizes. There must have been at least thirty of them, too many for Ella to count. They raced to the boneyard, snapping and yelping at one another, and sending the crows swirling up into the sky in a noisy, messy spiral.

The dogs fell on the mother's body, and Ella and Scarface sat up there in the tree, side by side, their feet dangling over the edge, watching the dogs and the great black crows darting down to pick up scraps. And Ella couldn't tell if this was a good thing or a bad thing.

The next thing she saw was definitely a bad thing.

There was a grown-up standing in the next field. A live one. It looked like a mother, but it was hard to tell from this far away. It was very still, like a scarecrow, its arms straight out. Ella nudged Scarface and pointed. He squinted at it, then slipped the pack off his back and dug around inside it until he found a pair of binoculars. Ella had stopped being surprised at the way he didn't behave like other grown-ups. She'd accepted him for what he was. Weird. He put the binoculars to his eyes and adjusted the focus, gently turning the wheel with his knobbly, bent fingers. He made a deep humming sound in his throat, almost like an animal growling. Like a dog.

The dogs had seen the scarecrow as well now and were acting all confused, whimpering, their ears going flat, hair up on their backs, crouching low to the ground. They started to move away from the mother they'd been eating, going in a pack toward the live grown-up. As they got closer, they seemed even more scared, holding back, running in yippy circles. Every now and then one would get braver than his friends, dart forward, daring himself to go up closer. He'd sniff the scarecrow, nip at its legs, then run back with his tail between his legs. Then another would try. Like little kids daring each other. In the end they all got near enough and started to circle the scarecrow, yelping, howling, running in and snapping at it, but never getting right up close. Eventually they ran off together in a pack, barking their heads off, back into the woods.

Scarface started down the ladder, Ella followed, and soon they were pushing through the long grass toward the scarecrow. When they got there, it was like they were copying the dogs. Neither she nor Scarface wanted to go any nearer. Scarface was holding both of his knives in his hands, the blades pointing down toward the ground.

Ella looked and saw that it was a father with long, stringy hair and man boobs. The skin had rotted away from the bottom half of his face, showing the bones and the teeth of his lower jaw. There were so many boils and swellings on the top half of his face, they'd blocked his eyes up. He must be blind. Maybe that was why he was standing like that.

He didn't look very dangerous to Ella, just ugly and horrible and old. Smelly. But what did she know?

"Go on then, Face-Ache," she said. "What are you waiting for?"

At last Scarface moved in closer. Went right up to the father and sniffed him, circling him just as the dogs had done. Finally he looked at Ella and mimed covering his eyes. Ella got the message and turned around. Behind her she heard a slicing sound, *slish* . . .

When she turned back, the father was gone, fallen over

and hidden in the long grass, and Scarface was kneeling down doing something to him.

Afterward Scarface showed Ella a sort of trail where the grass had been flattened by something walking along, probably the scarecrow. They followed it until they came to an area where the grass was trampled all over the place, with paths going off in every direction it seemed.

Scarface picked one trail and set off, moving fast along the edge of the woods. Ella couldn't always see what Scarface was following, and he sometimes stopped and went back and took a different path. He was sniffing like a dog, always listening hard, peering around with his one good eye.

They kept going like that for what felt like ages, and soon Ella was tired and bored and fed up. She started grumbling at Scarface, but he just ignored her. He was a dog with a scent and nothing was going to stop him.

Ella stared at the Nike bag on Scarface's back. Something was dripping from it. She looked closer and saw little gray things wriggling, like tiny slugs or worms. She was going to say something, that Scarface had maggots in his bag, but didn't. It was *his* problem. If he wasn't going to speak to her, she really didn't need to speak to him. Grumpy old grown-up.

After a time—maybe an hour, Ella thought, but she couldn't be sure, her aching legs thought they'd walked a hundred miles—they came to a big broken-down wire fence. A tree had fallen on it and squashed it half to the ground. Scarface inspected the wire where it was torn and snaggly. He found a scrap of clothing stuck on it. He sniffed it, nodded to himself, and climbed over the flattened bit of fence, holding on to the tree trunk for balance. Ella followed, picking her way and trying not to fall over. There were more trees on the other side, and then a wooden fence that was broken in a couple of places. When they went through it, Ella found that they were in some sort of park with paths winding among jungly trees and bushes. There were benches and trash bins, odd-shaped things she didn't quite understand, funny-looking statues, giant toadstools . . .

Then she stopped suddenly and tugged at Scarface's jacket, pointing up. There was a man in a tree. She instantly saw that it wasn't a real man, it was a plastic model, and she felt embarrassed. Thought Scarface would laugh at her, tease her, silly little girl, but then she remembered that he never laughed. Grumpy old man. Ugly, grumpy old man. Face-Ache.

The man in the tree looked old-fashioned, from the time of knights, and he was carrying a horn. And then Ella saw a tree with the words THE ENCHANTED FOREST written on it. The more she looked around, the madder this place was. There was a castle just showing above the bushes. Up ahead a walkway through the trees with a sign saying THE RAT TRAP, and a shield with a wolf's head on it. Memories were coming back to her. She'd been here before, she was sure of it, but she was confused; she hadn't been expecting any of this, and everything was all overgrown and broken.

Scarface set off toward the castle, and when they got there Ella saw that it seemed to be made of giant plastic bricks.

She finally realized where they were.

"This is Legoland!"

7

"Why have you brought me to Legoland, Face-Ache?" Ella squealed. "Are we having a treat?" And she laughed at her joke. Scarface didn't laugh. He just tilted his head to one side and stared at her through his good eye.

Ella had come here with her family, with Mom and Dad and Sam. A long time ago, it seemed, but she remembered some of the rides, how scared she'd been, how she couldn't go on them because she was too small and had cried, even though she was secretly glad, because she was really too frightened.

Frightened? Of a silly Lego ride?

That was a different world.

The past was Legoland. The future was Zombieland.

"There's the shop!" she shouted, and before Scarface could stop her, she ran off toward a sign saying TURRET SHOP. The doors to the shop were open and inside everything was as it'd been left, the shelves piled high with Lego toys. Dust and dirt and dead leaves and rubbish had blown in through the doors, birds had been in there and made a mess, but Ella didn't mind. She ran down the aisles, looking at the brightly colored boxes. She picked out a castle set, with a king and a queen and a princess and some knights, and held it out to Scarface.

Scarface sniffed, and then took the box from Ella and squashed it into the top of his backpack, with the end sticking out. She thought he might be annoyed with her, having to carry toys like this. Her mom and dad had never let her buy anything in any of the shops when they'd come here. "It's a rip-off, darling. Too expensive." Well, now everything was free.

"Can I get something else?" she asked. Scarface looked at her. He might be really angry now. But he didn't lose his temper; instead he went over to a rack and picked up a full-size Lego knight's shield, with the same wolf's head on it as she'd seen outside.

He sort of smiled. At least that's what Ella thought he was trying to do as his face twisted and wrinkled. She held the shield in one hand and her club in the other. The shield was just made of rubber, wouldn't really protect her, and the club . . . Well, she was never going to use it, was she? But it made her feel good, like a real warrior. She grimaced and roared at Scarface.

He made a weird gurgling sound.

Maybe he could laugh after all.

She was about to give another roar when Scarface put his finger to his lips and went very still. In a blink she was out of Legoland and back into Zombieland. Forget theme-park rides: this was what it was like to be frightened. When you didn't know what was going on. When you didn't know where the enemy was. When you knew that there were things out there. Monsters. Real monsters, who wanted to kill you. Who would eat you if they could. Cannibals. Flesh-eating sickos.

Scarface made a movement with his hands that Ella understood—*Go carefully, keep quiet, stay behind me*—and walked out of the shop.

Not that she needed to be told to be careful.

Scarface crept on, hunched over, his spear held out in front of him. She stayed in his shadow, making herself small.

They made their way through the theme park, Scarface listening, listening, listening, although Ella could hear nothing. None of the paths here were straight; they wound through the trees and past the attractions, so that it was very hard to know what might be up ahead.

At last they rounded a corner and there ahead of them was Miniland, a sort of shrunk-down version of the world with all the famous places made out of Lego bricks, with buildings and roads and mountains and cars and people and rivers and boats . . . and sickos.

Three grown-ups were walking through it, looking lost. She heard Scarface sigh. Was this what they'd been tracking all this time? These three? Was it really worth coming all this way?

But, to be fair, she was glad there weren't more of them.

They were going the other way and hadn't seen Scarface and Ella. Scarface crept closer. Ready for the kill. Ella had seen dogs behave like this. All stiff and concentrating. There was going to be blood. Ella could see the colorful box of the Lego set sticking out of Scarface's bag. It was always the same. Good things, then bad things, good things, then bad things.

Scarface got closer and closer, and still they hadn't seen him.

The grown-ups were crossing London now; they'd passed the weird skyscraper called the Gherkin and were going past the Tower of London toward St. Paul's Cathedral. They looked like giants, or monsters from an alien-invasion film, trampling the city. One of them, a big father wearing a long, dirty coat, brushed against Nelson's Column as they crossed Trafalgar Square. When they got to Buckingham Palace, Scarface suddenly ran in and attacked, stabbing one in the back.

Ella looked away.

She didn't want to see any more blood, any more killing, even though it had to be done. Every last grown-up had to die.

She heard the sounds of the fight—grunting, hissing, thudding—and when she looked back, one of the grown-ups was lying half in the River Thames, turning it red, and another was lying across the Houses of Parliament. The third, a mother, had made it to the pathway and was lying there, her arms and legs sort of wriggling. Scarface was squatting over her, cutting her with one of his knives. He spotted Ella watching him and scowled at her so that she looked away again.

If only it would be that easy to kill all the grown-ups in London. If only the three giants were all they ever had to deal with and Scarface was Jack the Giant Killer.

But Ella knew this wasn't the end. Not by a long way. This was just Legoland.

The next few days were the same. Wake with the sun. Feed the chickens and clean out their run. Check the traps. Follow trails. Track down grown-ups.

Kill them.

The grown-ups mostly went about in ones and twos. Sometimes there were more, sometimes there was only one of them, and every time Scarface was able to sneak up on them and kill them without being seen, without getting hurt. Most of them were asleep, hiding inside buildings, and Ella would wait outside while Scarface went in and did what he had to do. She would sit there, nervous, hoping there were no others nearby. She would try not to listen to the sounds of Scarface clearing out the nest, the sound of fighting, things crashing and breaking. Then Scarface would come out all covered in blood.

But sometimes the grown-ups were wandering lost and confused in the daylight. And every morning there were more out in the fields, standing like the first scarecrow. Arms stretched out. Once Ella saw a crow sitting on the head of a father, pecking into his earhole, and he didn't move at all.

Occasionally they found more scarecrows on their travels, and always Scarface would cut them down. They were the easiest ones.

Ella got to know the area around the farm very well on her travels. There was a big park nearby with trees laid out in long, straight lines. And lots of lakes—there seemed to be lakes everywhere. Sometimes in the distance she saw what looked like a city, with a real castle watching over it, but Scarface never went near it. He seemed to want to avoid towns and houses, unless he had to go in to find hiding grown-ups.

Ella thought they weren't really in the countryside at all, not the faraway countryside. There were roads everywhere, crisscrossing the fields and woods, with grass and weeds beginning to poke through the asphalt.

She spent the whole time feeling tired, but she was growing stronger every day, and was able to walk farther without her legs feeling like they were going to crumble. At least Scarface had good food. The best she'd eaten since she'd moved out of Waitrose all those weeks ago. There were eggs every day, sometimes a chicken. Sometimes animals Scarface had trapped. Rabbits and ducks and pigeons. Sometimes fish. Scarface had nets and traps all over the place in the lakes and rivers. He also had stores in another barn. There were big sacks of flour, and dried beans, a pile of potatoes, and onions hanging up.

When they were out, he picked lots of wild leaves and

what looked like weeds. They tasted bitter, but Ella chewed them and swallowed them down, because she knew they were good for her. Scarface even made a sort of flat, hard bread.

Ella was beginning to wonder if this was how her life was going to be from now on. Just him and her, not ever seeing another child again. Never having a proper conversation again. It wasn't too bad. She felt safe with old Face-Ache. He knew how to look after himself and how to look after her. But she did feel lonely and bored a lot of the time. She cheered herself up by reading some of the books on his shelves. She never saw him read; instead he would sit by himself for hours and hours, just staring at nothing.

And then one day they saw some other children.

Ella and Scarface were returning from a hunt and it had been a big waste of time. They hadn't seen any grown-ups, not even a scarecrow, and in the end Scarface had given up. They were a long way from the farm and it was starting to grow dark, so they'd turned and headed for home. Ella was looking forward to getting back; they always had something warm to eat, usually soup of some sort. Scarface was always cooking up chicken bones and stuff. Ella was picturing the two of them sitting by the fire as the smoke went up through the hole in the roof, getting nice and warm and cozy. Like how her mom had used to make her a mug of hot chocolate when she came home from school in the winter.

These thoughts had kept her going, and they were nearly at the edge of the woods when Scarface froze, as suddenly as if someone had paused a DVD. One moment he was walking along and the next he was still as a statue, in a sort of half-walking position. He stayed there like that, one hand on Ella's chest to stop her moving. Then, without any warning, he quickly pulled her to the ground. They lay there, peering out from behind some dead, scratchy brown bracken.

Ella couldn't see anything at first. She had no idea what they were supposed to be looking for. Some grown-ups, probably. Though she had never seen Scarface act like this before.

And then she saw them.

A group of kids striding through the fields, passing alongside the woods. They carried spears and clubs on their shoulders, and were laughing and chatting, one of them swiping the grass with a long blade as he went. They looked like kids just coming back from the sports field after a game of something, carrying their rackets and bats.

Ella wanted to shout out to them. She raised her head, but Scarface clamped his hand over her mouth and squashed her down into the dirt.

What are you doing? she wanted to say. She struggled, but it was no good, he was too strong. She could hardly move at all.

What are you doing? They're children. Only children. I can go with them!

And then she remembered what Scarface was. What he looked like. They'd try to kill him. When he was just . . .

What was he?

He wasn't an enemy, that was for sure. He could have killed her ten times over if he'd wanted. Instead he looked after her. She managed to wriggle around a bit and tap him on the arm. Got his attention, looked into his face, trying not to concentrate on his bad eye, the bloody one with the scars all around it. She tried to show him with her own eyes that it was all right, that she wasn't going to shout out, that he could remove his big, sweaty, mashed-up hand. He didn't let go, though, wouldn't take the risk. He waited until the kids were long gone before freeing her.

"I wouldn't have done anything," Ella said. "Not once I thought about it. I wouldn't have given you away. You're safe with me." Even as she was saying it, though, she pictured herself up and running through the long grass toward the kids. Wished she was going with them. Scarface wasn't her friend, he was a monster. A gnarly freak. She couldn't bear the thought of spending the rest of her life with him. Looking at his ugly face day after day. She started to cry, and he tilted his head like a dog, then got up and left her to it. Turning his back on her and staring off into the woods.

"I'm sorry," Ella said, with a big sniff. "You must think I'm a baby."

Scarface gave a little shrug, slipped his backpack off, and then squatted down and waited for Ella to climb on. Halfway home she stopped crying and let her mind go empty and numb. Tried to pretend she'd never even seen the other kids. That life was the same as it had been this morning.

That evening, as they sat with bowls of chicken soup, staring at the red glow among the white ashes of the fire, she allowed herself to think about the children again. At least she knew now that there were others around. There was more out there than just grown-ups. There must be other farms. Other safe places. This wasn't the end. Ella would wait. Maybe plan a way to run off, once she knew where the kids were. That gave her something to think about. Making a plan. Even if she never did anything about it, it would stop her from getting bored. She could lie there in the dark and have fantasies.

She just wished she'd been able to see them better, to talk to them. Even if only for five minutes. One minute.

She found a chicken wishbone in her soup and picked it out, sucked the scraps of meat off it and then, when Scarface wasn't looking, held it behind her back and gently broke it. Made a wish, with all her heart, that she would see some more children soon.

The next day she got her wish.

But like all good things, it came with bad things.

Very bad things.

It was better hunting the next day. There were two fat rab-bits in the traps in the morning. There was a scarecrow in the field that ended up on the bone pile to feed the dogs. Scarface soon found a fresh trail and picked up a scent. Before midday they'd found their prey, hiding out in a house, but they weren't finished there. Scarface picked up another scent and they were off into a small town, with posh houses among the trees, cars sitting in the driveways.

After he'd dealt with the sickos in the town, they set off for home. They were nearly there when Scarface suddenly got excited. He'd seen something. He paced around and around in circles, his good eye scanning the ground. Every now and then he'd stop and tilt his head up and sniff the air, and then he was off and moving quickly, not toward the farm, but back the way they'd come.

Ella wanted to tell him they'd done enough for one day, but she knew there'd be no stopping him, so she tagged along behind, watching his heavy pack as it bounced on his back and trying not to get fed up.

After a while he veered off into the big park. They jogged along the wide walkway that ran down the middle of it, trees lined up in neat rows on either side. The walkway ran dead straight. In one direction was a hill with the statue of a man on a horse on the top of it. In the other direction was the big castle she'd sometimes spotted off in the distance. And there, running down the path toward it, were three children.

Scarface got his binoculars out and watched them go. He made a sort of disappointed sound in his throat, like *mhmph*, and lowered the binoculars.

They looked in the other direction and Ella saw that a couple of scarecrows had appeared by the statue, standing there as if they were trying to stay as still as it was. And, as Ella watched, a group of grown-ups came over the crest of the hill next to them, stumbling along in a tight pack. Ella hoped Scarface wasn't planning to attack them. It was different hunting ones that were asleep, or from behind. These would see him coming before he got close.

"Come on," she said. "Let's go home, yeah? You can't kill them all. Not today."

Scarface just sniffed and lifted his binoculars again. Studying the grown-ups, who were walking steadily down the hill toward the start of the walkway.

"Let's go the other way," said Ella. "We've had a good day."

Scarface seemed to think for a moment, then he put his binoculars away and started to move toward the hill, getting faster and faster as he went. For a tiny fraction of a second, Ella had a fantasy of turning and running in the other direction, toward the children, toward the castle. It would be safe there. There would be other children.

But she didn't turn and she didn't run. She was too scared to risk going off on her own. Too scared to leave Scarface. Instead she ran to catch up with him like an obedient puppy.

In the end it didn't really matter that the grown-ups saw Scarface coming. They tried to be ready, some even hurried up and stumbled toward him in a sort of charge, but he was too fast for them, and he had his knives, and he stabbed them as he ran past, then he turned and went back and stabbed them again. Ella didn't want to watch, but she was running, so she couldn't shut her eyes. She hoped that was the end of it. The walking grown-ups were all knocked to the ground and bleeding. Scarface kept going, though, up to the top of the hill, and chopped down the two scarecrows and then stood against the skyline at the base of the statue, which was sitting on what looked like a pile of rocks and stones. As she got nearer, Ella saw that the statue seemed to be of some sort of Roman emperor.

She ran the last few steps up the hill and over to Scarface.

"Face-Ache," she said, sounding hot and bothered and grumpy, "can we *please* go home now?"

She tugged at his sleeve. He ignored her. He was staring through his binoculars again.

Then he made the *mhmph*ing noise in his throat again. What was he looking at now? Bloody old grown-up.

"What can you see?" She turned and looked for herself. It was like all three of them were looking now, she and Scarface and the Roman emperor on his green metal horse.

There was a long sweep of grass down the hillside, then woods and fields dotted about, roads and hedges and the occasional building. And there, about as far away as Ella could see, was a dark, moving mass. It looked like a shadow on the land, slowly turning it black, eating it up, like when a cloud passes over the sun.

"What is it?" she said. "What is that?"

Scarface passed her the binoculars and Ella put them to her eyes, fiddling with the wheel that adjusted the focus until she could see sharply.

Even then it took her a few seconds to make sense of it. This big, blurry, moving *thing*.

No. Not a *thing*. Not *one* thing. *Lots* of things. *People* . . . men and women, mothers and fathers, grown-ups. An army of them, tramping slowly and steadily toward her. They filled the ground they walked on. There must be hundreds of them. She wrinkled her nose. It was as if she could already smell them.

How awful must that be? The stink. So many of them like that.

And then Ella realized something.

"The farm," she said. "They're heading toward the farm."

10

Ella didn't think she'd ever run so fast. Down the side of the hill, nearly falling over as her legs ran away with her, and then cutting across the park toward some woods, Scarface holding back so that she could keep up with him, though she knew he would rather be racing ahead. He must be scared for his precious farm, his supplies, his chickens, his fire, and his bed and his books. His whole world.

She was glad of all the walking they'd been doing, strengthening her legs, but she soon had a stitch in her side and burning in her lungs. Her head was pounding, like someone was hitting her with a spade.

As they ran, Ella couldn't stop thinking about that big stain of grown-ups spreading across the ground, all the way from right to left, filling the world up, it had seemed. Surely nothing could stop them, not all of Scarface's traps. Even if he had fifty of them, a hundred. The only thing on their side was that the army had been going slowly, plodding along, only moving as fast as the slowest walker. The binoculars had made them look closer than they were. It would be a long time before they got as far as the farm. Even so, they'd get there eventually, and then what? Would they go around? Or would they plow straight on through, not caring?

What were they doing, marching along like that? She'd never seen so many of them all together in one place. She hated not being able to talk to Scarface about it. Just having thoughts rattling around in her head, getting bigger and scarier because she had no way of letting them out.

As they got to the trees, Ella took a last glance across the familiar fields in the direction the grown-ups had been coming from. You couldn't see anything from down here, though. All you could see were green grass, blue sky, wispy clouds, some birds. You couldn't imagine what was coming your way.

Then they were pounding through the woods, Ella desperate not to trip up. She could hear a weird sound, like screaming and wailing. She thought at first it was people, and then she realized it must be the dogs. They were spooked. She couldn't see any of them, but she could sense them in the trees all around, so that she couldn't tell where the noise was coming from exactly. They sounded like wolves in a horror film. She knew how careful Scarface was around them. He was scared of them, and if *they* were scared of something else, then it was bad. Very bad.

Ella saw some movement off to one side and was terrified that the army of mothers and fathers had caught up with them. But it wasn't grown-ups, it was kids, five of them, charging through the woods like rabbits running from a pack of hounds. They were going much faster than her and Scarface, and as they crashed past, Ella saw their terrified faces. Were they scared because they'd spotted Scarface, or was it the thought of the army, which they were obviously running away from? In a moment they were gone. Ella didn't even have the chance to call out to them.

Scarface slowed down and stopped. He was thinking about something. He looked pained. Was he wondering whether to change his plan? Abandon the farm and run away? He turned to Ella.

"It's all right," she said. "Don't worry about me. You have to save the farm."

Scarface suddenly scooped Ella up in his left arm and hurried on, clutching her to his chest, so that she was facing backward, going faster than she could run by herself. They burst out of the trees back into the sunlight. Ella twisted around to see where they were going, and there ahead of them was the farm, across the other side of the field.

And people.

At first Ella thought they might be grown-ups, and then she realized they were the children who had passed them in the woods. Three boys and two girls. They were moving toward the gate. The tripwires. Ella screamed, her voice high and thin and piercing.

"No! No. Stop! There's a trap! Stop there!"

The kids turned and froze, not sure what to do. Scared. Ella wondered what she and Scarface must look like, charging across the open ground toward them.

"Please!" she yelled again. "Just wait. It's all right."

But the kids were pointing and shouting something, eyes wide, mouths black holes in their faces, panicked. Ella looked back over Scarface's shoulder.

"Oh, no . . ."

The dogs were running.

They were streaming out of the trees from all sides, howling as they came. If she hadn't been up high on Scarface's shoulder, Ella might not have been able to see them, only the waving of the long grass as they pushed through it. Some were getting close enough for her to be able to make out the yellow of their teeth, their wide, crazy eyes.

"Faster. Go faster!" she shouted, but Scarface didn't need to be told. He'd moved onto the road and was sprinting, jolting Ella's face into his body. She looked down and saw a dog running with them, a mongrel with its tail between its legs, its fur up all along the ridge of its back, showing its teeth and gums, whimpering and yelping.

Ella twisted around and looked toward the kids at the gate. They hadn't moved. Thank God. They'd listened to her. But they would have had a good look at Scarface by now. What would they be thinking? Especially now that he had a gang of dogs coming with him. Which would they fear more, Ella's warning, or the things bolting toward them across the field?

One of the girls obviously decided to risk the gate. She walked quickly toward it, and Ella screamed louder than she had ever screamed before in her life, shrill as a referee's whistle.

A boy hurried after the girl and pulled her back, and at last Ella and Scarface were there.

"He's all right!" Ella shouted, wriggling down out of Scarface's arms. "He won't hurt you. He's not an enemy. He's been looking after me. But this is his home and there are traps."

Her words had come spilling out in a breathless tumble and she hoped it was enough. The kids were all armed and ready to fight. Scarface had his knives in his hands. He didn't trust them any more than they trusted him. The mongrel was zooming around them, jumping up, and snapping and yapping. Scarface kicked it away and risked glancing back at the field. The other dogs were still coming through the grass.

One of the boys pointed at Scarface.

"We know who he is," he said. "He's the Predator."

"Never seen him up close before," said another boy. "He's even uglier than I thought."

"He's a good person," said Ella angrily.

"Never mind that," said the girl who had almost gotten herself killed in Scarface's traps. "Those dogs are going to massacre us."

They all turned now, weapons at the ready, set to take on the pack.

The dogs were nearly on them, but they were slowing down, and at the last moment they began to split and turn to left and right, avoiding the farm, all except for one huge brute with a square head and short black fur. It charged toward the kids, who scattered. But the dog ignored them and ran on, not attacking, but retreating. It went right past them, barking like mad, and stumbled straight into the trip wires. Ella didn't manage to look away in time and watched helplessly as the pole came whipping out of the bushes and smacked right into the dog, taking it in the back of its neck as it jumped up to free itself from the wires.

One of the other girls screamed and a boy laughed. The shortest of the three, the one who'd been mean to Scarface.

"Did you see that? Sick!"

The dog died instantly and hung there on the spikes, its back legs twitching, as if it was still trying to run.

"Close one, Sonya," said the tallest boy.

"Ooh, I'd like to have seen that," said the short boy. "A Sonya kebab."

"Shut up, Harry," said Sonya.

"*Shut up, Harry,*" Harry repeated, mimicking Sonya.

The dogs were still circling the farm, seeming to want to stay close to Scarface, but scared to come *too* close.

"We're screwed," said the third boy, who had a bow slung across his back, a bandage over one of his eyebrows, and a big bruise covering half his face. "We can take our chances with the dogs, the grown-ups, or the Windsor bastards. But either way, *we are screwed.*"

"We should keep on running," said Sonya.

"*We should keep on running,*" Harry repeated.

"If you don't shut it I will smash your teeth in, Harry," said Sonya.

"*I will smash your teeth in, Harry.*"

"Just shut up, Harry," said the third boy, and he glanced at Scarface, not liking what he saw.

"Instead of being a total jerk, as usual," he went on, "why don't you tell us what you think we should do?"

"To be honest, I agree with Sonya," said Harry. "I think we should go on. When those grown-ups get here it's gonna be well crazy."

The other girl, who had been quiet up till now, turned to Ella. She looked very similar to Sonya; they could be sisters.

"We don't know what to do. Whether to keep on running. Did you see them? The grown-ups?"

Ella nodded.

Sonya was staring into the distance.

"How long before they get here?" she asked nobody in particular.

"Fifteen, twenty minutes maybe," said the boy with the bruised face. "We can't keep on running. We can't get around them. We need to hide."

Sonya was now looking along the road toward the gate.

"If you go carefully, you can get over the wires," said Ella.

Scarface grunted and gave her a look, as if to say, *Why are you inviting them in?*

"They can help us defend the farm," she explained, hoping he'd understand.

"I'm with Isaac," said the tallest boy, the oldest-looking one, who had a round face and pimples. "I say we hole up here. We're way off our turf and it'll be dark soon."

The short boy, Harry, eyed Scarface suspiciously. He was wearing a black North Face jacket that he'd painted with

slogans: KILL ALL ZOMBIES—LADIES' MAN—I WILL EAT
YOU.

"You sure Pizzaface is safe?" he said.

"Why would I lie to you?" said Ella.

"*Why would I lie to you?*" Harry repeated, and Ella felt her
face get hot. She wished she hadn't said anything. Wished
she'd just left these kids to look after themselves.

Sonya walked over to the wires.

"Show us the way."

Ella led them to the gate, carefully avoiding catching
Scarface's eye. He hung back, letting them get ahead, and
she heard him making some noise behind them. She knew
he'd be pulling the dog off the spikes and resetting the trap.

"You must never try to open the gate," she said when they
got to it. "Always climb over. And don't go in the bushes.
There are traps everywhere."

Once safely inside the farmyard, the kids stood around
awkwardly, taking it all in, unsure of themselves, trying to
act tough. Obviously scared. They were older than her, the
boy with pimples being maybe fifteen. He introduced himself as Daniel, the quiet boy was Isaac, and the other girl,
who looked like Sonya's sister, was called Louisa.

"So what you got here?" said Harry. "We gonna be safe?"

"You got food?" asked Sonya.

"Oh, yes," said Ella. "Lots . . ." She stopped herself.
"Well, not lots, some."

Stupid. She'd wanted to show off. What if the kids
were lying, though? What if they'd only really come here
to steal stuff? What if they found out about the barn full of

chickens? They might return with friends, with their own army. She wished Scarface would finish what he was doing and come back. She didn't feel like she could deal with this by herself.

"He got weapons?" Harry went on.

"Oh, yes," said Ella, the words coming out in a rush. "Loads. He's really good at hunting, he hunts grown-ups and he kills them, he's very good at killing, every day he kills people . . ." *People like you,* she wanted to add as a warning, but thought that might be going too far.

"Do you live here, then?" asked Louisa. "With Ghostface?"

"Duh," said Harry. "What do you think, Louisa? Oh, I forgot, you don't ever think, do you?"

Louisa blushed and looked at her shoes.

"I didn't always live here," said Ella, coming to Louisa's rescue. "I do now. Scarface saved me."

"Scarface?" said Daniel. "Him? The Predator?"

Harry let out a burst of nasty laughter. "You can talk, Daniel," he said. "Are those your zits, or are you looking after them for a grown-up?"

Daniel swore at Harry, who just laughed again.

"You are such an asshole, Harry," said Isaac, and Harry copied him.

"*You are such an asshole.* At least I'm not an ass*face* like your friend," he added, looking at Ella. "He's ugly as the Elephant Man."

"He got kicked by an ugly bastard wearing ugly boots," said Daniel.

"Whacked by the ugly bat."

"He won Britain's ugliest man competition."

"Britain's Got Ugly Talent."

Sonya joined in with them. *"Ugly Come Dancing."*

"Ugly on Ice," said Louisa.

"That's crap," said Harry. *"Ugly on Ice."* He turned to Sonya. "Tell your dumb sister not to try to join in with the jokes."

"Actually, I thought *Britain's Got Ugly Talent* was lame," said Louisa.

Ella heard something and looked around to see that Scarface had arrived without anyone noticing. He must have heard everything they said. She hated these kids being mean about him. Especially as he might be the only person who could keep them alive when the army arrived.

He was standing there, silent, not moving. The other kids were peeking at him out of the corners of their eyes, not wanting to stare. Pretending they hadn't been laughing at him.

"We should check out these buildings," said Isaac, looking around the yard, changing the subject.

"Yeah," said Daniel. "The farmhouse looks pretty solid."

"It's not safe," said Ella, almost before he'd stopped talking. "It was burned."

"We should still check it out, though."

"He won't even let me see inside," said Ella.

"We gotta do what he says?" said Sonya, her voice all sneery.

"He'll kill you if you try and go in there." Ella couldn't think of what else to say. She needed to change the subject. Besides, it wasn't necessarily a lie. It wasn't working, though; the kids were still looking over toward the farm-house. What if they searched everywhere and found the food, the chickens?

"There's a lookout," she blurted.

"What sort of lookout?" Isaac asked.

"In the trees," Ella went on quickly, pointing up to where one of the platforms was just visible. "We can see where the grown-ups are, maybe? They might not even be coming this way. We should check."

Ella led them over to a shed.

"Who's coming up?" she asked. Sonya and Isaac stepped forward. There was a ladder you put against the shed, then you climbed onto the roof, and from there you could lean over and reach the first wooden board that was nailed to a big tree.

"We've heard about the Predator," said Sonya as they began to climb. "Everyone talks about the creepy skulls and weird crap he has hanging up everywhere. But nobody really knew what he looked like. We keep away from him."

"He's not a monster," said Ella.

"Can he understand us?" Sonya asked. "Can he talk, or what? What is he?"

"He can't talk," said Ella. "But he *can* understand."

"I don't trust him," said Sonya. "I wouldn't live here with him. I'd be scared he might fatten me up and eat me one night."

"I'm not scared of him," said Ella.

"You should be," said Sonya. "We need him for now, but if you like, when this is over, we can try and get rid of him for you."

"Oh, no," said Ella, panicked. "No, you mustn't."

Sonya laughed. "I was only joking," she said.

But was she? Ella couldn't be sure.

There was only a small platform up in the tree, with just enough room for one of them at a time. Two ropes tied around the trunk led from there to another tree, then another. By using them as a bridge, they could get to the main viewing platform at the front of the farm. Sonya and Isaac went first, standing on one rope, their hands on the other, wobbling and swaying backward and forward, laughing to cover their nervousness.

Ella waited till they'd reached the next platform and went after them.

Once they were all on the main platform they looked out across the fields, but couldn't see anything of the grown-ups. The army must be hidden behind trees and small rises in the ground.

"Maybe they won't come this way," said Ella. "Maybe we'll be all right."

"They're out there," said Isaac. "We all saw them."

"One of us needs to stay up here as a lookout," said Sonya. "I think you should, Isaac. You can fire your arrows down from here."

"How many arrows have you got?" Ella asked.

"About twenty-five, thirty," said Isaac.

"And how many grown-ups did you see earlier?"

"Yeah, way more than that," said Isaac, and he gave a harsh laugh. "Better than nothing, though."

Isaac agreed to stay up there if they brought him something to eat, and Ella took Sonya back down.

When they returned to the yard, the other kids came over and crowded around them, asking loads of questions, trying to reassure themselves they'd made the right decision to stop here.

"We couldn't keep on running," said Louisa.

"'Specially as you run like a typical girl," said Harry, and he went into a silly run, all wobbly knees and flapping arms. "Look at me," he squealed in a high-pitched voice. "I'm a kind of crap dinosaur."

Sonya stepped up behind him and tripped him, sending him sprawling into the dirt. He swore at her, but she stood over him and held him down with the heel of her boot.

"If you have a go at my sister one more time, I will shove your head up your ass," she said. "And you can see what you had for lunch."

"What's the matter with you?" said Harry. "Lost your sense of humor? Besides, you're always having a go at her."

"She's my sister, that's different."

Ella left them to it and went to look for Scarface. She found him near the gate, rigging up more defenses. Pulling some vicious-looking farm machinery into place. She said hello to him, but he ignored her. He seemed in a bad mood, but whether that was because there was an army of grown-ups on its way or because Ella had invited the others in, she couldn't tell. When he was in one of his moods, he behaved like a little kid.

"Are you cross with me?" she asked.

He shrugged.

"I *had* to let them in," she went on. "You know that. We couldn't leave them out there to get killed, could we? And anyway, if the grown-ups *do* attack, it'll be helpful to have some more people to fight them off, won't it?"

Scarface just shrugged again.

"So what do you think?" Ella asked. "That I should have just let them get splatted by your trap? Would you have liked that?"

Scarface gave Ella one of his sort-of-smiles. That made her feel better.

"I didn't tell them about the food and the chickens," she said. "And I scared them. I told them how fierce you are. How you're the biggest killer on the planet. How they don't want to mess with you. Is that right? Did I do the right thing?"

Again all she got was a shrug. She hated it when Scarface was grumpy like this. She wanted to make him laugh.

"I didn't tell them about your books, and how you're secretly a wimp and into baking and ballet and Justin Bieber. How your name is really Face-Ache the Belieber."

Scarface gave two quick snorts through his nose. It might have been a laugh. Ella told herself it was.

"I'd better go and see what they're doing," she said, trying to keep busy, trying not to think about the grown-ups getting closer. She looked to see if he had anything to add, and just as she had expected, he shrugged again.

Bloody grumpy old Face-Ache.

Daniel and Harry were sitting on some old logs that Scarface had set up like seats in the middle of the yard. They were checking their weapons and chatting nervously. There was no sign of the two girls.

"Where's Sonya and Louisa?" asked Ella, trying to sound casual.

"Dunno," said Harry.

Ella strolled off, trying not to hurry. Where were they? What were they doing? She looked everywhere, as the shadows of night deepened, and eventually found them by the chicken barn, fiddling with the locks.

"You need to be careful," she said, going over to them. "He's got traps everywhere."

"What's in here?" said Sonya.

"Farm stuff, I think," said Ella. "Tools and that."

"There's a funny smell."

"That's a farm smell."

"Like animals."

"There were animals here before, I think."

"If we're gonna be safe, we need to get inside a building," said Louisa.

"We live in the big barn," said Ella. "That'll be the best place—we'll all go in there."

"Why not the farmhouse?"

"Oh, I never go in there."

"Why not?"

"You know . . ." Ella had no idea what to say next. Why couldn't Scarface deal with all this? "Shall I take something up to Isaac?" was all she could think of.

"Sure." Sonya dug about in her backpack and took out a bottle of water and a plastic box filled with what looked like trail mix—dried fruit and nuts and stuff. When Ella went to take it from her, Sonya held on to it tightly and put her face very close to Ella's.

"Are you holding out on us?" she said.

"What?" Ella was trying not to get scared.

"You're all nervous and jittery. Like you're hiding something. Like there's more here than you're letting on."

"I'm just scared of the grown-ups coming. That's what we should be thinking about. Not . . . you know . . ."

"Yeah, you're right." Sonya let go of the box. "I keep forgetting about the grown-ups, like everything's okay, and then I suddenly remember, and I'm like, oh my God. This is not happening. Isaac is gonna think we've forgotten about him. You take this up."

"Okay." Ella walked slowly away, carrying the box and the bottle of water.

When she climbed back up to Isaac, she found him sitting on the platform, reading a book.

"Can you see anything?" she asked.

Isaac looked up from the book and scanned the surrounding countryside.

"Nothing," he said. "No sign of them."

"No." Ella got the water and the food out of her backpack. "I meant, can you see your book? It's getting very dark."

Isaac laughed. "Not really. But I was bored. There's nothing to see, nothing happening. Maybe they've all gone another way. Maybe we'll be okay. That's what I'm praying for anyway. What's going on down there?"

"Getting ready." Ella handed Isaac the food and he started to dig in.

"What are you reading?" she asked, and he flapped the cover at her.

"It's the first Alex Rider book," he said.

"Is it good? I think Sam read it. My brother."

"Yeah. I've read it before. Loads of times. We need to get some new books. I'd go into Windsor, but . . . you know."

"What's Windsor?"

"Where the big castle is," said Isaac. "It's the biggest town around here. There's a load of kids living there, but they don't like anyone else coming close. Don't like strangers."

"Where are you from, then?" Ella asked.

"Bracknell. It's quite far from here. On the other side of the grown-ups. We were stuck. Windsor kids one way, who'd probably have beaten on us; grown-ups the other. It felt like we had no options. No choice. It's kismet."

"What?"

"Fate. Do you believe in fate?"

"I don't really know what that is."

"It's like there's a big book somewhere with your whole life written in it. Everything that's going to happen to you."

"I've never really thought about it like that," said Ella.

"I have," said Isaac. "I have this feeling. That if they're going to get you, then that's what'll happen—they'll get you."

"Is that fate, then?"

"I think it's my fate. That it's written down. They'll get me in the end. If I dodge it today, they'll get me tomorrow."

"It's better not to think about things too much," said Ella.

"Maybe you're right."

"What's the matter with the moon?" Ella asked, looking up at where it was appearing out of the darkening sky. It was turning red.

"Dunno," said Isaac. "It's not a good sign, though, is it?" He gave a bitter little laugh.

"What would make it red?" Ella said.

"Maybe smoke from a fire or something," said Isaac. "Or maybe dust or, I don't know, particles in the atmosphere, you know, like, refracting the light."

"I think it's pretty," said Ella. "So let's not worry about it, yeah?"

"Good plan. No worries. It's just . . . They're out there somewhere. I know they are."

Ella got Scarface's binoculars out and scanned the fields. It was getting too dark to see much. She passed them to Isaac.

"What else you got on you?" he asked. "Anything useful, like radar, or an RPG launcher?"

"Nothing really."

Isaac adjusted the focus as he scanned the horizon.

"So were you out looking for food and stuff today, then?" Ella asked, remembering the scavenger parties back in Holloway.

"Yeah. There's still quite a lot of stuff if you know where to look. Got a bit lost, though. Went farther than we meant to, strayed into Windsor territory."

"Are the Windsor children really that bad?"

"They're all bastards. Them and Slough and Maidenhead. We only have any dealings with them at the races, at Ascot. Then we all get together and . . ." His voice dropped. "Oh, shit."

"What?"

"They're coming. . . ."

12

Ella found the other kids sitting on the logs, not really talking to each other. She was glad to see that Sonya and Louisa were there. She explained what she'd seen from the lookout and saw them get all hunched up and scared-looking, though they were trying hard not to show it. Ella had seen enough kids like this before to recognize the signs. Daniel swore. Harry laughed. Ella had no idea what at. Maybe nothing. Louisa looked toward the gate and shook her head.

There was no sign of Scarface. He was still keeping to himself. Ella hurried off and tracked him down to the barn, where he was sitting in his favorite garden chair, poking the fire with a bundle of sticks that he'd tied together.

"They're nearly here," she said. "We saw them from the tree with the binoculars. We've still got time to run. We could try to get to Windsor. We'll be faster than them, I think."

Scarface shook his head. He was probably as scared of the kids in Windsor as the grown-ups. Maybe more so. And everything he had was here, on the farm.

"Sonya and Louisa, the girls, they've been trying to get in the buildings."

Scarface made the grunting noise in his throat and laid his sticks down near the edge of the fire. Ella could see that he'd made another couple of bundles.

"Are we going to die?" she asked him.

She didn't know why she bothered asking. She knew what he would do. Just shrug. That was all he seemed to do.

"Well, I don't want to die," said Ella. "So will you please get up and do something? Get ready!"

Scarface got up creakily from his chair and stretched. She could hear his joints popping, and he gave another little groan, deep in his throat. Then he found Ella's spiked club and her rubber Lego shield and gave them to her. Ella felt like throwing them on the floor.

"I can't do anything," she said. "I can't fight. Look at me. I'm no use. Why did you ever rescue me if you weren't going to look after me?"

Scarface shook his head and turned away, went over to a cabinet on the wall that was padlocked shut. When he opened it, Ella saw there was a shotgun inside it, the type that farmers used, and some boxes of shells. He bent the gun in half and slotted in two shells, then filled up his pockets with the boxes. He left the gun bent in half.

Out in the yard they were able to smell the grown-ups before they could see them. The wind was blowing toward them from the west and bringing with it the unwashed stink of a thousand diseased bodies. A countryside smell of manure and sour urine, mixed with a town smell of drains and sewers and rotting rubbish. Then they heard them, the steady tramp of their feet making a shuffling rumble, and their sighs and hisses, not a roar, just a depressing moan. Like wind rattling at a window, trying to get in.

The kids moved to the gate. There was still nothing to see in the darkness. The grown-ups wouldn't be visible until they got to the wire.

Ella and Scarface found them there, staring into the night. The noise of the approaching grown-ups made her shiver, and she wanted to be sick. The smell was suffocating. She heard Isaac calling out and looked up to see that he had moved back over the rope bridge to the platform in the nearer tree. He sounded scared and excited.

"They're almost here!" he was shouting. "You should see it. You wouldn't believe it. It's insane. There's hundreds of them. Unless they go around us we don't stand a hope in hell."

"They have to go past us, don't they?" said Louisa. "Why wouldn't they?"

"They have to go past us, don't they?" Harry mimicked her.

"Well, they do!" snapped Louisa angrily. "Some of them. They wouldn't all want to push in here."

"Unless they're hungry," said Harry, and he licked his lips. "Mmmm, a nice fresh Louisa."

Daniel didn't laugh. He looked scared. "Why don't we all just climb up there with Isaac?" he said. "They're not going to get to us up there. We could wait for them to move on."

"Yeah, and what if they don't move on?" said Sonya. "What then? If we go up top we'll be stuck there. Like a cat chased up a tree by a pack of dogs."

"Just like the hobbits in *The Hobbit*," said Ella. "And we don't have any kind of magic talking eagle to save us."

Harry spotted Scarface's gun.

"You got any more of them?" he asked. "That'd be really useful."

Scarface didn't respond in any way. Didn't even look at Harry.

"It's the only one he's got," said Ella.

"He's a miserable bastard, isn't he?" said Sonya.

"I'd be miserable with a face like that," said Harry.

"I'd be miserable with a face like yours," said Sonya.

Scarface put a finger to his lips to get them all to shut up. They stopped talking, and they could hear the grown-ups, closer still, a whispering noise like wind in the trees, or a wave coming closer and closer, just one wave that sounded like it was never going to break. A tsunami.

Ella stayed close to Scarface, looking at the faces of the other kids, just white streaks in the night.

"I can see them," said Louisa quietly, and they all turned toward the gate. There, across the open ground, was a moving black mass, the pale light from the moon outlining the tops of heads, picking out steam rising into the night air. They filled the space that was framed by the trees on both sides of the road, and they took up the whole width of the field.

One by one the children moved to the gate to get a better look. The stink of the grown-ups was growing stronger; it made Ella feel sick. She wanted to hide, to dig a hole and bury herself in the ground, let the wave wash over her. But she had to look. She had to know what was coming. She went over to the gate with Scarface and forced herself to look.

They were coming slowly, bunched together, shuffling

through the long grass, trampling everything in their way. A shapeless mass of people. Ella couldn't see their faces yet, but one thing was very clear to her.

They weren't going to stop. They weren't going to go around. They would come straight through the farm. . . .

"We need to get in the barn," she said, surprised that her voice didn't sound more shaky.

Scarface put a hand on her shoulder, holding her still. She looked up at him. He was staring at the grown-ups, unblinking. He wanted to defend his farm, but what could he do?

"Army ants," said Daniel. "They're just like army ants. They'll eat everything in their way. We should of run. Instead we're trapped here with a freak and a useless little girl."

He started shouting, swearing at the top of his voice, calling the faceless grown-ups all sorts of bad names, his voice getting hoarser and hoarser. And then he stopped shouting, shook his head, and dropped to his knees, pressing his face into the ground. He was crying. Harry snickered, and Sonya punched him in the arm. Scarface ignored them, just watched the approaching army, his gun hanging from his elbow.

A thin cloud moved across the sky, exposing the moon so that its full bloodred light fell on the fields.

And now Ella saw their faces.

Stupid faces, diseased, rotten, lumpy, and gray. They were all sorts—mothers, fathers, a few teenagers, their clothes greasy and black, some naked. Mostly so skinny they were just walking skeletons, but one or two were swollen and puffy, like fat grubs ready to burst. And there were bits of them missing—noses, ears, eyes, lips, fingers, hands, whole arms.

One of them was slightly in front, a mother who seemed

to be laughing, with wide, crazy eyes and two rows of gleaming white teeth. She wasn't laughing, though: she'd lost the skin and flesh from the lower half of her face, and there were two thick ropes of snot coming out of her nose and dribbling down across her teeth to where they hung off her chin, swaying from side to side as she walked.

Ella put a hand over her mouth as she retched, her throat gulping. Still Scarface would not move. Daniel had gotten up and he and the other kids were backing away.

Still Scarface wouldn't move and still the grown-ups kept on advancing. They were hissing. They'd seen the children waiting on the other side of the gate, heard Daniel shrieking, and they fixed their dead eyes on them, blank but staring, black holes in their horrible, stupid faces. The first of them were coming up the road toward the gate now, funnelling into the narrower gap, so that they were even more tightly pressed together. Any moment now they would be at the wires.

"We have to hide," said Ella. "We can't fight them."

Scarface calmly snapped his shotgun straight. Waiting.

And then the lead grown-ups got tangled in the wires, tripping and stumbling. Nothing happened. They kept trying to walk on. What was wrong? Why hadn't they triggered the trap? More and more of them filled the gap, plowing through the wires. Hadn't Scarface reset the pole? Had it broken? Ella was just about to say something when there was a creaking sound, a crack and a rushing noise, and then, with a great thud, the pole swung out. It chopped down a line of grown-ups and thwacked into the backs of the leaders, skewering them on the spikes. They wriggled and writhed there, trapped, five or six of them. Still the others behind them kept on pressing forward, so that the next rank was slowly pushed into the pole and on to the rear-facing spikes belly first.

It made no difference. It didn't stop the rest of them. They came trudging on, driving the trapped grown-ups deeper into the spikes and bending the pole. There were so many of them pushing that there was soon a splintering sound and a crack, and the pole broke and the front ranks went tumbling down.

It made no difference. The ones behind came trundling on, walking right over the first line of grown-ups, treading on them, crushing them beneath their feet. They were at the gate now, only a couple of yards from where Ella stood with Scarface. All around she could hear the sound of other traps being sprung among the trees and bushes. Bangs and thuds and grunts. Hissing.

It made no difference. The grown-ups were pushing at the gate now, their bodies crushed by the weight of other people shoving from behind, their flesh squeezing between the metal bars. She could hear the breath being forced out of them, ribs breaking. She remembered the Play-Doh set she used to have, the brightly colored plastic machines for squashing the dough so that it came out in long, wormy shapes. That's what was happening to these grown-ups as the ones behind kept pushing forward.

The gate couldn't hold. There was another crash as the gateposts broke and the gate came slamming down, spilling grown-ups into the yard and setting off more traps from the sides. Long spikes flew out, spearing more mothers and fathers.

It made no difference. It made no difference. Nothing made a difference. Nothing could stop them. Ella saw the laughing mother; she'd almost made it to the yard. And behind her was another mother, impossibly thin and impossibly tall, with a long, pale face that looked almost sad, her dark eyes sunk beneath jutting brows. She had long hair that hung down to her waist. Black and straight. Ella had never seen a woman so tall and thin. She swayed slightly from side to side as she walked, arms stiff at her sides, fingers pointing at the ground.

There was something about the woman. Maybe it was just how tall she was, towering over the other grown-ups. Ella wasn't sure. There was a power about her. The grown-ups around her looked like they were copying her, mimicking her movements. As if she were some sort of general and this was her army. As if she could somehow silently command them.

Her eyes fixed on Ella and seemed to look right inside her. Ella felt almost hypnotized. She couldn't look away. The mother raised an arm and beckoned to her with a bony hand, as if calling her over. Everything seemed to fall away and go quiet and still. Before she knew what she was doing, Ella took a step forward and another, and then Scarface grabbed her and the spell was broken.

She was back in the noise and chaos.

The first one of the army was through, stepping over the bodies of those who had fallen at the gate. It was a wiry father with a twisted mouth, his lower jaw broken. He held a club in his hand and he raised it, hissing at Scarface.

Scarface raised his shotgun to his shoulder and fired a blast directly at him, flattening him and several others around him. Scarface fired a second shot, taking out a few more of them, and now, at last, he decided it was time to retreat.

He took hold of Ella's hand and they were running.

13

They all bundled inside the main barn—it was the first time the other kids had been in here. There was some light from the fire, and Ella watched them looking around with feverish, wild eyes. Outside, they could hear the grown-ups moving through the farm.

"They won't stop," said Louisa. "Why would they stop? They'll keep on going to wherever it is they're going. They're not interested in us. Why would they stop?"

"Why would they stop?" Harry sneered.

"They'll stop," said Daniel. "They always stop."

"Why would they, though?" said Louisa, sounding desperate.

"Because we're here," said Daniel hopelessly. "Because there's food. I mean, did you see them all, how many there were? It would take a lot of food to feed an army like that. What have they been eating? They'll stop."

"No," said Louisa. "They won't."

"Just because you say it won't make it happen," said Harry. "You are such a *moron*, Louisa."

"They won't stop!" Louisa shouted and, as if in answer to her, to show her up for being wrong, there was a bang on the metal side of the barn. Then another. And then a third bang as something hit it hard enough to leave a dent.

"They've stopped," said Daniel. "We are *dead*."

Scarface went over to a ladder that led up through the opening in the roof. He climbed quickly up it and disappeared from view. Ella had been up there once to have a look. The top of the ladder was tied to a crossbeam and it looked out over the whole farmyard. The roof itself was too rickety to stand on.

"Screw this," said Sonya. "I have to see what's going on." And she started to climb up after him.

"There's only room for one," Ella shouted after her, but Sonya ignored her.

"They'll get in here," said Daniel, his voice a harsh whisper. "And they'll kill us. There's too many of them."

"There's too many of them."

"Admit it, Harry: you're scared."

"Shut up, Daniel," said Harry. "You're a real downer, you know."

Harry was having to speak quite loudly to be heard, because there was a banging on the outside of the barn that sounded like rolling thunder as a hundred hands battered the metal sheets. More and more dents were appearing, and Ella could hear grown-ups snuffling and sniffing at any gaps or holes. She wished she hadn't stayed to look at them as they came to the farm. It made them too real. It would have been easier if she had no picture of them and could pretend they weren't that bad, that they were weak and useless, not scary at all. The banging could be rain or hailstones. The movement outside? The grunts and moans? It could be a herd of escaped cows. Or horses. Or . . .

Anything other than diseased grown-ups. If they got in they would take her like they'd taken her brother and so many of her friends. She wished Scarface would come back down. She didn't feel safe without him. These kids were useless; all they did was argue. Daniel was too scared to do anything. He was walking about in circles, going from one wall to another, listening, looking up at the sky, muttering to himself, crying all the time, and thumping his chest with his fist. Harry was being mean to Louisa, calling her stupid, and she was giving it back to him. Every now and then Harry would break off the argument and go over to where the banging noise was loudest and smash the wall with his club. Swear at the grown-ups.

It made no difference. Nothing made any difference. The grown-ups kept banging on the walls—so loud that Ella couldn't think—and pushing against them so that they were getting steadily more and more bent in.

Ella had an image that the barn was her head and the grown-ups were hammering directly on her skull. She wanted it to stop. She wanted it all to stop.

There was a rattling at the door.

And then Louisa screamed.

One part of the wall had been bent in so far at the bottom that grown-ups were able to get their hands through. Ella could see their fingers scrabbling at the concrete floor and gripping the edge of the bent metal. Harry ran over and started kicking and stomping. Louisa joined him, stabbing with her short spear, cursing the grown-ups. She turned to Daniel, her face pale, eyes wide, mouth wide.

"Help us, won't you?"

"Yeah, yeah, sorry." Daniel hurried over to join Harry, stomping on the hands that came under the wall. Despite their efforts, the hole was getting bigger as the grown-ups clawed at the metal and forced it upward and inward. A mother stuck her head under, tongue flicking out and licking the floor, lips pulled back from her teeth, showing purple gums. Harry kicked her in the temple and then kicked her again, and she pulled back out, only to be followed seconds later by two more heads.

As they stomped on the heads, a section of wall right next to them was thumped so hard that a big piece of it was bent in. Ella turned to look at it and then saw with a shock that they weren't alone. While they'd been distracted by the hole at the bottom of the wall, some grown-ups had gotten in from somewhere else. She couldn't tell how many there were in the half-light, but in her panic they appeared to fill the barn. She'd seen them just in time. Her scream alerted the other three, who turned around to defend themselves.

That was all they could do, though: hold the invaders off. They were backed up against the wall with no room to use their weapons effectively. Ella hid behind Harry, clutching her club and her shield, hoping nobody expected her to fight. She was aware of a high-pitched wailing and realized it was her. She couldn't stop screaming.

"Shut up, why don't you?" Harry snapped, and Ella fought to control herself.

But the screams were building inside her, bursting to get

out. The stench of the grown-ups was even more awful close up. They were hot and damp and dripping, like old food left too long in a kitchen compost bin.

Finally she could stand it no longer; she opened her mouth wide to scream, but the noise was drowned out by an almighty bang, and there was a flash in the darkness.

14

Scarface had come back down the ladder and let off a blast from his shotgun. Sonya was with him, and they were attacking the grown-ups from the side. Scarface emptied his other barrel, and as he reloaded, Sonya got busy with her spear. Soon they'd cleared a path to Ella's group, and together they forced the grown-ups back the way they'd come.

"I'll deal with these!" Daniel shouted, returning to the hole under the wall, where three grown-ups had managed to get their upper bodies through.

"Kill them, Dan!" Sonya yelled. "Their dead bodies will block the entrance." Ella watched as Daniel picked up a spear and started to stab them, crying out with every thrust.

Scarface and the three other kids managed to clear most of the barn, working their way over to a side door that had been forced open. The clasp that held the padlocked bolt in place had been bent right off the wall. Scarface pushed his way to the front and fired two shots into the open doorway, and for a blessed moment there were no grown-ups there, just empty space.

"Give me a hand!" Sonya ran to the door and tried to close it, but already there were more grown-ups trying to get in. Harry battered them, knocking back any hands or arms that came through.

What's the point? thought Ella. There were too many. They would just keep on coming. Somehow, though, Sonya got the door closed, and then Scarface jammed an iron bar under the broken handle, wedging it against the concrete floor. Harry stayed there, leaning all his weight on the bar. He looked very tired. His jacket with the painted slogans was ripped.

But they hadn't completely cleared the barn. A laughing mother, who now had blood pouring out of her mouth and nose, rushed at Ella, fingers spread wide, like she was drying her nails. Before Ella could do anything, Louisa charged at the mother and shoved her into the fire, sending up a firework spray of sparks. The mother shrieked and jerked around before she managed to roll out, and Sonya stepped forward to stab her with her spear.

"Where have you been?" gasped Louisa, exhausted from the fight.

"Trying to see what's going on," Sonya replied.

"How bad is it?" Daniel asked.

"The whole yard's filling up with them," said Sonya. "Some are moving on, but most are trying to get in here."

"It's stupid," said Daniel. "We're trapped. It's just stupid."

Harry copied him. *"It's just stupid."*

"I hope they get you, Harry," said Daniel. "I hope they rip you to pieces and use your stupid bloody head as a football. I hope you die painfully."

"I hope *you* die painfully," said Harry.

"Please, both of you, stop it," said Louisa.

"Stop it," said Harry, and then he shouted as Sonya pushed past him, nearly knocking him over. He didn't say anything to her, though, because he could see that she had gone over to the hole where the dead bodies had been pulled away and more grown-ups were coming through.

And all the while the hammering went on, all around, on every wall, *bang-bang-bang-bang-bang.*

Scarface seemed to be completely ignoring what was happening. He'd gone over to where there was an old bit of machinery with pumps and pipes sticking out of it. He was fiddling with something, turning a wheel. Ella didn't know how long it went on like that, the kids trying to stop the adults from getting in, the adults beating on the walls, the kids bickering with each other whenever there was a moment's quiet, Scarface fiddling. And no matter how often they blocked up a hole, or a gap in the walls where they'd been bent, another one would open up, and another.

The kids were moving like grown-ups themselves now, slow and automatic and stiff. Zombies. There were dead bodies on the floor from when the grown-ups had gotten in before, and Ella tried not to look at them. Every now and then her eyes would play tricks on her, caused by the dim light and her own tiredness, and she'd think one of the bodies was moving. And she'd scream and run from it, and the others would curse her when there was nothing there. Nothing had moved. No corpse was going to rise from the dead.

When Ella did it for the fifth time, Harry completely lost it and started yelling at her, shoving her around, calling her all sorts of names. He only stopped when Scarface slapped him across the face. For a second Harry was so surprised and upset he looked like he might burst into tears. And then he turned all his anger and frustration on Scarface.

"That's right, go on, hit me, attack me, why don't you? You know you want to, because you're a bloody grown-up like them, aren't you? Why are we even in here with you? It's crazy. You should be out there with your own kind. You bloody grown-up scum. You scum, you bloody scum."

Harry spat at Scarface, who didn't respond in any way other than to wipe his face. And then a new gap opened up and they were all smashing at it with clubs and spears, and the banging noise was louder than ever, and this time they had to move a big cupboard over the gap. As they were sliding it up against the wall, Daniel got his hand caught behind it and he yelled.

"You've broken my bloody fingers."

And Harry copied him.

"You've broken my bloody fingers."

And Louisa laughed at him until Daniel hit her, and then Sonya hit Daniel and Daniel flipped.

"I'm not staying here," he croaked, his voice almost gone. "I'm not staying here to die. We're like sardines in a can. We should never have come here."

And then, before anyone could stop him, he pushed Harry aside and sprinted across the barn to the side door.

"No, Daniel . . ." Sonya screamed after him, but it was no good.

Daniel pulled the bar free, then wrenched the door open and stumbled out into the night.

"Stop him," said Louisa. "We have to stop him."

"It's too late," said Sonya. "He's gone."

Grown-ups were coming through the door. Scarface fired off two shots at them. He looked to Harry to help him, and Ella saw Harry still lying where he'd been pushed over.

"That bloody idiot has done it now," Harry moaned. Ella could see that he was hurt. He'd fallen against some concrete blocks and his pants were torn. His leg was glistening with blood. He started swearing and calling Daniel worse names than he'd called Ella. She put her hand over her ears. Grown-ups were streaming through the open door, and more were coming in the other side under the bent wall. The kids were being forced into the center of the barn. Scarface was blasting away with his shotgun, two shots at a time, each one sending a wide spray of pellets into the advancing grown-ups, and then he had to break it to reload. Sonya and Louisa were jabbing with their spears and using them to hold the grown-ups at bay. Harry had managed to get to his feet, and limping and clutching his side with one hand, he was swinging a spear with the other.

"We can't hold them back," said Louisa.

"*We can't hold them back,*" said Harry automatically, not even bothering to sound nasty.

The whole barn seemed to be filled with a grunting, hissing, shuffling crowd of them. Everywhere Ella looked, there they were. A father got close to Scarface before he could reload, and he had to use the butt of his gun as a club. He rammed it into the father's face and he went down, spitting out teeth.

And then Harry went down. Three of them had gotten in close and he hadn't been strong enough to hold them back.

"Harry!" Sonya yelled.

"Harry," he replied, still copying her.

Scarface battered the grown-ups off Harry and then pulled all the kids into a tight circle around him. He snatched a bundle of tied-up sticks from the fire. Ella saw that he'd made them into a flaming torch. He hurled the burning brand toward the open doorway. It turned in the air, end over end, and landed just outside. Instantly there was a *WHUMP* and a bright flare of flame. The sudden burst of light lit the barn as bright as day. Ella could clearly see the blood everywhere, the pale, filthy faces of the kids; the rotten, lumpy faces of the grown-ups. Through the gaps in the walls she could see flames circling the barn. Smoke was pouring in, and the stink of rotting grown-ups was replaced by the worse stink of burning clothes and skin and hair. A burning mother stumbled into the barn and collapsed. The grown-ups who had gotten into the barn had frozen, startled and confused by this new threat.

But as quickly as it had flared up, the fire outside died down. Although Ella was upset that their ring of fire was no more, she was happy that she couldn't clearly see the horror in the barn anymore.

The open door was still clear of people. Now might be their chance to run like Daniel. She'd seen a look of doubt on the girls' faces. They were all thinking about it.

"I can't move," said Harry. Ella looked at him. The grown-ups had made an awful mess of his legs. One of them looked like it had been chewed half off. Blood covered one side of his face from the wound in his scalp.

"It's gone quiet," said Sonya. Was she prepared to leave Harry behind?

"Should we . . . ?" said Louisa, but her words were cut off as something was thrown into the barn. It hit the concrete floor and bounced, then rolled toward the fire.

"Oh, no," said Sonya. "No."

It was a head. A boy's head. Daniel's head. One ear bitten off. An expression of surprise on his face.

This seemed to act like a signal to the grown-ups in the barn. They snapped back to life. They weren't alone. Scarface went into action. He grabbed Ella, dragged her over to the chemical toilet, opened the door, and shoved her inside. She clumsily fiddled and fumbled with the lock until she at last got it shut and then flopped down onto the seat. The stink of chemicals in here made her nose burn. Maybe, though, it would mask her own smell. Maybe that was why Scarface had put her in here. For her protection. And that meant one thing. That he was scared. That the battle was nearly lost.

Ella sat there on the toilet, shivering. She could hear the sounds of the fight—shouting, hissing, scraping, thudding, and now and then an explosion from Scarface's gun.

She wanted to know what was happening. It was almost scarier being shut in here, blind and helpless. Almost. She had hated it out there. Hated the grown-ups. Hated the blood and the fear and the stink. She had to look, though. She went over to the door, trying to find a spy hole of some sort. There was a tiny spot of light coming through part of the handle. There was a gap there. She put her eye to it, but then almost immediately jumped back as the point of a spear suddenly punched through the heavy plastic of the door, missing her face by inches. The spear was pulled free. She waited a moment, and then put her eye to the new hole, praying that another spear thrust wouldn't blind her.

She could hear the cries of the children, but all she could see was the glow of the fire, dark bodies going past it. She sat back on the toilet. Put the beads of her necklace into her mouth and closed her eyes. She clamped her hands over her ears again, rocking backward and forward. Rocking and rocking until she was too tired to continue and she leaned against the wall. In the end her tiredness was stronger than her fear, and she drifted off into a sleep where her nightmares were no more frightening, strange, or confused than her waking life had been.

15

"No, Mom, no, it's me, it's Ella . . . !"

But her mother wasn't listening. She was chasing Ella, fingernails like claws, trying to scratch her eyes out.

"Mom, no, please . . . !"

Ella woke with a start to the smell of smoke and blood. Feeling stiff. Sitting scrunched up, her head against a wall. For a moment not sure where she was, trying to throw off the last of the dream, still jittery, trying to convince herself it hadn't happened. But what *had* happened? Where was she?

And then it came back to her in a sudden, painful rush that jolted her fully awake.

The toilet. The barn. The battle.

She leaned forward and peered out through the hole in the door.

It was morning. The sun was up. Just. There was a haze of smoke drifting in the air. Otherwise the barn was still. The concrete floor was covered in bodies, like a thick, dark carpet. Whether there were any children's bodies among them Ella couldn't tell.

She listened hard. It was quiet. The sound of the grown-ups, that breaking wave, that humming, hissing, swarming noise, had gone. The army must have moved on.

Did that mean . . . ?

Was she alone?

She waited and waited, too scared to open the door. She didn't know what she'd find. She couldn't bear the thought of being the only one still alive. She'd rather have died.

And then she saw a movement. Something was rising from the pile of corpses, a body. She held her breath. It seemed to uncurl, like the speeded-up film of a plant growing, pushing up like a shoot from this mound of dead flesh. Whoever it was was covered in blood, black and sticky with it. It was twisted and misshapen, broken, but somehow still moving around.

It was Scarface.

Ella let out her breath and was just about to shout out to him when she saw another movement. Two people were coming down the ladder from the roof.

They got to the bottom and came slowly across the barn toward Scarface, said something to him. Ella couldn't hear through the door. He shook his head slowly. Ella could see that he held his two knives in his hands. They were dark red. Louisa said something else and Scarface shook his head again. And then Ella gasped as Louisa hit him in the back of the head with her club. He fell face-first to the ground. Sonya and Louisa went to his body and started searching it. Then Sonya gave a shout of triumph, straightened up. She was holding Scarface's big bunch of keys.

They hurried over to the main doors and went out into the early morning sunlight.

Ella carefully lifted the lock of the door and slowly eased it open. She stuck her head out and checked that it was okay. Worried that she'd see the girls. Worried that she'd see grown-ups. Living ones. There were more dead ones in here than she could have imagined. They were lying on top of each other everywhere she looked. In some places three deep. She was glad of the smoke, because it did something to hide the worst smells. Of bodies ripped open.

She went over to Scarface. He was lying where he'd fallen, on top of a pile of grown-ups. She felt him, shook him, put her ear to his mouth, listening for any breathing. Then she put her hand to his chest and she felt the tiniest flutter of a heartbeat, and worried that she was only feeling her own pulse. No. His chest was moving. He was just about alive. The back of his head was badly cut, and his own blood was mixing with the blood he'd been splashed with.

Ella ran over to the cabinet where he kept his medicine supplies, tugged the door open, nearly pulling the cabinet off the wall. She found a roll of bandage, unrolled it, and cut off a long strip. She tied it loosely around his head, hoping to stop the bleeding. Didn't know what else to do.

Then she remembered Sonya and Louisa. They'd taken his keys. What were they doing? She went over to the door and peeped out, scared that they would see her and come back to hit her over the head as well.

There was a scorched black patch all around the edge of the barn, and the smell of gasoline hung in the air, mixed with a barbecue smell of roasted meat. There were more dead bodies out there, close to the building, most of them burned. There was another pile over by the fallen gate, but otherwise the farm looked deserted.

So where were the girls?

The chicken shed. *Obviously.*

That's where they'd been sniffing around earlier. Trying to get in.

It had to be that.

Ella was just about to go after them when she saw a group of grown-ups come around the side of the farmhouse. So they hadn't all left. She pulled the barn doors closed, leaving a small crack to peep out through. Her whole body was trembling. She was cold and tired and hungry and terrified.

And alone.

A big mother broke away from the group and limped toward the barn. She had bare arms, huge breasts, and a fat neck, fatter than her head. As she got close, she belched and a stream of thin brown liquid washed down her chin and spattered onto the ground. When she reached the doors, she began to snuffle at them.

Ella shrank back from her, and as she did so she became aware of a howling and a whining and a snarling. Something moved fast across the yard and knocked into the mother. It was the dogs. Scarface's dogs had come back. There were no traps to stop them anymore. They tore into the grown-ups, pulling them down and mauling them. Their growls and yelps sounded unreal, something from a horror film about aliens. Three fathers were trying to get away, dogs snapping at their legs, hanging on with bared teeth.

Ella closed the barn doors fully and slid the main bolt across. She listened to the sounds of the attack, closing her eyes and resting her forehead on the doors. Glad she wasn't out there. Her throat was painful and dry. She tried to swallow. She needed water.

And then she heard a noise behind her.

There was somebody moving about inside the barn. For a tiny moment she hoped it might be Scarface, that he wasn't as badly wounded as she'd feared. But she knew in her heart it wasn't him.

She opened her eyes and turned around.

It was a father. He had his back to Ella and was reversing toward her, dragging something across the floor. His back was wide and the remains of his shirt were stretched tight across it. Where his lumpy skin showed through the gaps, it was black with dirt and grease.

Ella realized that the thing he was dragging was Scarface. The father had him by the ankles. Ella didn't know what to do. Even though she had her club, she couldn't fight this man. He was huge—to Ella he seemed to be a giant—and she was feeble. A little girl, Daniel had called her. *A useless little girl*. And he was right. Ella couldn't hit hard enough to hurt a fly.

There were flies in here. They swarmed around the father and over the dead bodies. Their buzzing set her on edge.

She looked down at her club. It was shaking so much in her sweaty hands, it looked like it was attached to a motor. She put a finger to one of the bits of metal that were stuck in it. It was sharp. If she hit the father in a soft place she might hurt him. She couldn't kill him with it, but she might slow him down, maybe make him let go of Scarface, give her friend a chance to escape.

It was that or watch him drag Scarface off somewhere to be eaten in private and then wait for him to come back and start on her. Where could she hit him, though, that would do enough damage?

The father was getting closer and closer. She could hear him grunting with the effort. His long legs stiff and awkward as he shuffled backward, kicking arms and legs out of his way with his heels. And then Ella had an idea, and, before she could talk herself out of it, she ran at the father and swung the club with all her strength at the backs of his knees. Ella let go of it and it stuck there, the spikes digging into him.

He gave a girlish cry and crumpled to the floor, letting go of Scarface. Ella was breathing so hard it hurt her chest. She was crying. But she'd done it. The father was down. . . .

He rolled onto his front, leaving the club behind, pushed himself up onto his hands like someone doing exercises, and stared at Ella. He didn't look angry or in pain, he just looked as if there was something he needed to do and nothing was going to stop him. He began to move, pulling himself along on his arms, eyes fixed on Ella. She went over to the door and started to open it, when she saw the huge head of a dog sticking its nose in the crack and snuffling like the mother had done earlier. She slammed the door shut as it started to bark.

Still the father was coming, hauling himself through the blood and the slime on the concrete floor, his face a mess of boils and sores. Much nearer now. Ella backed away from him. He was making a sort of brushing sound as the air came out through his blocked nose. His eyes all the while staring at Ella with that clear, serious look.

Unable to see what was behind her, Ella tripped and stumbled, went dancing back, and crashed into an iron support pillar. She slid down onto her bottom, too surprised to feel any pain. And still the father came on, one hand forward, then the other, dragging himself over the dead bodies.

Ella looked around for something to defend herself with and saw Daniel's head sitting on the floor. It was as if he were looking at her. His lips had shrunk back from his teeth so that he was smiling, laughing even. Laughing at the useless little girl who thought she could hurt a grown-up.

Ella closed her eyes. She'd finally had enough. There was nothing left in her. She gave a little laugh. There wasn't even any fear left in her. It had all been used up. Let him come. Let him do what he was going to do and then it would all be over. Maybe she'd see Sam in heaven. That would be nice.

The bang was so loud it left Ella's ears ringing. She wondered if the father had hit her. But she didn't feel anything. And there had been a flash behind her eyelids. She forced them open, forced herself to look. The father was lying on his side, blood leaking out of him.

He'd been shot.

"Scarface?" she said, looking around.

"No," said a voice, very close, almost at her side, and she saw Harry sitting propped up against the wall of the barn, holding Scarface's shotgun. Ella crawled over to him, too weak to stand.

"Harry?"

"He gave me the gun." Harry's face was white, spotted with blood.

"Your friend," he went on. "There were only two shells left. I was saving the last one. It's done now."

"Oh, Harry," said Ella. She couldn't think what else to say.

Harry nodded over to where Scarface was lying.

"He tried to save me," he said. "He's all right, you know."

"No, he's hurt."

"*He's hurt* . . . Idiot. I mean he's an all-right guy. All night he stood over me. Fighting them off. I couldn't move. Some of the bastards got to me. The girls ran away. Went up the ladder. I don't blame them. There was just too many of the bastards. And some of them, they could climb. Yeah. Couldn't believe that. Never seen it before. They tried to get up the ladder. Your friend, he pulled them down."

Harry grunted in pain and his eyelids flickered. Ella tried to focus on the boy, not what had happened to him. She stared into his eyes so she wouldn't have to look at the rest of him. She had caught a glimpse, though, just enough to see that his legs were missing.

"Are *you* all right, Harry?" she asked, and immediately felt stupid. Of course he wasn't all right.

"*Are you all right, Harry?*" he replied in his slightly sneery way. He couldn't help himself.

"You're bleeding a lot."

"*You're bleeding a lot.*" His voice was feeble.

"I hope you don't die, but I don't know what to do."

"*I don't know what to do. . . .*" Harry paused, looked like he was going to cry. "Just hold my hand," he said.

Ella held his hand. It felt cold and was trembling. After a while it stopped trembling and Harry smiled.

"Thank you," he said. "I'm glad you weren't hurt."

"That was a good shot, Harry. You fixed that bloody father all right."

"Fixed that bloody father . . . Didn't I just? BOOM!" Harry laughed.

"I think that was the last one," said Ella. "The grown-ups have all gone."

"The grown-ups have all gone," said Harry. This time not in a sneery way, but in a happy way, like it was a good thing. Which it was.

"They're someone else's problem now," he added, and then he closed his eyes and didn't say anything else, and his hand went stiff, and Ella knew he was dead without having to check.

Harry was all right in the end.

She made her way across the barn. Not looking. Not looking. Too many bodies. Wanting to be sick. Wondering how she was even still moving. She found Scarface sprawled on his back, arms flung wide. His bandage had come off and there was a thin trail of blood where the father had dragged him. She pressed her ear to his chest like she'd done before. And, like before, she heard a faint beating. She put her hands on either side of his damp head and shook him. His face looked worse than ever. Like an old toy the dogs had left behind. Mangled and chewed out of shape. He was a thing. But he was an *alive* thing.

And he was all Ella had.

"Come on," she said, shaking him harder. "You're not

dead. You can't just lie there. You're too big for me to move. We have to get away from here. I need you to look after me. You're only an ugly old grown-up, an ugly old thing, but you looked after me before and you have to do it again. I'll look after you, I'll help make you well, we'll look after each other—how about that? You need to wake up, though, you need to listen to me: I won't let you die. I can't have anyone else die, even if you are just a freak, a sicko, one of them, even if you can't talk and you're no use as a friend. You're just an ugly old hunter, a face-ache, but you're *my* hunter. You're *my* Face-Ache."

A tear rolled down her face and fell on Scarface, and she sniffed and wiped her nose. She hit his chest with her fists.

"I don't even know if you can hear me, but if you *can* hear me, you can understand me, and if you could talk, I don't know what you'd say. I don't know you, I don't know who you are, so what would you say to me? You'd probably tell me to shut up and not be such a little girl. Well, I don't mind what you think. I wouldn't mind whatever you said as long as you'd just wake up and help me. Wake up, Face-Ache! Wake up!"

But he didn't wake up.

It was no use. He was just lying there, slowly bleeding to death. Ella couldn't help him. She couldn't move him. All she could try to do was help herself.

She forced herself to stand up, turned her back on him, and headed for the ladder. She might be able to see a way out of here without being killed by the dogs.

As she put her foot on the first rung, she heard a voice behind her.

"I can talk," it said.

She turned around. Scarface had his good eye open and had raised his head enough to be able to see her.

"What did you say?"

"I said, I *can* talk. And I'm not a grown-up."

16

Ella was in the chicken shed. And she was crying. This place had always been so full of noisy life, and now it was quiet and still and dead. When she got there, she'd found the door open. The padlock hanging from the clasp with the keys still in it. The sisters had been there. And when they'd left they hadn't even bothered to lock the door. Which meant the dogs had gotten in. They'd gone crazy in there. Must have just run around and around killing the chickens, eating a few, but leaving most of them lying on the floor.

Dead.

Ella felt so sorry for Scarface. He'd tried to protect all this, and in the end it had been the girls who'd messed everything up. Ella picked out a few birds that weren't too badly mangled and put them in her carrying bag. At least they wouldn't *all* go to waste.

She went back out and rescued Scarface's keys from the padlock. Finding them had been the easiest thing she had to do. Going into the farmhouse was going to be the hardest.

The dogs had left. There were no more living grown-ups

on the farm. It was just her now. She walked up to the front of the farmhouse, key held out ready, and waited. Trying to get brave enough to open the front door. In all the time she'd been here Scarface had never let her go inside, although he'd sneak in there at the end of every day, and in her mind she'd built it up to be a big deal. There was something in there. Something bad. It wasn't just the fire. It was worse than that. She just knew it. Although she was finding it hard to think of anything that could be worse than what she'd been through in the last few hours. How she was still walking around and doing things she had no idea. Except that when you were busy doing things you didn't have time to think about other stuff. The quicker she got everything done, the quicker she could get away from this place. Already the stink from the dead bodies was foul, and it would only get worse as they started to rot.

"The dogs will eat some of them, the flies will lay their eggs, and their maggots will have the rest," Scarface had said. "And they'll spread disease. If we stay here we'll die from it."

Ella was still trying to get used to him speaking. Not that he'd exactly said a lot. His voice sounded croaky and cracked, and the words seemed to get stuck in his throat.

He'd only really said five things so far.

He'd told Ella that they couldn't stay here.

He'd told her that he had another hiding place, away from the farm, and together they were going to get there, whatever it took.

He'd told her that he had an emergency kit in the cellar of the farmhouse that contained all they needed to survive for a few days.

He'd told her where exactly to find the kit.

And he'd told her that she wasn't to go anywhere else inside the house.

When Ella had asked him if it was dangerous, he hadn't said anything.

That was it.

So now here she was. The windows of the house were dark and she wondered whether Scarface had boarded them up. All this time it had been sitting here, in the middle of the yard, with its black windows and black walls. And she was going inside it.

She slid the key into the lock. It turned easily and the door clicked open. As it did, she heard a noise. A sort of humming noise, as if from an engine, and she had the spooky feeling that the house was somehow alive.

She pushed the door open wider. Stepped over the mat. Wiped her feet out of habit. The noise was all around her now. It felt hotter in there than outside, and the feeling that the house was alive was even stronger. There was a stink in here as well. A stink of damp and mold. The stair carpet was green and gray from fungus, and more climbed up the walls like ivy.

Turn left into the kitchen, Scarface had said, and Ella did as she'd been told. The kitchen was neat and tidy, everything in its place, except that the walls were streaked from water leaking in and it was crawling with flies. They covered every surface and, as she passed the windows, a great swarm of them took off from the glass and swirled around her head in a black cloud. Light burst into the room. The windows hadn't been boarded up, they'd been covered in a layer of flies, like a living curtain.

She put her hands up to protect her hair and face and waved them around to keep the flies from landing. Some battered into her and she shook her head. She kept on walking quickly to the door on the far side like she'd been told, snapped on her flashlight, and opened it.

It'll be dark in the cellar. . . .

There was a short corridor leading to the cellar, with hooks along the wall for coats and a rack for shoes and boots. The door was at the end. When Ella got to it, she once again selected the right key and then started to go down.

She couldn't stop. Couldn't think about it.

Don't be scared. There's nothing down there. As long as you do exactly what I tell you, there's no way there'll be anything alive in there. . . .

Yeah. Except the flies, filling the place with their noise.

You won't be scared, will you?

No. *Of course not.* It was just her and the flies. But the light from the flashlight was jumping all over the place, and her teeth were clamped so tightly together to stop them from rattling that her jaw was aching. Halfway down Ella stopped to throw up, spattering the creaky wooden steps with watery vomit.

When she got to the bottom, she found a small dry cellar. Cobwebs covered the walls—the spiders in this house must be as fat as mice—and there, in the corner, just as Scarface had described it, was a large metal box with a padlock on it. Once again Ella selected the right key and tried to poke it in the lock with trembling hands. It took her several tries, and she swore at herself until she got it right.

Get the kit and get out. Don't look in any other rooms. . . .

Inside the box was a duffel bag. It was a big green army thing with a camouflage pattern, and it was almost too heavy for her to lift. The first few times she got it halfway out and let it slip back. Eventually, though, she managed to haul it over the edge and it fell to the floor with a thump, sending up an explosion of dust.

She dragged it across the floor and began to bump it up the steps. The dust and dirt in the house were sticking to her sweaty skin and she had to keep spitting it out of her mouth and trying to cough her throat clear.

It took her ages to get the duffel bag up the steps, but when at last it was up, she found it much easier to haul down the corridor and through the kitchen to the hallway. It got caught on something in the kitchen doorway, though, and she tugged and pulled until it came away with a jerk, and she staggered back, exhausted, and fell onto the main staircase, surrounded by a cloud of buzzing flies. Ella closed her eyes, let the flies land on her, ignoring the tickle as they explored her face. She pretended she was dead and nothing could annoy her. Nothing could hurt her. She could easily fall asleep now, but another gush of vomit woke her up, and this time it sprayed over her shoes.

She stood up. Head throbbing. Scarface was waiting for her outside the barn. Between the two of them they'd managed to get him outside into the fresh air and sunlight—half walking, half crawling—Ella struggling to hold him up and pull him along. She wondered now how on earth they were going to get the two of them and this heavy old duffel bag away from the farm and to the woods where Scarface's hide-out was.

Best not to think about that. Best to just keep going.

She looked up the staircase. The humming of the flies filled the house. Filled her head. She could just turn now and go out of the front door. Leave the house behind.

Don't look in any other rooms. . . .

Why not? What was in here? Why did he always come here after they'd been out hunting and never let her in? What was his secret? And he must have thousands. Like being able to speak. That was a big one. She really knew nothing about him.

Before Ella knew what she was doing she was climbing the stairs, following her flashlight beam like a moth as it slid up the moldy stair carpet.

The house smelled worse upstairs, and it wasn't just the smell of damp. There was something else. The charred, sour, smoky smell from the fire. The walls up here were black. Light came in through the broken roof, and she looked up at a cold gray sky. There was a closed and charred bedroom door right in front of her. Why was she here? This was stupid. When someone tells you not to open a door, you don't open it, do you?

All you can think about, though, is what might be on the other side. And this would probably be her only chance to find out.

She got her flashlight ready, pointing straight ahead, and pushed the door open. At first she couldn't figure out what she was seeing.

And then she understood.

17

The bedroom was full of heads. A great mound of them, carefully stacked. The ones at the bottom were not much more than skulls, with the flesh dried up and the skin stretched and brown, bones and teeth showing through. But, as each layer piled up toward the ceiling, the heads got fresher and fresher. Some of the ones on the top layer Ella recognized as grown-ups they'd hunted together. Not that any dead grown-up ever really looked *fresh*—they were rotten and eaten away even before they died.

There was a thick covering of flies crawling over the mound, and maggots everywhere, wriggling in the eye sockets and spilling out of open mouths. They were shiny and pale. Munching away. Plus, there was something else. That wormy gray stuff she'd seen dripping from Scarface's bag. It oozed here and there from the heads on the top row, trickling down to the skulls below.

Ella closed the door. She hadn't seen it. That's what she'd tell herself. It wasn't real. She glanced in through the open door of another bedroom and saw a similar sight. The house was full of them. She swallowed. Felt vomit rising up her throat again. They were only heads, only the heads of dirty grown-ups.

No . . . The house was empty, remember? Just an ordinary farmhouse. There was nothing in it. She hadn't seen anything. . . .

She went quickly down the stairs, picked up the duffel bag, and pulled it out of the front door, which she locked carefully behind her. The house and its secrets could stay there.

When Ella eventually got to him, Scarface looked to be asleep, but he opened one eye and peered at her when she got close.

"Water," he said.

"Okay."

She fetched a plastic bottle of water from the stash in the barn and tipped some into his mouth. His own head didn't look much different from the dead ones in the farmhouse. There were fresh cuts to add to the scars that covered his skin. There were so many chunks missing from him it was like the maggots had been at him already. He didn't seem able to open his bad eye anymore. That was okay. She didn't like that bloody, dead jelly.

When he'd drunk enough, Ella took a big swig herself and then sat down next to him.

"What are we going to do?" she said. "I can't carry you *and* the bag and *everything*. How far can you walk?"

"Not far. You?"

"Not far. I'm so tired."

"It's only five minutes away. In the woods. You know the tree that's split by lightning?"

"Yeah. I think so."

"Five minutes," Scarface repeated.

"If you could walk normally," said Ella. "Which you can't."

"We'll go one step at a time. You take the bag ahead. Then we'll catch up with it."

"I can't do it," said Ella. "I can't do anything anymore. What do you think I am?"

"I think you're a hero," said Scarface. "I think you're the bravest girl in the world."

"You're just saying that."

"I haven't spoken in nearly a year, Ella," said Scarface with his broken voice. "I'm not going to waste my breath on lies. Get me to the hideout and you can sleep for a thousand years. When you wake up, everything will be fine."

"I've seen things today," said Ella. "I'm not ever going to be normal again."

Scarface gave a little laugh and Ella glared at him. Angry.

"What are you laughing at?" she asked.

"Nothing," said Scarface, closing his eye. Laughing had tired him out. "It's just . . . I kind of know the feeling. Now take the bag to the shed near the gate, then come back for me."

"No . . ."

"Ella . . ."

Ella huffed and got up and lugged the duffel bag over to the gate, her legs aching, her back sore, her fingers going white where they tugged at the straps. When she got back, Scarface had somehow managed to get up onto his feet and was leaning against the wall, eyes closed again, sweat running down his cracked, leathery cheeks.

"I'm not sleeping," he said when he heard Ella. "Just

resting." And he put a hand on her shoulder. The hand with the missing fingers. His other hand was gripping the shotgun, which he was using as a sort of walking stick.

"Come on, then," he said, gripping Ella tighter. "We can do this."

Step by painful step, they crossed the yard, barely moving. They didn't stop, though, and when they eventually got as far as the bag, Scarface slumped down with a moan. It looked like he'd never get up again.

He mumbled something that Ella couldn't hear, and she shook him and told him to say it again.

"There's a wheelbarrow in the shed," he said, his voice not much more than a whisper.

"I can't take you in a wheelbarrow."

"Not me, the bag. You can wheel it down the road."

Ella found the wheelbarrow. It was quite wobbly and hard to steer at first, and she swore at it. It tipped over three times as she tried to get the bag in it. At last it was done, though, and she set off. It was even harder to steer with the weight of the bag inside, but slowly she got the hang of it. It was certainly much easier moving the duffel bag like this. She took it about a hundred yards down the road, then came back for Scarface, and on they went. Inch by inch by inch.

They'd gotten about halfway to the barrow, and Ella was wondering if they'd ever get there, when she saw someone approaching in the distance. Moving quickly down the road.

"There's a . . ." she started to say.

"I've seen it," Scarface interrupted.

"Is it a grown-up?"

"No. It's a kid. You can always tell. A boy, I reckon."

I can't always tell, thought Ella, but she didn't say anything. They stopped walking and stood there, waiting. They couldn't have run away even if they'd wanted to. As the boy got nearer, Ella realized that she recognized him.

"It's Isaac," she said.

"You mustn't tell him," said Scarface.

"Tell him what?"

"Anything," said Scarface.

Isaac seemed to take a long time getting to them. He wasn't running, just walking, tramping steadily along, head down. When he finally arrived, he looked the two of them over.

"Are you okay?" he asked.

Ella nodded.

"I came back," he said. "I couldn't leave you."

"What happened?" Ella asked. "Did you stay up on the lookout platform all night?"

"I couldn't get down," Isaac replied. "I tried and tried, but there were always grown-ups there. Waiting. Some even tried to climb up. I couldn't see into the barn, didn't know what was happening inside. But I had to watch it all, the grown-ups outside, circling, clawing at the walls. Then there was that massive fire. I thought they'd all be burned. There were so many, though. You couldn't count them. I saw Daniel come out. I tried to shout to him . . ." Isaac trailed off into silence.

"It was horrible," Ella said quietly. "I'm sorry about your friends."

"I saw Sonya and Louisa this morning," said Isaac. "I

didn't sleep all night. There were grown-ups still around. The girls got away just as the dogs arrived. I shouted to them. They ignored me. Luckily the dogs chased off the rest of the grown-ups. I guess they were scared of an army, but not a few stragglers."

"Harry died," said Ella.

"Oh." Isaac looked away. Not wanting to show Ella his tears. "We were at school together," he said, then sniffed and went all serious.

"I'm heading back to Bracknell. You need to come with me."

"I can't."

"It's too dangerous to stay here, Ella." Isaac looked desperate to get away.

"I can't leave Scarface," said Ella. "He's my friend. He's too badly hurt to go fast."

Isaac took hold of Ella and dragged her a little way away so that Scarface couldn't hear them.

"You have to leave him. We have to go right now."

"I can't." Ella was shaking her head. "He saved me. He looked after me. Now I have to look after him."

Isaac laughed. He sounded slightly crazy, almost crying.

"Just leave him," he said. "You have to. He's just a—"

"Just a *what*?"

"He's one of *them*," said Isaac. "If you bring him with us, they'll just kill him when we get there."

"Then I'm staying here," said Ella. "We've got another hiding place."

"Where?"

Ella remembered what Scarface had said—that she mustn't tell him anything. But Isaac could help them. Maybe if she just told him a little.

"In the woods," she said. "Will you help us before you go?"

Isaac thought for a second.

"Come on, then," he said, walking back and taking hold of Scarface. "Let's do this."

So the three of them set off. Ella wheeling the barrow, Isaac supporting Scarface. It was harder going when they got off the road and had to cross a field to the trees, but they kept on moving. Four times Ella's barrow tipped, and Isaac had to help her get the duffel bag back on board. They made it to the woods, though, and stopped to rest, Scarface leaning up against a big tree whose bark was as gnarly as his face. He caught Ella's eye and made a jerky movement with his head as if to say, *Get rid of him.* He obviously didn't want Isaac to know exactly where the hideout was, just in case.

"We'll be all right now," Ella said to Isaac. And he looked unsure, checking out the woods.

"Really?"

"Yes." Ella nodded. "There's a place we can shelter here."

"I'll get you all the way there."

"You need to go," said Ella.

"Well . . ."

"We're away from the farm," said Ella. "We've got food in the bag. We'll be fine."

"If you're really sure? Okay."

Ella could tell that Isaac wanted to be off. She gave him a hug and thanked him.

"If you ever make it to Bracknell," he said into her hair, "look for me. Isaac, yeah? Isaac Hills."

"Okay."

They separated and Isaac started to hurry away.

"Isaac!" Ella called out, and he turned around.

"It didn't get you," she shouted.

"Who?"

"That fate thing. You dodged it."

"I did this time."

"Good luck."

Soon he was gone and Ella wondered if she'd ever see him again.

18

Somehow the last part was the hardest, getting over the bumpy ground to the actual den, too tired to even think. Ella had to leave the barrow behind because it got too hard to wheel through the trees. Instead she would pull the duffel bag along the ground for a few paces, come back and help Scarface get from one tree to the next, then leave him leaning there and pull the bag a little farther on. Then back for Scarface . . .

Somehow they did it, though. Got to the lightning tree, its big gray trunk split down the middle but still growing. Scarface dropped down and sat on the ground. Ella looked around. She could see no sign of a hideout. She searched everywhere, in the bushes, in the shadows under the other trees, up in the branches, hoping they weren't going to have to do any climbing. Nothing. When she looked back at Scarface, however, he was scrabbling about in a pile of dead leaves and fallen sticks.

"Here," he grunted. "Help me. I can't do it."

Ella went to him and saw that he had partly uncovered

a door of some sort that he must have taken from one of the farm buildings. It was covered with dirt and leaves and stones. They managed to lift it just far enough for Ella to see that there was a hole underneath. First she pushed in the bag, and then she helped Scarface slide in and drop down. He found the strength to hold the door up so that Ella could fit under it, and she squeezed through. There was a short tunnel that they crawled along to where it opened out into a sort of burrow just large enough for the two of them.

Ella switched on her flashlight. They were right in among the tree roots that formed a cage around them. She saw bags and boxes tucked into gaps between the roots and some smaller animal holes going off to the sides.

"I think badgers made it originally," said Scarface, flopping down onto an old mattress. "Or maybe foxes. I dug it out some more. I always knew it would be useful one day. You've got to think ahead."

His voice was so quiet Ella could hardly hear it. It was a dry, rustling noise. She shone the flashlight in his face and he screwed his good eye shut.

"What are you doing?" he complained.

"You need a new bandage," she said.

"In the bag."

Ella went to fetch the duffel bag, undid the top of it, and started to take stuff out. She was amazed at how much was packed into it: weapons and tools and clothing and food and drink. About halfway down she found a medicine kit.

She cleaned Scarface's wounds again and wiped them with antiseptic. Then they drank some water and ate some stale chocolate in silence.

Ella started to shake, so she lay down next to Scarface and wrapped herself in a blanket, waiting for the shaking to go away. She closed her eyes, hoping to sleep.

After a few minutes she opened her eyes and pointed the flashlight at the roof. There were smaller white roots, like fingers, or claws, poking through the earth above her head.

"Save the flashlight," said Scarface, and she switched it off. It was dark now. She was still shaking. Scarface found her hand and held on to it.

"Thank you," he said.

"I can't sleep," said Ella. "I thought nothing could keep me awake, but lying here now, I can't sleep. My body won't let me."

"Me either," said Scarface.

"Tell me a story," said Ella.

"What story?"

"Your story. I don't know who you are. I don't know anything about you. You say you're not a grown-up, so what are you? Tell me."

"Okay. But it'll be our story, though, yeah? You'll not tell anyone else."

"There isn't anyone else here . . . except maybe a rabbit or a mole."

"Don't even tell the moles."

"I promise."

"Good."

"Go on, then. Who are you?"

"My name's Malik Hussein. I went to Rowhurst School in Kent. I'm fifteen years old. And most of the time I wish I was dead. . . ."

THE HUNTER

19

'd been hunting the night I found you." Malik's voice was quiet and scratchy in the darkness. "I'd followed a group of grown-ups to the river. Got half of them and the rest got away.

"I was on the bank of the river, under the highway bridge where it crosses over, and I sat down there and I stared at the water and it was dark, black, and I thought, *What's the point? What's the point of doing what I'm doing?* Night after night, day after day, hunting them down, killing them. And I was good at killing them. I'm the hunter. But I couldn't see a point to it anymore. There wasn't a bit of me that didn't ache, that wasn't tired or hurting. I just thought there wouldn't ever be an end to it and I would never be normal again. I was an animal. A kicked dog. Couldn't go near kids, and I wasn't a grown-up, despite what I looked like. I couldn't see any point to life. It was just hard work and pain.

"I was going to throw myself in the river. I thought about it, thought about drowning. Under all that black water. It would be an end to it all. *Jannah.* And then I saw another grown-up. He was one I'd been hunting for days, and he'd always gotten away from me. He was a big, ugly, dangerous bastard, and I thought, well, at least if I can kill him it would be one good thing before I died. I was like a dog who can't stop chasing a stick.

"So I followed him and he went over the bridge to Monkey Island, and I knew there were more of them around, because I can smell them. I can sense them. Sometimes I think I can even hear them, inside my brain. Chattering. Squeaking. Whispering. But I know that's just me being crazy. I knew there were lots of them, though, and *they* were hunting too. There was blood in the air. There was killing that night. They'd found some kids. I knew that much. So I went over the bridge and into the hotel. There was one down in the lobby, the reception area, a mother, eating something. I took her out quickly, then went up the stairs, following a trail of blood. Found another two in a corridor. They had your friend, the little boy."

"Monkey-Boy."

"Was that his name? Well, I put them out of action and was trying to help the boy when you ran around the corner, and I must've scared the crap out of you, because you fainted. Like you just switched off. So then I had some work to do. Taking them all out, finishing them off, and trying to keep you and your friend alive. And anyone else. I quickly found out there were no more kids in there—not alive, anyway— and I brought you and the boy outside.

"I'm sorry he died. I did what I could. Killed the rest of the grown-ups. And then . . . well, I couldn't chuck myself in the river then, could I? Couldn't leave you there all alone. There was nobody else around to look after you. So I brought you to the farm. I'd never let anyone else in my camp before. Thought I'd get you well and take you to Windsor or Bracknell. Leave you on someone's doorstep."

Malik stopped and made a noise. Ella realized he was laughing. For a while he said nothing, and she waited for him to continue.

"I'm sorry about what happened to your farm," she said, and squeezed his hand.

Finally he spoke again.

"It was stupid of me," he said. "Trying to defend the place like that. All I did was get those kids killed. I should have come straight here."

"No," said Ella. "It was worth fighting for."

"I knew it couldn't last," said Malik. "I knew I couldn't hold it by myself. Sooner or later someone was going to come along and take it all away from me. A swarm of grown-ups, or more likely some kids. They're spreading out more and more, the ones in Windsor and the ones at Bracknell. I tried to scare them away, but I always knew that one day there'd be someone brave enough to come take a look, and once they'd found the chickens in the barn, or the food, they weren't going to let me keep it all for myself.

"Never thought it would be quite as spectacular as what happened last night, though. That was mental. Never seen anything like it before, and I've seen a lot. Can't remember all the people I've seen die. Friends and enemies and strangers. But I've forgotten so much as well. Sometimes I can't even remember what I did the day before. My brain is full of clouds. I remember the start of it all quite clearly, being at school, down in Kent. The disease. When it all began to go wrong.

"Do you remember the 'Scared Kid' video? How we laughed when we first saw it, this kid terrified of real-life zombies or whatever. And then we realized it wasn't fake. He wasn't being punked. And then how we were all scared after that. The most scared I've ever been."

"I don't remember that time so well," said Ella. "It seems so long ago."

"You're much younger than me," said Malik. "I can remember it clearly. How we got through the first bit of the craziness, stayed at the school. The teachers tried to help us, but when they got sick it all got worse. I ended up hiding out in the school chapel with some kids from my House. Funny thing was, I'd never really been in there before. I wasn't exactly a strict Muslim, but I knew chapel was boring, so I got out of it 'on religious grounds.' A guy named Matt sort of took over, went a bit mental, actually. Started raving about God and the Lamb and how the Lamb was going to save us. I didn't really listen, and then the silly bastard poisoned us all with, like, carbon-monoxide fumes, burning stuff in the chapel.

"We nearly died. Probably would've if my mate Ed hadn't turned up with some other kids. Got the doors open and got us all out. All except one kid with asthma who died. Can't remember his name. We decided to leave the school after that and head for the countryside. Seemed like a plan of sorts. When we set off, we were in quite a good mood, to be honest. It felt better, doing something and not just hiding, not just waiting for the food to run out or the grown-ups to come for us.

"I remember walking along, chatting to Ed. I wonder what happened to him. He was a good guy. A good friend. Popular. Head of everything. A hit with the girls. Yeah, that's what we were talking about—girls—if you want to know. I can't remember exactly what we were saying, just a typical boys' conversation like we'd had a million times before. You know? Well, you wouldn't know, I guess. You're too young. And a girl. Anyway, it was silly stuff, because we felt sort of safe. Being all together like that. With a plan. We were going to find somewhere like my farm. With food and animals, you know . . . So we were just chatting and walking, and then, out of nowhere, there were grown-ups."

Malik paused, and when he went on, his voice was even quieter, so Ella struggled to hear him.

"They got me before I knew they were even there. Grabbed me and dragged me into a building, started ripping at me. Don't remember much more after that. Not even sure I remember anything, to tell you the truth. I've sort of pieced it together from dreams and memories and what people told me afterward. You know? Glimpses and pictures. Bits and pieces. Some other kids rescued me. I never knew what happened to Ed and the rest of the boys from my school. I hope they're okay. That they got away. I tried to find out, but nobody knew.

"The kids that found me weren't from my school, you see. There was another school in Rowhurst. The local public school on the other side of town. Brockridge Park. We never mixed with them. They were the rough kids. We were always told to keep away from them, but they saved me that day. The boy in charge, their leader, guy called Rav, he told me afterward that when they found me, I was so badly mashed up they thought I was dead. There's been a lot of times since when I wished I had died.

"They were looting my body, apparently, when I grabbed hold of one of them by the arm, like something out of a horror film. Freaked him right out. Nearly crapped himself. They didn't know what to do with me, but there was a doctor nearby who helped some of them. This was right at the beginning, when there were still some adults who hadn't gotten the disease yet. You remember, we all thought maybe some of them would be immune or something? So, anyway, this doctor, Dr. Catell—Chris Catell—he was trying to help us kids.

"He had a medical center near where we'd been ambushed. And they took me there. He'd barricaded it up, you see. Made it safe. He had two nurses with him and they were doing what they could. At first he didn't want to take me in, apparently. Told Rav that it was a waste of time; with wounds like I had, I was a goner. But Rav's group didn't want me either, so they dumped me on his doorstep and when I didn't die straight off, he kind of had to take me in.

"I can sort of remember it from there. This and that. Lying in one of the consulting rooms, all bandaged up like a mummy. This one nurse crying all the time. One of them was named Mel and one of them was Janey. I think it was Janey who cried all the time. Dr. Catell, unshaven, pumping me full of painkillers and antibiotics and stuff, cleaning my wounds, trying to stitch me up. It felt like all the nerves in my skin had been exposed, rubbed with grit. Like I'd been deep-fried. I remember a lot of screaming. He must've given me the most righteous painkillers he had. All pointless, he told me, but it seemed I wasn't ready to die yet. The Koran says everything that happens has been planned by Allah. It's all worked out."

"Fate," said Ella. "Isaac was going on about it. Something called a funny word, like Kermit?"

"Kismet," said Malik and he chuckled. "*Kermit*. Yeah, it's all the same thing. Fate, kismet, Kermit, Qadar. That's one of the main teachings of Islam—Qadar. It's all written down somewhere, everything that happens to you. Like we're all just characters in a book. So why do you think I wasn't allowed to die? Why do you think that is? I sometimes thought it was because there was something Allah wanted me to do. That I had a purpose. Other times I thought maybe he was just laughing at me. And lots of times I lost any faith I might have had. Didn't believe in anything. I'd have been happy to die back then, instead of screaming all night. Dr. Chris didn't know how I survived, said I'd lost so much blood I must've had only, like, half a quart left in me.

"I don't know exactly how long it went on like that, me lying there, him looking more tired every day, the one nurse crying, the other one going slowly nuts, the kids shouting out. Yeah, there were others. I wasn't the only one. There were six of us in all, me and another couple of boys and three girls. Time just sort of passed. Didn't know what was day and what was night, while Chris tried to look after me and the nurses, and his other patients.

"Then one of the boys died and there were five of us, and

then it was clear that a nurse had the disease, and Chris and the other nurse, the crying one, had to shut her outside. And she stayed out there, wailing and weeping and screaming and banging on the doors, saying she was all right, then making weird sounds and using made-up language. In the end she was just, like, grunting and swearing and sniffing at the doors and windows. And then one day Chris went out and hit her with something until she was quiet.

"The other nurse cried even more after that. I never saw her with dry eyes. She was nice, though. Nice but scared. Janey. Yeah, she was definitely Janey. We talked a lot. She wouldn't look at me, though. That only made her cry worse. Not that she could see much of me. I was covered in bandages, to tell you the truth. She'd talk about any kind of stuff. Her family, things she'd watched on the TV—she liked soaps—trips she'd been on, her boyfriend, who was dead. And then one of the girls died. I'd never met her. And the doctor accused Janey of doing it and they had this, like, massive fight, right in my room. Janey freaked out. Started climbing the walls and then she scratched the doctor's face, and he held her down and injected her with something. She went still and he dragged her out by her hair, and I never saw her again.

"So now it's just me and Dr. Chris, the other boy and two girls. And I didn't want to stay in that bed forever, waiting for bad things to happen to me. Of all the parts of me that the grown-ups had bitten and chewed, my legs were probably the least damaged. They hardly touched them. So, as soon as I could, I got out of bed and started trying to walk, hobbling around my little room. That's when I got a shock, though. My legs weren't too bad, but my ass hurt like you wouldn't believe where one of the grown-ups had taken a chunk out of it. I made myself keep walking, though, and Chris let me leave my room.

"I got to know the girls a bit. One had some kind of stomach infection, a split in her gut or something. She wasn't much older than you. The other one, Abby, had a badly broken arm. I only met the boy twice. Tommy, his name was. He didn't seem to be injured; he just sat in a chair all day, rocking backward and forward, humming to himself. I don't know if he was sick or he'd just wigged out. Chris wouldn't talk about him. I think maybe he might have had something wrong with his brain, you know, like a tumor or something.

"As I say, there was only the two times I saw him. After that first time the doc put him back in his room and said we weren't to disturb him.

"The power was off by then, but the doctor had collected a load of candles. He'd light a couple in the evenings, and we'd play cards and read magazines, the same ones over and over, and I tried to walk around and get my muscles working properly. But my stitches would pull and I'd be bleeding, and the doc said he couldn't keep giving me more blood, we were running out.

"The girl with the stomach problem, she got sicker and sicker. Went back to her bed. She shouted a lot for painkillers, and the doc was giving her all these, like, antibiotics, but she went green and died. Something burst inside her, the doc said. And we couldn't bury her, so she went outside like the others. Like putting the rubbish out.

"I eventually grew the balls to look in a mirror for the first time. And, well, I don't need to tell you what I look like. It was much worse then, if you can believe it. As well as the cuts and gouges, and the strips of missing skin, I was all swollen and bruised, and weeping with pus and crap. I'd been bitten and scratched and clawed at. One eye was blind. Bits of me were healing, but bits of me were gone and wouldn't ever be coming back. I looked like someone put together from spare parts, badly put together, stitched up like Frankenstein's monster.

"The doc said really I shouldn't have been alive at all. He couldn't work out how I wasn't dead. Maybe something got inside me when I was bitten. Only instead of killing me, it made me stronger. Kept me going. Like the grown-ups you see walking around with bits missing, terrible wounds, arms and legs gone, guts swinging in the breeze, their brains hanging out of their heads. But they're still walking around. How does that work? I mean, I know they're not zombies, but they might as well be, the way they look and act, the way you can whack them and whack them and they won't go down."

"Take their brains out," said Ella.

"Huh?"

"That's what you have to do to zombies. My brother told me—smash their brains out."

"Zombies don't make any sense," said Malik. "The dead can't get up and walk. Unless I'm one, one of the walking dead. A revenant."

"I don't think you are," said Ella.

"I don't think I am either. But why I'm here, how I survived, I can't tell you. And, like I said, Dr. Chris didn't know either. I got to know him quite well. We talked a lot. Well, *he* talked a lot. My throat hurt too much to mumble more than a few words at a time. The grown-ups had squeezed it, strangling me. They'd squeezed it and bitten it, and tried to rip my windpipe out.

"Chris told us something of what was going on outside, how things were just getting worse and worse. I guess I wouldn't be alive if it wasn't for him. Everything he did for me. And at first it was taking it out of him. Each day he was paler and thinner and darker around the eyes. He'd managed to stockpile some food when things had all kicked off, but it was steadily running out. He was giving us most of it, not eating much himself. He started to get spots and sores. I didn't know if it was the disease or if he was just getting rundown. He was always coughing.

"And then one night he was acting all crazy and manic, like he was high, might have been drunk for all I knew, or raiding his medicine cabinet. After that he seemed to turn around, started getting a little stronger. He started shaving and washing, became quite, you know, optimistic. I told myself that he was going to pull through. I didn't know then that there's no cure. You don't get better.

"Me and Abby, though, it gave us hope that maybe not everyone was going to die from the sickness. That guys like the doctor would be okay. He'd tell us, when we played cards, he'd say, 'Look at me. I've beaten it.'

"He hadn't beaten it. It was starting to eat away at him. You'd catch him looking at you funny. His eyes all swiveling around. And he'd say weird, random things. Made no sense. And you'd say, 'What?' and he'd just laugh—'Nothing'—like it was nothing. But it wasn't nothing. After a few days of washing and shaving, he stopped. Started getting careless, his clothes dirtier and dirtier, his hands not clean and his hair all greasy. His eyes, they got shiny. He was shaking. And one day he left Tommy's room unlocked and I went in to see if he was all right."

Malik stopped. His last few words had been shaky.

"Was it bad?" Ella asked, and at first Malik didn't say anything. He just squeezed her hand.

And then he continued on. . . .

20

Tommy was a mess. With all drips and bags of blood hanging off him. And, worse than that, he had these wounds all over him. Horrible cuts, bits stitched up. The doc had been eating him. Cutting bits off with his scalpel. From his arms and legs. Worst thing was—the boy was still alive. The doc was keeping him alive. So the meat was fresh, I reckon. But, man, he was a mess. Unconscious, luckily. I knew how bad that would all hurt. So I put a pillow over his face.

"When I came out, the doctor was looking at me crazy. I laid into him for what he'd done, and he broke down, weeping and sobbing and groveling. Down on his knees, saying all, 'Sorry, sorry, sorry,' and stuff. I'd liked the doctor, he'd been doing his best, but this thing wasn't him anymore. I had to be careful, though. I didn't know where Abby was. If he'd done something to her while I was in Tommy's room. He was clinging on to my shirt. I dragged him along. 'Where's Abby? What have you done to Abby?'

"He'd injected her like the nurse. She was lying on the floor in the waiting room as if she was asleep. Don't know what was in the syringe. Hoped it wasn't poison. I shrugged him off and went to her, and that was when he came at me with another syringe. But I was ready for him. I'd picked up a scalpel in Tommy's room. Cut his hand, across the back, and then I dug it in his wrist until he dropped the syringe, blood going everywhere. He was really sorry for himself now, whimpering like a little baby. He went off to his office and I heard him banging around, looking for medicine and bandages to fix himself up, I guess.

"I went back to Abby. She was still alive, though in a dead sleep. I tried to get her up, but it hurt too much. I was still pretty weak and my hands and arms were much worse than my legs. I could hear the doc moving about. Knew he'd be back soon. I did what they do in films. I slapped Abby, but it didn't do anything.

"So I hid. I picked up a fire extinguisher and I hid, around a corner near to where Abby was lying, and when the doc came out of his office and went to her, I hit him over the head. That wasn't like the films either. He just said, 'Ow,' and fell over, clutching his head, not knocked out at all. He'd dropped one of his syringes, though, and I grabbed it up and stuck it in his back and pressed the plunger down. And he jumped up, with the needle sticking out of him, and he stumbled about, ranting and raving, and I hit him with the fire extinguisher again and again, and in the end he sat down on the floor and blew bubbles and his eyes rolled up and went white. I dragged him into the room with Tommy and locked it shut, and as far as I know, he's still in there.

"Then I waited for Abby to wake up, too weak to do anything else. Sitting in one of the plastic chairs like I was waiting to see the doctor, and I thought about how weird the world had become and how horrible and depressing. I'll tell you, that was one of my low points, one of the very lowest, and I've got a lot to choose from.

"It took a few hours, but eventually Abby woke up, or at least she choked and puked herself awake. When she was feeling okay enough, we talked about what we were going to do and we both agreed we didn't want to stay there any longer. So twenty minutes later we were out on the street, carrying as much medical gear and drugs as we could.

"Turned out Abby had been brought to the medical center by Rav, same as me. She'd been hanging out with him. Part of his gang. They'd been hiding out in Brockridge Park, near his school. There was a building there called Brockridge House. Some rich family had once lived there and the park had been their land. The house was almost a sort of castle, and it had a garden with high walls. Rav had made a good choice. Easy place to defend. Open space around it. It'd been a place where you could get tea and pastries and things, and there were two big rooms you could hire out for parties and weddings. Upstairs was a gallery, I think.

"Now it was a fortress.

"It was about a half-hour walk to the other side of town. The streets were quiet, but that didn't make them any less scary. I knew what it was like to get ambushed, and so did Abby. She'd broken her arm when a load of sick teenagers had tried to kill her. Luckily we didn't see anyone. No kids. No adults, nothing. Like in cheesy old films where somebody says, 'It's too quiet. . . .' Only in those films the next thing that happens is some big-ass attack. None came, but we were still way tense, and by the time we arrived at Brockridge House, we were both exhausted. Abby was still throwing up from the injection, and I was hurt all over and bleeding through my bandages. Anyway, Rav was there with his little army of kids from the school. They were pretty amazed to see us.

"Rav said he'd had me down for dead. And there I was, walking around. Well, staggering and stumbling and bleeding all over the place. I really *must've* looked like one of the walking dead just then. They were excited to see us at first, especially Abby, as she was one of them. But I could tell they didn't like having me around. I freaked them out. I was too weird, too much like a diseased and rotting grown-up.

"I mean, for the first few days I was a hero, escaping from the mad doctor, bringing Abby home. Then, the next few days after that, I was cool, a curiosity, the boy who'd survived an attack, back from the dead. And then I was a freak. Ugly and mashed up and no use to anyone. Even Abby didn't want anything to do with me. She was back with her old friends. Siding with them. Soon there were whispers, people giving me dirty looks, complaining—you know, 'He's not one of us. Why should we feed him? What can he do to help?'

"You can't blame them, I suppose. They were looking after their own. Trying to get by, to survive. I got talking to a little group of kids I'd sort of made friends with. Kids on the edge. Ignored by the others. Guy named Andy, who had cerebral palsy and was in a wheelchair, his friend Susannah, who had the thickest glasses I'd ever seen and a permanently runny nose, a big wiry boy named Henry with a shaved head. Henry had some kind of learning difficulties and had been in a special school. Didn't have a mom or dad. Didn't really know what was going on. He had seizures now and then and kept swearing really quietly, muttering these rude words all the time.

"They didn't fit in, so I hung out with them, my new pals. We'd sit in the garden and talk. I was still recovering, trying to get strong, but hurting too much. I was really weak, slept a lot.

"We were like a weird little gang. I'd always felt a bit of an outsider at school, at Rowhurst. There were only a couple of Muslims in the whole place. I was expected to be friends with them just because we all happened to share the same religion. But we didn't have much else in common and I didn't really get along with them, to tell you the truth. I mean, there wasn't a lot of crap about me being a Muslim; for the most part the boys had been okay. Obviously there were moments whenever there was anything in the news about terrorists or troubles in the Middle East. Then there'd be comments, jokes, people taking jabs. Same as if we were playing Germany at football, the one German kid at school had to put up with a load of digs.

"But now I really was different. I looked like a monster. You can't deny it. I *am* a monster. I frighten people. And you know, when people are all squashed up together and things are going badly, they look for other people to blame. I mean, we had grown-ups for an enemy, but there was never enough food in the house. There wasn't enough room for everyone. So people got forced out.

"Rav was doing his best. He was a good leader as it goes, but it was hard for him to keep everyone happy. They were always trying to find more food. And when they went out looking, they were often attacked by grown-ups. Graffiti started appearing. The kids were spraying the walls. A sort of logo of a mouth with big lips, bared teeth, and a tongue sticking out. The words 'Too many mouths' next to it. Too many mouths to feed. In the end they had a meeting. Rav tried to fight for me. He was cool. But he was voted down, and he wanted to stay in charge."

"So did they throw you out?" asked Ella.

"Not just me. All of us. All our little gang. Me and Andy and Susannah and weird sweary Henry. They booted us all out. Told us we were on our own."

"Were you cross with them?"

"I just felt too bad to get angry," said Malik. "I thought that if it wasn't for me they probably wouldn't have kicked the others out. Felt it was all my fault."

"What did you do? What happened to the others?"

"First thing we had to do was find a source of food. I talked to the others. We were sitting out under a tree in the park, hadn't gone that far from the camp. They told me they knew about a supermarket full of food that nobody could get into. Sounded like a magic supermarket to me, but they claimed it was real. All locked up and the windows impossible to break. So I said we'd go there. Work out a way. It was something to do. The supermarket was just outside town, with a big parking lot and a gas station. It had been built with the same redbrick as the older buildings in Rowhurst, to try and make it blend in, but it was huge and out of scale and still looked like what it was—a big shed full of food—like it didn't really belong there.

"There were some cars in the parking lot and a long line of abandoned shopping carts. When we reached the supermarket entrance, we found three dead bodies lying there. A middle-aged woman and two younger men. They'd been half eaten. Whether by animals or by other humans it was hard to tell. One of the guys was missing both his arms. We all tried not to look at them, tried not to think about them. Pretend they weren't there.

"The shop doors were bolted firmly shut. We pressed our faces against the glass. It wasn't exactly full. That would have been too good to be true, but there did still appear to be *some* stuff on the shelves. How were we going to get at it, though?

"I asked if anyone knew how to hot-wire a car. Not something they taught at Rowhurst. Well, that set Andy off. He was one of those guys who knew everything about everything.

"He was all like—'It's very difficult with modern cars. Almost impossible with any model built after 2004. They have too many security systems. With earlier makes it's easier, but you'd need tools, wire-cutters and electrical tape and a screwdriver. I've never actually done it, but I've seen videos on YouTube. It's quite complicated.'"

Malik said all this in a squeaky, nasal voice, and Ella giggled.

"Yeah, Andy knew a lot of stuff," Malik went on. "Couldn't do a lot, stuck in his chair, but knew a lot.

"So I'm like—'What about those dead bodies? They might have driven here; they might have car keys on them.'

"'Go on, then,' said Andy, and he was almost sort of grinning. 'Why don't you take a look?'

"I told him no way, and he said it wasn't like *I'm a Celebrity . . . Get Me Out of Here*—I didn't have to eat them or anything. 'Just got to think of them like a dead fox or something, a dead bird.'

"Anyway, I couldn't do it," said Malik. "The way my hands were, I didn't want to risk infection. In the end Henry did it. I remember him going over to the armless man, mumbling and swearing. He leaned over him, covering his mouth and nose with one hand. He took hold of the zipper of his jacket between his finger and thumb and peeled it back. The jacket was stiff with dried blood. A cloud of flies flew up from underneath it and Henry fell back on his ass, swearing and spitting.

"The others laughed. Henry really went for it then. Searching all the man's pockets, but he couldn't find anything. Susannah suggested he try the woman's handbag. She still had it clutched in one hand, though the flesh had mostly been eaten, or had rotted away. I remember her hand was bony, the sinews showing like strings. Henry picked up the handbag and yanked it, trying to wrench it from the woman's grasp, and there was a snap as her hand broke off and came away with it. He flapped about, trying to shake it loose, and it flew away and hit the window. Then he opened the bag and tipped out its contents. There were all the things you'd expect to find in a handbag—a purse, house keys, makeup, a brush, mobile phone, tissues, and ta-dah!—a car key.

"He found a rag and cleaned it. Then paraded around the parking lot, aiming it like some kind of ray gun at the cars and pressing the UNLOCK button until at last a Ford Focus flashed its indicators and there was a *clunk* as the locks popped open.

"Everyone cheered and we crowded around the car. And then we saw what was inside."

21

"What was inside the car?" asked Ella.

"There were the bodies of two small children on the backseat. Holding each other in their arms. Long dead, they were covered in a fuzz of green and orange mold and had sort of melted into the seats.

"Henry dropped the key and walked away, squatted down, holding his knees to his chest. Nobody wanted to get in the car, so I stepped up. This was supposed to be my expedition, after all. I was supposed to be the one getting into the supermarket. I picked up the key and opened the door. The stink that came out was so foul that Susannah bent over and threw up all over the place. I quickly climbed into the driver's seat and just told myself to keep moving. I buckled up my seat belt and jammed the key into the ignition. One twist and the engine started. First time.

"I'd had driving lessons from an uncle in Iran when we went over there on a family holiday the summer before. It had been cool. We'd rolled around the countryside and I knew enough to get the thing going and keep it in a straight line. It wasn't as if I was going to be driving the Focus very far, after all. It was a short, quick ride into a large plate-glass window. Finding the bodies in the car had distracted me from the fact that this was a very dangerous stunt.

"Yeah, well, I tried not to think about all that and kept moving.

"'Mirror, signal, maneuver,' that was the drill.

"I looked in the rearview mirror and got a glimpse of the two corpses in the back. They were blackened, their lips shrunk back, showing their teeth, as if the two of them were grinning at a private joke.

"I looked away pretty quickly. I really didn't need to check my mirror or make any signals, did I? I was about to break all the rules. So I set off across the parking lot toward the front of the shop. It felt unreal, like I was a dad on some kind of warped family outing, with his two kids in the back.

"A family of crash test dummies.

"As soon as I had a clear run at the window, I accelerated. Not too fast—I didn't want to kill myself—just fast enough to break the glass. It felt insane. I was about to ram a car at full speed into Tesco. I had no idea what might happen. If it had been a film, the car would've probably exploded. . . .

"At the last moment I put on a final burst of speed, screamed like a kid on a roller coaster, and slammed the car into the window. It all went down so quickly I didn't really have any idea what happened next. I thought I might be dead, to tell you the truth. I couldn't see anything, hear anything, or feel anything. I think I probably blacked out for a moment.

"All I had was a memory of the impact, rather than the

actual feeling of it. The memory of a big bang followed by the sound of glass falling. The memory of something big and white punching me in the face. The memory of being kicked back into my seat and my head bouncing off the headrest. The memory of the two bodies in the back being thrown forward through the windshield and splattering messily across the hood.

"It was like a computer rebooting. First my vision came back into focus. There was smoke and steam and shiny bits of windshield everywhere. Then my hearing. Hissing, dripping, tinkling, a high-pitched whine inside my head. My nerves started to send pain signals to my brain. I had the beginnings of a monster headache. My face was sore, scratched, throbbing with each heartbeat, as if someone was hammering at it.

"I was slumped over the air bag, the car crumpled up against the check-out aisles inside the shop. There were bits of rotten flesh and wriggling maggots in a funnel shape over the hood, as if the car had thrown up something evil through its broken windshield.

"Then I heard voices . . . 'Are you all right? That looked amazing.'

" 'The whole window went, like, just *boom*. . . .'

" 'It was like a film or something.'

"They helped me out of the car and I, like, limped over to the supermarket shelves. A lot of them were empty—the shops had run out of food real quick when the panic set in—but miraculously there were still a few things left to eat, a few cans and packets—beans and sardines and cake mix. And in a back storeroom we found some water and some bags of rice and pasta. Plus a load of sweets and chocolate. Enough to last us maybe two or three weeks. And then what? What could the four of us do? We barricaded ourselves in the back room there and talked.

"Henry had nowhere to go. No family. He went on and on about someone called Mary, in between the swearing and the spitting, which he also sometimes did. I worked out that Mary must've been his, like, teacher, or nurse, or caregiver, or something. He kept asking where she was and when he'd see her again. At first I explained every time what had happened, how she was probably dead, and he'd understand and nod his head, and not long after he'd ask the same questions over again . . . 'Where's Mary? Where's Mary? Will she bring my tea?' So after a while I stopped explaining and just said she'd be coming soon, and that seemed to keep him happy.

"Andy said his family were all dead. He hadn't had any brothers or sisters. Only parents, and they went quick. Susannah said she had one sister, who was back at Brockridge House with Rav and the rest. I couldn't believe it. That her sister would let her go like that and not say anything. But Susannah just sort of shrugged, said her sister hated her.

"I told them about my family. Three sisters, all younger than me. I had no idea what had happened to them. I said I wanted to go look for them. See if maybe they were safe back home somewhere. I mean, I didn't expect much, it was a real long shot, but it was something to do, somewhere to go. What was the alternative? To stay there and wait till we either starved to death or were attacked by a group of grown-ups wanting to finish what they'd started. I told the others they could either come with me or stay there, it was up to them.

"Susannah just shrugged again; nothing seemed to be a big deal to her. It was like she had something missing. Andy said he wanted to come, but we'd have to help him with his wheelchair. He'd had an electric one before, but when his batteries had run down there was no way of recharging them. So now he had a fold-up one that we had to push for him. It was a bit rickety.

"And Henry? Well, Henry just did what he was told."

"Where was your home?" asked Ella. "Was it nearby?"

"No. Rowhurst was a boarding school. I had to do a load of exams to get in. It was my dad's idea. He couldn't really afford it, to tell you the truth, but he always said he wanted the best for me. He wanted me to be a doctor or a scientist. 'Something proper,' he always said. My dad worked at Heathrow, at the airport. Mom was an office cleaner. But Dad had been buying cheap properties to rent out around Slough, and I think he had some family money. I hated it at first, being away from my family, but I guess I got used to it. I grew up in Slough. It's not far from here, as it goes."

"I remember Slough," said Ella. "We passed it when we drove out of London. I remember saying that it sounded like a horrible place."

"Yeah. Imagine growing up in a place called Slough." Malik laughed sourly in the dark. "It's not totally horrible, though. I mean, it's not exactly great, it's just . . . *Slough*. Bad name, I know. It's about sixty miles from Rowhurst to there. Andy said the average human walking speed was three miles an hour. So we figured it would take us about twenty hours, give or take a bit. If we pushed ourselves we could do maybe ten miles a day. Get to Slough in a week.

"What did we know? This was early days. We had no idea what was out there. How dangerous it might be. It was just a school math problem. They never asked that in the exams, did they? Like, 'If John walks at three miles an hour from London to Brighton, and he's attacked by rabid grown-ups four times, and they bite his right leg off, how long will it take him to bleed to death?'"

Malik laughed again.

"We were just four dumb kids with a lot of stupid hope.

"It was Andy who suggested we look for some more car keys. I mean, it had gone so well before, hadn't it? I'd only been knocked out for a few seconds. So me and Henry searched the supermarket. Andy and Susannah stayed behind to guard the storeroom. Though what use they'd have been if anyone got in and attacked, I don't know. Susannah would just shrug, I guess.

"We found an upstairs and we found the manager's office, and we found the manager, hanging from the ceiling, with his belt around his neck, and his pants around his ankles. He hadn't thought about that. How he'd look if he took his belt off. I must admit I laughed. But Henry didn't really have a sense of humor. He was determined, though, I'll give him that. As I looked around the office, he went through the guy's pockets. I found his keys in his desk. House keys, work keys, car key. For a Volvo. We looked out the window that overlooked a staff parking lot behind the supermarket. Henry knew a bit about cars and he recognized the Volvo.

"Ten minutes later we were packing our supplies into the trunk. It didn't have a whole lot of gas in it. The dashboard said twenty-seven miles. We knew we probably wouldn't be able to find any more gas anywhere. It had run out quickly when the disease hit. The tankers had stopped delivering. Everyone ran dry, got stranded. But twenty-seven miles was better than nothing. It would get us halfway there. It felt like a good sign. We were learning how to get by. We felt like we'd sort of achieved something.

"It was a good thing we had the car, because five minutes down the road we ran into a big gang of grown-ups blocking the street. We braked hard and they came after us, but we managed to turn around and go a different way, and that felt like a good sign too.

"Do you remember what it was like in those early days? Crazy. There were fires everywhere. Kids and adults roaming the streets, all fighting each other. We'd been lucky not to come across any of it since we'd left Brockridge House, but now we were seeing it everywhere, the full-on madness of it. I just kept on driving, trying not to think too far ahead. I had my plan to get to Slough and that was it. Didn't want to think about anything else.

"It was hard work. At first I kept stalling the car, but I slowly got better at it and we made our way out of town. We figured we'd be better off on the M25. It was a good wide road, with not too many buildings near it. We found our way there and set off. There were crashed and burned-out cars all over the place: people had driven until their gas ran out, or they'd gotten too sick to carry on. As if you could escape the sickness by driving. I mean, there was nowhere to go, was there?

"There were dead bodies as well. In the road. In the cars. Lots of cars piled up. There wouldn't have been any police around, or fire brigade. People just went nuts. There were cars all twisted together. We even passed a convoy of army trucks stalled in the road. No sign of the soldiers. We stopped to look for weapons—nothing there, worse luck. Would have been good to get hold of some rifles, hand grenades, and stuff, like in the movies.

"So it was back in the car and more driving. Felt good to be moving. Even if I was a bit of a slow driver. These were scary times, but in a way, maybe they were the most optimistic. Because we were moving, it felt like we were winning. I thought, because I was driving, that it was down to me. I was saving people. We were just like the other drivers, though. We thought we could get away. We thought we were going somewhere. Instead we were just going around in a big circle, which is what the M25 is, isn't it? A big roundabout going all the way around London.

"We were chatting away. Excited. Except Henry, who talked to himself, swear words mostly. We really thought we might live forever. Well, we didn't, did we?

"Susannah was the first to go. We'd made it as far as some services, nearly ten miles farther than the gauge had said we'd go. But we'd been running on empty for a long way. We just made it and I parked up near the pumps.

"There was no power so I knew we couldn't actually use the pumps, but I wondered if there was maybe some way we could get some gas out. Gave up after a few minutes. It was hopeless. So the next thing was to look for another car. There was a sort of hotel place there—an inn, it was called— with brightly painted walls. There were some cars parked outside it. We searched the cars for keys but didn't find any. So we went in, me and Henry, the fearless key hunters.

"It was a mess inside, and upstairs we found signs of a fight. Some dead adults clustered around a door. The door had been barricaded up, but the attackers had managed to force it a little way open. Me and Henry forced it further. Inside the room we found a father and his son, at least that's what it looked like. Both dead. Henry did his thing—he was getting good at this—found the father's car key in his jacket pocket. A Citroën this time. We spotted it outside and there was still gas in it. We drove it back to where Andy and Susannah were waiting in the Volvo, and started to swap our supplies over from the boot.

"It was while we were doing this that the kids arrived. A gang of them appeared from nowhere, armed with sticks and tools and clubs. We quickly jumped into the Citroën and locked all the doors. Had no idea if they would be friendly or not. But we had a bunch of food and couldn't offer much of a fight.

"Susannah was in a state, though. The first time I'd seen her get worked up about anything. Like a different person. She started up about how we hadn't moved all the food, that we'd left some in the other car. Maybe I'd gone on too much about how important the food was. She was getting all anxious and hysterical. I think she was probably a bit unhinged to start with. Odd, you know. We were all odd. A real odd bunch. But this was freaky. She was going nuts.

"The kids got nearer, ignored us, and started getting the stuff out of the trunk of the Volvo, and Susannah just flipped.

She jumped out of the car before we could stop her and ran over to them and started to fight one of them over a box of cookies—cookies! The guy dropped them and they spilled all over the road, and she tried to pick them up and one of the other boys hit her with his stick, knocked her down.

"I got out of the car, but about five of them lined up and gave me a look that said, *Back off.*"

Malik paused. Sighed. Ella could hear him breathing heavily. She waited for him to continue.

"If it was today," he said, his voice almost a whisper, "I'd have taken them on. Smashed them to pieces. But I hadn't learned to fight then, and I was still weak and in a lot of pain, bleeding, limping, half blind, a useless piece of chewed-up meat. There was nothing I could do except stand there. There were too many of them; if I'd tried to do anything they'd have massacred us.

"I watched as Susannah managed to get up, and she got into the Volvo. She got it started. I'd left the key in the ignition. She went zooming off out of control, smashed right into one of the gas pumps and knocked it flat. No gas had spilled out, but you could smell the fumes pouring out of the damaged pump. The kids were running toward the car to get the stuff out of the trunk, laughing, jeering. And then Susannah must've tried to start the engine again and there must've been a spark, because next thing there was a big sort of *whoomph* sound and a fireball around the car. Some of the chasing boys were knocked over and I felt a hot blast, like a kick. That was enough for me. I was back in the Citroën. I turned the key and we were out of there.

"Andy was crying and Henry kept asking about Mary

and was she going to come and help and I felt sick. I'd hardly known Susannah, but I hated for this to have happened to her. You'd think you'd get used to it, people dying, friends getting killed, but somehow, for me, each new one is worse. I made a decision then that I was going to save people. Somehow I was going to save people.

"I didn't do a great job, did I? The next to die was Andy. In Slough. Not a great place to live. Worse place to die. The Citroën got us there. Only took us about half an hour. But when we arrived I wondered why we'd bothered. Why had we come here? What was I expecting to find? Happy families dancing in the street? My sisters rushing to meet me with big smiley faces? Yeah . . . Slough had been banged up much worse than Rowhurst. The whole town was ripped apart. It was chaos. Looked like there'd been a riot, or a war, or something.

"We should've expected it from the drive in. When we were on the highway, we saw these fields full of dead bodies, like they'd been dumped there and bulldozed into piles. You couldn't believe how many there were, rotting away, rubbish piles of bones and skulls and mangled flesh. The sky above was thick with birds, crows, and seagulls, and there were great clouds of flies. The mounds were crawling with rats and dogs. We kept the windows wound up tight. It was like passing through hell, and when we got to Slough . . .

"You know how some places, even now, they look normal, untouched, just like they always must've? Maybe some weeds have grown up, grass and that, but otherwise they look fine. Ascot and most of Windsor are like that. But Slough was a wreck. It was like everyone who lived there, everyone who hated the place, had finally found an excuse to trash it. Shops were smashed in, houses burned down, cars as well; there was rubbish and litter and garbage everywhere. Dead bodies piled up, skeletons and rotten corpses, half-eaten children, pets. Flies everywhere. So many flies, like they'd taken over the town. It stank something awful.

"We lived in the Castleview area. As Slough goes, it was one of the nicer parts—not anymore. Looked like there'd been a hurricane through there. It took me a while to even find our house, because I didn't recognize the place, and of course, by the time we got there I wasn't expecting to find anything. This was all just bad news.

"In the end I found the house and we stopped outside— we only just made it because the car was nearly out of gas. You know when a little kid draws a house? With a red pointy roof and square windows, a tiny front garden, a garage, chimneys? A typical English house? That's what our house looked like. Semidetached. Another Muslim family lived in the other half. The street was all the same. All these boring houses. And now we'd gotten here I didn't really want to go in. I mean, what was I going to find in there?

"It was Andy who persuaded me. Said if I didn't go in, it would be a waste of time and that Susannah would've died for nothing. I didn't want to say anything, but let's face it, she had really, hadn't she? No matter what I found inside. So all three of us got out of the car, and Henry helped me get Andy into his wheelchair.

"We'd passed a couple of gangs of kids roaming the streets, heavily armed, and we'd avoided them, but so far we hadn't seen any grown-ups. It seemed quite quiet at the house. We went up the path and in through the front door. It wasn't locked—the lock had been kicked off. The downstairs of the house was like the rest of Slough—wrecked. Broken glass, broken furniture, all my mom's photos on the walls scrawled over or spray-painted, books thrown everywhere, plates smashed in the kitchen. No signs of life, though.

"Or death.

"Until I went upstairs . . .

"I found my sisters in their bedroom. I only recognized them from their sneakers. It was just three dried-up corpses, all shriveled, lying on the bed next to each other. In a row. I sat down then, on the floor, and I cried. For the first time since this had all begun, I cried. Until I was too tired to cry anymore. I curled up in a ball and I think I fell asleep. I didn't care about anything much right then. About Henry and Andy downstairs. About me. I mean, I don't think I'd ever expected to find them alive, but the reality of it, seeing them there, their bright sneakers as good as new, their bodies . . ."

Once again Malik fell silent. And Ella waited, squeezing his hand gently.

"Did you find anyone else?" she asked after a while.

"No." Malik's voice sounded flat and unemotional. "And to tell you the truth, I didn't want to look. I just hoped that my mom and dad had gone to somewhere better. I bundled my sisters up in a sheet and carried them downstairs. They hardly weighed anything. My faith says you're supposed to bury the dead as soon as possible. It looked like Ameena, Nadia, and Zahra had been dead for weeks. They were good girls, though; they hadn't lived long enough to do anyone any harm. So I knew that if there was a heaven they'd already be there. God wouldn't worry too much about what they'd left behind. I couldn't bear for their bodies to be exposed like this, though. So I took them out the back to bury them.

"We had a shed at the bottom of the garden, where Dad kept his tools. I opened the door without paying attention. I was thinking too much about my sisters. And there inside the shed were about ten grown-ups, all squashed together in the dark, like a fresh litter of puppies. It was hot in there and the smell was rank. I stood there like, frozen, not knowing what to do. Then they started to move and I grabbed a spade from where it was hanging on the wall and backed away. The grown-ups sort of unfolded, expanded from the squashed-up lump they'd been, like when you pour water on to a balled-up, dried-out cloth and it swells like a flower opening. They were coming up off the floor, eyes opening, lips parting, all teeth and tongues and gums. And then they were coming after me.

"I tried to slam the door shut on them, but I wasn't quick enough, or strong enough. They forced it open and came out blinking into the light. I swung the spade at the first one, got him in the side of the head with a big *clang*, and he fell into a couple of the others, but he didn't go down. I swung again, this time with the sharp edge of the spade, and I managed to hit him in the neck. That stopped him all right. Couldn't stop the others, though.

"I ran into the house. Andy and Henry were still there. Andy in his chair. Henry waiting patiently on the sofa, his hands in his lap. I noticed he'd pretty much stopped swearing now. Seemed calmer almost.

"I told them we had to get out of there, and Henry helped me wheel Andy into the hallway and through the front door. Only the whole street seemed to be filled with grown-ups now. They were all around the car. We had no way of getting to it. We tried to charge down the street, Henry pushing the chair, me clearing the way with the spade. It was hopeless. There was nowhere to run to, and in the chaos and confusion, Henry crashed the wheelchair into a trashed car and tipped Andy out. Some grown-ups got close to them and Henry went crazy. He was a bit uncoordinated, but he was wiry and tough and mad, lashing out all around him.

"I kept the grown-ups away while Henry picked Andy up—he was stronger than he looked—and we ran back to the house. Where else was there to go? I saw that most of the grown-ups from the shed had come out of the front door and were wandering down the driveway, and we got past them and back inside. There were two still there, though, slower ones, both mothers, I think. I went crazy, chopping and hacking and whacking with the spade until they were both down, and I shoved their bodies out. We barricaded the front door and the back door and took Andy to the sofa where five minutes earlier Henry had been sitting so calmly. He was bleeding. He'd badly cut his side on the rusted metal of the car. I tried to clean the wound and gave him a pillow to press against it.

"I looked out of the front window. The grown-ups were milling about in the street. Some tried to get into the house but couldn't figure out how. I felt like a fool. We shouldn't have run. I should have just slammed the back door on the ones in the garden. I've learned a lot since then. Wouldn't make a mistake like that again. As I was looking out, one of the gangs of kids we'd seen earlier arrived; maybe they'd been following the car or something. Or maybe following all the grown-ups who were out there. I don't know, but the kids chased them away from our house and forced them down the street, and in a while it was quiet.

"So I went into the back garden and hoisted the dead father over the fence into the next-door garden. I didn't stop. I used the spade to dig a grave in a flower bed and put the girls in there. Said a prayer for them as best I could.

"When I went back in, Andy was in a bad way, crying and shouting and bleeding all over the sofa. Henry was just sitting there in an armchair, ignoring him. Hands in his lap. Like he was waiting. I looked at him and he asked where Mary was, and right then I wanted to hit him with the spade, though I guess he couldn't help how he was. I found another sheet upstairs and tore off some strips to make a bandage for Andy. Gave him some painkillers I'd kept from the doctor's. The wound was deep, right in below his ribs. It looked really bad.

"It *was* bad. We stayed there for a few days, eating our food and rationing the water we had. And Andy got worse and worse. The wound was infected and he went very pale and like, blotchy. Feverish. All sweating and shaking. He said he probably had blood poisoning. He knew all about that sort of thing. He was smart. Said if he didn't have antibiotics he'd die. I didn't have any antibiotics, did I? But I knew where the nearest pharmacy was. An uncle of mine used to run it. I didn't want to go back out on the streets, though. Not after seeing what it was like out there. I made excuses. Said I needed to make sure it was safe. Just scared, really.

"I spent ages at the window, peering out through Mom's net curtains. Waiting until I was sure it was quiet. Trying to man up enough to do it. Andy was getting worse and worse. I couldn't leave it any longer, so, armed just with the spade, I set off. Leaving Henry behind to look after Andy. Not that he was much use, sitting there asking, 'Where's Mary? When's she coming? Will I have my proper tea today . . . ?' But better than nothing, I guess.

"Amazingly, I made it to the pharmacy and back without seeing anyone else. I even managed to get in and find what I thought looked like antibiotics. It was hard to tell as all the pills and medicines had brand names, and I was in and out fast, dashing about like crazy, not wanting to be there any longer than I had to. Anyway, I was pretty sure I had the right thing, and I was thinking I was some kind of bloody hero, but when I got back Andy was dead. Lying there, curled up on the sofa. Henry sitting next to him.

" 'Where's Mary? When's she coming?'

"I went to hit him. I screamed at him and he stared at me. I sat down, said she'd be there soon, and he was happy.

"And I had to bury another body.

"So now it was just me and Henry. A weird life we had there; couldn't really talk to him about anything much. Andy had been good to talk to. He was funny and clever, even if he did talk weird, his mouth not working properly. Henry was different. He was damaged in the brain. No matter. I didn't really want to talk. I was shattered. Done in by it all. Still recovering from my own wounds. Why I hadn't ended up like Andy I had no idea.

"Good luck, or bad luck maybe, you tell me. . . .

"We stayed there, slowly working our way through the food. I had to hide it from Henry, otherwise he'd forget and just start stuffing his face with everything. I knew it wasn't going to last forever, though, and after that? I had no idea what we were going to do. I was too depressed to think. I just lay there all day on the sofa, staring at the ceiling, and every now and then Henry would ask about Mary and I'd say she was coming.

"I did find out a bit about him, piecing the bits together from what he let slip. I think he'd been abandoned when he was a baby. Maybe his parents found out there was something wrong with him and didn't want him. I don't know if he liked me, but we were together and he was staying with me because he didn't have anyone else.

"And then one day I woke up and he was gone. He must've wandered off in the night. I didn't try and figure it out. All I knew was he wasn't there anymore and I was alone."

"Did you ever see him again?" Ella asked.

"No," said Malik. "I never did. I have absolutely no idea what happened to him."

22

After Andy died I got sick. I thought at first I was imagining it. You know like when someone says they have a cold and you suddenly think you have one too? Or someone describes the symptoms of some terrible disease and you immediately think you've got it? I told myself it was that. Just imagining I was going the same way as Andy. Just my imagination. Or I was just hungry or tired, or not drinking enough water, or I don't know what.

"First I got the shakes. Then I got the sweats. Then I got the nightmares . . . real weird ones. Got so I didn't know what was real and what was in my head. Felt like I was going mad. Seeing giant bugs everywhere. Sometimes talking bugs. Kept seeing my sisters' bodies, up and walking around. Sometimes I thought Andy was there, sitting in his wheelchair in the corner of the room, and we'd talk for hours, and then I'd look around and he wasn't there anymore.

"I was really dizzy all the time, puking, kept passing out, couldn't get up, just kept a bottle of water by the sofa, although it was really difficult to swallow, like someone had their hands around my throat. It was horrible. I had lumps in my neck as big as tennis balls. I don't know how long I was like that. It still happens to me occasionally. I've had it off and on ever since—times when I slip away into Weirdsville. Probably something to do with being bitten by the grown-ups. Figure they must've put some of their sickness in me and my body's fighting it. I'm not a doctor. Never got that far in my studies. Even if I was . . . I mean, no one knows how this all works, do they, the sickness?

"You know what, though? Sometimes it's like they're talking to me, the grown-ups. I've got this, like, *sense* that they're there. That's why I'm so good at hunting them. I know where they are. These last few days, two or three weeks, it's been getting stronger and stronger. When that swarm of them hit the farm, it was like I could hear them buzzing, like locusts, right inside my head. But I'm half crazy, so it probably doesn't mean anything. The other kids around here, they think I'm the bogeyman; they think I'm a grown-up, a monster, and maybe I am in a way. I'm fifteen now. I'm one of them as much as I'm a boy.

"That was when I was most crazy, though, when I first got hit by the fever. Lost touch with the real world, and I was happy with that; it was cool as far as I was concerned. It was nice to drift off into another dimension and let this world take care of itself. I would've been happy to just totally freak out and become a nutjob. Live with the talking bugs and the dead people.

"My body had other ideas, though: fought it off, sweated it out. My immune system went into overdrive, and little by little, I threw off the fever and came in to land. Seems I still wasn't going to die. I stank like a corpse, though. My clothes were crusty and foul with sweat and I don't know what. They'd stuck to my wounds. I had no way of washing. I was worse than an animal, very weak, and my food was running low, not much water left. I knew I had to somehow find more. Knew I had to get help. Get food and supplies. And I knew there was only one way I could do that. I had to find other kids.

"But I looked in the mirror, the cracked mirror in our bathroom that the vandals had smashed. I was still a little feverish and I had a vision that it was me—my ugliness—that had cracked the mirror, like in a cartoon. I was worried that if I went out on the streets looking like that, any kids who saw me would think I was a grown-up.

"But I had no choice. I couldn't make it on my own. I knew I had to get help or die. So I grabbed my secret emergency food stash that I'd been saving just in case—don't know how I'd gotten through the madness without cracking and eating it all. I had some cans of Coke and some chocolate bars left over from our supermarket heist, Mars and Snickers and stuff. I filled up a carrier bag and went out on the street.

"It was the middle of the day. The sun was at its highest and brightest. From watching before, I'd noticed that this seemed to be the quietest time. There were way less grown-ups out and about in the day. I was still more nervous than you can imagine, expecting at any moment to be mobbed by a gang of mothers and fathers. I passed the car that killed Andy, a twisted metal skeleton, and went on down the street, limping along. I must've looked like Gollum's ugly cousin.

"I worked my way toward the center of town and at last, after what felt like hours but was probably only about twenty minutes, I saw some kids. They were throwing stones at a house, smashing windows, maybe thirty of them, all laughing, all armed, wearing hoodies, their pants hanging off their asses. They were the sort of kids my mom used to tell me to avoid when I was home for the holidays. They didn't like posh kids who went to private school. Muslim kids named Malik. I could see that some of them were holding beer cans.

"They didn't notice me until I was quite close. I wanted to shout out to them, but was worried my voice would be too weak; my throat was still really painful and swollen. In the end one of them turned and pointed, getting his mates' attention. I raised a hand to wave to them and tried to speak, but it just came out like a strangled croak, not like speech at all, like I was some crazy frog. I panicked that my throat was totally damaged, that the disease had broken it and I'd never speak again, and that made it worse. I tried again. Epic fail. And then they started throwing stones at me. Their aim wasn't brilliant, but a couple of them hit me. Not big stones, luckily, but it still hurt.

"I couldn't go any closer, they were keeping me away, so I grabbed a handful of chocolate bars out of the bag and I held them out as an offering, ducking my head to protect it from their stones, cringing in the road. They just threw more stones, laughing. I sat down, still holding the bars out, waiting for them to either stop or run out of ammunition. Feeling stones bounce off my shoulders. One got me on the top of the head and I heard them cheer. And I just sat there and waited for it to stop. At last one of them came over to me, prodded me with a stick, and I looked up, tried to smile, tried to speak, held the bars out to him. He looked at me like I was some weird animal in the zoo, head tilted to one side, checking me out.

"He was like—'What are you, then?'

"I croaked and shook the bars, showing him I had more in the bag. He took the bag from me, stuck his nose in it.

"'That for us, is it?'

"I nodded my head.

"'You can understand me?'

"I nodded again.

"'You a kid?'

"I nodded. He poked me once more with his stick, then turned and shouted back to his friends.

"'He thinks he's a kid.'

"Their leader came over, checked me out.

"'We don't want him,' was all he said. They took all the candy from me and left me there, just walked off. I tried to follow and they threw more stones to keep me away. I didn't give up, I had no choice. I followed them all the way back to their base. They were living in an industrial park—in an old factory that had a big metal fence all the way around it. They shut me outside the gates, laughing like it was a game.

"But I stayed there. Sat there all night with my back against the fence. And all the next day. Now and then some of them would come out to look at me, and they'd shout things at me, but at least they'd stopped throwing stones. I had my backpack with me, which had the last of my food and water in it. If the kids didn't take me in I'd eventually starve or die of thirst. There was nowhere else to go, though, was there?

To be honest, I didn't really care right then, because as far as I could see, it really didn't matter if I lived or died.

"And then, on the afternoon of the second day, a group of them came over to the gates. They opened them, and while two of them grabbed me and held me still, a third one put a big studded dog collar around my neck, attached to a heavy leash, like you might use for a Rottweiler or a bulldog or something.

"And that was how I became Tyler Keene's bitch."

23

Tyler Keene, I'll never forget him. I hated him from the start. I'd seen him before, figured out he was the guy in charge there. He was a fat kid with short curly hair and a face that looked like it was smiling but wasn't. He was a vicious psychopath, to tell you the truth. I'm not sure anyone there liked him, but they were all scared of him so they'd made him their leader.

"'You're my dog now,' he said as he put the collar on me, and he laughed. From that day until I escaped from him he made my life hell.

"He had a girlfriend called Josa—nasty, pinch-faced girl with no teeth, cruel as him. I don't know which one was worse, really. When the two of them got together, they could be really evil, like they were showing off to each other. See who could think up the worst things.

"They didn't take me inside just then; they were heading out on a hunting party, looking for food. They made me walk at the front, out on the leash like a dog, prodding me forward with their weapons, laughing at me, calling me names. I couldn't say anything. Sitting out in the open hadn't helped my throat. But they *had* taken me on, and I thought at least they might feed me.

"It was a miserable day. They spent the time breaking into houses, picking up anything useful, trashing everything else. I lost count of how many houses we went into, and always I was forced to go in first as they shouted things like, 'Sniff 'em out, dingo-boy,' and 'Take 'em down, bitch.'

"That's what they mostly called me, if they called me anything—'bitch.'

"We didn't find a lot: a few cans and packages of food. Some chips that Tyler scarfed up straight away. And then in one house there were grown-ups. They attacked me as soon as we went in, but I managed to duck out of the way and keep out of it, though I was still on the leash. The kids were too distracted to make me do anything else, as they hacked at the mothers and fathers who were hiding in there. Not laughing now, deadly serious. And I could see that Tyler was a mean fighter, lethal. It was pretty gross, fighting in there, close up, all packed in, the noise and the smell, the grunting and shouting and yelling.

"I got used to it gradually, over the weeks, got braver, I guess, probably because I cared less and less whether I got hurt. Bravery and stupidity are pretty close. And it's easy to be brave if you've got nothing to live for. I learned to attack as well, though they wouldn't let me have any weapons, treated me like an animal. I went in with my bare hands and teeth. Keeping low like a dog, going for the grown-ups' legs, biting them in the ankles, so they'd go down. I thought it might make the kids like me, accept me, if I fought well. Didn't make any difference, though. They kept me chained up the whole time, out in the yard at their camp. Fed me rotten scraps in a bowl, made me go on all fours to eat and drink.

"There were three girls came out now and then to give me some better food. I guess they felt sorry for me, but most of the kids would only come out to tease me, watch me squirm. I suppose they liked having someone in a worse-off condition than themselves, made them feel better. You know what? A couple of them I even recognized from elementary school. I knew them. But they didn't recognize me. I was just the dog, the bitch, the ratbag.

"Josa was the worst. She was clever. She really thought about it. About how to make someone feel like the lowest piece of crap on the planet. She was a very creative sadist. She'd lead me on and offer me hope and then . . . I can't tell you the things she did, Ella. Tyler was just a bully, a stupid bully. He loved to torment me, to torture me. He'd whip me occasionally with a piece of wire, just for fun, pretending I was a real dog. He'd kick me and make me do tricks like play dead and roll over. Once he actually pissed on me. The other thing he did, that he thought was hilarious, was use me as bait.

"They'd take me to a nearby area where they knew there were grown-ups hiding, and they'd chain me up to something and leave me out in the open. All I could do was sit there and wait while Tyler and his gang kept out of the way. For hours I sat out like that. And in the end the grown-ups would come crawling and sniffing from their holes, and when they came up to me Tyler would pounce, come yelling and screaming out of his hiding place with his boys and girls, and they'd kill the grown-ups.

"The thing was, Tyler left it later and later to attack, because he'd seen that the grown-ups wouldn't go for me. They'd come up, curious, they'd sniff around me, peer at me with their stupid diseased eyes, but they hardly ever actually tried to attack me.

"I've noticed it since. Grown-ups are like wild animals. They use smell more than anything to hunt. Children seem to give off a powerful scent that they can detect, and it makes them crazy. But my scent doesn't seem to be anywhere near as strong. That's how come I can hunt the way I do, because they don't know I'm coming. Doesn't always work. Not if they're *really* hungry. Mostly, though, they think I'm one of them. And, you know, sitting there, looking into their eyes as they tried to make sense of me, I felt in many ways that I *was* one of them. I certainly had more in common with them than a jerk like Tyler.

"The whole time I was there, living in the factory, I didn't speak. At first because I couldn't, and after a while, when the swelling went down in my throat . . . I didn't want to. I didn't want to be one of them, part of what they were. I didn't want to be a kid anymore. I was happier being a dog.

"Quite a few of them lived in the factory, and more came to join all the time. It was sort of balanced by some of them getting killed in fights, or else dying from illness, or doing something stupid like falling off a roof. I'd watch them carry the bodies out and dump them in the yard next door. They didn't try to bury them or burn them or anything, and of course that just meant that whatever illness had killed them was spread more. The kids who've survived, and there are lots around here, are the ones who were organized, the ones who were clever. Josa should've been running that place, not Tyler. Yeah, she was a psychobitch, but she had smarts.

"I heard a bit about what was going on in other towns. News spreads, gossip spreads. There was another gang in Maidenhead, the next town over, to the west, and more in Bracknell, where Harry and Sonya and the others came from; others farther out in Sandhurst, the old military academy there, and at Ascot.

"The biggest, most organized bunch of kids, though, live in the castle at Windsor, just to the south. Everyone knows about them. Their leaders are two kids known as the Golden Boy and the Golden Girl, the Golden Twins. Tyler used to laugh about them, calling them the Golden Gays. He thought that was pretty funny. But he had nothing on them. They were clever, they were twenty-first century, and he was just a Viking. A moronic thug. He didn't have a chance in the long run. Didn't know enough about staying alive. He was squeezing all he could out of the situation before things totally fell apart. Maybe even *he* knew the clock was ticking.

"It takes a lot more than being a good fighter to survive. You've got to understand how the world works. I mean, Tyler *was* a good fighter, he was awesome in battle—there's not many I've seen could've beaten him—but what he had going on at the factory, it couldn't last. As the weeks passed, his kids got paler and thinner and were getting ill all the time, coughing and sneezing, bad guts, diarrhea, puking; they started to look as sick as the grown-ups. Compared to them, I didn't look so bad anymore.

"What made it worse was a rival gang of kids in town, camped out in Arbour Vale School to the north, led by a kid named Kenton who was into DIY tattoos—thought it made him look tougher, I guess. Kenton's group and Tyler's group were squabbling over what few resources there were in Slough. Instead of joining together to get rid of the grown-ups, they were fighting each other, sometimes killing each other.

"It finally went into meltdown when the Arbour Vale kids found their way into a cold-storage place on the estate. It had been there all along, right under Tyler's nose, but he'd either never investigated, or thought it was too hard to get into. So Arbour Vale got in there first. We were setting off to search a new part of town one morning, taking a different route through the estate, when we heard them. It made Tyler crazy. This was his turf. That place was stuffed full of food. It was the jackpot. The Arbour Vale kids were busy hauling out anything that hadn't spoiled too badly. Boxes and boxes of stuff.

"So Tyler steamed in there, with me at the front as usual, and, well, I wasn't going to attack other kids and that made Tyler even madder, kicking and punching and calling me 'bitch.' Luckily, though, he was outnumbered, hadn't bothered to find out what he was up against, acted before thinking. All the best Arbour Vale foot soldiers were there, including Kenton, who was a pretty good fighter. They'd been prepared for trouble, and Tyler only had a small scouting party. He was just bright enough to send runners back to their camp, but he was soon in the middle of a really vicious battle, and I was only holding him back, because he had to keep me on the leash. He got so badly cramped in, he needed both hands free—and he let go of the leash. First time ever.

"Last time."

24

didn't wait. I bolted. Got well away from there. The Arbour Vale kids didn't know what to make of me, left me alone, and I was able to climb up onto the top of the warehouse. Right up onto the roof, where I hid, watching the battle below. It was bad. Lots of kids got hurt; half of them were wounded, some so badly it was obvious they weren't going to live much longer. It was all so stupid. Seeing them lay into each other like that. I was lucky to be out of it.

"In the end Tyler's reinforcements turned up and the Arbour Vale kids made a run for it, carrying as much as they could. Tyler acted like he'd won some major war, strutting about the place, punching his chest and bellowing. King of the rotten food . . .

"He left some kids there to guard the place twenty-four hours a day. They mostly camped out in a little office near the main doors. There were rows of giant freezers in there, big enough to walk into. Whole rooms kept below zero. When the power had gone off, they'd taken a long time to thaw. Most of the food had gone bad, but there was still a lot you could eat if you weren't too fussy, and water too, from all the ice that had melted.

"I found a crawl space, and for the next few days that's where I lived. I'd come out at night and go down while the guards were sleeping and steal food and water. They never knew I was there, the idiots. I'd eat whatever I could get my hands on. Just to stay alive. I'd long forgotten the idea of only eating halal—not that I'd been that strict before, unless I was with some of the more, like, devout members of my family. You know what? I figured that if there was a God, and He had a whole universe to look after, He wouldn't be too bothered about what we put in our sandwiches and what type of hats we wear.

"I'd mostly sleep in the day and explore at night, poking about in all the back rooms, picking up useful stuff. I found a load of paper bags and I used to crap in them, chuck the poo outside through a skylight, so that there was no evidence of me. I mean, I was a bit weird then, to tell you the truth. I'd been Tyler's dog for so long. I'd get flashes too, of the fever. See things in the dark. Talking bugs. My sisters. There were pigeons up there, flapping about and crapping and nesting. I used to talk to them. Imagined I'd made friends with them. For a few days I convinced myself that I was dead. A zombie. That my body was rotting. Luckily I never went completely over the edge, imagining I could fly or anything like that. I stayed alive. Alive, but weird.

"I played nasty games with Tyler as well. I'd get out onto the roof and wait for him. He turned up most days to organize the food collection. Well, not exactly 'organize,' more just standing there, shouting at people and showing off.

You could see he was still thinking he was Mr. Big Shot, and he was going to let the whole world know. He'd seen off the Arbour Vale kids and now had the biggest source of food around. Well, I found a good spot where nobody could see me and I'd wait for him and I'd lob bags of shit down at him. Twice I got him, and that was enough for me. Made a real mess as well. I still smile at that memory. It's childish, I know. But, oh, it was funny. You should have seen him. He went mental. Never worked out where it was coming from. Stupid idiot, probably thought it was giant pigeons.

"As I say, I hated him, but did I want him to die? I don't know. I dreamed of killing him. Pictured myself doing it . . . But it was never real.

"The Windsor kids fixed all that. I don't know, it might have gone on like that for ages if they hadn't showed up. It was all Tyler's fault. He'd been bragging so much about his stash that word got around. Windsor's not far from Slough, and one morning, while Tyler was lording it up, a shout went out.

"'Windsor! Windsor are here!'

"They were advancing down the street. A big group of them, tightly packed, moving in formation, well armed, three big pickup trucks at the back. And out in front two kids all dressed in gold, riding horses.

"I was up on the roof. I saw it all. How Tyler thought he could take them on and win, all puffed up and sure of himself. He called his troops together and he marched out of the yard into the street, Josa at his side. She wasn't all mouth: she was a tough little fighter, and dedicated to her man. Well, I wasn't going to miss this. I climbed down off the roof and followed them.

"The Windsor kids looked better organized all around than Tyler's mob. And the Golden Boy and the Golden Girl were pretty impressive. They were actual twins by the look of it, with long fair hair, and they were wearing gold armor. They must've found it in the armory at Windsor Castle; it was black steel with gold stripes and studs. They had swords at their sides, with gold decoration on them; even their horses had bits of gold armor. The horses were a matching pair—white. They looked like something out of a kids' picture book. I could see that Tyler had no fear of them. He lined his troops up across the road and started name-calling.

"The Golden Twins stopped and said hello. They were posh, well-spoken, with a kind of snooty air about them, looking down from their horses. Tyler had no respect for posh kids. Nor did Josa, who shouted some really filthy stuff at the twins. She had a grating, husky voice, like sandpaper. A slight lisp from having no teeth.

"'We've come to pick up some food,' said the Golden Boy. 'We've heard you've got some here.'

"'It's mine, Gaylord,' said Tyler, and his mates laughed, Josa loudest of all.

"'It's not really yours, is it?' said the Golden Girl. 'You found it, but that doesn't make it yours.'

"'Doesn't make it yours either, bitch.'

"'That's not how we see it.'

"'Yeah? Well, this is how I see it,' Tyler shouted, and he dropped his trousers and showed his ass to them, which his mates thought was the funniest thing they'd ever seen. And I'll admit I *did* smile.

"'Hey!' Josa shrieked at Tyler, her face mad with laughter. 'That's mine! Don't you go sharing it out with no Windsor slags.'

"The Golden Twins didn't know how to handle this. If they'd been expecting a serious discussion, maybe some negotiation, they were out of luck. They must've realized by then that they were dealing with a total moron. It was clear that Tyler wasn't the sort of person you could have any kind of sensible conversation with. They leaned over and talked to each other, and it was then, while they were distracted, that Tyler decided to attack. Bravely leading his men into battle. Well, not exactly 'leading,' just charging wildly into the fight, yelling his head off.

"At first, taken by surprise, the Windsor kids had a hard time of it. They were knocked back and penned in. There was just a lot of pushing and shoving and swearing and name-calling. But the twins had the advantage of being on horseback and they used their horses to push through Tyler's troops, and once they were out in the clear they could turn and ride along the rear of Tyler's mob, laying into them with heavy clubs. They could easily have used their swords and that would've meant a quick end to Tyler and his idiots, but I guess they didn't want to kill anyone if they didn't have to. They had some decency.

"The fight went on for ages. I couldn't tell what was going on. Kids were running everywhere and there was no shape to it. All you could clearly see were the twins, riding through the mass of bodies, whacking and hacking. Their kids were better organized. They had some idea of tactics at least, and gradually the fight started to break up. One by one Tyler's guys gave up—they were too bruised and battered—and either left the scrum and sat on the ground with their weapons at their sides or ran off. Tyler and Josa and their closest friends were still at it, though.

"The twins had probably been hoping that Tyler wouldn't hold out this long. In fact, I bet they'd expected that he'd simply surrender when he saw he was outnumbered. But Tyler wasn't the surrendering type. He was more of a fight-to-the-death kind of guy. And that day he got what he wanted.

"It was the Golden Girl who killed him. She was excellent on her horse, a real expert. Riding rings around him. He kept on going, swearing and calling her all sorts of filthy names, like a Duracell bunny—unstoppable. In the end I guess the girl just wanted it over with, and she sort of poked him in the neck with the point of her sword. It went down through his shoulder, must've hit his heart or something, because he dropped quick, like a butchered cow in a slaughterhouse. *Bap* . . . and he was dead. Just like that. Josa screamed and ran to him, and it was over. There were about four or five other bodies—whether they were dead or just unconscious I don't know. Josa was sitting in the road with Tyler's body in her lap, wailing like a madwoman. And all I thought was, *You got what you deserved.*

"That was it for me. I'd had enough of Slough. Should never have gone back there. And I wasn't going to Windsor. You see, the thing is, I don't want you to think that I reckon the Golden Twins were any better than Tyler just because they were more organized and knew what they were doing.

I didn't like them any more than him. They were looters, stealing other kids' food, and they were prepared to kill to get it. They cleaned that cold storage warehouse out. Didn't leave a scrap for the local kids. Took everything and loaded it on to the pickup trucks along with a couple of the bodies and marched out of there.

"It was time for me to get out as well."

25

didn't want anything more to do with kids if this was how they were going to behave. I cut and ran south, out of Slough, over the highway and into the countryside, such as it was. I mean, you know what it's like around here—it's not the deep countryside, but there are fields and woods and lakes."

"Where I found you?" said Ella. "You came here?"

"Yeah. Where I found *you*."

"Where we found each other."

"Yeah . . ."

Malik stopped talking again. Ella listened to his breathing.

"What happened to the children you left behind in Slough?" she asked after a while. "Without a leader?"

"I heard later they'd joined up with the Arbour Vale kids," said Malik. "Like they should've done in the first place. They're doing all right there now, I think. They've cleaned most of the grown-ups out of town. Made it safe. Apparently Josa's in charge now, with Kenton, the tattooed boy from

Arbour Vale, as her second-in-command. She was pregnant too. Had Tyler's baby. So . . . not somewhere you'd want to go. Maybe you should go to Bracknell, or Maidenhead—"

"No," Ella interrupted. "I saw what those children are like. I saw what Louisa and Sonya did. If you won't have anything to do with them, then I won't either."

"I don't know if I can keep you safe, Ella."

"I'm not leaving you."

"Listen, Ella," said Malik. "Sure, kids are still desperate, but it's a year since I was in Slough. That was all a long time ago. Things have settled down a lot since those early days. For the most part kids have stopped fighting each other and they respect each other's turf. That's what the races are all about."

"What are the races?" Ella asked. "Isaac was going on about them like I should know what he meant."

"It's what they call these games that the kids have over at Ascot. It's their way of competing against each other without anyone getting killed. Well, all right, sometimes there are deaths, but that's not the main idea."

"What sort of games are they?"

"I don't know. I've never been, Ella. Since I left Slough I've tried to avoid other kids."

"Have you been alone for all that time? Did you go straight to the farm?"

"Not right away. I wandered all over at first, but the countryside can be a harsh place if you don't know what you're doing, which I didn't back then. I had no idea how to live off the land, and there were still grown-ups about. The kids had stayed mostly in the towns, and the grown-ups had been forced out. So it wasn't safe anywhere. Funnily enough, though, it was grown-ups who looked after me. Saved me. Treated me better than the kids had."

"Grown-ups?"

"Yeah. There was a group of them, sort of survival nuts. They'd gotten out of town when everything started to go wrong. They'd been ready for it. Looking forward to it, I reckon. They had everything you need to survive: weapons, tools, medicine, armor, traps, tents, water-filtration kits, night-vision goggles. They were living here on the farm. They set up a lot of the traps and things. They'd stay indoors during the days and hunt at night."

"Weren't they sick?"

"Yeah, they were sick, but fighting it. Looking after each other. There were five of them when I first met them: Brian, Waggers, Mike, Roy, and Tomasz. There'd been more to start with, but they'd gotten the disease worse. The rest of them were going down slower. Learning how to keep it at bay."

"So how did you find them?"

Malik laughed. "I got caught in one of their traps one afternoon when I was out foraging. An animal trap. Big one. Nearly broke my leg. They found me that night. Like everyone else they weren't sure what I was—a grown-up or a child. I refused to speak to them. I was done with talking. In the end they decided I was just a kid and they felt guilty they'd trapped me. You know, they were, like, sorry for me, the way I looked, how badly mashed up I was, my leg all bruised and bloody. And I hadn't been eating well. What with that and the attacks of the fever and everything, I was just skin and bone. Skin and bone."

"So what did they do?"

"They took me in. Looked after me. They seemed to like doing all that first-aid, doctor-type stuff. They were good at it, actually. I learned a lot from them. In fact, I learned everything from them. Except for what I'd gotten from Tyler, I suppose, which was how to attack like an animal."

"You're not an animal," said Ella, and Malik laughed softly and hugged her.

"Thanks for reminding me. I don't know, maybe Waggers and Brian and the rest thought I was. They liked animals, when they weren't hunting them. They had horses. Three of them. Used to go out hunting on them. Tomasz taught me how to ride. He was really good on a horse. Showed me all sorts of tricks. I was rubbish at first, but I got the hang of it. There were more animals on the farm then. They'd collected them—a pig, a goat, the chickens, of course. They showed me how to look after them."

"What happened to the other animals?"

"We slaughtered the pig for the winter and the goat was killed one night when some dogs got in. She was a mean old ratbag. Killed a couple of them before they got her. The horses died too. They're useless, horses; they get so many diseases, they injure themselves easily, they eat the wrong things. Two of them died of some kind of horse flu thing. The third broke its leg and Tomasz shot it. But for a while it was like a proper farm."

"Weren't there any women?" asked Ella.

"Only the goat," said Malik with a laugh. "They seemed happy enough, the men. They had a big stash of beer and whiskey and they'd built their own still, made this foul spirit they called *nitrofuel*. Tasted like poison, which is pretty much what it was. Afterward I turned the still into a stove, to heat the place better. They had it well fortified and well guarded. They had all the animals and the food. Plus, they had this big metal barrel half-buried in the middle of the yard. Wouldn't talk to me about it. Wouldn't tell me what was in it."

"So was it their farm, then?"

"No. Not really. They'd killed the family that lived there. They told me the family were all diseased. They'd eaten their own children. Mike and Waggers and the rest went in there and shot them all. *Military-style*, they said. Executions. One bullet each to the back of the head. They tried to stick to army rules, army ways. Made them feel legit, I guess, excused what they were doing.

"They wore, like, full army gear—camouflage, make-up on their faces, black stripes and that. Sneaking around at night with their night-vision goggles, communicating with wind-up walkie-talkies, all that 'alpha bravo, target acquired, tango down . . .' stuff. They weren't real military, they were just playing at it, but they weren't bad. They had their guns and their crossbows, they dug holes and built hides and set nets and fishing lines and trapped small animals and birds, rabbits, ducks, swans. Once they got a deer. And they knew how to properly forage for stuff I'd never even heard of: chickweed and yarrow, fat hen, bittercress and elderberries. They taught me how important it was to get vitamins inside me. They kept me alive and healthy.

"They were sick, though. There was no getting around it. They knew it and I knew it. They were all coughing, runny noses, red-eyed. I'd been with Dr. Catell, watched him slowly get worse. I knew what it was going to be like, just a matter of time. But they never talked about it.

"One of them, the one I liked best, Roy, he was badly wounded in the groin. He'd been in a fight with some other grown-ups and one of them had stuck him with a spear. He had a real nasty wound there, couldn't walk. The others used to carry him to the river and he'd sit there all night fishing, his gun at his side. They'd bring him back in the early morning, before the dawn, when they'd finished hunting, and they'd sit in the yard and drink and play cards, and talk, and laugh. That's what I remember most, them laughing. God, could they laugh. Laugh till they were crying or sick or both. Roy laughing loudest of all. They'd laugh at anything. Telling jokes, making fun of each other, remembering things they'd done in the past—mostly involving getting drunk—and just laughing.

"I'd laugh too, though I wasn't always sure what at; you just couldn't help joining in. And they'd sing songs as well. Waggers had this battered old acoustic guitar. He could never get it in tune, but it didn't really matter. They'd have singalongs around the fire. I remember them as good times. You see, these grown-ups treated me better than any of the kids in Slough. And, speaking of kids, they stayed far away from the farm. They didn't want anything to do with the men. We were left well alone.

"Sometimes sick grown-ups came blundering in and Waggers or one of the others would shoot them. Oh, I wish I still had those guns, but they ran out of ammo eventually, or broke and I couldn't fix them. Tomasz buried a stash of weapons somewhere and died before he could tell me where they were, and I've been looking for them ever since. All I had by the end was my trusty shottie. And now I've run out of shells for that. So all I've got left is you."

"I'm sorry."

"I was joking, Ella."

"But what *are* you going to do?" said Ella, trying not to let her voice get too trembly.

"I've gotten this far, Ella," said Malik. "I've always come through somehow. As I say, maybe God has a plan for me. He's not going to let me die."

"And what about me?"

"I'll look after you, don't you worry."

"Yes, but . . . well . . ." Ella didn't quite know how to say it. "I don't mean to be rude, but everyone around you seems to die."

26

Malik was really laughing, his voice loud in the cramped space under the tree. Ella pictured the army men laughing; they must have sounded like this. She was hurt at first: she thought Malik was laughing at her. Slowly, though, she melted and then joined in, her own high little voice cutting through his great roar.

"Oh, Ella," he said at last. "I haven't laughed this much since . . . well, since those nights with the lads. You're right. Everyone I meet does seem to come to a bad end, don't they? Dr. Catell and the kids in his clinic, Susannah and Andy. Tyler . . . Waggers and Mike and Brian and Tomasz and Roy. They were tough. They held out for a long, long time. Fighting the illness. Trying different drugs and different plants, anything they could think of to keep it away. Nothing worked, or at least nothing did anything more than slow it down. They couldn't shoot it or trap it, or sneak up on it and stab it with a hunting knife. Weak or strong, short or tall, or fat or thin, it got you in the end, if you were old enough.

"Mike was the first to go. As the days passed, he talked

less and less, and when he did talk it didn't always make sense. And then one night he went berserk, kicked the fire all over the yard, cut poor Roy, who couldn't get out of the way, all the time ranting about something none of us could understand. Next night he was very quiet, and just before we turned in for bed he took Tomasz aside for a long, intense chat. And Tomasz nodded and the two of them left the farmyard and went out into the fields, and later we heard a single shot. And Mike never came back.

"I knew what had happened. *Military-style*. One clean shot to the back of the head. You'd think they wouldn't laugh so much after that, but if anything they just laughed more. Brian had even made a joke about it as Tomasz and Mike had left. Whispered, 'He's just going outside and may be some time.'"

"I don't get it," said Ella.

"Oh, it's a famous saying," said Malik. "From Captain Scott's expedition to the Antarctic, where they all died. They were stuck in a tent in the snow, freezing cold, and the food was running out, and one of them, Captain Oates, who was wounded, sacrificed himself, said, 'I'm just going outside and may be some time.' Walked out of the tent and was never seen again. It became their catchphrase after that, the lads. Whenever their time was up, one of them would say it and the others would know.

"About two weeks after Mike died, Brian said it, and Tomasz took him out into the field. It was Tomasz who was the next to go. He was from somewhere in Eastern Europe. He had an accent. He'd been a builder of some sort, I think. Made most of the platforms in the trees and things. He was younger than the others, with fair hair, and he was very strong and fit, always showing off, doing push-ups and stuff. Never took anything very seriously. And one night he tried to kill Waggers, just suddenly turned on him, eyes red, foaming at the mouth, snarling like a beast.

"Waggers was screaming for help and Roy couldn't do anything, because he didn't have his gun with him. It was next to me. So I shot Tomasz. Roy had taught me how to use the gun. Wasn't such a clean death. Not military-style at all. Took four shots, but I put him down. Waggers was quite badly hurt. I helped Roy to patch him up and bandage him, but I think his wounds weakened his immune system. He got bad real quick after that, and Roy smothered him in his sleep with a pillow.

"So now it was just me and Roy. As I said, he was my favorite. Roy Peachy. I liked that name. He was big and a bit fat, with a great red beard and a rolling, booming voice. Before his wound he must have been a really physical guy, crashing and roaring around like a bear. Now he was just a wounded bear. He reminded me of Brian Blessed."

"Who?"

"Never mind. Doesn't matter. But he was fun, and funny, and he was the one who looked after me the most, even though he had this horrible wound that wouldn't heal. Right in his . . . well, his *groin*. He held out for a lot longer than the others. I'd help him to the river. That seemed to keep him going. Something to do. A bit like you helping me along. Under one arm, him hopping and shouting out with the pain.

"It was late autumn. Winter was coming and he fussed

all over me, telling me how hard it was going to be and making sure I was prepared. I had to do everything now, which was a good way of learning. I slaughtered the pig. I couldn't feed it through the winter, but it could feed me. That was how Roy put it. He taught me to smoke the meat and to salt it. He went over and over what to do with the chickens, how all the traps worked, how to catch fish—that was his favorite part, he loved fishing. It was like he was the last adult and he was trying to pass on all the knowledge and information that humans had stored up.

"But each day he got a little weaker and a little less focused. He'd drift off. Staring at nothing. Stop talking halfway through a word. Coughing all the time, and sneezing and sweating. He got twitchy. Would suddenly laugh at nothing and then get scared or sad. Drinking more and more. Sometimes I'd watch him when he didn't know I was looking, and he'd be talking to himself. Eventually he couldn't leave the farm. He was too weak. So I put him upstairs in the farmhouse where he'd be safe. It got so I hated to be in there with him, listening to him shouting and screaming and muttering all through the night, screeching with laughter. I moved into the barn, left him alone in the house.

"I got used to it in there, with the sky above me, and I got used to being able to hear everything that was going on in the outside world. Birds in the trees, dogs in the fields, grown-ups coming past. Roy screaming. I felt at home there. I really was becoming half wild. Somehow Roy was holding on. Days went past. I'd go out in the day—I didn't need to stay hidden from the light like grown-ups—wandering in the fields and woods, fishing in the lakes. Keeping out of Roy's way. We ate together and that was about it. He stopped talking too eventually. We were like two animals sharing a kill.

"One morning I went down to the lakes at Virginia Water. You remember where those weird sort of Roman ruins are? It was beautiful. The sun was just coming up, and I undressed and washed myself. Something I never did. Took all my filthy, crusty clothes off and washed them too. And for the first time since the attack I saw myself naked, reflected in the water. Saw what my body looked like. It was awful. I was this broken thing. I was tempted not to get dressed again, to wade out into the lake and go under. I don't know, water always does that to me. Like it's calling to me. 'Malik . . . Malik . . . Come to me, let me give you rest. . . .'" He gave a little snort of laughter.

"But I'd made a deal with Roy, you see? Promised him I'd take him out before he went totally sick. So I told the water to get lost. When I got back later, I assumed Roy was asleep. The sun was high in the sky. But as I was sitting in the yard, reading a book, I heard something, and there he was, crawling across the ground, dragging his legs behind him, a look of pure murder on his face. The sun was burning into him. His skin was all red and blistered, and there were boils on him like you see on the really sick ones. They'd come up fast, hadn't been there the day before. I backed away from him. It wasn't difficult. I mean, he could only move slowly. And then I realized he was guarding something. He'd gotten it into his sick mind that he needed to protect the tank that they'd buried. The big metal barrel thing that they'd never told me what was inside. He was sort of lying on top of it.

"As I watched him, the look on his face went away. First

his expression went blank, then sad, then he seemed to recognize me. He smiled and I went to him. Crouched down. He was trying to say something. I could just hear the words."

"What did he say?" asked Ella.

"'I'm just going outside and may be some time.'"

27

Before I killed Roy, though, I had to know something. And I wanted to let him know something. So I spoke to him for the first time. I asked him a question."

"What did you ask?"

"I just asked him what was in the barrel and what it was for. He really smiled then, came alive. Laughed. Like a little kid. Happy for me, I guess. Pleased to be alive. Just like the old days, the old Roy. Told me it was full of gasoline. But they'd been paranoid that somebody would want to steal it, so they'd been keeping it secret and guarding it all this time.

"I helped him up and I moved him into the shade.

"'It's yours now,' he said. 'All this. The whole world is yours. Don't muck it up like we did.'

"I hugged him and he said I was a sly one. 'Always knew you were holding out on us,' he said. 'Now you stay alive for me, yeah? Make things right again.'

"I told him I would and I thanked him for everything and that made him happy, and then I shot him."

"You must have been sad," said Ella.

"I was alone," said Malik. "I knew that much. And I wasn't well again. I don't know if it was from swimming in the cold water, or the stress of losing Roy, but I could feel it coming back. I lost a few days. Couldn't remember anything after. Still can't. Just odd, weird flashes. Horrible things. And when I got my senses back I was lying curled up on the floor in the room of the farmhouse where Roy had been sleeping, and there was this sort of weird shrine thing there. I must've built it. Wasn't anybody else around. There were all these candles, and some little action figures, army types. God knows where I got them from. And Roy's gun, in pieces, all broken up and arranged in a pattern. Some dead birds and animals bones tied together. Bowls of beer and whiskey, gas. Some odd random words in what looked like red paint. Feathers and fur and food. And right in the middle, sitting there grinning at me, was Roy's head. I had a nasty flashback. Of cutting it off with one of the butcher's knives we'd used on the pig. Dragging the rest of his body out into the field for the dogs.

"Why I'd done all this I had no idea, no memory of it at all. It looked sick. Evil. I set fire to it all. Nearly burned the whole house down, except it started raining and that put it out. Didn't want to go back in there, but the next day some grown-ups got into the yard while I was resetting the traps and I had to put them down, and I was so cross I whacked all their heads off and without really thinking I took them into the house and upstairs and put them next to the burned remains of Roy's head. And since then, well . . ."

"I saw it," said Ella.

"Yeah," said Malik. "I know. I could tell by the way you looked at me back there. It was a crazy thing at first, a fever thing, and then it became a sort of, I don't know, like a compulsion. I had to do it. Felt like it gave me some control over the world. Got so that every time I killed a grown-up I'd cut off their head and put it in the farmhouse. It's mad, I know. But then I *am* mad."

"Why do you kill so many of them?" Ella asked.

"It's my job. I'm the hunter and they're the hunted."

"Really? Is that all?"

"No. It's because of what Roy said, I guess, about making the world clean again, about getting rid of the old world, the grown-ups. Making it right and making it so that we can build something new, something better. And because . . . Well, as I said, *because I'm mad*, I suppose. Mad at the world for what it did to me. And just plain mad. The mad killer. But it doesn't make me any happier. It can't change what I am."

"You're a good person," said Ella. "I know you are."

"Am I? I try not to think about it. It's just one day to the next, get by, stay alive. I scraped through the winter after Roy died. Trying to remember everything he'd taught me. Nearly starved to death, nearly froze to death, nearly killed by dogs, nearly poisoned by eating the wrong plants, nearly wiped out by the fever that kept coming back. And then I noticed that the days were getting longer. It was getting warmer. Life was coming back to the world. And I should've been happy, glad to be alive, but the water was always calling to me . . . 'Jump in the river and drown, Malik. Good night, Irene. Over and out.'"

"Who's Irene?" Ella asked, confused.

"Oh, it's this song," said Malik. "The lads used to sing it when they were drunk. Waggers on his out-of-tune guitar. Tomasz sitting on this wooden crate and banging it like a drum. 'Good night, Irene.' They were always singing it. I know it off by heart now. I always wanted to join in, but I couldn't."

"Sing me a bit," said Ella. "I like songs."

"Really? Seriously?"

"Yes. Really . . ."

So Malik began to sing, his voice weak and broken, but getting stronger the more he sang. It was a simple tune and Ella was able to join in on the choruses quite quickly.

> *Irene, good n–i–ight, Irene, good night,*
> *Good night, Irene, good night, Irene,*
> *I'll see you in my dreams.*

> *Last Saturday night I got married,*
> *Me and my wife settled down,*
> *Now me and my wife we're parted,*
> *I'm gonna take another stroll downtown.*

> *Irene, good n–i–ight, Irene, good night,*
> *Good night, Irene, good night, Irene,*
> *I'll see you in my dreams.*

> *I love Irene, God knows I do,*
> *I'll love her till the seas run dry,*
> *But if Irene turns her back on me,*
> *I'm gonna take morphine and die.*

Irene, good ni-i-ght, Irene, good night,
Good night, Irene, good night, Irene,
I'll see you in my dreams.

Sometimes I live in the country,
Sometimes I live in town,
Sometimes I have a great notion
To jump in the river and drown. . . .

Malik stopped. Let Ella sing the last chorus. And then there was silence. Until Malik's voice came quietly in the darkness.

"That night, when I rescued you," he said, "when I was down by the river, ready to jump in, the words were going around in my head. The river was calling to me. I was at my lowest just then, before I met you. I so wanted to jump in."

"Why didn't you?"

"I told you before. The grown-ups came. More of them. I got their scent and—"

"No," said Ella. "That's not it. Why didn't you jump in *really*?"

"I've always thought there was a very thin line," said Malik, "between doing it and not doing it—but there wasn't. It's a thick line, and it's a line I just couldn't cross. I guess some of us are wired for survival. We carry on. And now the thing is, you've given me a reason to carry on, Ella. I don't want to jump in the river anymore. I don't want to be an animal anymore. I want to return to the world. You showed me that it isn't only full of bad things. Bad people."

"From now on it's all going to be all right," said Ella, and Malik laughed.

"I hope you're right," he said.

"I'm right," she said. "I'm going to make you well and we're going to rebuild the farm and we'll live there like proper farmers. I'll plant flowers and we'll have a donkey, and another goat. I like goats. And we'll find a pig somewhere and make sausages out of him."

"You've got it all thought out, haven't you?"

"Yes. I have."

28

I won't go! I won't go! I won't go!"

"You've got no choice."

"I won't . . ." Ella beat her small fists against Malik's chest. He winced and coughed, then let her keep going a few beats longer before grabbing her wrists and holding her still. He glared at her through his good eye, the white stained red around the edges.

"You can't stay here."

"I can . . ."

They were sitting on a platform high up in the treetops in the woods. It was several days since they'd left the farm and gone to hide in the hole. Ella remembered crawling out after listening to Malik's story. She had had no idea what sort of time it might be, no idea how long they'd been down there, and it had been a shock returning to the real world. Since then she'd spent most of her time sleeping, woken only by hunger. That was how it had been. Day by day, just getting from one meal to the next, stretching out their rations, looking after each other.

Malik got stronger every day and was able to move around more and more for himself. Now he was even well enough to climb trees. He'd spent the morning showing Ella how to make animal traps and he'd found a rabbit in one he'd set nearby. Ella was so hungry she forgot to be squeamish about it and they'd eaten it for lunch, roasted over a fire that he'd let her make. Malik had also found some bitterweeds that she happily ate.

Then they'd come up here to try and see what was going on in the world. The sun was sparkling down through the branches of the surrounding trees, which had fresh, bright green leaves bursting out on them. Through the leaves they could see out over the tops of the lower trees to the fields beyond. It looked quiet and peaceful, and for a long while they'd just sat there, taking it in, glad to be alive, trying not to think of all the bad things that had happened.

And then Malik had ruined it by announcing that he was going to take Ella to a town. They'd gone around and around in circles arguing, and for the hundredth time Ella told him that she wasn't going.

"I'm not leaving you," she said, her voice husky from shouting.

"Who said anything about leaving me?" Malik asked. "I need you to look after me." He smiled at her with his ugly, twisted mouth and his one good eye.

"But I thought you'd never go back to where people were."

"I've got no choice, Ella. We're running out of food and I'm too weak and strung out to catch enough for us to both live on. We'll go to Bracknell."

"Where Isaac went?"

"Yeah." Malik nodded. "Provided he made it back there safely. He can stick up for us. He knows you, he knows me, he knows I'm not a threat."

"I'm not going."

"I'm responsible for you now, Ella. I have to make sure you're all right. So don't argue anymore. We're going. End of story."

"No. I said no."

"Ella, we'll die. Don't you see that?"

"And if we go to a town it'll be like before—they'll be horrible to you. Do you think I wasn't listening to your story?"

"It'll be different. I'll be all right. I've got you. You've shown me that I can trust people—*some* people. I've thought about this a lot and I've decided. I need to return to the world. I'm not an animal. I'm a person. It'll be a good thing. A positive thing. I *want* to do it, Ella. It'll be good for both of us."

Deep down Ella knew he was right. It had been getting harder and harder as their supplies started to run low. She felt feeble all the time and cold and scared. There was always the worry that they'd be attacked again. She never felt completely safe, not even when they were down in their snug hole. So far they'd been all right. There had been a couple of occasions when a pack of dogs came sniffing by, but Malik got rid of them. The dogs half liked him and half feared him, but they were hungry too and wild, and if they got the chance they'd come in for dinner. When dogs were in a pack, they behaved differently.

"When?" she said, sounding grumpy and glum. *Grumpy Glumdrops.* That's what her mom used to call her when she was in a bad mood, to try to tease her out of it. And it had always just made her worse. Grumpy Glumdrops. That's who she was.

"Tomorrow," said Malik. "No point in waiting any longer. I'm well enough to walk now. I've been thinking about this ever since we had to leave the farm, planning it. You need to be back with people, not stuck with a ghoul like me."

"You're not a ghoul."

"I'm hardly Johnny Depp, though, am I?"

Ella had to admit that there was a part of her that was lonely and a part of her that was bored, made worse by sitting thinking about food all day.

That and being attacked by grown-ups.

They hadn't seen any of them so far. Maybe they'd all gone, marched off with the tall woman and her army. Ella wondered where they'd been going.

"You're right," said Malik. "I'm not a ghoul. Which is why I need to go and live with people again. I'll have to do it sooner or later. If I don't go to them, they'll come to me. So are you all right with it, Ella? Can we stop arguing?"

"I suppose so."

"Good girl. You'll see. It's the right thing to do."

29

Next morning they packed up what they could carry, stowed the rest in the hole, and set off for Bracknell. As they walked through the woods, Ella asked Malik how long he thought it would take them.

"Shouldn't be more than a couple of hours, maybe three, as I can't go too fast and we might need to stop now and then, but we'll be there by lunchtime. It's the start of a new life, Ella."

"If you say so." There she was, doing it again—Grumpy Glumdrops. Couldn't snap out of it even though she knew this was the right thing to do.

It was a gray day to suit Ella's gray mood, and there was a thin, cutting wind that made her shiver. As they came out of the woods, the countryside looked flat. The wind was somehow hardly stirring the trees and bushes. They trudged on into a field overgrown with tall grass and weeds. She'd gotten to know the land around here quite well. Not so long ago she'd thought she might live here forever.

Already she'd forgotten what it was like at the museum.

Holloway was a stronger memory, though not a good one. That was where Sam had been taken by the greasy mother in the pink tracksuit. Ella wished she could remember happier things about Sam, and not that awful day. She could remember the mother better than him. His face was blurry. Like in a dream where things shifted and disappeared when you tried to touch them.

Don't think about the past and don't think about the future, that's what Malik told her, and that's how she was going to try to live.

She kept close to him, always scared when they were out in the open, even if it was daytime and the grown-ups would mostly be in their own holes. There were always the dogs, though, and other kids. She'd picked up on Malik's fear of them, even though she knew it was stupid. She was obviously one of them. A child herself. They'd never mistake *her* for a grown-up. Not like Malik. Something had made his body grow and bulge and get bigger like a man's. She was proud to be walking with him. He was strong and clever. He had all his tricks and traps and ways of beating the enemy.

"Malik?" she asked.

"What?"

The grass was up to Ella's chest and she tucked in behind him, walking in the path he'd trampled.

"That explosion, back at the farm, when the grown-ups came through and you burned up all the ones who were attacking the barn."

"What of it?"

"Was that gas?"

"Yeah." Malik nodded. "It was from the tank that the

lads left behind. I rigged up some pipes and valves and stuff so that I could empty it into a trench that ran around the barn. It was for emergencies. A ring of fire. I'd hoped I'd never need to use it. Last-resort sort of a thing."

"I wish they hadn't attacked us. I wish we were still living there with the chickens."

"We can't change the past, Ella, so no point going over it."

"Yeah, yeah, I know," she said. *"Don't think about the past and don't think about the future."*

"One foot in front of the other. Deal with problems as they come up."

"Burn the grown-ups with gas."

"Yeah." Malik laughed. "Burn the grown-ups with gas."

They reached a road and Malik stuck to it for a while. Every now and then he would stop and listen and sniff the air, and once he told Ella to hurry and darted off to the side to hide in the long grass. All Ella could see from their little flattened patch was grass and gray sky. They stayed there and lay low for what felt like ages, and in the end nothing happened.

They set off again, and a few minutes later Malik went through the same routine. He wasn't happy being on the open road and he was walking slower the farther they went. His injured leg was obviously giving him trouble. He was limping badly. Ella could see that he was in pain and trying not to show it. So that he didn't feel too bad, she started to say that she was tired and asked for frequent rest stops. Malik would gratefully sit down for a while and rub his leg.

And so they plodded on—stop-start, stop-start—Ella anxious to get there, but also anxious not to get there. Not sure what they were going to find. If they'd be welcome, or if the kids would treat Malik like all the others had done. Well, not if she could help it. She'd protect him. She'd fight anyone who was mean to him.

They'd been going for some time when Malik suggested they stop and drink some water. Ella wasn't particularly thirsty, but she realized that Malik needed another excuse to rest, so she didn't say anything. They moved off the road into some nearby trees and flopped down, Malik sitting back against a knobbly silver-gray trunk. He got his bottle out and took a small sip before passing it to Ella. She drank and offered it back to him, but he ignored her. He was staring straight ahead, but not seeing, just concentrating on listening. Listening and sniffing. She could see his nostrils twitching, going wide, then narrow. His mangled, battered face started to work itself into a frown. Then he hopped up on to his feet and squatted there, head tilted to one side.

"What is it?" Ella asked, and he shushed her. He was listening hard now, his head moving around like radar, trying to figure out which direction the sound was coming from. And then he suddenly grabbed her forearm and gripped it painfully tight.

"Run!"

He dragged her to her feet and pulled her along. Ella was fighting for breath, more frightened because she had no idea what it was they were running from. They pelted through the trees, Malik sort of skipping to keep the weight off his bad leg. Small branches whipped at Ella and scratched her face.

"What is it?" she gasped. "What's happening?"

"I'm not sure," Malik grunted, and Ella risked looking back. She could see figures among the trees, moving fast.

"It's people," she said, trying to keep the panic out of her voice. Now Malik looked back and swore.

"It's grown-ups, isn't it?" she said.

"Yes," said Malik. "And something else. Something I don't understand."

Ella screamed as a father came crashing out of some bushes next to her and she cringed, waiting for him to attack her, but he ran past. He wasn't interested in her. She realized now that the grown-ups weren't running toward *her*, they were running *away* from something. Two more of them went past. Now Ella was really scared. Malik was hobbling and hopping and they were getting into a tangle of trees growing closely together, slowing them down. Another grown-up barged past, and, distracted, Ella tripped and fell, pulling Malik down with her. She put her arms around her head to protect herself and looked up. There was no way forward and the grown-ups were having to get out of the woods into the open. She wasn't used to seeing grown-ups during the day, and she wasn't used to seeing them run like this.

"I don't like it," she said. "What's going on? What's going on?"

They heard weird yelps and a noise like thunder coming through the woods. A squealing sound. The howls of animals.

"Dogs," said Malik.

"Are they that scared of dogs?"

"And something else."

"You said. What is it? *What* something else?"

"I don't know. And I don't want to stay and find out."

A mother came stumbling and careering along, fell face-first next to them, and hit the ground with a screech. When she pushed herself up on her arms, her face was a mess of dirt and pus and blood, teeth missing, nose flattened. Malik kicked her out of the way and dragged Ella to her feet.

There was only one way to go. They had to run with the pack and follow the grown-ups out into the open. Malik set off as fast as he could go, Ella leaping over roots and stones to keep up with him. And they were out of the woods, into another field, long grass holding them back. Tracks through it where the mothers and fathers had gone. And Ella saw that there were more grown-ups coming out of the trees on the far side of the field, joining the others in a swirling, confused mass in the center, too spooked to go any farther, and Malik and Ella were sucked in among them. And the noise of thunder grew and the squeals and howls, and Ella put her hands to her ears and screamed.

Then a line of horses broke from behind a long hedge, came galloping toward them.

They were being ridden by children. Armed with spears and clubs and carrying nets. They were shouting and blowing horns, dogs running at their side.

Ella raised a hand and tried to shout to them, her voice lost in the chaos of noise and bumbling bodies. She raised both hands, called out, and was knocked to the ground by a fat mother. The breath went out of her and she felt light-headed and dizzy. As she tried to stand, another mother fell on her. It felt like she was at the center of a shoal of fish being attacked by sharks. The grown-ups were being herded into a tighter and tighter ball. And more and more bodies were trampling on Ella, falling on her, crushing her. She couldn't breathe—she couldn't speak—she couldn't see Malik.

Where was he?

What had happened to him?

There were bright flashes in her eyes, right inside her brain. Her vision was flickering and blurry. The stink of the grown-ups, the hot, close heat of them, was like a foul gas in her nose and mouth. She was losing touch with reality. Thought she saw two fathers scooped up in a net.

Two golden twins on horses.

Malik rising up . . . a sword swinging down.

Malik falling.

Her fault. It was all her fault.

And she was dying here.

Someone had to help her.

She opened her mouth wide and it was like she'd opened a door and her soul was sucked out of her.

She felt a terrible emptiness.

And slipped away.

19 DAYS EARLIER

30

"Don't put that in there, Macca, you moron. Stick it on the roof. It won't fit inside."

Ed was in a foul mood. He was getting ready to set off in search of Ella, and he still didn't know who was coming with him from the museum. If anyone. He had his mates from the Tower: Kyle and Macca and Will. They'd come this far together and weren't going to split up now. So it wasn't going to be some mad solo expedition. And they weren't going to be on foot this time.

They had a car. A people carrier. A lovely big fat blue Chrysler Voyager, large enough to seat seven comfortably, eight or nine if they were willing to squash up.

Getting a car had been the idea of one of the museum kids. Boy named Boggle. Apparently nobody could pronounce his name or spell it properly, and they reckoned it looked like a jumbled-up bunch of random letters, like in the word game Boggle.

Ed used to play it with his family. A long time ago. But Boggle himself had never seen it, let alone played it. Ed had asked Boggle if it bothered him, but Boggle told him he'd been called a lot worse.

He also told Ed that Ella and her friends had left in a car. Which was news to Ed. Boggle had made him swear not to tell anyone else.

"We found it months ago," Boggle explained. "Me and my best mate, Robbie. A big Range Rover. We'd been looking after it. He named it Raymonda. No one else knew about it, you see. Still don't. Robbie was worried that Justin would take it for himself if he found out."

At first Ed had been deflated. That meant Robbie and Maeve and Ella and Monkey-Boy could be miles away by now. They could be halfway to Wales. But then Boggle explained that there hadn't been that much gas in it. Only enough to get out of town, about twenty-five miles. Their plan had been to take the car as far as it would go, straight west on the highway, and then look for some other kids.

"So if you get yourself a car," said Boggle, "with enough gas, you can go twenty miles, maybe thirty. You can look on the dial to see how far that is, or, you know, like, get a map and draw a circle or whatever, and search around there."

Of course Boggle didn't have another car himself. That would have been too easy.

"So where do I get myself another set of wheels?" Ed asked.

"Ryan's hunters. They find things. They'll maybe barter with you. If you got something to barter with."

It all came back to Ed, getting rescued by Ryan Aherne and his gang near the Houses of Parliament the other day. Ed remembered thinking that he was glad that Ryan's hunters were on his side. They were an ugly bunch, street-hard, heavily armed, and with a pack of mean fighting dogs. Some of them wore masks—ski masks, leather gimp masks—and Ryan wore one made from a human face he'd carved off a dead sicko.

The hunters worked the local streets and traded between the various camps. Ed had to wait a couple of days for them to come by, and Ryan seemed pleased to see him again.

"Thought you was gonna die in the badlands, dude."

Ed explained what he needed—a reliable car with at least twenty miles of gas in the tank, preferably twice that, so he could get there and back.

"If I *could* get you a motor," said Ryan, "what can you offer me for it?"

"*Can* you get me one?"

"I can get anything," said Ryan. "But there's a price, soldier. I mean, what you got? Apart from that face that got stomped on?"

One step forward. Two steps back. Ed knew he couldn't rely on Justin to give him anything. And then he had an idea.

"How about alcohol?" he said. "What if I got you as much booze as you can carry?"

"Then, my friend, we have a deal."

And so it was that this morning Ryan had arrived with the Chrysler. The weather was fine and the hunters were still there, lounging around on the steps that led up to the front of the museum, sampling some of the liquor that Ed had gotten for them. They were all dressed in leathers and furs and looked like a heavy metal band posing for their latest album cover.

Ed was loading supplies into the trunk when Ryan came over.

"You heading out already?" he said, raising a can of beer in a salute.

Ed was glad that Ryan had taken his mask off—it gave him the creeps—although Ryan's real face wasn't exactly a pretty sight. It was covered in acne and battered from a thousand fights.

"I have to find someone," Ed explained.

"No rest, eh, dude?" said Ryan with a lopsided grin. "Not for us soldiers. *No Sleep 'til Hammersmith.*"

"Hammersmith?"

"Is an album. Motörhead. No, brother, you and me, we don't get to sit down and sip cups of tea, do our knitting. We're workers. We're soldiers. We're hunters. No rest for the wicked, yeah? We never sleep. Not till we're in our graves."

"You die if you want, Ryan." Ed smiled at him, knowing his own face would be pulled into a Halloween mask. "I intend to live till I'm a hundred."

"Good luck with that, my man. You want a drink?"

"Nope."

"Is good stuff. So tell me, where'd you get it all? Who's your supply?"

"That's confidential."

"Thought it might be."

"Where you want these, boss?" Kyle had come over, carrying a box of fifty crossbow bolts.

"Sling them on the roof." The bolts were part of the deal. Ryan had gotten them for Ed, and Ed was going to use them to pay for the booze. That's how the world worked now. Barter.

The liquor had come from a boy called Dylan, although no one but Ed knew his real name—to everyone else he was Shadowman. Ed had saved Shadowman at Piccadilly Circus a few nights ago, and Shadowman owed him. He had a hideout in an abandoned drinking club not far away. And there was more alcohol stashed away in its cellars than he could ever drink.

So they'd done a deal. Ed had taken a load of beer and vodka and cider and promised to come back with crossbow bolts. They'd have to drop them off for Shadowman on the way.

It had only taken Ryan a few days to find a car. Ed had gotten more and more frustrated waiting around for him, but knew that when it did arrive the car would save them a lot of time and hassle. Now that it was here he just wanted to be off and get this whole thing over and done with. Everyone was telling him it was crazy, stupid, pointless, dangerous. . . .

Everyone except Sam.

Ryan had parked the car outside the museum gates and Ed, Kyle, Macca, and Will had spent the last hour or so getting it ready. Packing supplies into the back and strapping their weapons and any larger items to the roof rack. They'd put in as much food as Justin would allow them, plus spare clothes, water, sleeping bags, and a decent first-aid kit. They were just about ready to leave now. Ed was delaying setting off, though. Hoping against hope that someone else would volunteer to come with them.

He looked up toward the main doors of the museum. A small crowd of curious museum kids had gathered there to watch. Ed couldn't really blame them for not helping. This didn't have anything to do with them, and anyway he'd heard that Justin had told them all not to go. He needed his fighters here.

But the Holloway kids: Ella was one of them. *Sam* was one of them. Hell, none of Ed's crew even knew what Ella looked like.

He was just about to turn away when he saw movement. A small delegation was coming down to speak to him.

Was it going to be good news or bad news?

A step forward or a step back?

31

Ed recognized the red-haired boy, Ollie, but the other three he hadn't gotten to know yet. There was a round-faced black kid; a sleepy-looking guy with an Afro, who was wearing what looked like bits of samurai armor and carrying a katana; and a younger, pale-faced girl, who had a haunted look about her. When they arrived, she stared at Ed with scared, black-rimmed eyes, her lips pressed tight together. He noticed she was carrying a big leather-bound book under her arm and was keeping close to Ollie, who put a protective arm across her shoulders.

"What's up?" Ed asked, trying not to sound aggressive. "You come to wave me off or join up?"

"I would come with you," said Ollie, "but I've promised to look after Lettis."

He gave the pale-faced girl a squeeze. Ed realized who she was now. He'd heard about how she'd been left abandoned in a church and all her friends had been killed. Ollie had saved her and now it looked like she wouldn't leave his side.

"No way she's ever going back out there," said Ollie. "Not after what she's been through. But Ebenezer here, he's good. He wants to come."

"I don't like it here," said Ebenezer, the round-faced kid. He had a strong African accent. "Too many dead things in glass boxes. And those Twisted Kids. I don't like them being here. They are not right. They are not in God's image. They are not right."

Ed had to admit that the kids Blue had brought back with him from the last expedition out of London made him a little uncomfortable as well.

"The disease did something to them in the womb," said Ollie. "It's not their fault."

"They are mutations," said Ebenezer.

"They're kids," said Ollie.

"You were on Blue's expedition, Ebenezer?" Ed wanted to change the subject.

"Yes. I will go again. It does not scare me. I have seen what is on the road."

"Ebenezer's good with a javelin," said Ollie. "And he knows Ella well from Holloway days."

Ed looked to the last member of the group, who seemed to be half asleep.

"What about you?" he asked and the boy lazily opened his eyes just enough to give Ed a once-over.

"Lewis," he said and scratched his bushy Afro. "I'm in, dude. I got to know that little girl on the way over here. She's brave as they come. I liked her. I'll do it for her and the boy. Small Sam. He done well an' all. Staying alive. Is all cool. I'll come."

Ed smiled and they bumped fists. Lewis might be sleepy-looking, but several people had told Ed what a good fighter he was.

"So that's six of us, then." Ed counted on his fingers. "Including my group. Not exactly an army, but the car only seats seven anyway. You ready to leave now?"

Ebenezer nodded and Lewis shrugged.

"I'd really hoped we could persuade Achilleus. He seems like a pain in the ass, but he'd be really useful from all I hear."

"Akkie definitely won't go with you," said Ollie.

"You know that?"

"Yeah."

"I thought nothing fazed him."

"Nothing does," said Ollie, and he took Ed to one side.

"Akkie, he's like me and Lettis," he said when they were out of earshot of the others.

"Yeah?"

"Yeah." Ollie nodded. "You see that little Irish kid he always has with him?"

"Yeah. Bit of hero worship there."

"Kid's called Paddy. We picked him up on the road. He'd been living with some nutjobs in a crappy camp in Green Park. A right wild bunch. Paddy jumped ship and came with us. He's a tough little bastard, but like a lot of kids, he's not as tough as he'd like everyone to think."

"What do you mean?" Ed asked.

"I think he was having a hard time of it before. Not coping well. He ran away, basically, from the kids he was living with. Achilleus is like a dad to him now. Looks after him. They went out and got caught up in the madness near Heathrow, and since they got back Paddy's been having real bad nightmares. No one says anything, but we've all seen it. All heard it. Paddy wakes up screaming and Akkie has to calm him down. Akkie tries to pretend he ain't got no heart. But underneath . . . he's just protecting Paddy. Making it look like it's his decision not to go. He knows Paddy wouldn't hold up out there, and he wouldn't leave him behind. Like me and Lettis here, and you and Sam, I guess."

"Okay." Ed rubbed his scar. "Listen, Ollie," he said. "You seem switched on. Can you keep an eye on Sam while I'm gone? I don't want him doing anything stupid. He ran off once before."

"No problem," said Ollie. "I'm on it. God knows how the little shrimp did it, though. Got across London like that."

"And the rest." Ed laughed. "That boy is something else, I tell you. You know, there's even a group of kids living over in St. Paul's Cathedral who think he's some kind of a god."

Ollie laughed. "I wouldn't go that far."

"I'll tell you about it one day." Ed looked around as Kyle leaned on the car horn and yelled out of the window.

"Get a move on!"

As they walked down to the car, Lewis had a word with Ed.

"He driving, is he?"

"It's between him and Macca. They both reckon they know how. Why? You drive?"

"Some."

Ed mentioned this to the others, and the three of them, Lewis, Kyle, and Macca, argued about who was going to be in the driver's seat. In the end they all three had a turn, driving up and down the stretch of the Cromwell Road that ran along the front of the museum. Kyle showed off, tried to go too fast, and didn't look like he was in control at all. Macca went the other way and looked too cautious, nervous even. Macca was quite small, with a screwed-up face and untidy hair. He was a great shot, and had perfect eyesight, but he sometimes reckoned he knew more about the world than he actually did, and he had a habit of biting off more than he could chew.

Driving was evidently not one of his skills.

Lewis was the best and Ed gave him the job. Kyle moaned until Ed told him to shut up, and that was that. Lewis was the designated driver.

At last they were ready to go.

32

Ed sat in the front passenger seat, studying a big road map while Lewis adjusted his seat and checked all the controls. The route was simple—follow the road west until they joined the M4, and then just keep going until the odometer had added twenty miles.

"All set?" he asked Lewis without looking up.

"Hold up, boss," said Kyle from the back, and Ed saw Brooke coming down the long ramp from the museum entrance. She'd changed out of the weird old-fashioned dress she'd been wearing since Ed had arrived, and was wearing jeans and sneakers with some kind of rugged, zip-up jacket. She had a small pack slung over one shoulder and was carrying a sword in a scabbard in her free hand. She still had a bandage across her forehead, probably as much to hide her scar as to protect it. And she had a knit cap jammed over it, half covering the white of the bandage. She looked almost boyish. About as different from the girl he'd first met last year as you could get. Back then she'd been a fashion victim, overdressed, overly made-up, mouthy, and cruel. In a funny way Ed almost missed the old Brooke. At least he'd known where he stood with her.

"You going somewhere?" he asked when she got to the car and leaned in his window.

"I'm coming with you," she replied.

"You're what?"

"You heard me." Brooke had a very determined look about her. She wasn't going to be told no. "I owe you, Ed. If it wasn't for me, DogNut wouldn't of got himself killed."

"You don't owe me. You don't have to come."

"You scared I can't look after myself?"

"I didn't want to say it, but . . ."

Brooke stepped back, yanked the sword from its scabbard, and swiped it through the air.

"Since we were attacked near Green Park I've been practicing," she said. "Jackson's been showing me how to fight. Lewis even gave a few tips."

Ed looked to Lewis, who shrugged.

"She all right," he said. "She won't hold us back none."

"Besides," said Brooke, putting the sword away and giving the lads in the back of the car a once-over, "I think you could do with having a girl along. This is in danger of looking like a gay day trip. I mean, I don't want to spoil your bromance at all, but really . . ."

"I'm not gay," said Ebenezer seriously. He looked put out.

"I was joking," said Brooke, and she laughed, which only made Ebenezer more angry.

"That is not funny," he said. "Not something to joke about."

"Ooh, hit a nerve there," said Brooke.

"It's all right, Ebenezer." Ed shot Brooke a dirty look. This was more like how she used to be, stirring it up.

"We can fit you in," he said, and Brooke leaned in again.

"It's not just me," she said quietly.

Ed looked back up toward the museum entrance. "There're others who want to come?" he asked, though there was no sign of anyone else. "We can't fit too many more in the car. Who is it?"

"I thought you wanted more."

Ed sighed. "That was before I got the car. Who is it, anyway?"

"Come on." Brooke turned and walked back up the way she'd come. "Follow me."

33

Ed followed Brooke up to the birds gallery in the green zone. This was the room that Ed had prepared for Wormwood to live in, but lately the Twisted Kids had moved in with him. And they were all there when Ed arrived, sitting patiently on plastic chairs. It felt weird being in here with them all together. The stuffed birds didn't help. Ed had always found birds a little freaky, and they had some real crazy ones in the gallery—dodos, vultures with naked faces, an ostrich watching him from behind the glass with giant staring eyes, a whole bush in a cabinet, its branches filled with hummingbirds. And there, sitting in a semicircle surrounded by all this, was the strangest collection of humans Ed had ever seen. They really should be in their own museum somewhere.

At the back was Wormwood, the Green Man himself, still wrapped in the blanket he'd arrived in and wearing the green bowler hat he'd picked up at Shadowman's hideout. Otherwise he was naked. Ed wondered if it was a trick of the light, but the fuzz of green mold that covered him looked like it might be clearing up a little. Ed still didn't trust him, though. He had a way of staring hungrily at you with his pale eyes, and clicking his long, horny fingernails together.

Next to him was his daughter, Fish-Face, with her flattened head, the eyes squeezed around to the sides. She was crushingly shy and hardly ever spoke. She sat there with her neck bent and her face turned to the floor. She wasn't scary, but she still freaked Ed out, because she appeared to have the ability to read your thoughts. That made him twitchy and uncomfortable, as if he could actually feel her inside his head.

Then there was Skinner. Skinner didn't spend much time with the other Twisted Kids. He'd made friends with Achilleus and Paddy. He was the most friendly of the Twisted Kids. He just wanted to get along with everyone and join in. He was always asking questions and trying to help, though his folds of loose skin made him clumsy.

Finally there was Trinity, who looked like a girl and a boy fused together. They had a third smaller body on their back that they mostly kept hidden. The girl, Trio, and the boy, Trey, were always arguing with each other and could be quite mouthy, especially the girl. Ed had initially thought the third body on their back was dead, but they assured him he wasn't. He was called Mr. Three, and he woke up every now and then in a bad mood apparently. Ed didn't want to be around when that happened.

And what did he look like to them? he wondered. A freak, perhaps, with his scarred face pulled out of shape on one side. Brooke didn't look much better. One day she was going to have to take her bandage off and show the world what had happened to her.

"Is this going to take long?" Ed leaned against a cabinet with his arms folded, making sure they knew how impatient he was.

"Not at all," said Trey.

"You hope," said his "sister," Trio.

"So?" Ed just wanted to be out of there. On his way.

"When we left Heathrow . . ." said Trio, "the Warehouse Queen gave us some orders, which was, like, *typical*. We were to learn as much as we could about, you know, what you might call the *outside world*. And what I'm saying, and I don't mean to be rude, yeah? This is, like, all very impressive and that, but it's just, really, you know, like, a *museum*. It's hardly the big wide world. So we think one of us ought to come with you."

Ed sighed. Looked at his shoes. They were wearing out. He'd need to find some new ones soon.

"With all respect," he said, "we need fighters. I can't take passengers."

"We have skills," said Skinner.

"Yeah? Like what?" Ed didn't want to sound harsh, but he was worried they'd hold things up and he'd have to nanny them all of the way.

"Well, not me personally . . . obviously," said Skinner, sounding defeated. "I'm pretty useless. I can't really do that much." He gave a little laugh. "But the others."

"I'm waiting."

"We know what's going on," said Trey.

"You mean your mind-reading thing?" Ed looked at Trey and Trio, wondering if they knew what he was thinking right now. "The way you can get inside our minds?"

"Not yours," said Trey. "We can't read minds as such, ordinary minds."

"I thought you could." Maybe Ed had gotten it wrong. "How does it work, then?"

"Sickos," said Skinner. "That's what you call them, yeah?"

"Yeah."

Ed found it slightly disconcerting that Skinner had a cat stuffed inside his sweater, its head sticking out of the neck opening, staring at Ed. When Ed had first met Skinner, he'd thought for moment that the cat was part of him, some kind of growth—anything was possible with these kids—and he'd been relieved to discover that it was just a harmless kitty. It still freaked him out, though.

"Some of us can sort of hear them," said Skinner. "The sickos. Well, we all can, a little. It's hard to explain, but we can all sort of . . . It's like we share thoughts with them. I'm not so good at it. Fish-Face is brilliant. She's like a radio set. She can tune herself right into what's going on out there."

Ed turned to Fish-Face. "How do you do it?" he asked. "What happens?"

Fish-Face looked embarrassed and turned away, blushing. She wasn't going to say anything.

"Fish-Face could always do it," said Trio. "Her and the Queen. And Pencil Neck. He was the worst. He even knew what the rest of us were thinking, and we were like— 'Hello? Get out of my head, thank you very much.' And Mr. Three . . ."

Trinity turned around, showing the small and shriveled-looking third body that was curled up on their back, poking out of a hole in their sweater, like Skinner's cat.

"He can virtually talk to them," said Trio. "Like he was calling them on a mobile phone. 'Oh, hello, you sick bastard, how are you doing?' But he's hardly ever awake and it tires him out."

"Lately, though," said Trey, "we've all been starting to pick up the grown-ups a bit. Not exactly their thoughts. I mean, they don't exactly think, do they? But it's more like, I don't know, a radio, and if there's lots of them the signal's louder. . . ."

"It's like we *know*," said Skinner. "We just *know*. We're connected. Like we're all sharing one big brain."

"So to answer your question," said Trey, "we're not sure how it works, but we reckoned it'd be really useful for you to have one of us along."

"Maybe." Ed wasn't entirely convinced.

"Doesn't every military unit need a radio operator?" said Skinner.

"It's not really a radio, though, is it?" Ed protested. "You can't completely communicate."

"You got anything better?"

"I've got fighters. With weapons. I understand that. There's no voodoo in it."

"Listen to them," said Wormwood, his voice surprisingly normal, coming from such a messed-up-looking guy. "*Out of the mouths of babes*. They're speaking the truth. They know more than you ever will, and they can help you more than sticks and knives. They can protect you from my kind."

"If I was going to take one of you along," said Ed, scanning the row of kids, "and I'm not saying I am, which of you would it be?"

"I'm no good," said Skinner. "And Fish-Face is too shy."

"That leaves . . ." Ed looked at Trinity.

"Us, I'm afraid." Both of them nodded, grinning. "Reckon you can squeeze us in?"

"I was thinking I could maybe take one more." Ed was already picturing how cramped it was going to be in the car. "No offense, but you're more like two, if not three. And Ebenezer ain't gonna like it."

"We'll charm him."

"You're gonna have to. Guy's a bit of a fundamentalist. Thinks you lot are an abomination in the eyes of the Lord. This is going to be one interesting trip."

"Well now, you wouldn't want life to get boring, would you?" said Trey.

"As a matter of fact," said Ed, "I *would*. I'd like nothing more. A boring, boring life in which nothing happened. But you know what? I've had to accept that that is not gonna happen. So let's get this show on the road."

34

Y ou're too bony, girl, you're digging into my ribs like a bag of knives. It's like sitting next to a skeleton."

"Yeah, well, at least I don't stink like a sicko. Jeez, you got no soap at the Tower? Or do you just bathe in pig scat?"

"Oh, you'd know about that, wouldn't you? I heard you used to go out with a pig."

"Oh, that is so funny, I almost laughed."

"Shut it, you two," Ed shouted from the front seat.

It had been like this all the way from the museum. Brooke and Macca getting on each other like a couple of little kids bickering. Ed like a fed-up dad, getting angrier and angrier. He was beginning to wish he'd left Macca behind. It had almost happened. He'd gone from having not enough people to having too many. Macca had offered to give up his seat, but Will had persuaded him not to and volunteered to stay behind himself. He'd pointed out that Macca was better in a fight than him. Will said he'd be more use at the museum working with Einstein.

Ed had reluctantly agreed with him. He relied on Will, who was sensible and bright, but if it came to a fight, Macca was definitely the stronger of the two. Ed just wished he wasn't such a pain in the ass sometimes.

"You tell him to behave himself," said Brooke. "He's being a prick."

"Takes one to know one," said Macca.

There were three of them squashed in the backseat. Macca, Brooke, and Ebenezer. Ebenezer was trying to keep out of it, but he would occasionally snap and weigh in with some unhelpful remark. None of it was clever, and most of it didn't really make any sense. It was incredibly tiring, though, having to listen to it.

Brooke *was* quite thin, to tell the truth. They'd all lost a lot of weight since the disease struck. There was never enough food. But she was lean and muscular rather than anorexic. And it had to be said that Macca was a bit of a mess, and hygiene had never been his strong point. He was almost proud of it. He had several layers of clothing on, and Ed had never known him to change them. In the cramped confines of the car he was giving off a warm, ripe aroma. He never cut his hair either, kept it tied back in a loose ponytail, with bits sticking out all over the place, and that was causing Brooke problems. She kept leaning away and trying to keep it off her.

"I thought the biggest problem on this trip was going to be sickos," she said. "Not Mr. Stink here."

"What's your plan, then?" said Macca. "You gonna bore them sickos to death, or scare them to death with your supernatural ugliness?"

"I am so far out of your league you can't even *see* me, you dirty tramp," said Brooke.

"Who said that?" Macca laughed and shook his hair at her.

"Get your DNA out of my face," Brooke shrieked and shoved him away.

Ed couldn't be bothered to tell them to shut up again. He had a bad headache and it was making his scar throb and itch horribly. Too many mixed-up memories were coming back to him, of trips in the Rowhurst School minibus to play cricket or football at another school. Trips to Sevenoaks and Tonbridge and Rochester. The other boys on the bus making too much noise, farting as if it were an Olympic skill, teasing each other, telling filthy jokes, telling filthy lies, boasting about things they'd never done with girls. And another bus trip—a year ago. When Greg the butcher had picked up Ed and his friends after they'd escaped from Rowhurst. Brooke had already been on it, with her two friends, Courtney and Aleisha. The three of them sitting at the back, teasing the boys, winding him up. Seemed like a million years ago. How many of them on that bus had died? Jack and Bam and Piers; Courtney, Aleisha; Greg's son, Liam; the French girl with the cat, Frédérique . . .

Ghosts.

All those friends of his from school he'd never see again. Some hadn't even gotten as far as the bus. He'd lost one of his best friends, Malik, walking out of town. Bang. Just like that. One moment they'd been talking, and the next . . .

Gone.

He sighed. Brooke had changed a lot since then. Grown

up. Chilled out. Something had come over her since she'd joined this expedition, though. She was in the back row of the bus again, being mouthy. He couldn't blame her. Macca was an asshole at the best of times. It was crazy, though, crazy and stupid. Here they were, driving off into God knows what—probably a world of pain and terror if the past was anything to go by—and the two of them were behaving like a couple of ten-year-olds. Getting on each other's nerves. Oblivious to what was outside the car.

Maybe that's why they did it. So as not to think about where they were going. Also he knew Brooke was uncomfortable. Unsure of herself among these kids, half of whom she didn't really know. She'd always held to the philosophy that attack was the best form of defense.

And Macca? He was one of those boys who was unsure of himself around girls, and the only way he knew to flirt with them was to be rude.

Ed smiled to himself. God help Macca if he secretly had a thing for Brooke.

Lewis was driving at a calm, steady speed, showing nothing, eyes on the road, half closed, but not missing a thing. Cool. Not even listening to the chaos in the back. Behind them were the middle seats, like two big armchairs. Kyle and Trinity had these, as they were the biggest. Kyle wasn't helping. Every now and then he'd lob a comment back like a grenade and enjoy the reaction. Brooke and Macca yelling. Ebenezer getting angry and righteous.

For the fiftieth time Ed looked at his big road map, trying to shut out the noise, pretending to read it, but not able to concentrate. He hardly needed it anymore. They'd eventually made it onto the highway after a few detours. There was one tricky bit that Ebenezer had warned them about where the whole elevated section that carried the road had collapsed. So they'd had to avoid that. But Lewis had kept his cool and Ed had consulted his maps, and between them they'd managed to get on to the M4 farther along, and now it was easy going. Ed was keeping an eye on the odometer; as soon as it showed that they'd gone twenty miles, they were going to leave the highway. That was when it was going to get interesting. That was when they had to seriously start looking for Ella and Maeve and the others.

The reality of it was only now just hitting him. The realization of just what a huge area they had to cover. Having the car was a bonus, but still, when it came down to it, this was a fairly hopeless mission. Living in London, hemmed in by buildings on all sides, you lost the sense of how big the world was. How much there was of it. Driving out of London along the M4, Ed had watched the world unfold and open out. First houses and office buildings and factories had whizzed past, then they'd started to see trees and greenery, grass and bushes, the beginnings of the countryside, and then wide-open spaces.

And all along the way they'd seen sickos—sentinels—standing in the road, eyes closed, arms raised, faces turned up to the sky, skin burned and blistered.

"Why they doing that?" Lewis asked as he drove around one standing in the middle of the highway.

"They're carrying the signal," said Trey. "Like telephone poles."

"What signal?" said Lewis. "What they saying?"

"It's not words," said Trey. "It's more like a hum, a buzz, a homing signal."

"Who's it for?"

"They're gathering, I reckon," said Trio.

"I don't like them," said Ebenezer. "I hate them."

"We should run them down," said Kyle.

"Yeah," Macca joined in. "We should go GTA on them."

"We've got to keep moving," Ed protested. "Not waste time. If we stop to deal with every stray sicko we see, we'll never get anywhere."

Indeed, there seemed to be sentinels every few hundred yards, even out here on the highway—mothers, fathers, teenagers. . . . Ed calculated that if they were like this on all the roads leading out of London, there must be thousands of them. And how many more were they calling in?

He remembered the conversation he'd had with Shadowman when he'd gone to get the alcohol from him.

"You really gonna head out west and look for this girl?" he'd said, incredulous.

"I owe it to Sam."

"If it was me, I'd either tell him to shut it, or I'd lie to him," said Shadowman. "Pretend I'd looked. Give it a day or two, then go back and get on with your lives."

"Well, you're *not* me," said Ed.

"No," said Shadowman. "I'm not. You're like a dad, Ed. You think you need to look after everyone and keep them safe. But you can't look after everyone. You'll end up going crazy. And, besides, we need you here."

Shadowman had told him all about the sickos' general

he called Saint George, who seemed to be gathering all the grown-ups in London.

"They're massing, Ed," he'd said. "Something big is going down. Sooner or later they're gonna make their way into the center of town. And then it gets serious. We need to be ready for them. I can't do it alone. The kids in London, they're all in their own camps, their own little worlds, and they fight and argue and compete with each other. I've seen what they're like. We need to unite, we need to join together and deal with this, or it's going to be beyond bad."

Shadowman knew more about sickos than anyone else around. He'd made a study of them. "You've seen it yourself, Ed," he'd said when Ed had questioned him about whether he really thought they could get organized. "The change in them. The way they're wandering in from all over the place, as if something was calling them. And it's Saint George who's doing the calling."

"So what are they waiting for? Why don't they attack?"

Shadowman didn't know the answer to that one. He wanted to find out, though. He wanted to be back out on the streets watching them. And as soon as his sprained ankle was better—a couple more days he reckoned—that was where he was going.

"Maybe they're just waiting for more to arrive," Shadowman had said as Ed was leaving. "The call's gone out. The London sickos have gathered. What if they've put out a shout? A big shout out to the rest of the country. What if there's more coming from all over? From out where you're going."

"You know what?" Ed had grinned at Shadowman, trying to appear more unconcerned than he was. "Don't worry about shit until it happens."

"But it *does* happen," said Shadowman. "Shit *always* happens."

The more sentinels he saw on the road, the more Ed thought Shadowman was right. Something big was going to happen. Something big and something bad. He hoped they'd find Ella soon and not waste days searching for her. His place was back at the Tower with his people. He needed to tell General Jordan Hordern everything he'd talked about with Shadowman. Everyone had to join up, work together.

So what was he doing here, miles out of London?

This was all because of Sam, that stubborn, extraordinary little boy.

"Lord preserve us," said Ebenezer, and Ed turned to see him crossing himself.

"What is it?" he asked. Ebenezer pointed to their left.

"It was in there," he said. "The church where the little ones died. It was horrible. We left them alone and they were slaughtered. That is a bad place. A place of death. I pray for them every night. I hope they have gone to a better place."

"You want me to stop?" Lewis asked, slowing down.

"No way," said Ebenezer. "Not here. There is nothing here anyway. We burned the church down. We set it on fire to destroy the bodies of the fallen."

"Suit yourself. We go on."

"We go on." Ed stared out of his window, trying to see through the trees, feeling ghoulishly curious.

"Three churches," said Trey.

"What's that?" Ed asked.

"Rule of three," said Trey. "There will be three churches. Everything comes in threes. Way of the world."

"Don't start on that," said Trio. "We don't want to hear your stupid theories about—"

"You said something before," Brooke butted in from the back of the car. "When Ed first arrived at the museum. I heard you. You said something about three scarred faces. I didn't understand at the time . . ."

"Yeah," said Trey. "I remember that. I remember thinking there's Brooke, and now there's Ed, and there'll be a third. Can't wait to see what *that* looks like."

Ed was about to protest, more for Brooke's sake than his own, that he hadn't chosen to look this way, that it wasn't remotely fun, that he wasn't part of a carnival freak show, when it struck him that if anyone in the car looked like a freak it was Trinity. He guessed that gave them the right to comment on how other people looked.

"Yeah," said Macca, and he giggled. "But I doubt you'll find anyone more messed-up-looking than Miss Brookie Zipface."

Brooke gasped.

The car fell quiet.

Macca realized he'd gone too far.

That was wrong. No two ways about it. Macca didn't have the right to say anything about Brooke's disfigurement. After a few moments' stunned silence, everyone started shouting Macca down until he made a sort of half-sarcastic apology, laughing as if to show he wasn't that bothered.

Nobody said anything for a while after that. They left

the church behind and passed Heathrow Airport, heading farther west, and now they came to a small cluster of sentinels standing in the last Heathrow turnoff. In a clump, still as statues.

"Hey, look, Brooke," said Macca. "Your family's come out to wish you luck."

Ed swore inwardly. Macca just wasn't going to give up.

"Macca?" said Brooke. "Can we call a truce, yeah? It's getting to me a bit. You've been quite hurtful as it goes. Please. Just lay off me, okay? I can't take any more of it."

"You surrender to my greater wit and general awesomeness then, yeah?" said Macca triumphantly. "I knew you were weak. A weak girl."

"Seriously, yeah?" said Brooke. "I'm quite scared, actually."

"I knew it."

"And the thing is, to tell you the truth, Macca, I quite like you really. I quite fancy you."

"I knew it!"

Ed had to suppress a snort of laughter. Poor old Macca. He was walking into a trap. He wasn't the brightest kid on the chopping block. Brooke was way out of his league. He was a dick, but did he deserve what was going to happen?

Probably.

They came to the junction with the M25, the big highway that ringed London. Ed glanced at the odometer—nineteen miles gone. He had some idea now just how far twenty miles was. He'd had it in his head that you could walk it in a day. But the thought of walking all this way from the museum was nuts. It would take forever.

Next turnoff, though, they'd leave the highway, start their search for some local settlements.

"That was the main reason I came along on this thing." Brooke was pressing on. "As soon as I saw you turn up with Ed the other day, I thought, well . . ."

Ed had to hand it to Brooke. She was a pretty good actress.

"It's been quite lonely at the museum. You've seen what the guys are like there."

"Nerds and gays," said Macca.

"Exactly."

"It's only . . ." Macca was walking blindly into it. "I thought you liked Ed. I thought you two had a thing going on."

"Ed? You're joking. God, no."

Ed tried to hide his smile. Hoping Macca couldn't see him. Was he the only person who didn't know what was going on?

"Cool," said Macca. "You know all that stuff I was coming out with? I was just mucking about. Playing with you. That's how I show I like someone."

"Really?"

"Truly. I mean, you're not ugly and that."

"Do you think I'm pretty?"

"Well, you know . . . You're not ugly."

"Guys," said Trio quietly. "I've got a funny feeling."

But everyone was too caught up in Brooke's game to pay her any attention.

"You're pretty buff yourself, Macca," she said, sounding horribly sincere.

Ed was wondering how long Brooke was going to keep this up before she dealt him the killer blow. She was obviously enjoying it too much to stop now. It was cruel, really. Macca had no defenses against this kind of thing. He needed to be taught a lesson, though; he'd gone too far with Brooke.

Ed kept his head down, pretending to study the map, enjoying the show. Waiting for the drop.

"Seriously," said Trio. "We need to stop the car."

"What's up?" Ed asked, looking back at her, and then he heard Lewis swear and felt the car slowing.

"What?" Ed faced front. Lewis didn't need to answer. The road ahead was thick with sickos. They filled it from left to right and were stumbling along toward them. Lewis brought the car to a stop.

"What you want me to do?" he asked, his voice quiet and sleepy, unconcerned, bored even. Like he'd just woken up.

"Ram them," said Kyle.

"Yeah," said Macca. "Let's splatter them morons."

"There are too many of them," said Ebenezer, leaning forward for a better look. "We will just get stuck."

"There's a lot of them," said Trio. She and Trey both had their eyes shut. "A whole lot of them. We should go back."

"Where they going, anyway?" Lewis asked. "Where's the party at?"

"They've got the call," said Trey. "All they want is to get into town and meet up with the others."

"Ram them," said Kyle. "We go fast enough, they can't stop us."

"No," said Trey.

"A body can do a lot of damage to a car if it's going fast," said Lewis. "I saw a kid get run over at the junction near our school this one time. He *bounced*, man. Went flying. Was in hospital for, like, a year or something. Don't know how he wasn't killed. But that car, *whoa*, you shoulda seen it. All dented up, crushed, like the geezer had run it into a wall. Nice car and all."

"Yeah," Ed agreed, twisting around in his seat. "We don't want to wreck the car. Without it our job would be a whole lot harder."

"All right. We go slow, then," said Kyle. "Plow through them, like an icebreaker." He mimed the action with the edge of one hand, slicing the air.

Ed looked at Trinity.

"How many of them, you think? Can we force a way through?"

"Too many," said Trio, pinching her lip nervously. "Can't give you exact numbers. We're only seeing the front of them."

"Give it a go at least," said Macca. "Even if we only take some of them out, it'll be a few less sickos in the world."

"It's not about taking sickos out." Ed was trying not to get wound up. "It's about doing what we've come to do and getting safely back to the museum."

"Stupid question," said Brooke, "but can we go around them?"

"Stupid question," said Kyle, and he laughed.

"Another stupid question," said Brooke, "but how did you get to be such a moron, Kyle?"

"We can't go around them," Ed butted in, trying to kill

the argument. Brooke had stopped Macca from being a pest with her lovey-dovey act, and now Kyle was in danger of starting up a whole fresh round of bickering.

"There's no way off the highway here," he went on. "And they're filling the whole road. However, there *is* a turnoff to Slough not too far ahead. We could try pushing through them."

"We should go the other way, Lewis. Really we should." Trio was sounding very anxious.

"Didn't we just pass a turnoff?" Ebenezer asked.

"That was for the M25," Ed explained, and he double-checked his map. "If we go that way we have to do a big loop up to the M40 and along before we can get back to where we want to be."

"Then I vote we ram them," said Kyle. "Ten points for each one you splatter, Lewis. This'll be just like one of them challenges off of *Top Gear*."

Ed wished Will was here. He'd know what to do. He always thought things through, worked out the consequences.

Will wasn't here, though, was he? Ed had to make the decision alone. He looked at Lewis.

"Might as well give it a try, I suppose."

"Hold on to your hats," Kyle shouted. "It's going to be a bumpy ride!"

35

Lewis nodded.

"Cool."

He'd gotten away with it so far. They hadn't called him out on his driving. He'd only driven a real car a couple of times before. He'd picked up most of his driving skills from his PlayStation. He loved driving games. Used to have a state-of-the-art steering wheel controller. Man, he missed that PlayStation.

The two times he'd driven a real car it had been totally illegal. He'd had a friend named Altan who'd been obsessed with cars, kept nicking them, and twice he'd let Lewis have a try. Only up the street and back. Altan had gotten himself killed riding a stolen scooter one night, and after that Lewis went off the idea.

He hoped the others hadn't noticed what a crappy driver he was. They hadn't said anything, too focused on other things. At least he hadn't crashed.

"Look at the bastards," said Kyle, leaning forward between the front seats.

"Sickos?" said Lewis. "Is what you call 'em, yeah?"

"That's what they are," said Kyle. "Not human no more, just bags of pus and bad blood."

"Sickos. Yeah . . . I get that."

It was a good name for them. Felt right.

And now Lewis had to steer into them.

Driving into a mob of people. That was something else. Wasn't sure if he could pull this off. He'd give it a try, though. Never let anyone know you had any doubts. That was the game. Stay cool.

He looked in the rearview mirror. Trey and Trio had their hands clamped over their ears and were rocking in their seats, muttering to themselves. They'd tried to warn him. Maybe Lewis should have listened to them.

Ed was giving him instructions, and he was only half listening.

"Not so fast that you lose control and damage the car . . . Not so slow that they can crowd in on us . . ."

Lewis's throat felt dry. He needed something to get him through this. And then he remembered the CDs he'd brought along. Had kept them all these months in his backpack, in case he ever got the opportunity to hear them again. He jabbed the power button on the radio. There was a hiss of static, then he dug a CD out of his pocket, snapped the case open, and slotted the disc into the little slit. After a quiet start, "Crank That" by Soulja Boy Tell 'Em started to blast out, and the car was magically filled with noise.

He heard Ed tut, but the other kids cheered.

Lewis was ready.

Stay cool.

"Let's go," he said, and pressed his foot down on the accelerator.

The mothers and fathers ahead had seen the car but hardly reacted to it. They knew where they were going, and nothing would tell them otherwise. They were staying cool too. Focused. Marching forward, following the call, whatever heavy bass throb was drawing them in. It was pretty clear as the car got nearer to them, that they were not getting out of the way.

Lewis had seen a video on YouTube once of these crabs migrating on some island somewhere. They were all red and there were millions of them. Crazy. They just set off and crawled from one side of the island to the other, across roads, through gardens, schoolyards, fields, and forests. Nothing could stop them, and so cars would drive over them, crushing them under the wheels. And still those crabs kept going. Off to spawn.

These grown-ups, these *sickos*, were no different.

Closer and closer the car got and Lewis was holding his breath. Should he go faster or slower? The grown-ups were pretty tightly packed.

"I'm gonna need more speed," he said.

"Go for it." Ed sounded wound up tight.

"You're the boss. This is your gig."

A little faster. More pressure on the pedal. Just a little . . .

"There's too many!" Trio shouted.

"We need to clear them out the way," said Kyle.

"It's my plan," said Lewis, and he pressed harder. The car sped up and . . .

Thump. They hit their first one. A father. He was batted

off to the side. Kyle cheered. And then they were in among them. Grown-ups were smacked off left and right. Behind the first row were some teenagers, *thump, thump, thump*. The car forced its way through them. Then a mother went down and there was a lurch and a bump as the wheels went over her. Kyle cheered again. Macca joined him.

"Nuts," said Lewis. "They won't move for us."

The car was surrounded by grown-ups now. Lewis finally had their attention. They saw the car as a threat and started to crowd in on it, pawing at the windows. Shutting out the light.

"Faster, Lewis." That was Ebenezer in the back. He was a tough kid, not much fazed him, but he sounded worried, scared even.

"Can't go no faster," said Lewis. "It's like driving through heavy mud, man. Like driving through trees."

"This is stupid," said Brooke, and Lewis looked at her in the rearview mirror. "We need to get out of this."

You're telling me, thought Lewis. Trying to speed up didn't make any difference. There were just too many of them. A mother was right up on the hood, squatting there, legs bare and scabby, and she was beating on the windshield with her fists.

More grown-ups climbed up next to her. Lewis turned to his side window. It was jammed with faces, pressing against the glass, gums exposed, smearing their head juices everywhere.

And then the car started to sway from side to side.

Lewis remembered the riots. Watching TV footage of police vans being rocked. Tipped over.

"Go back!" Brooke shouted. "Lewis, go back. Get it in reverse. We can't drive through this. This is crazy."

Lewis didn't need to be told twice. He pulled the gear lever back, finding reverse. Trying the accelerator. Nothing much happening.

Nobody was talking inside the car now. Everyone was feeling the tension, worried that they'd be trapped. Lewis turned the volume up on the sound system to drown out the thunder of beating fists and skulls and boots and whatever else the sickos were slamming against the car.

The engine whined as the car slowly eased its way backward. There were more bumps underneath as they went over fallen grown-ups.

Stay cool.

He could see nothing out of the rear window. It was black with bodies. The three kids in the backseat were twisted around, hoping to see daylight, a break in the wall of flesh.

"Screw this!" Kyle shouted, and before anyone could stop him, he wrenched his door open and was jumping out of the car, clutching the big battle-ax he'd had between his knees.

36

haos. Kyle butting grown-ups with the ax handle. Shouts from the other kids. Ed trying to call him back. Trio screaming. Trey telling her to shut up.

There was a spray of blood across the back window. The flash of a blade chopping down. Light was getting through. Had Kyle cleared a path? Only thing was, if Lewis sped up and reversed away, there was a danger he'd leave Kyle behind.

"What do I do?" he said.

"Bloody Kyle," Ed muttered. "Bloody idiot."

"There he is!" Brooke shouted, and Macca leaned across between the seats and grabbed hold of Kyle as he tumbled back in through the open door.

"Floor it, man!" he yelled, and Lewis stamped down hard. The car surged backward. More thumps, bumps, and rattles underneath. It skidded and swerved.

"It's okay," said Ebenezer. "The road is clear. Kyle did it."

"Ebenezer's right," said Trio. "It's empty; you can go."

Lewis pulled the steering wheel around, and the car

slewed sideways into the median in the center of the highway. He shifted the gear into drive, gave it some gas, and they steamed forward, taking a wide arc across the asphalt. Slamming into some grown-ups who'd caught up. Spilling them off to the side.

"Just go," Ed shouted. "Head for the M25 turnoff."

"I'm going, man," said Lewis, staying calm. Staying cool.

"Bad call. My fault," Ed added. "We should have gone that way before. No more risks."

"Was worth it," said Kyle. "Worth a try, and at least now we know our limitations—this car ain't no tank."

"There's something wrong," said Trey quietly.

"There's a whole lot wrong," said Kyle. "Tell me something new."

"Are we okay?" Brooke asked. "Have they done any damage?"

Lewis shrugged. "She's handling okay." As if he knew what he was talking about. It did seem to be all right, though. It was steering straight and felt like it was responding to the pedals properly.

"There's more of them," said Trey. "I can feel it."

"We keep moving, we'll be okay." Ed leaned over and turned the music down a little. The guy was just like a parent or a teacher. He had his head on straight, but Lewis wondered if he'd be any good in a fight. Somebody had certainly gotten the better of him one time. Given him that ugly, dirty scar down his face. He was posh and all. Not from the streets of Holloway where Lewis had grown up. Still, if a hench-kid like Kyle could accept him as the boss man, he must have something going for him.

That had been some stunt the big guy had pulled. Leaping out like Thor and cutting a path.

Cool.

Lewis kept the car at a steady speed, and they soon arrived at the M25 exit. It was a little complicated getting onto the ramp as they were approaching it from the wrong direction and there were no signs, but they managed it okay and were soon heading north.

"Keep on here until we get to the M40," Ed explained. "That'll take us west again, and then we'll look for a turnoff that'll swing us back south."

"Whatever you say." Lewis settled back in his seat, feeling the tension ease away. It was an open road again. Danger over. Close one, though. Real close.

"We're still not safe." Trinity had been banging on about danger all the way. Lewis was tired of it. Wanted to tell them to shut up. In the end Macca did it for him.

"You've made your point," he said. "So how about you change the subject? I mean, it's not as if any of them tossers are gonna be able to keep up with us. I'd like to see that—a hundred-mile-an-hour sicko."

They cruised onto the M40, but it was a good few miles before they found a way off it, a turning to Beaconsfield, Amersham, and Slough.

"This'll do us fine." Ed was consulting his map again. "We'll try Slough first. It was on my list, one of the places to check out."

They left the highway and were very quickly into countryside, narrow roads, fields and hedges and trees and woodland off to the sides. Long grass, huge weeds, and bright wildflowers growing everywhere, even up through cracks in the road, so that they brushed the underside of the car with a swishing noise as it drove over them. Lewis hadn't been anywhere like this for months, years even, had almost forgotten that the rest of the world even existed, he'd been so used to buildings all around him. The city. Now nature was taking over. He relaxed another couple of notches. He liked it here. Was glad he'd come.

"Look at that," came Macca's voice from the back.

"What is it?"

"Stop a minute."

Lewis slowed the car and brought it to a halt in the middle of the road. Didn't have to pull over to the side. No danger of any other vehicles coming along here. Ed switched the power off on the music system. Silence.

"What is it?" he asked. "What did you see?"

"Over there," said Macca. Lewis could see in the mirror that he was pointing to something.

"What am I looking for?" Ed asked.

"Smoke."

"Yeah." Lewis could see it now, a thin gray column rising up above the trees in the distance and fading out as it blurred into the sky.

"What you reckon?" said Macca. "No smoke without a fire, they say, don't they?"

"Yeah," said Brooke, pretending to be impressed. "They *do* say that, don't they?"

"And a fire means people," said Kyle, ignoring her sarcasm.

"Not necessarily," Ed butted in, peering at the smoke.

"Could just be . . . like, I don't know. A tree on fire. Fires start."

"Usually, though," said Macca, "a fire means someone's lit it. And these days that means kids. Sickos ain't got the brains for it."

"Brains . . ." said Brooke, impersonating a cartoon zombie.

"Is it worth checking out, do you think?" Trio asked.

"I don't know." Ed didn't sound convinced. "My plan was to check the towns out first."

"We've come to find people, ain't we?" said Kyle. "I vote we check on the smoke. Otherwise we're just driving around blind."

Ed turned to look at Trinity.

"What do you reckon?" he asked. "Can you sense any big crowds of sickos around here?'

"There's something out there," said Trio. "But the signal's thin. Not crowds . . . I don't know what. We should be careful. I mean, we're never alone."

"You're never more than two yards from a rat," said Kyle. "Or a sicko."

"What would any sickos be doing around here?" Macca asked. "Except maybe camping." He laughed at his joke.

"He's right," said Brooke. "Except maybe camping."

"If there's kids around, there's likely sickos too." Ed really was a cautious type. "That's what they prey on. Everyone's after the same thing. Food and water. Staying alive. Lewis, what do you think?"

"Worth a look," said Lewis. "We got the car, we're

mobile. If it's a waste of time, we can move on quick. And if it's dangerous, no probs, we easily just roll away."

Ed pressed the power button and brought the music back up, but still keeping the volume down.

"Head for the smoke," he said, and Lewis set the car rolling forward.

37

It took them some time to find where the smoke was coming from. It wasn't as easy as they'd assumed. There were too many trees in the way to get a clear view, and it felt to Lewis that for a lot of the time they were driving around in circles. It didn't help that none of the roads went in a straight line, and they had no idea of just how far away the smoke was. But eventually they thought they had a bead on it.

The road they were on went through thick woodland. Their view was cut off as they got nearer, so they had to trust that they were heading in the right direction. When they finally came to a junction and broke clear of the trees, they saw a gateway in a high wall leading to a private road. It was trashed. A car had driven into one of the posts and knocked the gate down. It must have started a fire, because the sign explaining where the road led was all burned and blackened. There were the charred remains of two skeletons in the front seats.

"Yeah, well, that's a good sign," said Macca. "Very welcoming. What is this? The gates to hell?"

"If this was hell there'd be a three-headed dog waiting for us," said Trio.

"Yes, well, you would know all about that," Ebenezer muttered.

"What are you saying?" Trio sounded none too pleased with Ebenezer's comment.

"I am not saying anything."

"Oh, okay, fine," said Trio with heavy sarcasm. "Only a more sensitive person than myself might have thought you were making a comment about us having three heads."

"I didn't mean anything by it."

"It's the law of threes," said Trey.

"Oh, don't start on that," said Trio.

"Cerberus, the dog with three heads," said Trey. "Or there's the Chimera, with the head of a lion, a snake's head for a tail, and a goat's head coming out of its back. Or the three Furies, the three Norns, the Morrígan, Hecate? The Holy Trinity. Take your pick. Which do you want us to be, Ebenezer?"

"I don't know what you are talking about."

"Me either," said Lewis. "You want me to drive on?"

Ed slapped his hand on the top of the dashboard. "Let's do this," he said.

The driveway wound along through trees. The weeds and wildflowers had grown up all around and were starting to invade the road from both sides, leaving only a narrow strip to steer down. At the end of the drive was a big old house with smoke rising from one of the chimneys.

"Don't look much like hell to me," said Kyle. "Unless the devil's inside, getting his butler to toast sinners for him."

"Toast crumpets, more like," said Brooke.

Lewis drove up to the front of the house, where there was an overgrown parking area. He switched off the engine. Studied the building. It was tall and grand, three floors high, with a wide, square porch held up by six big pillars. It looked to Lewis like a shrunk-down version of Buckingham Palace. The white painted walls were grubby and streaked with dirt and rain.

There were blinds and shutters and net curtains covering all the windows at the front of the house, and no sign of any lights inside, so it was impossible to see if there was anybody in there. Lewis had to admit, though, that if he was hiding out anywhere around here this was the sort of place he'd have chosen. It was solid and well built. A brick wall enclosed the gardens. There were clear lines of sight all around. Only thing was—if he'd been living here he'd have repaired that gate. So what was up?

"Is it safe, do you reckon?" asked Ed.

"Please be careful," said Trio. "The signal hasn't changed. Like something following us."

"Relax," said Brooke. "It looks civilized. I mean, come on, what sicko is going to light a fire in a fireplace?"

"Even if it's kids it doesn't mean we'll be welcome." Ed undid his seat belt. "As Trio says, let's go careful. Nobody do anything stupid, okay?"

"Oh, *please*," said Kyle. "Let me do something stupid."

"Seriously, Kyle. If it *is* kids, and that's obviously what I'm hoping, they may have defenses, traps."

"Why don't we just go knock on the door?" said Macca.

"You all sure about this?" said Trey. "I've got a humming in my head and it's not going away."

"Sure as I can be." Ed opened his door. "At some point we all knew we were going to have to get out of the car."

"I already did," said Kyle, sliding his door open and climbing out. "Back there on the highway. Or didn't any of you losers notice?"

He got out and walked over toward the house, swinging his bloody ax idly in one hand. Lewis shoved his own door open and jumped down. Next out was Trinity. Lewis was impressed with how well the kids moved around, joined up as they were. They had two normal legs, one each, with smaller shriveled legs tucked up in between, under their body. They didn't wobble or stumble at all, and seemed to use one brain when it came to maneuvering. They walked over to join Kyle, and Lewis saw the third body on their back, sticking out below their pack. It looked dead, like an old mummy or a goblin, or something.

He thought he caught a movement in the corner of his eye and threw a look to the house. Sure he'd seen a face at a window, pale, like a ghost. No. Stupid. There were no ghosts. Zombies, yes. At least grown-ups who thought they were zombies. But no ghosts.

There was nothing at the window now. If there ever had been.

Next out were Brooke and Macca.

"You cool with this?" Macca asked Brooke, hovering too close to her.

"You'll look after me, won't you?" Brooke simpered.

Macca grinned, puffed up. "Sure," he said. "You don't need to worry about anything as long as I'm around."

Lewis grinned. That boy was so dumb. Couldn't he see when someone was winding him up? Taking him for a ride? Getting ready to dump on him.

Lewis caught Brooke's eye. She made a face behind Macca's back and pointed at him—*Can you believe this?*

Lewis was waiting for it. The moment when Brooke dropped the bomb on him. Looking forward to it. Must be any second now.

"I'll get my crossbow down off the roof," said Macca. "I'm a really good shot."

"One thing, Macca," said Brooke. Macca turned and hesitated.

"Yeah?"

This was it. He was gonna get it now.

"There's one thing I want to say to you. . . ."

"Yeah?"

But Brooke never told him, because at that moment something dark unfolded itself from the roof of the car, leaned over the edge, and half fell on Macca.

He yelled in fright and jerked as if he'd been electrocuted.

It was a father. He must have been holding on to the roof rack. How had none of them seen him? He had Macca's head locked in his arms and had sunk his rotten yellow teeth into his throat.

Macca screamed and groaned. There was a gush of bright red blood. And then Lewis was moving fast. He was closest. He smashed a fist into the side of the father's face. His jaws were wide apart and Lewis felt the lower jaw break, teeth come loose. Then Lewis grabbed one of his arms and yanked him down from the roof.

The father flopped to the ground with a wet thwack. And now Kyle was there. He swung his ax at him and got him in the neck, nearly cutting his head off; another swing and the head rolled free.

Macca had dropped to his knees and was clutching his bleeding throat. He was sobbing and raving, his voice sounding strangled, like he was drowning in his own blood.

"Oh Jesus, oh Jesus, no, not this, oh, help me, Jesus, help me, Mom."

Brooke went to his side and held onto him, looking around at the others with a helpless expression. Meanwhile, Ed had dropped his bag to the ground and unzipped it, dug out a first-aid kit. He unscrewed the top from a bottle of disinfectant, pulled Macca's hands away from his wound, and splashed liquid over it that caused Macca to hiss and groan. Then Ed ripped open an antiseptic bandage wrapper, pulled a white, square wad out of it, and pressed it to Macca's neck.

"Hold this," he said to Brooke, already scrabbling to open a bottle of painkillers.

Lewis was impressed by how quickly and expertly Ed did all this. He went to the car and checked the roof rack, making sure there were no more of the bastards up there. It was clean. He freed up his spear, a short wooden pole with a sharpened end, and grabbed one of Ebenezer's javelins and chucked it over to him. Lewis had his katana in the car, but he still preferred the spear. He was scared of the Japanese sword, worried it would cut him worse than his enemies.

Macca had gone very white and was shaking. Lewis had seen enough when Ed had pulled Macca's hands away to know that the sicko had chomped a fair-sized chunk out of him. Ed forced some pills into Macca's mouth, and Brooke made him swallow some water from a plastic bottle.

"You'll be all right," she said. "You'll be okay."

"Will I?" said Macca. "You're not lying to me."

"You're all right."

"Oh my God, we should have known." Trinity had gotten out of the car. They stood there, not sure what to do, rubbing their hands.

Ed was staring over at the building. "We need to get him inside," he said.

"We don't know what is in there," said Ebenezer.

"Well, let's find out. If it's people, they can help us." Ed walked around to the back of the car and fetched his sword from the trunk. It was a big heavy-looking old thing. He started toward the house, calling out commands as he went.

"Lewis and Kyle, you come with me. The rest of you stay here. Look after Macca. Protect him."

Lewis and Kyle hurried to catch up with Ed as he hammered on the front door.

"Hello," he called out. "Open up. Please. We know there's someone in there."

Lewis went over to one of the windows, pressed his face to the glass, and shaded it with his free hand. He could see nothing inside past the net curtains, just darkness. He was considering whether to smash the glass when Ed shouted—

"It's open."

Lewis ran back to him. Sure enough, the front door had opened a crack. It was impossible to see anything beyond it. He looked to Ed. Ed shrugged.

"Let's go for it."

Ed stepped up to the door and carefully pushed it wider. Still nothing visible beyond. Lewis walked in, his spear ready. It was dark in the hallway, a short, wide corridor leading to a larger hallway, a room off to either side. As Lewis walked farther in, he became aware of a brief movement off to his left. Something alive. Holding still now but definitely alive. He could sense it.

A person?

He tensed. Waiting. Held a hand out in warning as Ed pushed the door wider and came in. More light was thrown down the hallway and Lewis saw the person move, ducking into the room off to their left.

"What is it?" Ed asked.

"There's someone here," said Lewis. "Must be them's opened the door."

"Hello?" Ed called out. "It's okay, we're kids . . ."

"What if *they* ain't, though?" said Lewis.

"Then we murder them," said Kyle, pushing past with his heavy ax.

Ed was sniffing the air. "Does this feel like a sicko den to you?" he said. "Does it smell like it?"

"No," said Lewis. It smelled of soap and flowers and hospitals. Hadn't smelled anything like this in a long time.

"Smells clean," he said.

"I don't like it," said Kyle. "Ain't natural."

"Hello?" Ed called again and then turned to Lewis. "Which way did they go?"

"In there." Lewis pointed to the door on the left and Kyle advanced toward it. Ed held him back. This time he was going in first. Kyle and Lewis stayed close behind.

There was just enough light coming through the closed shutters to see that they were in a large sitting room, with sofas and chairs, all very neat and tidy. And there was another door that must lead through to the main hallway. Ed pulled the shutters open, filling the room with dusty light.

A quick scout around showed them that there was nobody in there.

Whoever had come in had obviously sneaked out through the other door.

"It's all right," Ed was shouting again. "We're kids. We don't want to hurt you, but one of us is injured. We need help."

Still no reply, but Lewis had heard movement from outside the door.

"There's definitely people here," he said. "They let us in, so now what? We got to go play hide-and-seek."

"I say we stop the nice-guy routine," said Kyle, and he put on a moist, lisping voice. "Oh, hello, do *please* help us, we're really nice. . . ."

Ed sighed and looked at his friend. "Kyle," he said, "it's not an act. I *am* really nice."

"Bullshit," said Kyle, gripping his ax tightly in both hands, ready for action. "You're a monster, Ed, and you know it."

"You two lover boys stay cool," said Lewis. "I'm going on through. I'll find whoever's here. You stay back."

He opened the second door into the hallway. Took a quick look to check it was all quiet. Stepped through.

It was a grand space. Sort of place you expected to see big paintings and suits of armor, like in old movies. Nothing like that in here. It was almost bare. Doors off everywhere, big old wooden stairs up the back, with high, dirty windows letting in a feeble light. Not enough to lift the murk and gloom. He scanned the area for any signs of life.

Nothing.

Just his own breathing. Sounding noisy in the big empty quiet. And then he saw a yellow flicker, coming along the landing at the top of the stairs, throwing shapes and shadows on the walls. A candle appeared, in a candlestick, someone holding it, walking slowly, a long gray dress, white hair, white face.

A ghost. Slowly coming down the stairs. A second figure, tucked up close, hiding behind the ghost's skirts.

Lewis swore, got his spear ready.

"You see anything?" Ed called through from the sitting room.

"Maybe."

"What is it?"

"Sickos," said Lewis bluntly.

38

Ed took a deep breath. He didn't want any more trouble. He'd been praying that this trip wouldn't end in disaster, in more deaths. He didn't want to know what was on the other side of the door, but he didn't want to leave Lewis there alone.

He hurried over. Went through. Saw Lewis standing ready. Saw two people slowly coming down the stairs. Old people. Old like he hadn't seen in a long time.

Two women, one holding a candle, walking stiff and upright, the other sort of hiding behind her, very small, bent over, a frightened look about her, like a baby animal.

"What do we do?" said Lewis. "Do we kill them?"

"Wait." Ed was thinking, trying to take this in. The old women didn't look diseased. There were none of the usual signs—boils or blisters or sores—and their clothes were clean. Their eyes showed intelligence.

They didn't look like a threat.

But they probably weren't alone.

He had to be careful. Mustn't make any more mistakes. Take no risks. Driving into the sickos on the highway had been dumb. His fault they'd ended up with one of them on the roof rack. His fault Macca was hurt.

Should he just kill these old women and be done with it?

They looked impossibly old. He'd never seen people this ancient and wrinkled. Even before the disease. Their hair was white and wispy, their skin hanging off their bones, thin and dry, blue veins showing through it, their skulls all too obvious beneath.

They came closer and stopped near the bottom of the stairs, eyes fixed on the three boys.

"What do we do, Ed?" asked Lewis. "What do we do?"

"Kill them," murmured Kyle.

Ed waited, trying to read the faces of the two old women. The one with the candle looked more alert, more intelligent, her eyes glinting.

He had to do something. Say something.

"Hello," he said at last, feeling foolish. "My name's Ed."

"Hello, Ed," said the woman with the candle. "I am Amelia. Sorry about the pantomime at the door. I wanted the chance to see you up close before I spoke to you. And my sister is nervous of strangers."

"This is weird."

"I'm sure it is."

"I don't know what to say," Ed went on. "Are you sick? What are you?"

"We're not sick," said Amelia. "We're just old. The sickness didn't bother with us. We weren't worth it."

"How can we trust you?" said Lewis.

"Do we look dangerous?" asked Amelia, and she smiled at him.

"There might be more of you."

"Oh, there *are* more of us."

Lewis tensed. Kyle stepped forward, his ax slightly raised.

"There's no need for that," said the old woman. "Follow me."

She came fully down the stairs and crossed the hall to a doorway opposite.

"It'll be a trap," Kyle muttered darkly.

Ed put a hand on Kyle's shoulder, urging him forward. "Then we'd better be ready for anything," he said.

Amelia opened the heavy door and waited there for the boys.

"After you," said Lewis as they drew near, and she led the way through. It wasn't as dark in the next room. There were three large bay windows down one side that let in a lot of light. Burning logs in the fireplace added an extra glow. Ed took it all in quickly.

It wasn't a trap.

That was clear.

There were about twenty people in there, sitting in armchairs and at small tables, all ancient, shriveled and shrunken. Some alert, watchful, others dead-eyed and slack-jawed. One or two lost in their own private worlds, rocking backward and forward, babbling.

"See?" said Amelia, and she blew her candle out. The smaller old woman was still clinging to her, not understanding what was going on, fearful. Amelia gently stroked the woman's hair as she talked. "I told you there were more of us. But we're all the same. All just old. Harmless."

An old man had gotten up from one of the tables and headed for them. He was bent over, walking with the help of two sticks, what was left of his silver hair neatly combed over his scalp. A smart blazer with a handkerchief folded in the top pocket. Glasses so thick they magnified his eyes.

"Hello," he said when he got to them, turning to peer at all three boys in turn. "How splendid to have some visitors. I won't shake your hands. I'm liable to fall over."

He chuckled.

"This is freaky," said Lewis. "I ain't talked to a grown-up in over a year."

"And I haven't talked to a child," said the man. "Not for a long while. They leave us alone here. They've forgotten us."

"What is this place?" asked Kyle.

"It's called the Beeches," said Amelia. "It used to be what you would call an old people's home. I suppose it still is. A *very* old people's home. And what brings you all here? I wonder."

Ed had almost forgotten about the rest of his group, still waiting outside. They'd be getting worried.

"Our friend is hurt," he said. "Can we bring him in? Do you have any medical stuff?"

"I saw from the window," said the woman. "A bad business. I do hope he's all right. We have some bits and pieces here. There's a medical wing, not as well stocked as it once was. And Norman here used to be a doctor."

"A very long time ago," said the man.

"He still remembers some things, don't you, Norman?"

"A little. But I forget more. I remember my training better than I remember what I had for breakfast this morning, to tell you the honest truth."

"You know perfectly well what you had for breakfast, Norman," said Amelia. "You had what you have every morning. What we all have. Porridge oats and sweet tea."

"What happened to your friend?" asked Norman, his goggle eyes blinking at Ed.

"He's been bitten."

"By one of *them*?"

"Yes."

Norman tutted. "Then I'm afraid there's not a lot I can do for him. I'll try my best, but my best is not what it was. He doesn't stand much of a chance, the poor devil. You'd better bring him inside."

39

"Y ou won't leave me, will you, Brooke? You won't leave me here alone?"

"No, of course not. I'm with you."

Macca was in a bed, with clean white sheets, in a clean room. Ed hadn't seen anywhere this clean, this gleaming white, for ages. It all felt like a dream. A dream of the old days. Norman—Dr. Norman Hunter, to give him his full name—was sitting at Macca's bedside. He'd tried to clean and close the wound, bandaged him up, and had stuck a thermometer in his mouth. He was waiting for the result now, slowly rubbing his dry hands together. The old doctor looked tired, his eyes drooping shut behind his thick glasses. Ed knew that it was bad. He'd read it in Norman's face when he'd inspected the wound. Macca needed a proper hospital, with serious drugs and proper surgical equipment if he was to have any chance.

Brooke was sitting on the other side of the bed, holding Macca's hand. Ebenezer stood awkwardly by the window, not sure what to say or do. The other kids—Kyle, Lewis, and

Trinity—were waiting downstairs in the empty front room. Amelia stood at the foot of the bed, her sister still stuck to her side. Amelia nodded to Norman, who gave her an uncertain look.

Amelia made a *hmm* noise and came over to where Ed was hovering in the doorway. She touched him lightly on the chest with her fingertips.

"There's nothing more we can do here," she said gently. "We're just getting in the way. Come along downstairs. There's a lot we need to talk about."

When Ed followed Amelia into the front room, Trinity and the others looked at her as if she were an alien. They were still getting used to the fact that there was an adult who didn't carry the disease. And Amelia stared back at Trinity in a similar way. This was strange for all of them. Amelia's little companion shrank away from the children, evidently scared.

Amelia plumped up some cushions and settled onto a sofa with a weary sigh, and her shadow sat down beside her, holding on tightly to her hand.

"I expect there's a great deal you all want to know," said Amelia. "And there's much I want to know as well." She looked at Trinity. "Particularly about you two, my dears. But we shall come to that in good time. Shall I go first?"

"Please." Ed nodded.

"My name is Amelia Dropmore and this is my sister, Dorothy. She is eighty-seven years old, and I am ninety-two. Don't mind her, she's living a second childhood. The diagnosis was Alzheimer's. She has been what they describe as 'demented,' charming word, for twelve years. It's a mercy for her, in a way, because she has no idea what's going on. Her mind is stuck in the past. She thinks it's the 1930s and she's a little girl and there is no sickness. . . .

"I am *not* demented. Before the sickness came, Dorothy had been living here for eight years. I was still independent, but I knew the place well. I visited her whenever I was able. Like everyone else, I'd thought that was it. The world would carry on as normal, Dorothy and I would grow older, and pretty soon one of us would pass on, and then the other. Nothing to write home about. Just a slow dying of the light.

"And then it happened. Our world did not carry on as normal. It was thrown off its axis. Altered beyond recognition. At first the staff here were really very good. They did what they could for the old folks. But one by one they either took sick, or simply stopped coming in in the mornings. Who can blame them? They all had loved ones. Families to be with. So in the end it was left to me to look after the ladies and gentlemen who live here."

"Why aren't any of you sick?" asked Lewis.

"She don't know, do she?" said Kyle. "How could she know? She ain't no scientist."

"I'm afraid you are quite wrong," said Amelia patiently. "I *am* a scientist."

"You're joking me."

"What? You don't think a woman can be a scientist? Or you don't think an old person can be a scientist?"

"For real? You're a scientist?"

"Yes. I trained at Cambridge before the war, in the Department of Experimental Medicine. And when war broke out I went to work for the government at the Medical

Research Council in Mount Vernon in Hampstead. Churchill was terrified that the Germans might use chemical or biological weapons—"

"I knew it." Kyle slapped the arm of his chair, sending up a tiny cloud of dust that hung in the air.

"You knew what?" asked Amelia.

"That's where the disease came from, innit? It was a weapon that got out, that went wrong."

"No," said Amelia and she slowly shook her head. "It wasn't that. It would have been easier to deal with if it had been. We'd have known what it was. And we had no idea. It was a peculiar disease, like nothing any of us had ever encountered before. It came from nowhere, appeared overnight in a fully virulent form. And it seemed choosy—the young were spared, anyone under the age of sixteen, and the very old."

"That's news to me," said Kyle, shifting uneasily in his seat.

"I'm not surprised," said Amelia. "When the world went to pieces, the old were vulnerable. No one to look after them, easy prey for looters and house invaders. Most were simply killed. In the fog of war it was hard to see what was going on."

"Maybe you're right," said Kyle. "I had some grandparents living in Wood Green. Lost touch with them when it all kicked off."

"You're saying older people aren't affected by the disease?" Ed asked.

"Yes. People in their late eighties and over do not seem to have been affected. Several of us here are over ninety, and three are over a hundred. It passed us by. Why?"

"Do you know why?" asked Lewis.

"We had theories. Perhaps old people had some degree of natural immunity to it, from some past infection. But that didn't explain why no young people got it. Perhaps it only bothered with people who were strong enough to carry it. But that would assume that the disease had a degree of intelligence. Which is impossible. Or so we thought. Ah, but I'm getting ahead of myself." She gave a stern look to Kyle that softened into a smile.

"You interrupted me," she said. "Got me off the subject. An old schoolboy trick."

"Sorry."

"As I was saying," Amelia went on, "I worked for the government during the war, doing my patriotic bit, and after that I moved around. I worked in Germany for a period, and America. For a few years I was at the Courtauld Institute of Biochemistry at Middlesex Hospital. I was even on the Board of Health for a spell . . . Oh, you don't need to know all this. Just listen to me! I'm a typical rambling old person, showing off how much I can still remember. Suffice to say, I spent my entire adult life researching diseases and the beautiful mysteries of the human body.

"And thirty years ago I retired, although I remained on various boards and charities and health advisory committees. And I got old. And I thought my usefulness was over. Aside from looking after Dorothy here." She touched her sister's hand and Dorothy smiled back at her.

"So when the disease came into the world, I looked on helplessly, wishing there was something I could do, some way I could help. Be careful what you wish for, that's what they say, and they're right, because the disease worked its evil magic. Doctors were dying, scientists, researchers, nurses . . . everyone except the very old and the young. Hospitals and laboratories were having to close down because there was nobody well enough to work in them. That's when I got the call. Me and hundreds like me. Retired scientists, and doctors, and nurses.

"It wasn't publicized. Imagine the panic if it got out that the future of the world was in the hands of a bunch of rickety senior citizens. But it was the only way they could keep the labs going, keep the hospitals going; they had to bring us out of retirement. They asked for volunteers at first, but when it got completely desperate they made it clear that we had no choice. I was here when they came for me, looking after Dot. I hated to leave her, but there was no way around it.

"When I went into the laboratory, I was shocked by what I found. It was desperate, simply desperate: sick and dying people trying to keep on working. And it was all no use: several of them went mad and did terrible damage to people and to equipment. It got so that if anyone showed even the slightest signs of illness they were barred from the labs. I tried to keep up—so much had changed since my day, there had been so many advances in technology and knowledge—but even so, nobody had the faintest idea where the disease had come from, how it worked, and how we might stop it.

"The basic techniques were unchanged. We took blood samples and tissue samples. We worked with rats and guinea pigs and monkeys, and one by one, we died. It was a race against time and we lost. The younger ones among us were the first to go. It was like a sort of ripple effect, working upward through the ages. Until there were only us old crocks left. There were five of us in the end, all over eighty-five, all women, trying to run the laboratory. We didn't stand a chance. We knew that even if we somehow did find a cure, there were no doctors left, no nurses, no infrastructure. What could we do? We five old crones?"

"And did you find a cure?" asked Kyle, leaning forward now, looking hopeful.

"No, dear. We did not."

Kyle slumped back in his seat.

"Did you find out how it worked, even?" he asked.

"I probably know more about the disease than anyone else in England," said Amelia. "And here am I, ninety-two, weak and feeble and helpless. I haven't got much longer on this earth. How I've gotten to ninety-two, quite frankly, I have no idea . . . and all I know will die with me."

"Unless you tell us," said Trey, and he and Trio crossed the room to sit next to her on the sofa. "We could write it all down, or something."

Amelia smiled at him and placed her hand on top of his. She stared into his face, trying to make sense of him, and was just about to ask him something when Lewis butted in.

"Is it like this all around the world?" he said. "Is it this bad everywhere?"

"As far as we know. Everything looked hopeless. We gave up in the end. We closed the labs, and I came here to be with Dot. By then all the staff had gone. Dead or run off. It was just the old people. Left to die. But we didn't die. Because, before I left the labs, I was able to do one last thing. I had ultimate authority: the government had given orders that anything I needed I should have. The work I was doing was that important. So I made one last order."

"What was it?" Ed asked.

"Come along," said Amelia, struggling up off the sofa. "I'll show you."

E d was reminded of the secret liquor stash in Shadowman's basement at the club in London. Only the shelves in the cellar here weren't piled high with alcohol. It was food. Rows and rows of boxes and cans and bottles and jars and bags and plastic containers, all with identical packaging: plain white with black lettering—EMERGENCY FOOD SUPPLIES—with the date and contents and various government stamps and labels and warnings. There was fruit, vegetables, rice, pasta in sauce, meatballs, Spam, noodles, condensed milk, long-life milk, fruit juice, cookies. Anything you could think of, it was here. All kept neat and in order.

"Three trucks turned up one morning," said Amelia. "And men in gas masks brought the food down here and put it on the shelves under my supervision, and I signed for it and they went away, and that was that. No questions asked. Just following orders. We've been living off it ever since. We have fresh food as well. There's a large vegetable garden and an orchard. We keep a few chickens and ducks and pigeons."

Ed looked along the shelves. He was reminded that those

who had the food had the power. He remembered Mad Matt's warehouse near St. Paul's. But what happened when it ran out? Could any of them grow enough food to live on?

"You have to tell us what you learned, Amelia," he said. "Is there any hope?"

Amelia clutched Ed's arm with her thin, bony hand. "*You* are our hope, Ed," she said. "You children. You are not infected. I learned that much. The young, like *us*, are not infected."

"Why?" asked Lewis. "Why aren't we infected?"

"Let's go back upstairs," said Amelia, her voice fragile and fluttery. "I'm getting tired. I need to sit down."

They made their way back to the front room. It took a while for Amelia to get her breath back. She was strong, though. Ed could see that she *had* to tell them what she knew.

"You were born after the infection spread across the planet," she explained once she was settled. "You must think of it like spores. Did you ever see a mushroom pop and spray a little cloud into the air? Spores. Like tiny, tiny little specks of dust. *Poof!*"

She looked at Kyle, who was not really following any of this, sitting there bored, spinning his ax in his hands and picking dried blood off the blade.

"You reminded me of it earlier," she said.

"Huh?" Kyle gave her a vacant, dumb look.

"When you clapped the arm of your chair."

"What have I done now?"

"Nothing wrong. But do it again."

"Do what?"

"Bang your chair." Amelia mimed the action.

Kyle did what he was told—thumped his hand down on the arm of his chair, sending up a cloud of dust that was picked out by the sunlight coming in through the windows.

"There," said Amelia. "You see it? If it didn't catch the light it would be invisible to you. That's what happens when a mushroom puffs out its spores. Up they go, into the atmosphere, spread by the wind, and by animals and people. Up into the clouds, down into the lakes and rivers. We think that the disease was spread in a similar way. It must have happened very quickly. And it certainly happened without anyone noticing.

"The disease would have originated somewhere isolated, and there must have been an incident, something that exposed it and introduced it into the wider world. It broke out of wherever it had been hiding, and it was carried to busier places and incubated unknowingly. And then—*pop!*—like spores on the wind, it spread itself, and anyone infected became a carrier until—*pop!*—they passed it on. More spores."

"All this happened before we were born?" Ed asked.

"It's the only explanation." Amelia looked out of the window, lost in her thoughts for a moment.

"The modern world," she said quietly after a while. "What a place it was. We were all linked via roads and shipping lanes and airplanes. We did the work of the disease for it . . . *Pop, pop, pop.* It spread across the planet until nearly everyone alive must have been a carrier. And then, some sixteen years ago, it stopped spreading and started to grow. So, you see, anyone born after that first infestation was untouched. That's you children. You are free of the disease. My fear is, though, that when it has reached a certain stage it will emerge again. *Pop!* The spores will be on the wind once more."

"They're massing," said Trio.

"What's that, my dear?"

"The sickos, the diseased adults, they're massing. All grouping together."

"Perhaps they're getting ready for the final stage," said Amelia. "But I don't know. There's still so much I can never know."

Amelia was growing tired, her body slumping. She gave in to small yawns that she tried unsuccessfully to hide behind her hand, and her head kept tipping forward.

"South America," said Trey. "That's where it came from. The Amazon rain forest, the big green."

Amelia seemed to come awake suddenly, to come alive.

"Are you sure of this?"

"Yes. Because our parents were the carriers. The people who first brought it out of the jungle and into the wider world."

"I knew you were special when I saw you," said Amelia, her eyes glinting. "You and I are going to need to have a long talk."

Framed by the bedroom window, the moon was riding high in the sky, thin clouds drifting in front of it, lit up a ghostly gray. A few stars showed through the silver veil, but there was a mistiness to the night that blurred and hid things. Brooke wondered how many other children might be looking up at the moon right now.

She was focusing her attention out there, in space, because she was finding it hard to think about what was going on down here. Right here, in this room where Macca was slowly dying. Little old Norman had done what he could, but Macca had lost a lot of blood and an infection had gotten into his body, and the doctor didn't have the drugs to fight it. Macca was burning up, his skin turning blotchy. He was feverish, slept most of the time, a restless, fidgety, troubled sleep, and would wake up babbling.

The only thing that seemed to calm him down, to make him happy and peaceful, was Brooke. She hadn't left the room since they'd arrived.

Ha! Big joke. She'd been winding Macca up in the car,

playing him for a fool, lining him up for a great big smack in the mouth. And it had never come, because the stupid bloody fool had gotten himself bitten. Five days they'd been here now and Brooke had hardly left his side.

Before they'd known just how bad the wound was, Ed had promised Macca that they wouldn't leave him behind. Ed was going crazy now, desperate to be moving on, but a promise was a promise.

And, whatever happened, Brooke knew she couldn't leave Macca. If she wasn't there when he woke up, he'd scream and rave and thrash about, accuse other people of trying to poison him. Brooke wasn't even sure if he really knew who she was anymore, whether she was his girlfriend or his sister or his mom, or some angel with fluffy wings who'd come fluttering down from heaven. There was just some part of him that seemed to need her.

She'd only come along on this stupid journey so that she could spend time with Ed, get closer to him, and she'd hardly done that at all. He was downstairs helping the crumblies, keeping his mind off the delay, the endless bloody waiting. Amelia had given him work to do in the garden. And they'd all been talking to the crocks about the disease, learning stuff, all except Brooke, who was stuck here with Sickboy.

She'd lost count of the times she'd thought about leaving him. She hardly knew him after all. He'd been nothing to her. Just some smelly, mouthy kid who'd come shuffling through the door behind Ed when they showed up at the museum. She didn't owe him nothing.

Brooke put her hand to his forehead. It was damp and burning up. Like touching a hot oven. She got a wet washcloth from the bowl of water on the chair next to the wall, dabbed at his face like Norman had shown her. Macca didn't react, didn't move at all, not even to flinch or try to push her away, like he used to do in the first couple of days. His breathing was heavy and raspy and broken, with no proper rhythm to it. Occasionally he'd have these fits of sucking in air in great gulps, his whole body shuddering.

She felt like weeping. What was she doing here? What were any of them doing here? She should be back at the museum with her friends. Not stuck here with these old people and this sick boy. Nobody cared. They'd dumped her here. *Oh, Brooke, she can look after our friend.* She stood up and walked quietly to the door. Maybe if she could just get out of here for a few minutes, go and walk in the garden in the moonlight, *anything*. It was driving her crazy.

"*Mom?*"

She stopped in the doorway.

"Mom? Is that you?"

She turned. Macca was sitting up. His eyes were very shiny, haunted. She walked over to him and eased him back down onto the pillows.

"It's all right, Macca," she said. "It's all right, go back to sleep."

"I don't want to go to school tomorrow, Mom. I don't feel well. Is it all right if I don't?"

"Yeah, of course it's all right. You don't need to go to school if you don't feel up to it."

"Okay. Is it all right if I go on my PlayStation, though? I know I'm supposed to be ill, but I'm well enough to go on the PlayStation, aren't I?"

"Yeah. Why not? You can do whatever you want, Macca."

"Yeah . . . of an . . . And could I . . . and I . . . and is there . . . why is there? Where are you? Why am I here?"

Brooke looked at Macca. He was crying. She wiped the tears away with the washcloth. His eyes seemed to focus. He stared intently at her.

"I'm really scared, Brooke," he said, back in reality.

Brooke found this harder to deal with. She didn't want to tell him the truth.

"I'm hurt really bad," he said. "I can't swallow and I'm scared that I'm going to die."

"Don't think about it, Macca. Worrying won't help. You just need to rest and get stronger."

"Do you believe in God?"

"I don't know. That's a weird question."

"And that's a terrible answer."

"It's the truth. I never think about all that. I don't know if there's a God."

"Me either. But I'm scared there's nothing there. Just nothing. Like blankness."

"Don't think about it, Macca."

"Billy."

"What?"

"Billy, it's my name. William McIntyre."

"I never knew that."

"Nobody does. Everyone calls me Macca. Or Maccy. My mom used to call me Billy, no one else."

"Do you want me to call you Billy?"

"Don't matter. I'm not bothered . . . I just, I just wanted you to know . . . what my name was. My real name. It's important. You see, if you bury me, will you write my real name? On a stone, or something? I don't know how it works, I never went to church. I don't know how it is, with, like, God and all that. How you get into heaven. But they should know my real name at least, I think. William McIntyre."

"Don't think about all that, Macca."

"It's not fair, is it really? I'm only just fifteen. It's not really long enough for a life. There was lots of things I wanted to do."

"Oh, Macca, will you stop it now? You'll have *me* blubbing. And I *never* cry."

"You know when we was getting out of the car . . . ?" said Macca. "When that sicko . . . Was it recently or was it last year? When was it?"

"Just a few days ago."

"Yeah? Okay. It must of been a dream, then?"

"What?"

"Us doing all them other things together. You and me. We went traveling all over. Fighting sickos. Must of dreamed that bit. Never mind. It was still cool. But you, when we were getting out of the car, there was something you were going to tell me. What was it, Brooke? I've been thinking about it."

"I don't know, Billy. I can't remember."

"For real?"

"Yeah, for real. Go to sleep and stop worrying about stuff."

"But was it a good thing or a bad thing?"

"A good thing, obviously. Why would I say a bad thing to you?"

"I've never been up to much. I've always been a bit small

for my age. I never had a real girlfriend. Girls never went for me, so I used to bad-mouth them. If I get well, will you be my proper girlfriend?"

"Of course I will," said Brooke without blinking.

He closed his eyes.

Brooke threw the washcloth back into the bowl and it hit with a splash, spilling water onto the floor.

Despite what Norman had said about him having no chance, she wasn't going to let Macca die. She was going to keep him alive. She'd make him well. She'd do everything she could.

So that when he was fit enough, and knew what was going on, she'd tell him exactly what she thought of him.

Yeah.

She realized she was crying.

"Now look what you've done," she said.

42

Lewis was chopping wood with Ed. He'd been enjoying it out there in the garden, practicing his ax skills, feeling good when the blade bit into an upended log and it fell into two neat halves. Feeling frustrated when his aim was off and he only sliced a pathetic splinter of wood from the log or sent it spinning away into the long grass. He hadn't realized how stressed he'd been before. Oh, he put on a front to the world that he was Mr. Cool, half asleep, that nothing bugged him. But he was human.

It was different for boneheaded Kyle. Kyle was bored. Kyle was restless, wanted to be out there cracking skulls. Kyle was your basic psychopath. He was over there now, on the opposite side of the garden, doing some target practice with Ebenezer.

Lewis was happy to lose himself in work. Have a little holiday. Driving the car, pretending he was on top of it, on the edge of panic the whole way, had been hard. So it was nice to just chill for a bit. There was a lot of violence in his past, and there would be a lot in his future, he was sure of that, but for now it was Zen, brother. Peace and love and happiness. Chop that wood. *Thock, thock, thock.* Pretend that there was nothing outside these walls. That the world was okay. Chillax, get his strength up, refill the ice in his cool box.

He prayed that Macca would hold on, because as long as he was alive they were going to stay put. How long had it been now? A week maybe? Ed getting more miserable every day. Lewis knew it was selfish, that he mainly wanted Macca to stay alive so that he could stay here in the garden, but you had to be selfish, didn't you? Had to look after yourself. There was no one else to do that for you. No Mom and Dad, no teachers or doctors or police. He definitely knew his own mom and dad weren't ever going to look after him again, because he'd killed them both. Strangled them in their beds when they'd gotten sick.

That seemed a way long time ago.

Best not to dig up any of them old memories.

There was a shout from across the garden. It was Kyle, throwing a spear into his target—an old door that they'd painted a crude picture of a sicko on. Ebenezer cheered and Kyle cackled. The spear had gotten the sicko in the crotch. Kyle had been making weapons out of old gardening tools and bits of wood and scrap metal they'd found around the place. Apparently, when Kyle had first met Ed, he'd been armed with a garden fork. He'd come up in the world since then, raided the armories at the Tower of London. His ax was a mean killing machine.

Lewis looked over to where Amelia was sitting with Trinity at a garden table under a wooden structure that was covered with a climbing rose. Jug of water and bottle of lemonade sparkling in the sunlight. Like something out of an old ad. Happy families. The grandchildren visit their granny . . . except that Trinity looked really odd, the two bodies, boy and girl, joined together, like something out of one of the Percy Jackson books Lewis had been into when he was younger, before football took over.

Trinity wasn't no monster, though. He mustn't think that. They could read minds, couldn't they?

"That'll do for now," Ed grunted and chucked a split log into a wheelbarrow.

Lewis still wasn't sure about Ed. He was together enough to be a leader, but was he a fighter as well? "You see your man Macca?" said Lewis.

"Yeah?" Ed was stooped over, picking up logs and lobbing them into the barrow.

"Reminds me of this guy Arran, yeah? Was one of the kids led us out of Holloway. I never really knew him that good. Blue was my general. Anyways, he got bit in the neck, same as Macca."

Ed started to wheel the barrow away. "You're going to tell me he died, aren't you?" he said.

"Yeah," said Lewis, following. "But not from the wound. He got hit by an arrow. Right in the chest. Was an accident. This girl, Sophie, shot him by mistake. That's what did it for him. Only thing is, maybe it was for the best. Quick, you know?"

"You suggesting I go up and shoot Macca with a bow and arrow?"

Lewis yawned, scratched his Afro, untangling a knot, staying cool.

"No way, man," he said. "I'm just saying . . ."

"What are you saying?"

"Dunno."

"Yeah."

Lewis felt uncomfortable around Ed. Knew he wanted to be gone from here. So he left him to stack the logs on the log pile and walked over to the table. Pulled up a chair. Helped himself to a glass of lemonade.

Trinity was deep in conversation with Amelia.

"So, if I understand you right," Trey was saying, "the disease is parasitical."

"That's right," said Amelia.

"What, you mean like a bug?" Lewis butted in. "An insect thing?"

"Along those lines, yes," said Amelia.

"It moved from this tribe in the rain forest into the scientists who were studying them," Trio explained. "Scientists from Promithios, from Medicines Without Frontiers, and loads of other organizations out there."

"From all around the world," said Amelia.

Lewis remembered the Twisted Kids talking about Promithios back at the museum. It's where their parents had worked and where they'd been hiding out when Blue found them.

"They were immunized and screened for all known diseases," said Amelia. "They were the experts in their field."

"So how come no one spotted this new sickness?" said Lewis.

"It was able to hide," Trey explained. "Amelia thinks it's in some ways intelligent."

"What? Like an intelligent tiny bug thing from outer space?" Lewis nodded his head, grinning. "Cool. I mean, *bad*, yeah, but cool."

"Well, maybe not intelligent like we'd understand it," said Amelia. "But it knows how to survive."

"When the parasite gets into you, it can control you," said Trey. "It was like the bugs hot-wired themselves into people, started becoming part of them, part of their brains, part of their bodies. They were able to mimic human cells, disguise themselves as, like, blood cells or whatever."

"Individually they're nothing," said Trio. "But once they get inside enough bodies, once there's millions of them out there, they create a sort of superbrain. A neural network. Like how scientists sometimes link up loads of different computers to work together solving massive problems."

"And hackers," said Lewis. "Mate of mine was a hacker. Used to link up computers from all over."

"That's exactly it," said Amelia, and Lewis felt proud he'd understood some of this.

"Think of the parasites as hackers," Amelia went on. "Or as a computer virus, a Trojan horse, getting inside every computer in the network and controlling it, able to stop any antivirus software from detecting it and destroying it. It was most important for the disease to hide, to keep itself secret until it was strong enough. That's what was going on with Promithios. We used to have dealings with them, and I always felt that there was a lot they weren't telling us. I could never have known that what they weren't telling us about was *you*."

Amelia was looking at Trinity with a look of sympathy and wonder.

"It was only our parents," said Trey. "Nobody else in the company even knew. Our moms and dads realized there was something wrong with us even before we were born, and they closed up tight, hid themselves away. Hid us away . . . the Twisted Kids."

"It was the disease working," said Amelia. "Controlling their minds. And it's almost as if you were a sort of experiment, as if the disease was . . ." Amelia suddenly stopped speaking, gave a little gasp, and put her hand to her mouth. She half rose from her seat, staring at Trinity.

The Twisted Kids had collapsed, so that they were bent double, their faces resting on the table.

Amelia slumped back into her seat, too exhausted to get up.

Ed came over, looking concerned.

"What's happened?"

"They suddenly went all wobbly and faint," said Amelia. "Their eyes rolled back in their heads and down they went. I think they've passed out. Are they all right? I hope they're all right."

And then she gasped again. There was something moving on Trinity's back.

"Oh. My. God," said Lewis.

Mr. Three had woken up.

43

Mr. Three had a shrunken, shriveled-up appearance, with a squashed nose, a few strands of greasy hair, and little gray teeth. His skin was so wrinkled that he looked older, like a little old man, or a goblin, but Lewis knew that must be an illusion. The guy was the same age as Trey and Trio. Had to be. He was part of them, had been born with them. He was twitching and blinking, coughing to clear his throat. He blinked again and peered around at everyone with bloodshot eyes.

"What are you looking at?" he said in the nasal, hard-edged voice of a teenager whose voice was changing. "You never seen a talking growth before?"

Nobody knew what to say to this.

"So? What am I, late for the party?" he said. He had two skinny arms that flailed about and thrashed in the air as if he wasn't used to using them.

"What's the matter?" he said. "Didn't expect me to show up? Law of three, peeps. If you want Trey and Trio, you get me as well. We come as a set."

"What have you done to the others?" Amelia asked.

"Done, Granny? I haven't *done* anything. We're just readjusting, kind of recalibrating, yeah? I mean, when all's said and done, we're one. Don't worry. I won't be here long. They'll come around in a minute. I've had a sudden rush of blood to the head, if you see what I mean, and they've had a sudden drastic oxygen shortage. Once in a blue moon I get a chance to sing—*I'm coming out!* That's me. Jack-in-the-box. Mr. Three. It's demeaning, don't you think? That name. Like I'm some kind of a freak. Circus performer. The Amazing Mr. Three! You know what I always wanted to be called?"

"What?" said Lewis.

"Colin," said the little creature. "Call me Colin."

"Why Colin?" Lewis asked.

"Why not? You got a problem with that name?"

"Nope."

Mr. Three coughed again, retched, and then spat out a sticky yellow gob of phlegm, laced with blood.

"Are you all right, Colin?" Amelia asked. "Can I get you a glass of water?"

"Oh, stop it, stop it," Three cackled. "I can't take it anymore. Stop with the Colin stuff."

"But you said . . ."

"Stupid old git!" Three shook his head at Amelia, laughing horribly. "'Course I don't want to be called Colin. Who'd choose to be called Colin?"

"Well, *what*, then?" said Lewis. "What you want us to call you?"

"You can call me anything you bloody well like," said

Mr. Three. "It doesn't make any difference really, does it? I'm not going to be around for long. These little spurts of consciousness never last. They'll start to take control again, them two, the sleeping beauties, and I'll be sent back to Coventry. I'm just trying to take it all in, sorting through all their new thoughts and memories, but it seems like you've been filling their heads with all kinds of crap. There's too much for me, it's overloading my circuits. And the damned fallen, they are loud today! Woke me up with their singing. Never known anything like it. . . ."

"What do you mean?" Ed looked anxious, wanting to know more. "You mean sickos? Grown-ups? What's happening?"

"There's a lot of them on their way. There's a wave breaking."

Trio was stirring. She started to rise, pushing with her hands on the tabletop, dragging up Trey, whose head lolled down on a floppy neck. Trio looked drowsy and confused. She fixed on Lewis and tried to focus.

"It's him, isn't it?" she said. "He's woken up. *Embarrassing.* I'm like a drunk at a teenage party who's been at Daddy's vodka. Oh wow, that is some monster headache. Ciao, Mr. Three, how have you been?"

"You can call me Colin."

"Yeah? Last time it was Neil."

"Ha-ha, yeah. That was a good one."

"Nearly as good as Roger."

"Roger and out . . ."

"You going so soon?"

Mr. Three stretched out his arms and yawned.

"I don't want to nod out, Trio. Truth is, I want to stay forever, but you two are too strong for me. I was just telling your friends here about the wave."

"What wave?"

"The fallen, they're coming, sister. We need to be careful. . . ."

"Please. You need to tell us what you mean exactly." Ed reached out toward him, as if he was going to shake him to keep him awake, but he held back at the last moment, unsure about touching him.

Now Trey was coming around. His eyelids fluttered. He groaned, put a hand to his head, and squeezed his temples with thumb and fingers.

"I feel sick," he said.

"At least you're awake," said Mr. Three, and he sounded sad and disappointed. "You can smell the coffee. . . ." He yawned again. "Be careful. . . ."

He closed his eyes, curled up, and folded himself into Trinity's back.

Ed swore, then looked at Amelia, who pretended she hadn't heard him.

"Well, that was special." Brooke was standing in the doorway from the house. Lewis had no idea how long she'd been there. All their attention had been on Mr. Three.

"Sorry," said Trio. "He doesn't get out much. Not a lot of social skills."

Brooke took a few paces from under the climbing rose and stood in the sun. Lewis realized he hadn't seen her here in the garden before. She spent all her time with Macca. . . .

He felt suddenly cold.

"Is he asleep?" he asked. Brooke shook her head, said nothing, looked like she'd crack into pieces if she tried to speak.

Ed put his arms around her and she collapsed against his shoulder, shaking with sobs.

So that was it then. The vacation was over.

44

"We're thinking we're going to stay here."

"Yeah? You sure? We could really use you guys." Ed looked at Trinity. He was still trying to get his head around the memory of the little guy on their back coming alive.

"Well, you'll have to admit we haven't exactly been a lot of help so far," said Trio, and she looked down at her feet embarrassed.

"You mean Macca?" Ed asked.

"Yeah."

"To be fair, you *did* try to warn us."

"It wasn't good enough."

Ed shrugged. He wasn't going to argue the point.

"The thing is," said Trey, "we think we can be more use here. There's so much Amelia knows, and together with what *we* know about Promithios, and, well, how we *are* and everything."

"It's your decision." Ed turned away. He was trying to get the car ready. Packing supplies into the trunk. Trinity followed him, walking fast on their two good legs.

"Amelia's old," said Trey. "She might not live much longer. This is our last chance."

"Last chance of what?" Ed asked, hefting a box of beans that Amelia had given him into the back of the car.

"Of finding a cure," said Trio.

"You really think that's possible?" Ed stopped what he was doing.

"There's a chance," said Trey. "A chance we might be able to work out a way to fight this thing. It's got to be worth it."

"You mean it's more important than chasing off around the countryside looking for Ella?"

"That's not what we meant," said Trey.

"It's true, though." Ed held out his hands in a hopeless, empty gesture. "I don't even really know myself why I'm doing this. So I'm not arguing with you. You're right. Stay here. Talk to Amelia. Work out a way to kick the disease in the balls. Do it for Macca, and all the other kids who've died. Once we've found Ella—*if* we find Ella—we'll come back and pick you up before heading back into town."

Ed smiled, trying to reassure Trinity. It all seemed so simple and straightforward. But so far one of them had been killed and they hadn't even begun to look for Sam's sister.

Trinity hurried back inside, passing Ebenezer, Kyle, and Lewis, who were bringing more gear out. As Ed was stashing his sword in the trunk, Lewis came over and asked if he could take a look at it. Ed shrugged and passed it to him.

"It's called a mortuary sword," he explained. "From the Civil War."

"American Civil War?"

"English."

"Never knew we had one." Lewis was swinging the sword through the air, feeling its balance and weight.

"Heavy," he said.

Ed couldn't believe Lewis had never heard of the English Civil War. "You know," he said, "Oliver Cromwell, Roundheads and Cavaliers? Royalists versus Parliamentarians?"

"Yeah? Take your word for it. Who won?"

"Cromwell. He beheaded the English king, Charles the First."

"Cool. Never was too bothered about history at school. This is a really solid blade, though."

Ed took it back from him and put it into the trunk.

"It's almost a club, it's so heavy," he said. "It'll smash through anything. But it takes some lifting, and if you get caught up in fighting too long it feels like your arm's gonna fall off."

"I like my spear," said Lewis. "I'm not so sure about swords. I picked mine up with all this samurai gear back at the museum. You know, the place next door with all the old crap in it. The other museum?"

"The Victoria and Albert?"

"Yeah, that's the joint. I mean, it's okay, my katana. I thought it was gonna be my piece for life, but I'm more used to a spear. Sword is hard to control, man. Takes some practice. Training. A spear . . . A spear is a spear."

"You need an ax, like good old Brain-biter," said Kyle, coming up behind them and doing a demonstration that nearly took Lewis's head off, like Charles I all over again.

"Watch yourself, man," said Lewis, backing away, scratching his Afro. "You ain't got no finesse with that thing. It's a mad weapon."

"It's a great weapon," said Kyle, and he kissed the blade. "Beats a gay sword any day."

"How can a sword be gay?" Ed protested.

"This is a man's weapon," said Kyle.

"Still reckon a spear's the best," said Lewis.

"A throwing spear is best of all," said Ebenezer, attaching his own stack of lighter javelins to the roof rack. "You won't let the sickos get close to you with their stink and their germs."

"We'll see," said Kyle. "We will see."

"I hope we won't," said Ed. "I hope we won't have to use any of these weapons again for a long while."

"That'd just be boring," said Kyle.

"What about what that mad thing on Trinity's back was babbling about?" said Lewis. "A tidal wave of sickos coming?"

"We've seen them," said Ed. "Marching into London from all around. Joining up. Shadowman reckons they're forming an army."

"What if there's more coming?" said Lewis.

"I don't know." Ed slammed the trunk shut. "This has all gotten way complicated. Did Mr. Three mean the sickos already in London, or something else? Or was he just babbling? I asked Trinity—they didn't know either."

"Babbling is right," said Kyle. "I ain't gonna listen to no shaved monkey. Now let's get rocking, shall we? You driving, Lewis? Or do you want me to take over?"

"I'm driving," said Lewis, and he settled into the driver's seat. "Where we headed?"

"From what Amelia said, our best bet's to try Slough." Ed climbed in the passenger side and picked up the road atlas from where it was lying on the seat. "She thinks there's a settlement of some kind there. Makes sense, it's a fairly big town. Anyone seen Brooke?"

"She's coming," said Ebenezer, getting in the back.

Ed looked over to see Brooke walking slowly from the house, deep in thought. She'd been quiet since Macca had died, but after her first breakdown she hadn't cried again. She looked older somehow, tired. Halfway to the car she tugged off her bandage and chucked it away. The skin on her forehead was pinched and puckered, shiny. She pulled her knitted cap on, not bothering to cover the scar with it. She got in the car and sat in one of the single seats.

Plenty of room now.

"Where's Trinity?" she asked, without looking at anyone.

"Staying here." Ed didn't feel like going into any long explanations right now, and nobody pressed him.

"We ready, then?" said Brooke.

"Yeah." Lewis started the engine and eased the car forward, steering it around the gravel area in front of the house and back onto the driveway. With new leaves out on the trees, everywhere looked pretty and peaceful in the bright sunlight. Ed certainly appreciated being in the countryside and realized how much he'd missed it, living in the city for the last year. The only thing was, he'd grown used to the city. He understood it. He knew its dangers. The countryside felt different, new. It was too easy to think there was nothing to fear out here. It all looked so nice and green and empty. But what dangers did it hide? He couldn't read this environment as well as he could the streets of London.

They were soon on the main road and heading through the woods toward Slough. It turned out the town was only a few minutes' drive away, and before they knew it they were in among houses and shops as they passed through the village of Burnham, which blurred into Slough itself, with nothing to show where one ended and the other began.

Slough seemed deserted. They found the main road through the town and drove all the way to the other side, looking for signs of life. The road was a long, dreary drag of car showrooms, DIY stores, builders' merchants, low factory blocks, and offices. They briefly passed through a more residential area of small, ugly, redbrick houses before finding themselves back at the M4, at the turnoff they would have taken if they hadn't found the road blocked by sickos. They had a brief discussion about what to do and then turned around and headed back into town. This time, when they were halfway through, they turned off to the right when they came to the first major road. It was as depressing and deserted as everywhere else, and they were just about to give up when Brooke started pointing and shouting.

"There, there, there . . ."

Ed looked around. Just in time to see a kid scampering off the street and ducking out of sight between two houses.

"Well, there's people here, then," said Kyle, who had also spotted it. "Not very friendly ones, though."

Ed banged the windshield. "There's another one," he said as a girl stuck her head around from the back of a truck and then quickly jerked it back. "Keep going up this road, Lewis."

The houses were thinning out, and it looked like they were heading for open country, but there were signs of life at last. Graffiti all over the place, painted on the houses and on the road, on cars and walls, on rotting advertising billboards, covering street signs, sidewalks, storefronts. They were mostly mindless slogans—SLOUGH RULES, SLOUGH RUDE BOYS, WINDSOR SCUM KEEP OUT, ZOMBIE FREE ZONE, WE WILL KICK YOUR ASS, MACNAMARA IS CHAMPION KILLER, WE ARE THE YOUNG, DIE, SICKBAGS, DIE, GO BACK TO YOUR SLUM, BRACKNELL—plus the usual swear words next to pictures of guns and knives and severed heads and the occasional obscene body part. Here and there was some more imaginative and artistic stuff, fancy tags and decorations, but mostly it was just rubbish.

And then they came to a school, the sign too defaced to be able to read its name. It was modern looking, made of a central, taller, ring-shaped building with other wings coming off it in a sort of star shape. There was a fence around the grounds that had been reinforced, and someone had built a rather rickety lookout tower by the main gates. Two kids watched them from the platform at the top, and others were clustered at the gates, safely on the other side.

"Looks like they heard us coming," said Kyle. "Hope they've baked a cake."

"What you want me to do?" Lewis asked.

Ed thought about it. "Stop here. I'll go over to the gates and talk to them."

"What if they try and attack us?" Kyle said.

"Why would they do that?" said Ed.

"From their graffiti, they don't seem too welcoming."

"From their graffiti, they seem like a bunch of halfwits."

Ed got out of the car.

Got his sword from the trunk.

Walked to the fence.

45

The kids by the gate were a mixed bunch. All ages. There were a few very small, grubby-faced ones, a larger group of eleven- and twelve-year-olds, and also some older, tougher-looking ones.

None of them were smiling. All of them were armed.

"Where you from?" a little girl shouted at Ed as he got close.

"London."

"What you doing here then? You get lost or something?"

"I'm looking for someone."

"Who?"

"Girl called Ella."

"Never heard of her."

"She was with some other kids. Maeve, Robbie . . ."

"Never heard of them. What you really doing here?"

"Who's in charge? Not you, I imagine."

Another voice cut in— "No, *I* am. At least until Josa gets back."

Ed looked over to where a tall boy with a shaved head

was approaching the gates. He was carrying a shotgun and had a sleeveless denim jacket and badly done homemade tattoos up his arms and over his face.

"Why don't you drive inside the gates, where it's safe?" he said, trying to appear friendly, which was difficult with his tattooed face. "Then we can talk properly. I can tell you everything that's going on around here if you ain't in't local."

"You sure?"

"Wouldn't say it if I wasn't. If you want some help we can give it you, but I ain't shouting through the gate, and you'll be a lot safer on this side." The boy sounded reasonable, even if he didn't look it. Ed returned to the car.

"Not sure we're in luck with Ella," he said through Lewis's open window. "But they said we should drive in, at least. What d'you reckon?" He aimed this last question at Lewis, who, along with Brooke, seemed the most sensible of the kids.

"Gotta be better than staying out on the street," said Lewis.

Ed switched his attention to Brooke. "You okay with that?"

"Guess so. Even if Ella's not here," said Brooke, "we can find out more about where to look. They got to be more clued in than Amelia and her lot. The old geezers ain't had no dealings with the outside world for months."

"Good point." Ed got back in the car, and Lewis eased it forward as the local kids opened the gates.

"Go careful, driver," said Kyle, with a smirk. "We wouldn't want to run any of them over when they been so nice and friendly."

The kids formed two lines on either side of the gate, watching in silence as the car drove in. The tattooed boy showed them where to stop, in a parking lot at the front of the school. There were a few cars parked there, and Ed spotted others that had been moved to the fence and turned on their sides to reinforce the barricades.

He wondered why these few had been left. Maybe they had gas in them.

Tattoo Boy walked over to them as Ed and Kyle got out. He sized Kyle up. Swinging his shotgun around like it was nothing. Not bothered about any threat. Several of the larger boys had formed up in a wide circle, two of them carrying crossbows.

"So you're the head teacher, are you?" asked Kyle, glancing over at the school building.

"Deputy head," the boy replied with a grin. "Girl called Josa runs the joint, but she's out hunting right now. When she gets back, we'll have a talk, yeah?"

"You can't talk now?" Kyle asked.

"Can't do nothing without Josa's say-so."

"We'll come inside, then."

"Nah," said the boy. "Best you stay out here till we know what Josa wants to do."

"How long's that gonna be?"

"As long as it takes."

"You got a name?" Kyle asked.

"Kenton."

"So you want us to hang here for a bit, do you, Kenton?"

"Something like that, yeah."

Kenton checked out the car. Brooke was sitting staring out of the window. Behind her Ebenezer was tapping out a rhythm on the back of the seat, ignoring them. Lewis looked like he was nodding off. His eyes were half shut and he was zoned out, miles away. They hardly looked like the most dangerous gang in town. Kenton obviously wasn't taking any chances, though. He was going to keep them isolated.

"We'll see you later, then." Ed walked back to the car and got in. No point in arguing. Kyle followed, and Kenton went back to his mates, had a conversation with them, turning now and then to check out the car and its passengers.

"They don't seem quite so friendly now they've got us in here," Ed explained. "Looks like we're sitting it out until the girl in charge gets back."

"And then what?" Brooke asked.

"And then we don't know what. I'm hoping they're going to have some useful info for us, though."

"Ella and her friends are either here or they're not," said Ebenezer. "We are wasting time. Can't one of these boys tell us what is what? Why do we need to wait?"

"Because it's what they want."

"What else do they want?"

"We'll find out sooner or later." Ed slid down in his seat and closed his eyes. Thought he might try to sleep, like Lewis.

"This is boring," said Brooke. She was sitting with her feet up on the back of the seat in front of her. "They really gonna keep us here all day? Why won't they at least let us into the building?"

"We're all right out here," said Kyle. "We got a good line of sight. Anything dodgy we just—"

"Just what?" Brooke interrupted.

"Smash our way out through the gate like in films."

"You reckon we can?"

"Dunno."

"I was asking Lewis, not you, Kyle."

"Dunno," said Lewis. Not asleep after all, taking it all in. "Wouldn't want to risk it, though. We damage the car, we're stuck."

"Does *anyone* have an exit plan?" Brooke looked around the car.

Only Ed replied.

"We wait," he said.

"That doesn't answer my question."

"I'm thinking about it."

"Well, while you're thinking, I'd like to talk."

"Surprise, surprise," said Kyle. "Typical girl. What you want to talk about? Fashion and that? Shoes? Boy bands? Makeup tips. You got any makeup tips, Ebenezer?"

"Shut up, Kyle," Ebenezer snapped. "I am a man."

"I don't doubt it," said Kyle. "I know, let's talk about feelings. How are we all feeling? How are you feeling, Ebenezer?"

"Oh, I am *so* laughing out loud," said Brooke. "Actually, I want to talk about what the old folks told you. What Amelia knows. About the disease. What did you find out?"

"Dunno," said Kyle. "Wasn't really listening."

"Wasn't asking you," said Brooke. "I was asking Ed."

"You want the short version?" said Lewis.

"I want any version."

"It's bugs. Parasites. They've gotten into the adults and they're controlling them. Plus, they can communicate with each other. It's a hive-mind deal. They're all on the same network. The word has gone out on Facebook, and they're all meeting up for one monster party."

"I'd rather talk about shoes and boy bands, to tell you the truth," said Kyle, and Ebenezer laughed.

"I don't get it," said Brooke, ignoring them. "How do they do that? How do they communicate? Telepathy?"

"Amelia reckons it's probably, like, an ultrasound thing," said Lewis. "Insect noises we can't hear. That's what the sentinels are for, to amplify the signal and pass it along. Come join the fun."

"But what are they massing for?" Brooke asked.

"They getting together for the big pop," said Lewis. "The next infestation. Happens every sixteen years, when their spores are ripe. They planning to get inside anyone who wasn't around the first time. Namely us."

"Nice," said Brooke. "They're gonna shoot their germs into the air and try to infect us all?"

"Something like that."

"So, if it's going to happen every sixteen years or whatever, that means this goes on forever. Each new generation getting infected. If we ever had kids, they'd have to go through what we're going through now. . . . God. I was hoping that learning about this stuff would make it less scary. It's the opposite. . . ."

"I ain't having no kids," said Kyle. "No way, man."

"Oh, I am so disappointed," said Brooke. "I wanted you to be my baby daddy."

"You're funny," said Kyle, and he actually laughed, a genuine laugh. "I like you."

"That's really made my week," said Brooke. She was silent for a minute. Then she said, "Seriously, though—we've got to stop them. Otherwise, us kids—we're never going to survive this, are we?"

46

Ed was aware of the day slipping away. Of losing time. Everything he'd learned about the disease had terrified him. He should be back in London, not chasing around out here. Brooke was right—they had to stop Saint George's army. He had a good mind to simply drive out of here and head toward town. Tell Sam he'd tried and failed.

He decided this would be his last shot. If the kids here were no help, then it was time to steer east instead of west.

The sun moved steadily across the sky. Kyle and Ebenezer couldn't stand the tedium and got out of the car. They found an old tennis ball in the long grass near the fence and spent ages chucking it to each other, gradually moving farther apart. Lewis really did nod off this time, and Ed moved into the back of the car to sit with Brooke.

This was the first real chance they'd had to be alone together since Ed had arrived at the museum, and it was a good opportunity to catch up. If nothing else it would kill some time. They both talked about what they'd been through in the last year, good times and bad. Brooke really had changed a lot. Grown up. Gotten some sense into her head. She'd always been smart—street-smart—but she'd never been exactly *wise*. Here in the car, alone, with nobody to score points off, she got through to Ed.

Ed tried to keep the conversation light and to steer clear of any of the really heavy stuff that had gone down. He didn't want her to know how he'd changed as well. It seemed to him that what she'd gained he'd lost. She'd become more human and he'd become less. He'd become harder and more cynical. To the outside world he was good old Ed, sensible and *nice*. To himself . . .

He sometimes felt almost as if he'd died somewhere along the way, and only came alive when he had his mortuary sword in his hand. Was that why he was pursuing this mad quest? To show he still had a heart?

Eventually they got around to what had happened to DogNut and Courtney, and Brooke told Ed the details of the awful battle by Green Park tube station for the first time. Ed felt an acid burning in his guts, wished he could have been there to smash those sickos to pieces.

Brooke was crying, remembering DogNut and Courtney. Ed put his arm around her but stayed dry-eyed. He didn't think he'd cried since Jack had died.

That was a bad day. The worst.

Losing Jack and Bam, his best friends.

He still remembered the sicko who'd done it. Would never forget him. Greg the butcher, who'd been driving the bus that had rescued them in Rowhurst and driven them to London. The bus where he'd first met Brooke. Greg had claimed he couldn't get sick, and had then killed his own boy before . . .

Bastard.

Ed would give anything to see Greg again. To cut him into bits. He knew he never would. That had all been a year back, far away. Chances were, Greg had died a long time ago. . . .

A massive thump on the side of the car snapped Ed back into the here and now. He looked around to see a dirty splotch on the window and Kyle and Ebenezer both laughing. One of them must have thrown the ball at the car.

Children.

Ed was going to say something boring and fatherly about being careful not to break the windows when he realized that Kyle had been trying to get his attention. He looked over to where the big hench was pointing.

A group of kids was coming in through the gates. This must be Josa returning from the hunt. There were about twenty of them and they were dragging along what appeared to be a group of four or five sickos. The sickos' hands were tied behind their backs and there were chains around their necks.

Ed got out of the car, feeling stiff and cranky. He looked up at the sky. The sun was far over in the west. It was late in the day. The moon was showing in the sky. Bloodred, like the circle on the Japanese flag. He kicked a wheel in frustration. He hated being dicked around like this.

"Stay with the car," he said to Kyle and Ebenezer. Kyle was too much of a liability. He was in a worse mood than Ed and was likely to shoot his mouth off and try to wind someone up. Ed didn't need a fight now. Instead he asked Brooke to come with him, and Lewis must have woken up, because there he was, standing next to them, even though Ed hadn't noticed him get out of the car. His eyelids were still drooping as if he was fighting to stay awake, and he was scratching his head and yawning.

"Whassup?" he said. "They gone and caught theirselves some grown-ups?"

"Let's go and find out." Ed started walking.

The three of them crossed the parking lot toward the new arrivals, who spotted them coming and formed into a defensive line. Ed smiled. Did they really think they were under attack?

This was one paranoid bunch of kids, and it had made them mean and suspicious and not to be trusted. Ed paused, hung back, not wanting to appear threatening in any way. Lewis shuffled on a few paces and then stopped as well. He yanked up his pants, which had been hanging off his ass, showing his underwear. They immediately slipped down again.

Kenton came out of the school building and approached the new arrivals. Ed saw him talk to a small, wiry girl with her hair tied back in a viciously tight knot. This must be Josa. She had a sicko on a leash and was carrying a spear. She looked mouthy and sharp. Someone you wouldn't want to pick a fight with. Ed thought it might be safe to approach now that Kenton must have explained what was going on, and he kept on walking.

Josa watched them come every step of the way, checking them out, sizing them up.

"All right?" she said as they got close, her voice husky and rasping, and she grinned at Ed, showing him that all her front teeth were missing. She had a pointed face, a pointed nose, and small, clever eyes that didn't miss a thing.

"Yeah." Ed smiled back at her. Polite. Aware that his face wasn't the most welcoming sight. "I'm all right. You must be Josa."

"I must be, yeah." She looked from him to Brooke. "You two been scrapping, have you?"

"Yeah." Ed knew that she was referring to the scars they both carried. Decided to let it lie. "But not with each other."

Josa looked pretty beaten up herself. It wasn't just her missing teeth. She had a scar on her top lip, as well as a twisted, mangled ear.

There was a gang of big bruisers around her, like a personal bodyguard. Ed noted that they were all well armed.

"Kenton here tells me you want our help," said Josa.

"Kind of."

"We're looking for some people," said Brooke. Josa switched her attention, holding Brooke's stare, daring her to look away. Ed knew Brooke well enough to know that she wouldn't be faced down, and in the end it was Josa who broke the stare, turning her head to fix on Lewis. She managed to do it in such a way that it looked like her choice.

Lewis didn't try to eyeball her. He lolled there, staring at his shoes, yawning and looking sleepy. Ed had no idea how much of it was an act. Josa gave him barely a second before dismissing him and returning to Ed.

"Some girl called Ella, yeah?" she said. "Am I right?"

"Yeah," Ed replied. "D'you know her?"

"Well, she ain't here. I can tell you that much. But I'm gonna go talk to some people, quiz my top dogs, see if we can't come up with something for you, yeah? We got, like, scouts out all the time. Ain't nothing we don't know about what's going on out there."

"Can we join the meeting?"

"Nah. I don't think so. This is my yard. Don't want you snooping around, checking us out. We don't know where you been. You might just be spies for the Golden Twins down Windsor, or the gaylords down Maidenhead. You're a funny-looking bunch, so in my mind you belong down Ascot with the weirdos."

"We're from London," said Brooke.

"We ain't had anyone come out of London in a way long time."

"We're not spies." Ed held out his hands in an empty gesture.

"Don't matter whether you is or whether you ain't. You ain't coming inside, you get me?"

"What're you doing with them sickos?" Brooke asked.

The grown-ups were a sorry bunch, bruised and battered and bleeding, with burst boils on their faces. The chains around their necks were fixed to long wooden poles so that the kids could keep them at a safe distance, and all the fight had gone out of them.

"We're rounding them up," said Josa. "For the races. And now you're gonna pretend you don't know what the races are, 'cause you claim to be from the smoke."

"We *are* from London," Ed insisted. "And we genuinely don't have a clue what the races might be."

"Well, you're missing out then, ain't you?" said Josa, and she cackled. "Now run off back to your wagon before I change my mind about being nice. We gonna go in and sort ourselves out, then we'll let you know. Okay?"

"Okay." Ed didn't have any choice. He watched them go around the other side of the school building and followed them far enough to see that there were three big pens built out in the open ground, where about twenty more sickos were locked up. They were sitting on the ground, mostly, looking defeated. Ed wanted to go nearer, but some of Josa's boys swaggered over menacingly.

Ed headed back to the car, already working on a plan B.

If Josa was going to mess with him, she had made a big mistake.

47

rooke had a few choice things to say about the local kids on the way back to the car. Lewis didn't seem to be bothered. He'd removed himself from what was going on, shifted to another level. Whether that was a higher level or a lower one, Ed had no way of knowing.

Kyle and Ebenezer were mad as hell, shooting off about being treated like this, swearing, and calling the locals all the filthy names they could think of.

Which was quite a lot.

"We should go in there and bust a few heads," Kyle protested.

"There's too many of them, Kyle," Ed pointed out. "And they don't look like wimps. It'd be stupid. We can outsmart them if we need to. And maybe they'll give us something useful."

"We're gonna lose a whole day at this rate," said Kyle. "It's gonna be dark soon, and I doubt they're gonna let us stay here."

"You think I don't know all that?" Ed shouted. He'd

finally lost his temper. "You think I want to hang around here while they play their stupid games?"

"We should never have come in here," said Ebenezer.

"Thanks for stating the obvious, Ebenezer. But there's no easy way out."

"Ed's right," said Lewis. "I been checking out the gate. There's always two guys up on the platform in the watchtower and another couple guarding the road."

"Turn the car around anyway." Ed forced himself to calm down. Getting angry didn't help. "Face it toward the gates, just in case. Then let's see what we can come up with."

They sat in the car and discussed their options. Kyle's suggestions all involved extreme violence, but Ed wanted to get out of this without hurting anyone, if possible, despite having recurring fantasies of cutting Josa's head off with his mortuary sword. Lewis had some better ideas. He was more a fan of stealth, which fitted with Ed's way of thinking.

It was growing dark and they were still talking when Kenton banged on the roof of the car.

"You wanna talk?" he shouted. "We'll talk."

Ed was first out of the car. His legs felt stiff and his back hurt. He tried to ease his muscles and loosen his joints. Lewis was next out. He shambled away from the car and took a piss in the long grass. As he did so, Kyle shifted into the driver's seat, and Ebenezer slipped out of the door on the far side without anyone paying him much attention.

Last out was Brooke. She slid her door back and sat on the step, watching.

"So what have you got for us, then?" Ed asked. No harm in being optimistic.

"This and that. Patience, dude. Josa's on her way."

"Great. I can hardly wait."

Kenton took stock of Ed. Probably had him down as just some useless rich kid who'd lost one too many fights and gotten himself carved up in the process.

Kenton had no worries. He had his shotgun with him. It annoyed Ed the way he played with it, swinging it around in one hand like a toy, showing it off, but trying to look like it was no big deal. The message was pretty clear. He had a gun and Ed didn't. No contest.

Ed and Lewis were unarmed, though there were weapons within reach on the roof. They didn't want to risk provoking the locals.

Josa arrived with her team around her. Her boy band. She looked full of herself, enjoying the situation, being in power. She strutted across the parking lot, laughing and joking with her boys.

"It's been a long day." Ed kept his voice polite. "We want to get going."

"Yeah, yeah, yeah," said Josa. "We've had a chat. I've asked my guys what they know."

"And?"

Josa opened her hands in an empty gesture, an amused glint in her eye.

"They don't know nothing. Sorry and that, yeah? We ain't seen no one from your gang up this way. Or out in the field. Ain't heard nothing from any of the other camps."

"It took you all this time to find that out?"

"I had to wash and get something to eat and put my little

boy to bed and catch up on all the goss. The world don't revolve around you, Mr. Funny Face."

"No," said Ed. "It appears to revolve around you."

"Mm. But listen, we ain't gonna let you leave with nothing."

"That's good of you."

"Your best bet is to go to Windsor. They got the biggest camp, the most kids. If I was coming out of London and wanted to hook up with anyone around here, I'd head there. They got the castle. They're sitting pretty."

"Our friends wanted to move to the country, to get away from cities."

"There's Sandhurst, then. Is a smaller place. Or Bracknell. The smallest camp of all, though, the most country-style, is Ascot. But they ain't nobody lives out in the open, talking to the trees and flowers, playing FarmVille. Too dangerous. You get me? All the kids is in towns."

"But Ascot's the smallest camp?" Ed asked.

"Yeah. They all nuts in Ascot, though. Seriously, I was you, I'd try Windsor first."

"It's just over the way," said Kenton. "Other side of the highway. Go down through Eton and you're there. Three, four miles at most. If you're quick you can make it in, like, an hour or so. 'Course, we're sorry it's got so late and that, and dark with it. Should make it more exciting for you, though, yeah? More of an adventure."

"Yeah," said Josa. "We might even put some bets on how long it takes you and which of you don't make it."

"What do you mean, a couple of hours?" Ed asked,

although he was pretty sure of the answer. He'd been wondering about Josa's plans. Had discussed it with the others. Why she might want to keep them here. Whether she'd been balancing the risks of a fight. Why there were a few other cars in the parking lot and they hadn't all been carted over to reinforce the fence. Wondering what might count as treasure around here.

"Why would it take us a couple of hours to drive four miles?" He was doing all the talking, letting them forget about Lewis, who had hung about on the edge of the parking lot for a while, fiddling with his Afro, staring at the sky, and generally looking like a dope, before wandering over to stand with some of the Slough kids. He was chatting with them, as if he had no interest in the main conversation. Even Ed kept forgetting about him, and hoped he could be trusted to do his part if it came to it.

So Ed was by himself. Out in the open. Exposed. The center of attention.

Kenton was waggling his shotgun, some of his team holding back like before, watching, with their crossbows. It was all locked down. Josa was confident. Unafraid. There was no threat.

"We could drive there in ten minutes," Ed went on.

"That's the other thing we wanted to talk to you about," said Josa. "That sweet motor of yours."

So there it was. No big surprise. These kids wanted working vehicles. The other cars in the parking lot must have gas in their tanks. That's why they kept them. A big car like the van—that was a useful piece of equipment.

Which is why he was prepared.

"Yeah?" he said, acting innocent. "I don't get it."

"Well, see." Josa exchanged a look with some of her boys, who smiled back at her, enjoying this. "We like the look of your motor. And we was wondering if you, like, wanted to, like, borrow it to us."

"The thing is . . ." Ed was trying hard to stay calm, neutral. There was a crowd of spectators forming. Wanting to see these intruders made to look small. Lewis was lost among them somewhere.

"The thing is what?" said Josa.

"The thing is, we really need this car. We've got to get back to London when this is all over, and before that we've a lot of ground to cover looking for our friends, you know?"

"That's not really our worry, though, is it, Funny Face?"

"I appreciate that, Josa. But I've got my guys here who I'm responsible for. We can't just walk off out of here into the night unprotected. Without that car, we don't stand much of a chance."

"I certainly wouldn't bet on you," said Josa, and she laughed, her gang joining in. "As I say, you're not my worry. You don't mean nothing to me. My job is to look after my people here."

"And my job is to look after my people here. So it's stalemate, I guess."

"Not really," said Josa. "I mean, you do the math, Funny Face. You're kind of outnumbered. And outgunned. And out everything."

"Is that what you think?"

"It is. And I ain't gonna discuss it no more, it's too boring, and it's past my bedtime. Put it like this, posh boy, you can walk outta here as you are—we'll even let you take some of your weapons. Or you can take us on and get whipped and go crawling outta here in your boxers."

"Or we can go out the way we came in." Ed was sounding quite cheerful now. "In the car. Nice and easy. Toodle-pip."

"I ain't offering that. That's not an option."

"Oh, but it is an option, actually."

"Ain't no option," said Kenton, and he laughed, doing a silly twirling move with his shotgun.

"You think we haven't learned how to look after ourselves in London?" Ed asked Josa.

"I think you're all mouth, Funny Face, and I've heard enough of what comes out of it."

"Yeah," said Kenton. "Just give us the keys and be on your way. Or Mr. Shottie here will tattoo you worse than my face."

Once again he did the silly twirling thing, only this time Lewis moved in. And he moved much faster than Ed could have imagined. He seemed to come out of nowhere.

"Say good-bye to your little friend," he said as he twisted Kenton's wrist and snatched the gun out of his hand before he really knew what was going on. A shout of protest went up from the gathered kids, but Lewis turned on them and leveled the gun, which shut them up.

In the confusion, and while everyone was distracted by Lewis, Ed made his own move. He barged past Josa's boys and grabbed her, getting an arm around her neck. She tried to bite him, but her lack of front teeth meant she didn't manage to do anything worse than slime his arm. Brooke chucked

Ed his sword, and he held it out to the side, daring any of the kids to attack him as he backed toward the car.

"I'm sorry about this," Ed murmured in Josa's ear. "But it was kind of your idea."

Lewis had come to his side now and they stepped in time with each other, almost as if they'd spent days rehearsing this. Now came the tricky part, trusting Kyle to drive the car to the gates without losing control. He fired up the engine and started to trundle forward, Ed, Lewis, and Josa walking in front, illuminated by the full beam of the headlights. Josa was kicking and screaming and trying to wriggle free. Ed ignored her. He'd developed enough muscle in the last year to have arms like steel.

They kept in a tight bunch so that nobody would be tempted to take a potshot at them with a crossbow, and the other kids were all too scared of Kenton's gun to risk getting up close and personal.

Kyle was trying to keep the car steady, but Ed was nervous. They were almost in more danger of being run over by him than of being attacked by the Slough kids.

Would they really let them walk out of here, though, without putting up some sort of fight?

That's where Ebenezer came in. It was all up to him now.

48

Ebenezer was supposed to have dodged through the long grass to the fence and worked his way around the back of the building, using the undergrowth as cover.

Had he done it? Ed had heard nothing yet. No shouts from the locals. That was a good thing, wasn't it? It meant he hadn't been spotted. Ed clung to that hope. Without Ebenezer's help, they might not make it to the gates. It was only a matter of time before the locals got up the courage to rush them. Kenton was really mad. He was stalking alongside them, shouting insults, but didn't have the guts to come for his gun. He'd been made to look like a fool and caught off guard. He'd let his boss down.

As for Josa, she was keeping up her own string of abuse, calling Ed every name in her arsenal while shouting at her kids to do something. Ed figured he'd heard enough and tightened his grip, choking off her whines.

If Ed got away with this, there were going to be some nasty arguments in school tonight.

Come on, Ebenezer.

At last there was a shout. High and shrill. And then another, and another. The knot of kids was starting to break up. Confusion was spreading.

Now Ed saw Ebenezer running toward the main gates, carrying a javelin in each hand. Nobody was bothering with him, though. Their attention was elsewhere.

It was a drastic plan, but the locals had been prepared to kick Ed and his friends out with no car and no protection in the middle of the night. They were only getting what they deserved.

The shouts were growing louder, some screams, and then the locals were running in all directions, some toward the danger, some back toward the school building. The fighters among them were grouping together. They had a bigger threat than Ed and Lewis on their hands.

Sickos.

Ebenezer had opened their pens.

Ed could see some of them now, wandering about on the other side of the road that led to the gate. He loosened his grip on Josa. Her usefulness was over.

"What the bloody hell have you done?" she shrieked.

"A little diversion." Ed laughed. "You wanna go deal with it? Your troops look a little headless."

"Don't hurt 'em!" Josa yelled at her guys. "We need 'em for the races. Don't hurt 'em. Round 'em up."

"You wanna go help?" Ed repeated.

"Let me go, you asshole."

"Tell your guys not to even think of shooting, or you're coming with us."

Ed hardly needed to say this. Josa's boys seemed to have

completely forgotten about her and were charging about, try-ing to shut down the sickos.

"Let me go."

"Anyone shoots at us I *will* shoot back," said Lewis.

"Let me go!"

Ed shoved her away, and she went stumbling over the ground, trying not to fall over, then ran off toward the sickos, shouting at her team not to hurt them.

Ed and Lewis jumped in the moving car, Brooke hauling them aboard, and Kyle sped up toward the gates. The kids were still guarding it but were in a standoff with Ebenezer, who had his javelins at the ready. As the car got closer, Lewis jumped out, raising the gun.

"Open it," he said, nothing sleepy about him now, and the kids hurriedly scrambled to unlock the gate and pull it open. Then Ebenezer and Lewis were back in the car, and they were speeding away down the main road.

A lone crossbow bolt bounced off the roof, and Ed's team cheered. He twisted around in his seat to see kids at the gates waving their arms and shouting at them, throwing stones and javelins.

"Idiots," said Ebenezer.

"Luckily," said Ed. "Or we'd still be there."

They drove down to the M4, where Kyle pulled over and reluctantly gave the controls back to Lewis.

Kyle kept saying, "I did all right. I reckon I did all right." And no matter how many times Ed agreed with him, he continued saying it, probably in the hope that he would be allowed to keep on driving the car.

Ed was trying to study the map, using the reading light.

He had no idea how late it was. It had been particularly sadistic of Josa to keep them waiting until it got dark.

"Where we heading then, boss?" Kyle asked.

"I think we're gonna have to go back to the old folks' home."

"*Whaaaat?*"

The car was filled with noisy complaints.

"What else can we do?" Ed protested. "It's late, it's dark. At least we've found out a bit about the other settlements."

"Yeah," said Brooke sourly. "From what I can make out, there's six groups of kids around here, in Windsor, Slough, Sandhurst, Maidenhead, Bracknell, and Ascot, and they all hate each other's guts."

"So it's not a great idea to be rocking up in the middle of the night," Ed pointed out. "We'll go back to Amelia's and start out again tomorrow—avoiding Slough—pretend today never happened."

"No way," Kyle shouted. "We've gotta have something to show for all that crap."

"What difference does it make?"

"I'm with Ed," said Lewis. "We ain't gonna achieve nothing driving around in the dark like this. We start again tomorrow. In the light."

Kyle swore. In the end he always did what Ed told him, though, so despite constant grumbling, they drove west along the M4 toward the next junction. Above them the red moon hung in the sky.

"We'll be back in less than ten minutes," Ed tried to soothe Kyle.

They left the M4 and headed north on the country roads.

Until Ed saw something ahead, caught in the car's headlights.

The night was going to be longer than any of them had expected.

"Oh, great," Lewis muttered. "Just what we need."

"What is it?" asked Brooke, leaning forward between the front seats.

The road ahead was completely blocked by sickos.

49

"What do we do?" asked Lewis. "I ain't gonna risk driving through them. Didn't turn out too good last time."

"We'll try to get around them." Ed was twisting in his seat to check that the road behind them was clear.

"Is this it?" said Lewis. "The fresh wave that Mr. Three warned us about?"

"Don't think about that," Ed snapped. "Just get us out of here."

The next few minutes were tense and confusing. Every road they tried seemed to be blocked by sickos. There must have been hundreds of them out there. In the end the kids found themselves going back over the highway and into the open ground to the south.

"Looks like you're gonna get your way, Kyle." Ed sounded gloomy. "Somebody doesn't want us to go back to the Beeches."

"Thank you, God," said Kyle.

"So where are we going to go, then?" asked Ebenezer. "Maybe we should try to go back to London."

"I thought about that." Ed was trying to read the map and figure out where they were. "But we can't get back onto the M4, and all the roads that way are blocked."

"So, what then?" asked Lewis.

"We need to get somewhere safe and sit this thing out. You heard what Josa said about the open countryside. Look for signs to Ascot or Sandhurst. That's our best bet."

"Didn't they used to do horse racing at Ascot?" Brooke asked.

"Yeah," said Kyle. "My dad lost a load of money on the horses. Silly sod."

There were still sickos on these country roads, but only in ones or twos, and the occasional sentinel.

"Where are they all going?" Ebenezer asked.

"Let's hope Slough," said Kyle, and he laughed.

"That wasn't it, then?" said Brooke. "The wave? And if it was, it wasn't so scary. There's hardly any of them."

Ed kept his mouth shut. No point in freaking anyone. He was looking out of the window, trying to calculate how many sickos there must be on the march. There may not be that many here right now, but if you added them up, multiplied them, all around London, all heading in . . .

That was too many to think about. He glanced up at the moon, partly covered by wispy clouds. He'd never seen it look so red. It wasn't a good sign. Blood on the moon.

"I reckon we've got past them," said Lewis, eyes on the road.

And that was when it got really bad.

As they rounded a bend, they almost ran into a pack of them, swarming across the road. Lewis had to slam on the brakes, and Kyle, who didn't have his seat belt on, went sprawling onto the floor with a curse.

The headlights lit up a massive force of sickos, tramping across the countryside. Lewis tried to back away, but there were more sickos coming out of the bushes along the side and filling the road behind them. They began to flow past the car like a flooding river.

Now Ed cursed. He remembered what it had been like the other day, how quickly they'd gotten bogged down when they'd tried to plow their way through. And there were many, many more of them in this mob.

"What do we do?" Brooke asked.

"I don't know." And Ed didn't know. At night, in the dark, on a narrow road, their options were few. So far the sickos were ignoring them. But for how long?

They were bunching up around the car, which was creating a bottleneck in the road. Ed could hear the thump of bodies hitting it.

"There's some buildings over there," Kyle shouted, and Ed could just make out some roofs where the moonlight was shining on them. They looked like factory buildings.

"Can you drive there?" he said to Lewis.

"This hulk ain't built for off-road," said Lewis.

"Then we've gotta get out," said Ed.

"What?" said Kyle. "Are you *insane*?"

The car was rocking now, sickos trying to push it out of the way. Lewis swore and tried to move it forward, but they hadn't gone five yards before they were completely stuck.

And now the sickos had noticed what was inside the car. They were pressing their faces against it, pushing from one side, and the car actually began to slide sideways across the road. It dropped into a ditch and started to tip.

"If we go over we're stuck here." Ed was getting up out of his seat. "Most of our weapons are on the roof. I can't use my sword inside the car. It's too cramped. We have to get out now and get to those buildings."

"No way," said Brooke. "I ain't going out there. Why don't we just wait for them to go away?"

"Do they look like they're about to go anywhere?" Ed shouted.

There were faces squashed against all the windows now, slathering them with gunk. The faces that had filled Ed's nightmares for the last year. Rotten, pustulant, bloated, hideous, deranged.

Inhuman.

"I ain't doing it."

"Me and Kyle will clear a path." Ed was reaching for the door handle. "It'll be all right. The rest of you follow and watch the sides."

"I'd be better up front," said Lewis. "I got the gun."

"You've only got two shells," Ed pointed out.

"Yeah. Hadn't thought of that."

"We can still use it." Ed had his hand on the handle, ready. "When I open the door, you blast a way out. Then drop the gun and use your katana. But only once me and Kyle are out. We'll hold them back. Brooke, you follow Lewis. Don't get tangled in the door. Ebenezer, you last. Okay?"

"Okay. My javelins are not going to be much use. I need space to throw them."

"Use one to stab. Leave the rest. We stay in a tight group. Understood? On my word, Brooke, pull the door back and we're on. You all do exactly as I say and I'll get us out of this."

Could he keep his promise? Ed wondered. Did they have any hope in hell of getting across the fields to the buildings they'd seen? Or were they all going to get killed as soon as that door opened?

Only one way to find out.

"Do it."

Brooke was trying not to look at the faces at the windows. Trying to pretend there was no one out there. A stroll in the park. All she had to do was follow Ed and he'd look after her and everything would be fine.

Yeah, right.

Lewis had shown her some tips on how to fight back at the museum after she'd taken him to get his Japanese armor and weapons. She'd practiced with her short sword, but she wasn't exactly an expert. And there was a whole world of difference between attacking some stuffed garbage bags and a real human being—who moved and fought back. A few times the two of them had had mock battles using sticks and she'd always ended up dead within about twenty seconds.

Okay, so Lewis was young and fit and clever and hadn't had his brain rotted by disease. One-on-one with a sicko she just might stand a chance of doing some damage. But two on one, ten on one, a hundred on one?

No chance.

And it was thick with sickos out there. This was worse

than Green Park. They were five kids against a frigging army. She had a lot of respect for Ed, but what she remembered of him from last year was that he'd always been slightly wary, not the first to get into a fight.

Oh Christ, girl, stop thinking. It didn't help. She had to get out there and do it. Fear was good. Fear was okay.

She remembered Macca. Glad she'd been able to keep her promise to him at the end. Had buried him in the woods with a little stone marker that just said "Billy" on it. In the last few hours he hadn't known where he was or what was going on. He'd lost all touch with reality. Seemed almost happy. The painkillers Dr. Norman had been pumping into him had obviously helped. He'd been kind of floating. Blissed out. In a dream world. What was better? To die like that, not knowing what was going on, not feeling any pain or fear? Or to be alive, right up to the last second? In the moment. Even if you were scared and in pain and desperate . . .

Brooke guessed the trick was not to die at all.

"Do it."

Ebenezer was praying. Silently. Some kids made fun of you if you prayed out loud. It was the only thing that gave him any courage. Sending up a little message to God. Asking the old man to watch over him, to let Christ's love shine down on him. Surely he deserved it. Not those freaks out there. Those abominations, they were against everything God believed in. They were possessed, taken by demons. He was God's instrument now.

He fingered the little silver crucifix he wore around his neck under his top.

I am a soldier of Christ, he thought. *He will be my shield.*
"Do it."

Kyle was gripping his battle-ax, pumped up and ready to go. He didn't care how many of them were out there. He didn't think like that. Didn't really have much of an imagination. He could see the ones at the windows—he would deal with them first. They would be the first to die.

And then . . .

Let it come down. See what happened next. Deal with it.

It would be him and Ed, side by side, like it had always been, ever since they'd teamed up at the battle of Lambeth Bridge. All Kyle had had as a weapon back then was his trusty garden fork. It had been enough. The two of them had slaughtered the sickos. No problem. It had been a blast. And there had been an army of them then as well. It would be no different tonight. They'd cut their way through and show those sickos who was boss.

He was ready.

Ready for anything.

He made a face at the window-lickers. Gave them the finger and swore at the stupid bastards.

"Kiss my ax," he whispered, and laughed.

"Do it."

Lewis was studying his shotgun, making sure the safety catch was off, checking the two triggers, one behind the other, so there were no snags. One pull for the first barrel, another pull for the second. He'd never fired a shotgun before but had seen enough films and played enough computer games to understand the concept. It was pretty straightforward. Not a lot to go wrong. As long as he remembered to keep the butt tight to his shoulder. He'd seen a million hilarious YouTube clips of people firing guns who didn't know how to hold them right. Got smashed in the teeth, knocked over, knocked out.

He knew the kick these things had.

Two pulls.

Bam-Bam . . .

And then what? There were four other kids in the car and he'd only ever been in a real fight with one of them before. Ebenezer. A good missile merchant. A key member of Ollie's team from Waitrose. This was going to be a dirty fight, though, close up, a melee, no room for fancy long-range missile tactics.

Brooke he knew about. She was okay. Not the world's greatest fighter, but he could count on her to hold her own and not run screaming and put the rest of them in danger trying to look after her.

Kyle. Well, as far as Lewis could tell, Kyle was a psycho. And psychos were useful in a fight. As long as they were on your side.

It was Ed he was most worried about.

Good at giving orders.

Could he fight?

Well, they were about to find out.

"Do it."

Brooke muttered something under her breath, tugged the handle, and slid the door all the way back. A waft of hot, stinking air came into the car, and the noise of them, a murmuring, hissing, gurgling sound. There was a solid wall of grown-ups standing there, surprised by this sudden change. Lewis jammed the butt of the shotgun into his shoulder, squeezed the first trigger. Rocked back.

The blast was deafening. There was a bright flash and a whole section of the grown-ups fell away in a confusion of smoke and blood.

He kept on pulling, felt the second trigger, squeezed.

Another bright flash, an ear-popping bang, a gout of smoke as the pellets from the shell sprayed out in a widening cone, and another load of grown-ups simply weren't there anymore.

For a brief moment there was emptiness by the side of the car. Silence, except for the ringing in his ears. Above it all, Lewis could see the moon, a strange red color, like someone had painted it with blood. And then Ed and Kyle were out of the car. Ed with his sword, Kyle with his ax, roaring a battle cry, already swinging the big heavy blade to the right and left.

Lewis tried to remember who was next out, what was the plan? It had all happened so fast, and the gun blasts had rattled his brains.

Was it him or Brooke out next?

"Go!" Brooke shouted. "Go, Lewis, go."

That was it, yes. Drop the gun. Grab the sword. Get out. Fight.

The grown-ups had fallen away at first but were now surging back toward the car, attracted by the noise and movement. Lewis chopped and slashed and stabbed, forcing his way through them, making space for Brooke and Ebenezer, who pulled the car door shut behind him with a heavy *clunk*.

Brooke looked panicked. The reality of so many rabid grown-ups was overwhelming. They pressed in from all around, hot and damp and putrid. Lewis was aware of eyes and teeth, grasping hands with long fingernails, drool and snot and pus. His katana, sharp as a razor, cut into them, chopping off bits of flesh, drawing red lines across faces, ripping through clothing, sinking into soft bellies and spilling guts.

"This is too much," Ebenezer shouted. "There are too many."

He was holding his javelin two-handed, jabbing with the point, keeping the grown-ups back but not doing a lot of damage. Brooke was scared, but working her short sword, holding her own. This was defense, not attack. They needed to move.

And then a space was opened up again. Ed and Kyle had cleared a way through up front, and Lewis wondered why he'd ever had any doubts about Ed.

The two of them were a killing machine, cutting through the grown-ups like a piece of farm machinery, not stopping, not seeming to think, working together in sync as if they shared one brain, protecting each other and timing their swings so that they didn't get tangled. There was an open area all around them, carpeted with fallen bodies. Their blades and clothing were already wet with blood, and they were shouting for the others to catch up.

Lewis, Ebenezer, and Brooke fell in with them. Ed and Kyle driving on at the front, Lewis and Brooke taking the flanks, Ebenezer turning to face backward and protect their rear.

The grown-ups didn't have the brains to hold back, just kept on coming, throwing themselves onto the kids' weapons. They blundered in too close and got cut, or stabbed, or blinded by a slash across the face.

Lewis could hear Kyle laughing and Ed grunting with

each strike, as step by painful step they forced their way toward a gap in the hedge.

Brooke was wailing like someone on a roller coaster, waving her sword madly, all idea of technique forgotten. Ebenezer was calling out to God. Lewis kept quiet, concentrating, getting into a rhythm, learning the best way to use the katana—a slash to the right, to the left, back to the right, and then in with the point.

Somehow Ed got them off the road and into the fields, where the grown-ups were less tightly packed. They could move faster now, driving through the scattered mothers and fathers, leaving behind a trail of dead and wounded. Lewis was already shattered. This was hard work—running and fighting. He could hear Brooke screaming with each swing of her blade, moving closer to panic. They had to hold it together. If you lost your nerve you were dead.

He risked glancing ahead. There were the buildings they were aiming for, on the other side of the field, a cluster of them behind a row of low trees. A long way, though. Two hundred yards, maybe. With grown-ups all the way.

And then he heard a cry as Ebenezer stumbled. Jogging backward over this uneven ground was much harder than on the road. Lewis had to stop and haul him up, leaving their side unprotected for a moment. The grown-ups weren't fast, but they were coming steadily from every direction. It was like trying to hold back water. You swept it away and it just flowed right in again. He got Ebenezer to his feet, but he could already feel hands grabbing at his armor. He was glad of it. It made him feel slightly clumsy, but it kept him protected. The grown-ups were near enough for him to feel the heat of their breath and hear the saliva rattling in their throats. The fat, bloated body of a father pressed against him, and Lewis pummeled it with his elbow. There was no room for him to get his blade up, and all he could do was hammer at the grown-up with the pommel. Ebenezer was having similar problems. His javelin was even harder to use this close up. He was using it like a staff and shoving grown-ups away with it.

Lewis was amazed by how quickly they'd gotten swamped. The field had looked half empty to begin with, and now he couldn't move. Brooke came to him, yelling at the grown-ups and whacking them with her sword, and for a few seconds Lewis thought he was saved, and then he was down, knocked over by a bald mother carrying a branch. Now they were on top of him, and he was lost in a tangle of legs and shuffling feet. It was too dark to see anything and, as he thrashed about, he felt fingers rake his face.

And then a shout.

"Keep your head down." It was Ed.

Lewis pressed himself to the ground, not wanting to be decapitated by that heavy sword, and got a faceful of grass and dirt. There were thuds and shrieks from above him. Bodies fell away and blood showered down on him. An arm fell at his side. Two legs, not attached to a body.

"Up! Up! Up!" Ed again, and he heard Kyle's voice too, bellowing obscenities at the grown-ups. Lewis got to his feet and forced himself up. Ed and Kyle had cleared a patch around him, cutting bodies down like grass. Ed was swinging his sword with both hands, his scarred face something out of a horror film, splashed with blood. His eyes had taken on a crazy gleam. He looked like a completely different person.

"Move it!" he shouted, no hint of friendliness in his voice. It was a barked command. "This way!"

The field had opened up a little. The grown-ups had formed into a clump where Lewis and Ebenezer had stopped, leaving the rest of the ground relatively clear. The mob was milling in a confused knot, tripping over the fallen, unaware that Lewis and Ebenezer and Brooke had gotten away.

The five of them were running now, Ebenezer no longer bothering to watch their backs. They had to get to the buildings. They needed to get under cover, somewhere they could defend. Lewis knocked down a grown-up who got in his way. Ebenezer stabbed him with the point of his javelin as he leaped over the body. Brooke swiped her sword into the face of a mother who wailed as she spun away, hands over her eyes.

Up ahead, Kyle's ax was swinging like a pendulum in front of him, grunting with each swing, daring any grown-ups to come close. And right at the front was Ed, sword held high over his head, yelling a wordless chant of death. Lewis saw him swerve toward a mother, bringing his sword arcing down, and cutting her head clean off her shoulders. It flew through the air and bounced as it hit the ground.

Ed didn't stop running.

They were going to make it. The trees were getting closer and closer.

Ed had dragged them clear and achieved the impossible.

They crashed into the tree line, scrambling through low branches, high-stepping over bushes and brambles.

And then stopped dead.

There was a twelve-foot chain-link fence on the other side, topped with vicious overhanging lines of razor wire.

51

ewis stared at the fence. Ed swore. No way through here.

Kyle took a swing at the fence with his ax, which sparked and bounced off harmlessly.

"Huh!" he said, turning to grin at the others. "Did you see that? Cool."

Nobody else laughed.

No way through at all.

"We'll have to work our way around to the gate." Ed's voice was harsh and croaky. "There must be a way in. Stay together, we're doing well. Keep it up. We'll get in there."

"Did you see my ax spark like that?" said Kyle.

"Shut up, Kyle." Ed strode back out into the open. Lewis followed. There was a line of grown-ups advancing toward them, strung out all the way across the field. Stumbling, moronic, relentless, only one thing on their minds. No way of reasoning with them. No way of stopping them. Ed was good, but he couldn't kill them all.

And there was nowhere to run. Wherever they turned there would be more of them. It was like every grown-up in the world had come out tonight, under the bloodred moon.

Lewis saw a mother who seemed to be leading them. She was very tall, with long, straight black hair that hung down to her waist. She tottered on, slightly ahead of the rest, arms straight and stiff at her sides. Her face narrow, nose like a great fin, eyes bulging and dark. They locked on Lewis and he felt a weird shiver of nausea pass through him. For a moment his fingers went all tingly and his brain buzzed. He thought he was going to faint, or throw up, or freeze. . . .

He wasn't there anymore.

He was just watching a film of all this.

Not real.

The tall woman came on.

She was on a screen.

"Lewis!" A shout from Kyle brought him crashing back to reality. He'd been left behind by the others. He swore and ran to catch up. They were hurrying alongside the line of trees. Lewis could see the end maybe thirty yards ahead. A corner. But what was around the corner?

More bloody grown-ups, no doubt. What else?

And the ones in the field were moving toward the corner as well, to cut them off. They weren't running, but they were seething across the open ground from every direction.

And when Lewis rounded the corner all he saw was pretty much what he'd been expecting—more of them. Only closer. And once again the kids had a fight on their hands. Lewis's arm was sore. The blade wasn't heavy, but he had to keep working it, using both hands mostly on the long handle. Right, left, right again, and stab. Twist and out and start again. The blade was horribly sharp and seemed to be able to cut through anything without much problem. Clothing, skin, muscle, sinews, bone. He swung and slashed and stabbed and swung again, slicing a father's hand clean off. He kicked another in the guts, elbowed a third.

"I can't keep this up," he heard Brooke gasp. Tried to see where she was. Saw her surrounded by a gang of mothers and fathers, poking at them with her sword. Ebenezer had seen it too, and the two of them steamed in, pulling bodies away, chopping at them, until they'd got Brooke clear. And there were Ed and Kyle, tirelessly harvesting the bastards. Lewis looked around. All he could see were grown-ups, plodding toward them. The kids were stuck here now, unable to move in any direction, and no closer to finding a way into the buildings.

He had a sickening urge to just drop his sword and give up. Stop fighting. Let it be. How were things ever going to be any different? Even if they somehow got away from this lot, there would be others. And others. More and more of them, too many to kill. But then he saw Ebenezer get in trouble, and he was running toward him, sword at the ready. He cut Ebenezer clear. And now Brooke was surrounded again.

There was going to be no end to this.

And then he saw bodies falling, out in the fields, as if they were tripping over some hidden wire. Or puppets having their strings cut. Grown-ups were going down all around them. He heard hard thwacking sounds, like someone beating a leather sofa with a belt. Missiles were streaking through the air.

Someone was shooting at them. He saw an arrow whiz across the field and embed itself in a mother's chest. Then another hit her as she fell.

More and more of them were falling, and Lewis saw figures advancing from the left. An organized fighting unit. Must be other kids. Orders were being shouted. More grown-ups going down, the rest of them milling in confusion, not knowing which kids to attack.

Lewis smiled for the first time that night.

Maybe they were going to make it after all.

52

Ed was in a killing frenzy. He'd shut down his conscious brain, withdrawn into the dark space where he let his animal side loose. He was aware, though, that something was going on. The rhythm of the fight had changed. The sickos were losing. Ed was being helped. There were arrows in the air.

He turned to look where they were coming from.

A group of archers was coming toward them, with smaller, more agile girls and boys running ahead of them, darting in and out of the sickos, picking up arrows from the ground, and plucking them from fallen bodies.

"This way! Over here!" A girl wearing a leather jacket shouted at them. She was tall and slim, with long dark hair and pale skin, and appeared to be in charge. Ed moved mechanically in her direction.

"Go to them!" he shouted to his team, his voice painful and hoarse in his dry throat. And they were running again, smashing sickos out of the way. Ed didn't check whether the others were with him. He just had to trust that they were. At least Kyle was at his side, keeping up. Always wanted to be at the front.

"Looks like not all the local kids are assholes," he shouted, and Ed didn't reply. He didn't want to speak. He didn't care. The blood moon was in the sky and in his heart.

There were maybe twenty-five kids there, not counting the younger ones who were still hopping around, picking up arrows, too swift for the sickos to catch. And the archers were keeping up a steady rain of arrows.

"Get in behind us," the girl in charge yelled, and Ed did as he was told, finally checking that all four of his crew were safe. There was Kyle, then Brooke, Ebenezer, and Lewis, bringing up the rear. Alive and alert, wild-eyed, laughing manically.

Saved.

Ed wished he felt something more than emptiness.

"When I say run, we run," the girl commanded.

"Where to?" asked Brooke, bent double and gasping for breath.

"Just follow us," said the girl. "This is the rear of the grown-ups' army. If we head in the right direction we can get away from them. You ready?"

"Do it," Ed grunted.

"Now!" the girl shouted. "Run."

And the archers turned and started running, around to the back of the buildings, through an open gate into another field, where there were only a few scattered sickos. One or two standing like sentinels. The kids pounded through the long grass and weeds. Ed's group was worn out, but something kept them going and they managed to keep up at the front of the pack. The archers crossed the field to a lane. They seemed to know where they were going. And once on the lane they could go even faster.

Ed felt the blood on his skin drying from the heat of his body. It was itchy and uncomfortable. It caked his clothing.

After running down the lane for what felt like fifteen, twenty minutes, the archers veered off into a field through a farm gate and up the side of a low hill. They hadn't seen any sickos for some time, and Ed could see that the hill would give them a good view of the surrounding country-side. There was also a clump of trees up here, and as soon as they arrived, three of the archers threw down their bows and started climbing to get a better view. The rest of the group slumped down onto the ground to rest, and Ed gratefully joined them. The girl in charge stayed standing, peering out across the darkened landscape.

Ed looked in the direction they'd come from. He could just make out the roofs of the factory buildings. And there was a black stain across the land that could have been the sickos or just the shadows of clouds across the moon, which was still a diseased red color.

Ed was fully aware of his body now. His heart was racing. His head ached. His arms ached. His legs ached. His chest ached, rising and falling quickly, his lungs burning with lactic acid. As far as he could tell, he hadn't gotten any fresh wounds. They'd been lucky. If these archers hadn't shown up, they could all well be dead. They couldn't have held out much longer.

He looked at the rest of his little gang, sprawled out on the ground, exhausted. Brooke looked pale and haunted.

Ebenezer was muttering to himself and had his hand around a cross on a chain. Kyle had a big drunken grin on his face. Somehow Lewis had managed to put his cool back on. He sat there, leaning back against a tree trunk, eyes half closed, just hanging.

Ed struggled to his feet and walked stiffly over to the tall pale girl, who had a pair of binoculars out now and was scanning the land to the east.

"Thanks," he said.

"That's okay. It was pure luck we came across you." She had a polite, middle class accent. Similar background to him, probably.

"What were you doing out there?" he asked.

"Scavenging. We'd been out all day and on the way back we got caught up with that lot." She waved her arm vaguely in the direction of the factory buildings. "God knows where they all came from or where they're going. We've been trying to get around them for hours. It's going to be a long march home from here."

"Where's home?"

"Ascot. You?"

"London."

"London? You're a bit far off your turf, aren't you?"

"Yeah, we're looking for someone."

"Well, good luck with that," she said with a touch of sarcasm.

Ed was going to question her further when Brooke called to him. He went over and dropped down next to her. She put an arm around him and held him tight. She was shaking.

"You all right?" he asked unnecessarily.

"I never want to do that again."

"Hopefully you won't have to."

"They're all going toward London, Ed."

"Maybe."

"You know it. You've seen it before, you told me. All the sickos you saw going past St. Paul's. They're massing in London. So I *will* have to do that again. We have to get back there, Ed. They're an army."

"We will get home." Ed folded both arms around her. "Just not tonight."

He was covering her in blood from his soaked clothing. At least it wasn't his own. He was numb and confused. Couldn't work out a plan. Couldn't think more than ten seconds ahead.

In the end a plan was made for him.

"Okay," shouted the girl in charge. "It's all clear ahead and it's safe to go. We have to keep moving. We've a lot of ground to cover."

53

It had taken a long time for Lewis to realize that he knew the girl in the leather jacket. Trying to put the pieces together. Watching her with Ed. And then it had come to him.

They were covering the ground at a fast walk, sticking to streets so the going was easy. Lewis had settled into a loping rhythm, his long legs eating up the miles. He felt like he could keep this up all night if needed. He worked his way up through the ranks of kids. Nobody was talking much, saving their energy. All you could hear was the slap-scrape-thud of their boots.

He got to the front of the column. Fell in beside the girl. He could hear her leather jacket creaking as she walked. It was the jacket that had done it.

"Hello, Sophie," he said, and she turned to look at him, surprised and more than a little curious.

She frowned, trying to place him.

"Do I know you?"

"I'm *hurt* you don't remember me, girl."

"Remind me."

"Camden Road, Regent's Park, Buckingham Palace . . ."

"Oh my God, you're one of the Holloway kids."

Sophie's face lit up in a smile and then instantly went sour.

"You're not . . . You weren't a friend of . . ."

"Of Arran? No. I was with the other camp. One of Blue's crew. You disappeared when we got to the palace."

"I didn't feel welcome there. Not by David and not by Maxie and her people. Not after what happened with Arran."

"Was an accident," said Lewis. "We all knew that. Weren't your fault. He was dying anyways, I reckon, seeing what's gone down with other kids as got bit. You did him a favor."

"I still felt awful. Shooting him like that. Tell you the truth, we wanted to get out of town as well; it had always been our plan. We came out west. Been moving around ever since. A little while at Windsor to start with, but the setup there reminded me too much of David at Buckingham Palace. Too many rules. Obnoxious bastards in charge: the Golden Twins, they call themselves. A pair of right pains. We were in Bracknell for a bit, but then we linked up with a gang of archers from Ascot. It was a better fit. Been there a couple of weeks now. It's okay there. Some of the kids are a bit weird, but we get along okay. They're organized at least. Might move on in the summer, though."

Sophie paused. Smiled again. "It's Lewis, isn't it? I remember now. The hair."

"You *do* remember me. Cool."

"I didn't really register you all in the dark. You're not all from Holloway, are you?"

"No. We a mix. Ebenezer come out of Holloway, but we've left the palace and moved to the Natural History Museum. We was like you, couldn't stick that David dickhead. See the girl there, with the scar?"

"Yeah? Was she from Holloway?"

"No. You remember, just before we got to the palace we found some kids being massacred close by Green Park tube station?"

"Yeah. It was pretty horrible."

"She was the one we rescued."

"No way! You're kidding."

"Straight up. You got to meet her, girl. She's way cool."

"I will. God, this is so freaky. Your guy said you were looking for someone?"

"Yeah."

And so Lewis explained about Ella and Sam and Maeve and Robbie and Monkey-Boy. And Sophie thought maybe she remembered Ella. Although Lewis thought she probably didn't. One thing was certain, though: Ella wasn't at Ascot, and Sophie hadn't heard anyone talking about a gang of kids coming out of London.

So they walked on through the night, and it felt good to talk, to remember all they'd been through since leaving Holloway.

At last Sophie said they were getting close to Ascot, and Lewis wondered what turn their lives were going to take now.

"What we gonna find when we get there?" he asked Sophie.

"The races, Lewis. It's gonna be the races. . . ."

THE RACES

54

It was the day of the races. It was warm and sunny and there was a party atmosphere. Ed was up in the grandstand of the Ascot racetrack with all the other kids, waiting, praying that somehow he was going to pull off his plan. It had been a risk. He'd had to balance waiting a few more days here in Ascot against hurrying back to town and seeing what was going down with the sicko army.

In the end he'd decided to risk staying here. If it went his way it would mean he could return to London with a real fighting force.

And Ella.

All the best fighters from all the kids' settlements were going to be here. So that meant two things. If Ella *was* around in this part of the world, someone here would know about it. And if Ed wanted to put together a crack squad, this was the place to do it.

Only thing was, he was going to have to somehow win the races.

• • •

At least he'd had some time to get things ready.

A couple of days after they'd arrived, once they'd felt rested enough, Ed's team had joined up with some of Sophie's archers, and they'd gone out to find the car. It was much quicker and easier in the daylight, with no sickos around; the countryside seemed mostly empty. They'd spotted one stray grown-up in the distance, limping across a field, and that was it. When they got to the car they were glad that Ebenezer had thought to shut the door behind him when he got out.

The car was a mess. It was covered in filth from the sickos, dried pus and blood and crusty streaks of saliva, as if it had somehow caught their disease. There were dents where the sickos had taken out their rage on it, plus some unidentified lumps of pinkish gray stuff that looked like growths on the metalwork.

But none of the sickos had had the sense to open the doors.

Lewis climbed into the driver's seat and fished the key out of his pocket. "Hope it starts," he said, putting the key in the ignition. The kids had all cheered when the engine rumbled into life.

Lewis put it in reverse and as many kids as could get around it had pushed and shoved until it came up out of the ditch and onto the road.

A load of them had crammed inside it, and the rest had walked behind as Lewis had driven it slowly back to Ascot.

When Ed left Ascot, he hoped to have a lot more vehicles with him. And a lot more kids.

For the last three days they'd been arriving from all around. Mostly on horseback or on foot, but one or two in cars, usually the leaders of the various camps, showing off. They'd marched in from the surrounding countryside, bringing sickos with them. The sickos were kept in the racetrack stables across the road. When Ed had found out exactly what the sickos were for, he'd at first been appalled. He'd kind of come to terms with it now. Saw that there was a twisted sense to it. He still hadn't made up his mind if he was going to join in that part. The rest of the setup was pretty straightforward, a mixture of horse races and fights.

Most of the kids stayed in tents they'd put up in the middle of the giant racetrack. It looked like an army encampment, or a rock festival like Glastonbury.

This had been the most famous racetrack in England. Where the Queen visited every year for Royal Ascot. There were notices and signs and information boards about the event everywhere Ed looked. Photos of the Queen and Prince Philip arriving in an open-topped carriage escorted by soldiers in old-fashioned uniforms, riding matching horses. Photos of the aristocracy enjoying themselves. Celebrities. The rich and the famous. He remembered seeing things on the news about it; women parading around in stupid hats.

Now it had been taken over by children.

The locals lived in a big old hospital behind the track, and the guy in charge was known as the Mad King. In the past he would have been described as having a syndrome, or a condition. You weren't allowed to call people mad then. But that's what he was. He didn't say much, and most of what he said made no sense. A guy called Arno Fletcher looked after him. He went everywhere with the king and interpreted everything that came out of his mouth. Ed could see that the whole thing was a scam. Arno was the real boss man, hiding behind the Mad King, twisting his words to mean whatever he wanted.

The king was huge—unnaturally so. His head was big and bony with a heavy brow. He walked stiffly and awkwardly as if he was in pain all the time, and he looked at you with deep-set, wary eyes. Arno was about Ed's age, small and skinny and clever, with long hair. He was always laughing and joking and came across as being friends with everyone.

Ed recognized him as a born politician.

There were a lot of kids like the Mad King here at Ascot, ones with conditions and syndromes. It was like they'd been collected, or, more likely, dumped here by other kids. There was a general air of craziness about the place, and Ed sometimes thought it was appropriate they lived in a hospital. Once he'd gotten used to it, though, it was fine. The kids looked after each other, and their combined strangeness gave them a sort of power.

It was Arno who'd come up with the idea for the races. And it was Arno who'd given Ed the idea for his plan.

Ed had eaten dinner with him the night after he'd arrived, sharing some cider and scavenged food.

"I don't like kids fighting other kids," Arno had said. "The races are a way of letting them compete without killing each other. At least most of the time. You see how football used to be? Or the Olympics? They were a way of waging war without too many casualties. Things around here are much better than they used to be. Plus, it stops us from getting bored. That's the worst thing about the disease. Nothing happens for weeks, and then there's some sudden mad fight against marauding grown-ups, and for a short time you're absolutely bloody terrified, and then it's back to the grind and the boredom."

"But what happens exactly?" Ed asked.

"Each camp puts in a team. Simple."

"And what do you get for winning?"

"Whatever you want, man. You get to choose. Until the next games your camp becomes top dog. Like Ancient Rome. You are the emperor."

"Does Ascot ever win?"

"What do you think? You've seen what we're like."

"Fair point."

"But the thing is, Ed—we don't need to win. We make a profit from the races. Everyone coming here, betting. Just don't tell anyone, yeah?"

"But if you did win the races . . ." Ed wasn't going to let this go. "You could choose your prize?"

"Yeah."

"Who's the captain?"

"Can't be me. Girl called Veda did it last time. But she ran off to Windsor. Never really fit in here. I was going to ask Sophie; she seems sensible."

"Would you let me do it?"

"We never win, Ed."

"So you've got nothing to lose."

And that was why Ed was sitting there, wearing a baggy white T-shirt over his clothes, anxious to see how his team was going to do.

It was like a medieval tournament. Each of the six set-tlements had their own colors. If kids didn't have jackets or shirts of the right color, they put T-shirts over their other clothes, like Ed, or carried homemade flags, or wore ban-danas. Some had even painted their faces.

Ascot wore white, Bracknell was green, Sandhurst was black, Slough was red, Maidenhead was blue, and Windsor was yellow, or gold if they had it.

Ed had been there when the Windsor kids had arrived. At their head were the twins he'd heard about, riding match-ing white horses, and wearing gleaming black-and-gold armor that must have been specially polished for the event. They also both wore a plastic wreath on their heads, spray-painted gold, to show that they were the winners of the last races. There was something arrogant and lordly about the Golden Twins. They had a snooty look to them, like they thought they were some prince and princess arriving at a rival's castle.

Behind them came their troops, well drilled and well behaved. A few of them had horses, and there were four pickup trucks loaded with sickos, all securely tied up or chained. A group of smaller kids brought up the rear, ner-vous but excited. This was the biggest group to arrive.

The next largest group was the kids from Slough. Ed had watched them come in as well, keeping himself well hid-den in the crowd of onlookers. Josa and Kenton had been at the front, Josa carrying a baby that must have been about a year old, her boys behind her, trying to look mean and tough, some of them succeeding. Ed reckoned they'd been lucky to get out of Slough without sustaining any serious damage from the wave of sickos passing through. It looked like they'd managed to round up most, if not all, of the ones that Ebenezer had released from the pens. They were being herded along in a group, chained and kept at a distance by Josa's long wooden poles.

The Sandhurst kids were the smallest group, but they were a hard-looking bunch, dressed in denim and leather, with big boots, as if they'd modeled themselves on a biker gang.

There wasn't much to distinguish between the Bracknell and Maidenhead groups. They looked like any bunch of kids arriving at another school for an event, a football match or whatever, excited, slightly nervous, sticking together. In the past there would have been teachers herding the kids, making sure they didn't misbehave. Now it was the other way around: the kids were herding the adults, and the adults were the problem. Diseased, violent, anarchistic, and stupid.

All the arrivals had a few horse riders among them, and there were more horses kept here at Ascot. Some of the new kids negotiated with the locals for extra mounts. There was a barter system in place. Kids were exchanging food and drink, weapons, armor, clothing, shoes, books, footballs and sports equipment, seeds and fertilizer, anything that was considered valuable and hard to get hold of. And some of this stuff was then exchanged for tokens to bet with. Arno Fletcher really did have a good system going on.

There must have been a few hundred kids here, but so far Ed hadn't had any luck finding anything out about Maeve, Robbie, Monkey-Boy, and Ella. Everyone had been busy organizing their teams, setting up their camps, getting settled in. He'd had a short chat with one of the guys in charge at Maidenhead, who said he hadn't heard anything, and he'd spent a wild but similarly blank night with the Sandhurst kids, whose leader was a friendly psycho named Dara.

Despite their looks, the Sandhurst kids seemed to be the most welcoming. While other groups kept to themselves and even posted guards to keep outsiders away, the Sandhurst kids were here to party and didn't much mind who joined them. They'd gotten hold of several cases of beer and a whole load of cigarettes and vodka. They never appeared to eat anything and instead had all gotten stuck into drinking, wrestling, kickboxing, and general free-for-all fighting. Kyle had joined in and held his own pretty well.

So that left Bracknell and Windsor. There was no way Ed was going to get anywhere near anyone in the Windsor camp. There was so much security there it might as well have been Guantánamo Bay.

Ebenezer had found out that most of the kids from Maidenhead were practicing Christians. Sandhurst had become Hell's Angels, Slough was a bunch of obnoxious yobs who spat at the world, the Ascot kids were misfits, Windsor was trying to act like royalty, and it seemed that the Maidenhead kids had gotten religion. They reminded Ed of Mad Matt and his acolytes at St. Paul's.

Everyone had found their own way of coping with this new world; they were free to create their own identities. The kids around here were only doing what teenagers had always done—trying to find out who they were and how they fit in.

Whatever helped you make it through the night.

And here they all were, sitting in different sections of the grandstand. Six blocks of color. Red, white, green, black, blue, and gold. The Ascot kids were sitting right in the center. To their right were Maidenhead, past them Bracknell, and then Slough. To their left were Sandhurst, and then Windsor. Ed was glad that he was a good distance from Josa's mob. He didn't want the complication of having to deal with them right now.

A few kids were warming up their horses, an equal number of girls and boys cantering up and down the straight length of track in front of the grandstand. Others were trying to form up in a line at one end. Some of them looked steadier in their saddles than others. A couple of the horses were already out of control, their riders yelling at them to hold still, and kicking them uselessly with their heels. One girl's horse had taken off and was galloping madly around the track in the wrong direction.

A ragged little band of musicians was playing tunes on trumpets and trombones, drums and cymbals, anything that could make a loud noise. It reminded Ed of the band that used to play at England matches, blaring out "Rule Britannia," *The Dam Busters*, and *The Great Escape*.

Right now the Ascot band was playing the national anthem because the Mad King was coming out onto the track, being pulled along on a little wagon by four kids. Another kid, a little scary-looking, was riding at their side. He had a shaved head and a blank face and made a point of not looking at anyone. The king was wearing a little plastic crown on his massive head, a child's toy, and had a cloak draped around his shoulders. He was happy, grinning and laughing. Ed didn't know what to think. Was he being presented as a freak, a figure of fun? Or was he having the time of his life?

Maybe both.

In front of the wagon strutted Arno Fletcher, with a long staff in his hand.

"My lords, ladies, and gentlemen," he called out, and miraculously all the kids in the grandstand grew quiet. "Welcome to the fifth New Ascot Race Meeting, which promises to be the biggest and best ever. Just you wait and see! So give it up for the Mad King himself, King Nutjob the Thirty-first!"

The grandstand erupted.

The races were getting under way.

55

Once the whooping and cheering and stamping had died down, Arno raised his staff for silence again and walked over to the king.

"And now a word from our sponsors," he shouted. "From the host of this world-famous event. Tell us, Your Majesty, how doth it hang?"

The king turned to the crowds, his mouth lopsided, and he wailed at them, a jumble of vowels and no consonants, more like an animal howling than human speech.

"He says you are all very welcome," Arno shouted. "Even if you are a bunch of useless, scum-sucking delinquents and special-needs cases."

Kids laughed and stamped their feet.

"And please place your bets with the royal bookies."

Boys and girls were making their way through the grandstand, taking bets off the kids, while down on the track the king was bellowing at the crowd. Once again Arno stepped up to translate.

"His Royal Highness has decreed that today is a good day to die. So let the mayhem commence!"

And mayhem it was. The first few races were simple sprints along the straightaway in front of the grandstand, with two riders from each camp in every heat. They careered down the track, frantically whipping their horses and each other. There didn't appear to be any rules. The riders were allowed to do whatever they wanted to win the race.

Some of the horses collided with each other, with the riders trying to knock their rivals out of their saddles. There was lots of shouting and laughter coming from the grandstand mixed in with hurled insults and obscenities. The biggest cheers of all came when riders fell off their horses, and often a race would end with a group of riders dismounting to punch and kick each other at the finish line. Sometimes they wouldn't even get that far and would sit in their saddles, halfway down the track, trying to smash each other to pieces.

The crowd loved every minute of it, cheering, jeering, laughing, winning bets, losing bets. And Ed cheered just as loudly as anyone else for the Ascot runners. He needed Ascot to do well if his plan was going to work.

There were ten races in the morning, with some riders racing more than once. Maidenhead won four, Windsor, Ascot, and Bracknell won two each. Slough and Sandhurst had so far won nothing. Ed wasn't sure that horse racing was their thing. So Ascot was comfortably in the middle, but until they moved on from the horse racing there wasn't anything much Ed and his team could do to help out.

The main horse race of the morning was the Big Kahuna,

a complete circuit of the track. Arno had told Ed it was about a mile and a half long, and it was in the shape of a giant triangle.

There were mostly different riders out for this one, three per camp, and these looked to be more confident and in control. Ed saw that the Golden Girl was racing for Windsor, and he was interested to see if she was as good on a horse as she wanted everyone to think. He also recognized one of Josa's boys riding for the Slough team.

As before, the riders lined up behind a rope that was stretched across the course by two kids. The king had his arm raised, and the two kids holding the rope were watching him intently. He wailed something. It could have been "On your marks, get set, go!," it was hard to tell, but when he dropped his hand the kids dropped the rope and the runners were off, thundering down the straightaway, their hooves throwing up clods of earth behind them.

There weren't as many of the dirty tactics as in the earlier races; this one was obviously taken more seriously. As they neared the first bend, however, two of the Sandhurst horses came in from either side of a Maidenhead rider and sandwiched him, lashing out at him with their whips and terrifying his horse. They eventually broke away, laughing, and the horse they'd hemmed in veered off to the side and jumped over the low fence at the edge of the course, where it went charging into the field of tents.

For a while the horses got smaller and smaller, racing away down the second side of the triangle, so it was hard to see what was happening. A couple of them dropped out at the next bend and came trotting back down the track, but most of the horses were now coming back toward the grandstand.

The track was massive, and most of it was only separated from the road by hedges, trees, and a low chain-link fence. A few kids had been placed as guards at several points around the edges, but it was too large to make fully secure. As the horses came thumping down toward the final bend, the Golden Girl was comfortably in the lead. She sat well in her saddle and was by far the best rider. She looked like one of those horsey girls who'd grown up hanging around stables. The Windsor kids were standing up, cheering her on. Not even a dirty trick could stop her now, surely? And then a gasp went up as a sicko wandered out on to the track, right in front of her.

"Kill the bastard!" someone yelled from the Slough section of the crowd, and a chant started.

"Kill the bastard! Kill the bastard!"

Golden Girl's horse was spooked. It shied away and went skittering across the track, kicking up its back legs. The next horse slammed into the sicko, which fell under its hooves and was trampled. Two other horses went right over it. The rest swerved around it. Golden Girl fought to get her horse calmed down and back into the race, but three riders had gone past her before she was up to speed. She didn't give up, but rode heroically, urging her horse on, and as they rounded the bend she was neck and neck with the number three runner. Now they were on the home stretch, galloping along toward the finish line. The screams and shouts from the crowd were deafening, and Ed was trying to drown them out, yelling his head off—the rider in front was wearing the white colors of Ascot.

Golden Girl edged past the second horse and was biting at the tail of the front-runner. The Ascot rider, another girl, probably couldn't believe her luck. Her mouth was open wide and she looked half terrified, half elated. Golden Girl edged forward, forward, forward . . . but just couldn't quite make it—and Ascot was first over the line.

The Ascot kids went mental, half of them running on to the track and crowding around their winner. Golden Girl looked deeply pissed off. She was complaining to anyone who would listen and nudging her horse over to where Arno Fletcher was standing with the king. When she got there, she started a massive fight, other kids joining in as a party from Windsor went over to argue their case.

Ed glanced up the track. Two of the Ascot guards were beating the sicko's lifeless body with clubs. The boy on horseback with the shaved head who had ridden in with the king, and who Ed thought of as the king's bodyguard, was sitting there, watching them expressionlessly, like a supervisor. Nobody else was paying them any attention.

The bodyguard turned around, noticed the commotion by the king, and galloped back. As soon as he got there, everyone backed off and stopped arguing. They were evidently scared of him. He was still blank-faced, though, and not looking directly at anyone. His presence there was enough, by the look of it. Now Arno was able to get everyone quieted down, and he raised his staff to get the attention of the kids in the grandstand.

"The king has made a ruling. Ain't that right, Your Royal Bigness?"

The king wailed, nodding his head.

"The result stands. Ascot wins. Zombies on the track is a natural hazard. And what the king says goes. Now get back to your seats and prepare thyselves for the next event, loyal subjects and honored guests and bums! For now we present, in all its gory glory hallelujah—the King's Road!"

Ed looked at Kyle, and they nodded to each other and stood up.

It was time to go to work.

56

Ed and Kyle walked down the aisle toward the track with Sophie and a tall, well-built kid named Sean, who seemed to be the closest thing the Ascot camp had to a champion. They weren't used to winning anything, but Ed and Kyle were hoping to change that.

Ed knew a little about the King's Road event; it was a variation on British Bulldog. Sean ran through the finer points as they made their way to their start position—a section of track marked by two ropes on the ground.

"We'll be there," Sean explained. "In the catchers' box. There'll be five kids from each camp, and we can't leave the box. Up to ten kids from each camp set off from the starting line." He pointed to the far end of the track, where a large group was starting to gather. "We don't usually field more than about seven. And they have to try to get past the catchers to the finish line."

"Is that it?" Ed asked. "Are there any tactics?"

"I guess," said Sean. "As a catcher, you've got to decide whether to protect your guys going through, or try to catch runners from other teams. Also, if a runner gets through they're allowed to go back to try to free their friends, so watch your backs. Winner is the team with the most runners past the line when the music stops."

"How long is that?" Ed asked.

"No idea. Arno and the king decide. Never soon enough. I warn you, it's fun, but pretty brutal."

"This is gonna be a blast," said Kyle, grinning in anticipation.

They were joined by a rather large kid who introduced himself as Green and high-fived them. Ed reckoned he'd make a solid enough barrier, but wondered how fast on his feet he'd be.

"You have any tactics?" Ed asked.

"We normally just make it up as we go along," said Sean. "And try not to get hurt too much. It's basically chaos."

"Okay." Ed looked down toward the runners. "Any of our guys get to us, we form up around them and escort them through the box."

"*If* any of them get to us," said Green. "We tend to be a bit useless."

"Gonna be different this time, soldier," said Kyle, and he slapped palms with the kid.

"Oh, there is one rule," said Sean. "You mustn't step outside the lines or you'll get disqualified and pulled out of the game. That's only catchers, not runners, obviously. You can tell who the runners are, because they're wearing black armbands."

Arno was over at the side of the track, chatting to the

king and the musicians, the king's bodyguard sitting nearby on his horse. Arno looked up at the sky, nodded, said something that made the king laugh, and they approached the barrier.

"Okay," he shouted, raising his staff. "May the best team win, and may the worst team lose, and may the good Lord keep you all safe and sound, you filthy rats."

The king tipped back his head and howled, and the band started playing, belting an out-of-tune but enthusiastic version of the *Carmina Burana* theme that they used on *The X Factor*. Ed was so busy listening he forgot this was the signal to start the game. By the time he'd turned to look, there were about sixty runners belting down the track toward him.

Some of them were already fighting, a few stronger runners trying to take down weaker ones. Two girls had stopped completely and were laying into each other. There were collisions, shoving and punching, but the main body of runners kept on coming.

Ed had faced enough rabid sickos in his time not to be scared by a bunch of kids, and was more amused than anything. He got himself ready, shutting down any outside distractions. He knew that the hardest part of taking on a pack was choosing which individual to go for and not being confused by too much choice.

The Windsor kids had formed up into a sort of ram, with two large boys at their head and the rest massed behind them in a column. It looked like they were going to try to blast their way through over to Ed's right, so he didn't have to worry about them for the moment. The Sandhurst kids were relying on their size and strength and intimidating look. They were singing a song to the tune of *Carmina Burana* as they came.

> *We're Sandhurst* kids.
> *We're Sandhurst* kids
> *And we will* kick *your* asses!

The rest of the runners were coming in an unruly mass, the Ascot kids scattered among them. Ed saw one stumble and fall and get trampled on, and he wondered whether any of them were even going to make it as far as the catchers.

And then there was no time to think as the two groups clashed.

Ed saw a blur of faces and bodies and picked out a slightly smaller kid, a boy wearing the green shirt of Bracknell. He was nippy, dodging about between the catchers, and had easily slipped past Sophie. Ed lunged at him, got ahold of his shirt, swung him around, and slammed him to the ground, slightly harder than he'd been meaning to. The kid cried out and was too winded to get up. Ed saw that Kyle had grabbed another Bracknell kid and thrown him down as well. Now Ed had to decide whether to hold on to his captive or try to knock down another.

Before he could make a decision, though, a Bracknell catcher nipped over, grabbed the boy, and pulled him into the Bracknell area. Ed was going to go after him when he saw that the Slough catchers had caught one of the Ascot runners. Two girls had hold of his arms and looked like they were trying to tear him in half. Ed barged into the Slough section and slammed the two girls into each other. They were so surprised they let go of the Ascot runner, and Ed and Kyle cleared a path through to the back of the catching area and sent him on his way home. So that was at least one they'd gotten through.

While they'd been distracted, Kyle's captive had gotten to his feet and was stumbling through the catchers. Kyle threw him to the ground again and told him to stay there.

There was a major brawl going on over at the left-hand side, and Ed saw that some of the stronger runners who had gotten through were coming back to free trapped friends.

Still the band played on.

And then Ed saw Kenton and Josa piling their way through the catchers. Josa was snarling like a cat. She head-butted a girl who tried to get hold of her, and the girl dropped to her knees clutching her face, blood pouring out from her shattered nose. Kyle made a move on Josa, and she butted him, too. Ed grinned. It would take more than that to stop a bonehead like Kyle.

Suddenly, though, Ed had problems of his own to deal with. Kenton was coming straight for him, his tattoos making him look like he was wearing a mask.

Ed froze. Kenton wasn't going to stop. He was knocking other kids out of the way as if they were straw dummies. Ed made a frightened face and ducked to one side. Kenton gave a shout of triumph and spat an obscenity at Ed, but as he sprinted past, Ed calmly stuck out a toe and tripped him so that he came crashing down face-first into the hard ground. He lay there, stunned.

Ed spotted Green and dragged him over.

"Sit on this one for me, mate," he said. "Whatever happens, don't let him up."

Green grinned and did as he was told. Ed turned to see if Kyle needed any help, and saw that he was running down the track toward the start line, with Josa over his shoulder, kicking and screaming and pummeling his back.

Everyone except the kids in the Slough section of the grandstand was laughing and cheering. Kyle was going to be disqualified, but surely the game would be over soon? He didn't stop until he was right down at the bend, where he dumped Josa on the ground.

And then Ed was almost knocked over as two of Josa's boys came running in to try to free Kenton. They barged into Ed, and one of them stood guard while the other started to kick Green, who was trying to protect himself with his arms wrapped around his head.

The boy standing guard dared Ed to make a move. But he didn't have to. Sophie came flying in and rugby-tackled the boy to the ground, giving Ed the chance to dash in and pull the kicker over by his leg. A major scrap looked like it was about to break out, when suddenly there was silence. The music had stopped. Once the crowd realized it was over, they broke out into loud cheering.

Slough had lost five kids to the Ascot team, so their score was pretty low. Sandhurst had done the best. They'd gotten seven runners through, by the simple use of force. Ascot only had two, but they had the respect of having taken out four of the heavily favored Slough team, plus the Bracknell boy who Kyle had taken down earlier and was sitting obediently where Kyle had left him.

Kenton got to his feet, slapping dirt and grass off his clothes. He gave Ed a filthy look.

"You ain't heard the last of this, shitface," he spat, and Ed laughed.

"You better go and see if Josa's all right," he said, and laughed some more as Kenton and his two mates trotted down the track to where Josa was yelling and screaming at Kyle and trying to pummel him. Kyle was casually keeping her at arm's length and singing the *Carmina Burana* tune.

Sean came over and high-fived Ed.

"Nice work, Ed," he said. "That's two more runners through than we've ever had before."

"Is your name Ed?"

Ed turned to see that the Bracknell runner they'd caught was staring at him.

"What of it?"

"Help me up."

Ed hauled the boy to his feet. He grunted with the effort, looked like he'd twisted his knee. No wonder he hadn't tried to run on.

"I was caught out in the open the night of the blood moon," the boy said, trying not to put any weight on his bad leg.

"Yeah?"

"The night the grown-ups went through."

"I know what you mean. So?"

The boy held out his hand and Ed shook it warily.

"My name's Isaac Hills," said the boy. "Someone said you were looking for a girl named Ella. . . ."

57

This was stupid. Stupid fighting. When everything was going wrong, why did kids want to fight more? And it wasn't just the boys, but the girls as well. Wasn't there enough hurt in the world?

Ella was sitting right up at the very top of the grandstand behind the Windsor kids, as far away from the fighting as she could get. She'd quite liked the horse racing, except the bits when they cheated and the fighting, of course. And she *really* hadn't liked it when the grown-up ran out onto the track. That had been horrible. It had brought back bad memories.

She'd felt safe since being at Windsor—safe, but not happy. The castle there was probably the safest place she'd been since the illness started. Probably the safest place in England.

She was lonely, though. She missed everyone. Sam and her friends from Holloway: Maeve and Robbie and Monkey-Boy, poor Malik . . .

She'd been knocked out when the Windsor kids caught her in their nets, and when she woke up in a bed at the castle, she'd lost a couple of days—and Malik.

She hardly remembered being captured. Although that's not what the Windsor kids called it. They said they'd rescued her. Saved her from a mob of grown-ups. Said she could have died.

Ella sometimes wished she *had* died.

It had all been her fault. What had happened to Malik. All her fault. He'd risked everything to take her to safety. She couldn't go anywhere without bad things happening. Maeve and Robbie and Monkey-Boy. *All her fault.* In her worst moments she imagined she was to blame for everything—the disease, the grown-ups, her parents dying, Sam being taken, Maeve and Robbie and Monkey-Boy . . .

Around and around in her head it all went until she was too tired to care anymore. It was like she'd been at the bottom of a deep black hole and had climbed out and found herself in a world without color. Nothing mattered to her. She couldn't connect; stuff just went on around her. She was numb. Couldn't feel anything.

In different times Ella would have been very happy at Windsor Castle. It had reminded her of Buckingham Palace. Not surprising really, as it had been one of the Queen's homes. Only this one was a proper castle, like out of a fairy tale. A castle full of children.

There were even a prince and princess there, the Golden Twins: Golden Boy and Golden Girl. She'd met them early on, and they'd been nice to her. Nice, but not really that interested. She was just a little girl who'd gotten caught in their nets, a shrimp, a sardine. She'd tried to tell them about Malik, but they wouldn't listen.

Most of the kids at Windsor had been kind to her.

They'd looked after her and fed her and given her pills for her headaches. And she'd made a friend, a girl who seemed to be in charge of everything inside the castle, organizing the medicine as well as the food and the armor and the weapons and the people.

She was a teenager who called herself Go-Girl. At first Ella thought her new friend was called Golden Girl, who she'd heard so much about. Thought that Go-Girl was the queen of the castle, and Go-Girl had pretended to get angry.

"I'm not Golden Girl," she'd said. "I'm Go-Girl. Don't you forget it—Go-Girl! I had the name first; Golden Girl stole the idea off me. I was always called Go-Girl back in London. We had a gang, we were going to form a band, we were like superheroes. Go-Girl was my rock-star name. There was me and the Fox, and Cool-Man and Shadowman and Magic-Man and one more. . . . Oh yeah, Big-Man. Mostly all dead now. But they can't kill Go-Girl!"

She tried to make Ella laugh, to trick her out of her mood. She really tried. But Ella stayed in her mood.

"You know what?" Go had told Ella. "Golden Girl even had the front to try and get me to change my name. Yeah! That's right. Even though I had it first. I mean, do you know what Golden Girl's real name is? Jessica Roberts-Wilding. Boring name. No wonder she changed it. And she was just copying me, but trying to go one better. *Golden* Girl."

Ella had said it was strange, calling someone Go-Girl, and Go-Girl told her that most people just called her Go. And that was all right. So that was what Ella called her. Go had said that she was going to adopt Ella and make her her own, and they went everywhere together. Except when Go had been riding in the races. She'd been in a sprint and the Big Kahuna, and Ella had cheered her on. Go wasn't the best rider, and she hadn't won anything, but she said it had been fun. She tried to get Ella excited about things, tried to make *her* have fun as well.

It wasn't fun.

Nothing was fun.

All her fault.

Maeve and Robbie and Monkey-Boy.

And Malik. She'd thought and thought and thought about Malik, how he'd been so ugly, so mashed up, like a wounded beast, but he'd had a brave heart and a good soul.

She watched now as Go came walking up the steps between the rows of seats. She'd been a runner in the King's Road and was all red-faced and sweaty and out of breath. She was sort of glowing as well, happy-looking. Alive. And Ella was jealous of that. She knew she had a permanently grumpy face, because Go teased her about it. Called her "misery guts." And Ella remembered how she used to call Malik Face-Ache. There was no hiding from the bad things. Always something there to remind her.

"That was great," said Go, flopping down into the seat next to Ella.

"Was it?" Ella hadn't wanted to sound quite as grumpy as it came out.

"Yeah." Go sort of half hugged, half shook Ella.

"It just looked like fighting to me," said Ella.

"It's good to get it out," said Go.

"Well, I think it's stupid and dangerous."

"Listen," said Go, "if you didn't like the King's Road,

you're really not going to like what's happening at the end of the day."

"Why, what is it? More fighting, I expect."

"Yeah." Go had a little laugh to herself. "It's all fighting from now on. We go to the Colosseum and they let the gladiators out. For some people that's what this is all about. I'm not sure."

"Are you going to join in?"

"I'll see—it's pretty hardcore. I'll check out the opposition first."

"That's what the grown-ups are for, isn't it?" Ella asked and sniffed.

Go looked at her.

"Yeah," she said.

"I can't stand it." Ella was crying. She hadn't wanted to, but she was. "I can't stand it, I can't stand it, I can't stand it. I don't want anyone else I love to get hurt, or killed. I can't stand it."

"Hey." Go wiped Ella's face. "It's all right. If it bothers you so much, I won't go in for it."

But it wasn't Go that Ella was thinking of.

58

So this Isaac kid saw her?"

"It's weird." Ed was shaking his head. Still trying to make sense of it all. "He says she was living with a sicko on a farm."

"That's more than weird," said Brooke. "That's like . . ." She thought about it. Gave up. "I don't think there's even a word for that."

It was the afternoon and the spectators had all moved around to the back of the grandstand to what Arno called the Colosseum: a large, oval-shaped arena with banks of seating all around it.

There had already been one event, Smackdown, where kids armed with lengths of wood wrapped in foam rubber had beaten the hell out of each other, like some sort of gladiatorial combat. Ed and Kyle had played for Ascot, and as a result, the white team was now in second place, just behind Windsor. Something unheard of in previous race meetings.

This was the first chance Ed had had to speak properly with Brooke. He'd had to join in Smackdown to keep Ascot near the top of the competition. Isaac's news had changed everything again, and not for the better. Ed had hoped to kill two birds with one stone here—find Ella and recruit an army. He was glad Ella was still alive, but if she was out there in the countryside somewhere, hiding, it was going to be that much harder to find her.

"Isaac left her the morning after the night of the blood moon, when the wave of sickos went through."

"What about the others?" Brooke asked, a note of desperation in her voice. "What about Robbie?"

Ed kept forgetting that Robbie was a friend of Brooke's. He'd been head of security at the museum, and she'd been living there with him for the past year.

"Nothing." Ed wished he had better news for her. "He only saw Ella. Not Maeve or Robbie or Monkey-Boy. He's offered to take us back there to look for her after the races, but . . ." Ed trailed off.

Brooke squeezed his arm.

"It's never-ending, eh?"

"We have to get back to London, Brooke. We're needed there."

They were interrupted by the band parping out a slightly stumbling version of the *Star Wars* theme.

The spectators were settling down all around them, ready for the next event.

"What happens now?" Brooke asked.

"This is where they wheel in the sickos." Ed ran a finger down his scar. "I'm sitting this one out. I've fought enough of them in my time."

Kids were marching into the arena. Two from each camp.

Mean-looking, grim-faced, serious. They all had weapons, real weapons this time, swords and spears, one with a spiked mace. And there, with his baggy white T-shirt already filthy from the day's action, was Kyle, carrying his ax. Beside him was Sean. The crowd was cheering loudly, but the gladiators all looked like they were in a world of their own. Concentrating. Some wore pieces of body armor and helmets. Some of them looked like they were from a paintball site, though a couple had boxing helmets and a few had snowboarding ones.

The two Windsor boys even had shields. Ed spotted Josa and Kenton, wearing the red of Slough. Sticking close to each other. Ed didn't recognize any of the others. They hadn't been in any of the races until now. These were specialists. Killers. The two Sandhurst guys reminded Ed of Ryan and his hunters. They were dressed all in leather—jacket, gloves, boots, even pants—glittering with sharp studs and chains. One even had a string of dried ears hanging from his belt, just like Ryan. He was the only fighter who raised his face and acknowledged the crowd. An ugly, battle-scarred face, with missing teeth and a broken nose. He looked like someone who was good for nothing except this.

"My money is on him," said Ebenezer. "He is going to punish the rest of them."

"Surely they're not going to fight each other?" Brooke was wide-eyed with disbelief. "Not with those weapons."

"Don't worry." Ed put his arm around her shoulders. He had to admit, though, that he really wasn't sure about this event. He had a sick, cold feeling in the pit of his stomach. The games had taken a darker turn.

Arno stepped up to the barrier, climbed into the arena, and stood in the middle. The king was sitting in a sort of makeshift throne in the center of the seats, grinning happily and turning his head from side to side like a clockwork toy.

"My lords, ladies, gentlemen, and whatever the hell the rest of you are," Arno called out, "we here at Ascot Entertainments and Extreme Sports Unlimited proudly present the highlight of our race meeting. The event you've all come here for. The Royal Tournament, presented in two parts. The champion of each part, gladiators and conquistadors, will be decided by you, the people. Although points are scored for kills and maimings. Who will be the champion this time in our battle royal?"

59

Kyle looked around the arena. His dad had brought him to Ascot once. He remembered coming back here to watch the horses being paraded around the arena before races so that punters could check them out and see which ones they fancied betting on. His dad had been showing off, telling Kyle all about "form," which horses were fit, the right weight, running well.

He still lost all his money betting on the wrong ones.

Well, the arena was being put to a very different use today. When Kyle had heard what this event was all about, he'd begged Sean to let him join in. The fat kid, Green, had been going to fight with Sean, and Kyle could see that he was secretly glad to be out of it.

Kyle asked Sean about the scary-looking guy with the shaved head who stuck to the king like glue. He'd seen how everyone was a bit scared of him. He was obviously handy. So why wasn't he on the team instead of the likes of Green?

"The only event he goes in for is the last part of the Royal Tournament," Sean explained. "Dunno why. Nobody questions him. Nobody ever really talks to him. He is what he is. Has his own way of doing things. Nobody even knows his name."

"Yeah? So what do you call him, then?"

"We don't call him anything. As I say, he is what he is."

Kyle was high on excitement. This was almost a medieval tournament, like something from *Game of Thrones*. He'd always liked stories and films about knights when he'd been little, and *The Lord of the Rings*. One Christmas he'd been given a Playmobil castle. Wondered where it was now. Would have loved to get it out of its box and set it up and have another battle. This was better, though. All the kids arriving at Ascot on their horses with their weapons and armor. The racing, the fighting. Shame there wasn't gonna be any jousting. Maybe he'd suggest it for the next meeting.

Not that he'd be here, he supposed. He'd be back in London by then, back at the Tower. So how about he get Jordan Hordern to set up his own races? His own Royal Tournament?

That'd be very cool.

Kyle was at home here. He liked fighting. It was that simple. All the other problems in the world disappeared when you were fighting. Nothing else mattered. It was just beat them before they beat you. His brain was clear in a fight. It was when the fighting stopped that things got complex. Confusing. Difficult.

He looked across the arena and saw Josa and Kenton. They were gonna be really sore from this morning. He hoped they wouldn't try anything stupid. Kenton had a club, and Josa carried a narrow-bladed sword.

Kyle realized the crowd had fallen silent. Arno was standing there with the king and old baldy, the nameless one. Arno waved his long stick in the air, like Gandalf on the bridge at Khazad-dûm, and the king started yelling something that Kyle couldn't understand. Then Arno cut in.

"His Royal Highness, King Loopy-Lou the Ninety-ninth, thanks you, noble fighters," Arno shouted. "I thank you, and the crowds gathered here today thank you, you mighty morons, you brain-dead dummies, prepared to suffer for our enjoyment. In a moment our merry band of musicians will give a crappy fanfare and then you will drop-kick the bogey-man!"

Arno dropped his staff. Trumpets and trombones blared, tambourines rattled, drums thumped, and the gates opened to let in the enemy.

60

A father limped into the arena carrying a length of metal piping, confused and blinking, his seminaked body a mess of sores and boils and weeping gashes. Ed rubbed his scar, which had started to throb. He hated sickos. Hated them more than anything else in the world. He had no problem slaughtering them.

So why did this feel different?

"I'm not sure I want to watch this," said Brooke.

"Remember the golden rules of this contest," Arno called out from his seat next to the king. "There are no rules. This is war now. And we can't let any of them live."

Behind the father came two more fathers, then a mother, then a whole group of them, the last being prodded in by Ascot guards carrying long spears and pikes, until there were thirty-five, maybe forty of them in the arena, huddled together. Some armed with crude weapons. Most unarmed. Aside from their fingernails and teeth.

The gate was pulled shut across the entrance. The only

way these grown-ups were getting out of there was being dragged by their heels.

The gladiators now turned to the king and raised their weapons in a salute.

"They honor you, crazy Caesar," Arno shouted. "And we offer you the blood of these bastards to make us stronger, and to help us win in the weeks ahead, until the next games. Now go to it, brethren, do it for your king, the King of Chaos. This is the death of all bad things, the triumph of the cool. You who are about to die, we salute you!"

The king tipped back his head and howled at the sky, and the howl was taken up by all the kids, like a pack of wolves, and the big bruiser from Sandhurst strode across the arena toward the sickos and cut one down with his sword and a great cry.

"*Rahhhh!*"

Ed was both horrified and fascinated. Next to him, Brooke was hiding behind her hands like a little kid watching *Doctor Who*. Ed noticed that the crowd had thinned out a little. Some kids had left, unable to watch the slaughter.

"Do you want to leave?" Ed asked Brooke.

"This is sick," she said. "And not *good* sick. I mean bad sick. Real sick. I never thought I'd feel sorry for one of 'em. But this is wrong."

"If it keeps the peace . . ." Ed didn't really know what else to say. "If it keeps these kids from killing each other, then . . ."

"This is cool," said Lewis. "It's really sick. And I mean sick as in a good thing." And then he jumped out of his seat with half of the other kids as Josa cut a mother's arm off. Ed had never seen Lewis this lively outside of a fight.

It was a full-scale massacre now, and it was hard to keep up with the action as the arena became a riot of swarming bodies. Kids running in and chopping at the sickos, stabbing, kicking, gouging. The adults fighting back now. They'd looked like a scrawny, mangy bunch, made stupid by disease and being out in the daylight, but they fought like banshees, roaming in little packs.

Ed had never watched a battle like this before; he'd only ever been in the middle of one. He figured that people had always liked watching violence, from the Romans throwing Christians to the lions, to the public executions of the Middle Ages, to slasher movies and awful stuff on the Internet.

This was still shocking, though. The grass was starting to turn red.

Those kids who had stayed to watch were loving it. This was revenge. Payback for everything that had happened in the last year.

Ed tried to pick Kyle out in the confusion.

Couldn't see what had happened to him.

He turned to Lewis.

"Can you see Kyle?"

Kyle was in among a tight bunch of sickos. They'd gotten around him quicker than he was expecting, and he was too hemmed in to swing his ax, so he was having to use it to shove them away to make some space.

He gave an almighty shove, swore at the ugly bastards, and now there was room. And then he felt the world shift sideways. He was reeling. It took a moment, but then his head exploded with pain. Something had smashed into the side of it. Must be an armed sicko. He'd seen one with an iron bar just now. He staggered in a circle, looking for him, worried that he might black out. Instead he puked, and that seemed to clear his head. The next moment, however, he felt a terrible, cold, aching jolt up his right arm, and he dropped his ax.

He'd been hit again. This time on the bicep. His whole arm had gone numb. He could barely move it.

Bastard sicko, where was he?

And then he heard a voice.

"You gonna pay for this morning, wasteman." It was

Kenton, looming out of the melee with a grin on his ugly, tattooed face, casually swinging his club in the air. Was it Kenton who'd hit him? He picked up the ax Kyle had dropped so that he was now holding two weapons, one in each hand.

"And you gonna pay for the other day an' all." Josa had come up behind Kyle. "That car was ours."

"Well, I ain't got my wallet on me," said Kyle, maneuvering for space. "So I can't pay you right now. How about I just kick your asses?"

"How about you try?" said Josa, and she lifted her sword. It glinted in the afternoon sun. It was two against one, and Kyle was unarmed.

The sensible thing to do would be to run. You can't argue with a blade. Stab wounds were bad. Hell—*any* wound was bad. He didn't want to end up bleeding to death in some stinky bed like Macca, as his poo leaked out of his punctured guts.

Trouble was, Kyle wasn't a bolter. He had too much bloody pride. To run now would be a loss of nerve, a loss of face. Fighting was his thing. The only thing he was good at. The thing that made him who he was.

An idiot, sure. But a fighter too.

Well, if it meant dying with his boots on.

Bring it on. . . .

Kenton certainly looked impressive with his two weapons. Like some ninja, kung fu warrior, or a badass *World of Warcraft* dude. But Kyle remembered him at Slough, twirling that damned shotgun. How easily Lewis had taken it off him. And two weapons at once were hard to control, especially when one was as heavy and hard to control as Brain-biter. Kenton wasn't the worry, though. Josa was.

Kyle badly needed something to defend himself with, give him an edge. What could he do? His arm still hurt like hell. He doubted he'd be able to use a weapon even if he could get ahold of one. There wasn't time for that anyway. If he switched his attention to look for something, Josa and Kenton would be on him like dogs on a bone.

A thought came to him. All sorts of things can be weapons.

He moved.

Ran hard at Kenton, getting inside his swing, going to his left, where he was struggling to raise Brain-biter with his weaker left arm. That put Kenton between Kyle and Josa. Kenton swung the ax feebly and the shaft batted harmlessly off Kyle's back. And Kyle was in. He grabbed hold of Kenton by the shirt with both hands, ignoring the pain that clawed at his wounded arm. Kenton hadn't been expecting this and had no hands free to do anything, unless he wanted to drop a weapon. And Kyle was giving him no time to think. He shoved hard, piling Kenton backward and into Josa, who couldn't get out of the way quickly enough and was now being forced back into a knot of sickos. Kyle kept moving, and as he felt the two of them start to go down, he gave one last push and they collapsed.

As they fell, Kyle grabbed Kenton's club, twisting it. Kenton, falling backward, had two options: let go or risk having his arm broken. Kyle helped him make the decision by kicking hard at his elbow. Kenton cried out in pain, and the cudgel was free. Kyle jumped over the falling bodies and ran clear, tensed, ready. Kenton, who had landed on Josa, was first up, fumbling with the ax. Kyle didn't give him a chance. He gripped the club in both hands, feeling a stab of pain that shot up his arm into his head, and swung.

He got Kenton full in the mouth. It was like hitting a tomato with a baseball bat. Bright red blood splattered out, and Kenton was down for good. The shock wave up Kyle's arm made him scream. It was shuddering and twitching in spasm.

He gritted his teeth and looked at Kenton, who was kneeling on the ground, moaning, Brain-biter dropped and forgotten.

"Now you're a matching pair," said Kyle. "The toothless twins."

Josa was up, though, and coming at Kyle in a low crouch, the blade ready in her hand. Kyle was about to lift the cudgel to a strike position with his left arm when he was grabbed by two fathers. If he hadn't been hurting so much already, he might have thrown them off, but he was powerless to do anything except curse and try to avoid their teeth.

Josa moved in for the kill. She had Kyle just where she wanted him.

And then Ed was there. And Josa went down again, punched in the side of the head. Stunned. Ed picked up Kyle's ax, cut the sickos away, and brought it around on Josa as she tried to get up.

"This ends now," he snapped. He had a look of cold, hard fury on his damaged face that even Kyle found frightening. Lots of people had made the mistake of thinking that Ed was a nice, gentle guy who wouldn't hurt a fly. Kyle knew him better. He knew that, if it came to it, Ed would drive that ax right through Josa's skull. And Josa knew it too. You could see it in her face.

"You shouldn't even be in this fight," she said.

"Show me the rule book." Ed hacked a mother aside as she came close, and Kyle could see that Josa was scared that she'd be next.

"All right," she said. "It's over."

62

Brooke was desperate. Couldn't work out what had happened. Trying to see what was going on. One moment Ed had been sitting beside her, looking for Kyle in the battle, and the next he'd sworn, leaped up, and gone racing down to the arena, completely unarmed.

He was somewhere out there. She scanned the arena and then felt relief flood over her. There he was, helping Kyle to the side, holding his ax, and swiping it at any sickos who came close.

He got to the barrier and Brooke went down to meet him. Kyle was clutching his arm and grumbling that he was all right. Ed kept telling him to shut up. Brooke helped them to climb over, and she could see that Kyle was having difficulty using his right arm.

They went back to their seats, where Lewis and Ebenezer asked them what had happened.

Brooke looked back down at the arena. The last three sickos standing, the fastest and strongest, were moving around the edge, trying to get away. Guards behind the barrier pushed them back with their weapons. Some kids in the front seats kicked out at them, laughing. The gladiators attacked in a pack and down the sickos went, one, two, three, in a flurry of flashing blades and flying blood. The Sandhurst boy even managed to finish on a high note: he swung at the last mother and took her head clean off with one blow.

"He's just showing off," said Kyle through clenched teeth.

The cheering from the crowd was the loudest yet at the races. The Sandhurst boy paraded around, holding the mother's head up by the hair, dripping blood everywhere. The guards moved in and started to drag the dead bodies clear.

Just another afternoon's sport, thought Brooke. But she knew it wasn't over yet.

Sophie had been standing at the barriers with some of her team, bows at the ready in case they needed to put down any sickos. She walked up to Ed's group.

"You ever seen anything like that?" she asked. Brooke could see there were spots of blood on her face.

"No," she said. "And I never want to again."

"Then maybe you won't want to stay for the last event," said Sophie. "They've saved the biggest, toughest, ugliest grown-ups for last."

"It just gets better," said Kyle. "See you around, Brooke."

But Brooke stayed put.

"What do you do with them bodies?" asked Lewis as two kids pulled away a fat father, one leg each.

"There's a big bonfire tonight and a big party apparently," said Sophie. "They go on that. I guess it's like a Guy Fawkes made of real people."

"Nice," said Brooke.

It took a while for the arena to be cleared of corpses, and while it went on, the gladiators took the cheers from the crowds. Lots of the kids threw things down to them, soft toys and bits of clothing, scarves that the gladiators tied around their wrists. Brooke could see that already this event was developing its own rituals as the kids celebrated their triumph over the enemy, making the nightmares go away, showing that the sickos weren't all-powerful, weren't all to be feared.

As they were sitting there, Josa came over, carrying her baby. She was alone. None of her boys around. To Brooke's surprise, she offered to shake Ed's hand.

To her even bigger surprise, Ed shook it.

"Respect," said Josa, and she offered Ed a toothless smile. Then she turned to Kyle.

"Clean slate, yeah? I know when I'm beat. You all could of come and joined us, you know. We need killers like you."

Ed shook his head, hardly believing what he was hearing. "If you'd been a bit more welcoming, maybe we'd have considered it," he said.

"You know what it's like." Josa gave a shrug. "We gotta survive. We don't trust no one. And I *do* like to play games."

"You're a bastard, Josa." Ed said it almost politely.

"Ain't I just?" Josa laughed. "Respect to you, though, yeah? From one warrior to another."

"Are you apologizing?"

"Maybe."

Ed nodded. "I guess *maybe*'s good enough for me."

"I was just doing what I had to do," said Josa. "Like I learned it."

"You've kept your people alive. You've pulled them through some hard times. I know how tough that is. Just remember what Arno said—the grown-ups are the enemy. If we're ever gonna make anything of this whole big mess, we're gonna have to work together to rebuild."

"You think that'll happen?" Josa asked. "You think any of us got a chance?"

"Maybe."

"*Maybe*'s good enough for me too," said Josa.

"That army has to be stopped first, though."

"What army?"

"The sickos that came through the other night."

"That was way heavy, man. Was all we could do to keep them out."

"They're massing. But I've got a plan."

"A man with a plan."

"Yeah. Can I rely on you to help me out, Josa?"

"Is like you said, Funny Face." Josa stared at Ed. *"Maybe."*

Her baby struggled in her arms and gave a little cry.

"What's his name?" Lewis asked.

"Tyler, after his dad." Josa poked a dirty finger in the baby's mouth. "His dad was a bit of a moron, to tell you the truth, but, you know, he *was* his dad. He died early. Golden Girl killed him. We ain't never liked them Windsor kids. Hope they don't win the cup again this year." She lifted her baby's little arm and made him wave at Ed and his gang.

"Say good-bye to the nice people, Tyler."

Brooke watched her go. She was understanding all this better now. Arno was clever. These games made sense. They were a neutral place where kids could get together and sort out their problems, and if a few sickos got mangled along the way, well, then. She shouldn't be so squeamish.

As Ed said, they were the enemy.

She just wondered what was going to happen to the rest of them in the final event.

63

Malik was sitting on the floor of his cage, just outside the arena. He was watching some kids haul a cartload of dead adults away along the road. He'd known what to expect. He'd heard the kids talking about it enough. The reality, though, seeing those carved-up bodies, made him doubt, not for the first time, whether he was doing the right thing. But his mind was set, and when he decided something he stuck with it. He'd decided to stay silent and hadn't said a word since they'd caught him in their nets.

Right now he still wanted nothing to do with the world of children. He'd known when it was time, when it felt right to go back, and being hunted and trapped like an animal hadn't made him like these kids anymore. So let them think he was a grown-up. Let them think he was diseased and good for nothing. He knew inside he was better than them. He wasn't going to give up. He was going to teach the kids a lesson. He was going to win.

Yeah, right . . .

When the Windsor kids had caught him, they'd beaten him unconscious and he'd woken in the back of a pickup truck with several comatose adults, one of whom had died on the journey. That was the only time he'd wobbled, the only time he'd tried to speak. There'd been a boy sitting in the back of the truck, holding a gun. Malik had lifted his head and croaked at him. Talking to Ella for all that time down in their hole in the ground had destroyed his voice. It was sore and dry and cracked. And a rope had tangled around his neck in the attack, making it worse.

He couldn't get any words out and the boy had kicked him and he'd fallen unconscious again. That had made his mind up. It was the last time he'd tried to talk. If he was going to get out of this, he was going to do it on his own terms. His own way.

His mom always said he was stubborn, and now it was probably going to get him killed.

Just so long as he made his mark along the way.

At the castle he'd been locked in what had once been the dungeons with all the adults they'd captured. It had been filthy and stinking and vile. They'd fed him on rotting vegetables and bits of rancid meat, and he'd become feeble and sick. The kids weren't that bothered. They only needed to keep him alive long enough to bring him here to be killed. For the most part the adults had left him alone. One night, however, a hungry father had gotten too close. He'd bothered Malik for hours, and in the end Malik had strangled him. When the kids came in in the morning to check them out, they found the man half eaten. The others had been at him all night. Malik had stolen his clothes, disguising himself more fully, covering himself in their smell. Now he hoped they'd all—adults and children—leave him in peace.

It wasn't to be, though. He was picked out and moved with a smaller group of adults to another part of the dungeon, where they were looked after better, given proper food and cleaner water. And then they were moved out of Windsor altogether. They'd been sold to Maidenhead. Seemed the kids there hadn't caught enough adults of their own to make it to the races. So Malik had been exchanged for fresh food and gasoline.

So he was a thing. Not even a person. An ugly, broken thing. Buried deep down inside him was a dark, festering thought; it chewed away at him. Was there another reason he kept away from kids? Was it the real reason he wanted nothing to do with them? Was it shame? Dirty shame.

He'd become a freak. Someone to be laughed at. They feared him because they knew they might end up like him, and, *because* they feared him, they hated him. As far as they were concerned, he was a monster. So why not behave like one? None of this would change if they found out he was a boy, would it? He could never properly be one of them. So that's what he was going to be. A dangerous monster. He would turn their hatred back on them ten times worse. A hundred times. He would make them pay for his shame.

There was only one person who didn't make him feel ashamed. Ella. She'd accepted him for what he was. And what made him lie awake at night, staring into the blackness, his guts sour with worry, was the thought that he had no idea what had happened to her. Whether she was all right.

When they'd first brought him to Windsor, and he was

lying there, sick and puked out, too feeble to even move, he wondered if they'd brought her here to the castle, and he wondered what he'd do if she came looking for him. He'd wanted to hide from her. Decided that she'd be better off with him out of her life. He'd only make things miserable for her. He was bad luck. She'd said it herself.

She didn't need to be saddled with a dog's dinner like him.

But at the same time he hadn't wanted her to see him dead. And he'd known that if he wanted to survive he had to get well, to eat more, to look after himself. So when the kids brought in buckets of slops, he'd made sure he was first to the trough, kicking back the other vermin down there, searching through for the best bits.

And this will to survive had remained strong at Maidenhead, where they'd been penned up outside. He'd killed another father soon after he'd arrived. The diseased old pus-bag had been top dog there before the newcomers from Windsor had been herded in. He'd wanted to fight Malik when he shoved to the front to get the best scraps. Malik had waited until he was sure no kids were around and strangled him like the other one, squeezing the life out of him with his bare hands. No one argued with him after that. The adults left him alone.

He could sense what they were feeling, as if he could soak up their thoughts and emotions through his pores, getting a weak pulse from their dull minds. They were hungry and confused and angry, in a sullen, sulky, depressed kind of way. And he was depressed from being among them for so long like this. He was used to hunting them, stamping them out; that's all he'd ever thought of. Lashing out against the world that had made him what he was. He couldn't kill all these, though—the kids would notice that something was wrong. Being with them, soaking up their pathetic, tiny, animal thoughts, he'd wondered if he'd been right. He didn't belong among children, but he didn't belong among adults either.

And now here he was. A pig. About to be taken to the slaughterhouse. Already the cage was being opened. A kid was poking through the bars at the back with a spear to herd them all out of there. It was starting.

This was his last chance to try to speak.

He looked at the boy and he looked at the adults, and he kept quiet.

Stubborn.

Stubborn and stupid and ashamed.

But they weren't used to taking on someone like him. He would show them today how to fight.

64

Ella was sitting with the Windsor kids. Waiting. Not sure if she wanted things to happen quicker or slower. She'd made herself watch the horrible gladiator fight, straining to see if Malik was there. So relieved when he wasn't. And now here was the last event. *With the last of the grown-ups.* Was he going to be among them?

She'd lost him when they'd been attacked near the woods, and the same thoughts had kept going around and around in her head ever since Go had told her about the races . . . Had he been killed? Had he escaped? Had he been captured and treated like a grown-up? Was he going to be here today?

She'd told Go all about him, explained that she'd been with a friend, a boy who looked like a grown-up. Asked Go to find out if he'd been picked up when they'd found her. Find out if anyone had seen him.

Go said that as far as she knew, no one had.

"His face is scarred," Ella had said. "People think he's a grown-up. But he's not, he's just a boy."

"We didn't find anybody," said Go. "I was there. I'd of

seen if there'd been any other kids. We almost didn't find you. You were buried under a pile of dead ones."

"Dead grown-ups?"

"Yeah. A lot got killed in the attack. We couldn't bring them all back here."

"So Malik could have been killed?"

"There were no other children, Ella. Just you."

Ella had begged to be allowed to see for herself, to look at the grown-ups in the dungeon. See if Malik was among them.

He wasn't.

He'd gone.

She prayed that he was safe somewhere.

The raggedy band started playing Darth Vader's music, "The Imperial March" from *Star Wars*, and kids were riding into the arena.

Golden Boy came in first, arm in the air with a clenched fist. Half the kids were cheering, half booing. He pulled his sword from his scabbard.

"This is my sword," he shouted. "This is it! I shall not return it to its sheath until it is stained red with the blood of the fallen."

"He can be such a jerk," said Go.

Behind Golden Boy came the scary-looking Ascot boy who was usually guarding the king. He was wearing a white sweatshirt over his clothes, the hood up and half covering his face. Then, from Sandhurst—Ella had quickly learned the colors of the different camps—a big boy in leather on a horse that was a bit too small for him. He was sitting uncomfortably and looked all wobbly. If Ella hadn't been so anxious she would have laughed. From Slough there was a girl with a ponytail, her head shaved around the sides. Then there was a boy from Maidenhead and a girl from Bracknell, both with lances.

They all went around and around the arena, encouraging the kids to cheer for them and throw more stuff into the ring. All sorts of rubbish was fluttering down. The Maidenhead rider speared a teddy bear on his lance and held it up in the air, grinning.

At last the band stopped, and the people stopped cheering and making so much noise, and the riders got ready, drawing their swords, patting their horses' necks to calm them down.

Everyone was waiting now. Ella wanted to be sick. Time had slowed down until it felt like it had stopped.

And then a great shout went up as the grown-ups were forced into the ring, shielding their faces from the light. These ones were bigger and stronger-looking than the first group. They didn't seem so scared and confused. They were angry, ready for a fight, the pick of the pack. Most of them were fathers, but there were some nasty-looking mothers among them, baring their teeth at the kids. One ripped down her top and bared her breasts at the crowd, who screamed with laughter. Ella just felt embarrassed.

The grown-ups spotted the riders and formed a group, waiting. Ella searched them, looking at their faces, the way they were standing, what they were wearing, trying to see if Malik was among them.

No, just ugly, diseased grown-ups, mothers and fathers and . . .

There. Right in the middle of the pack, trying not to stand out.

Ella wished that time really had stopped and would never start again.

Malik. His movements so familiar to her. Sniffing the air, his head turning and twisting to check out the whole area, thinking, planning, getting ready.

What could he do? What plan could he have? What hope did he have against these kids with their horses and their sharp weapons? Their swords and lances.

All her fault.

Golden Boy raised his sword and charged, shouting, "Windsor . . ."

And the rest of them followed. All shouting except for the bald boy.

"Bracknell . . ."

"Maidenhead . . ."

"Sandhurst . . ."

"Slough . . ."

65

The horses were coming, thundering across the arena, and Malik was moving. He wanted to stay in among the pack, where he'd be a harder target to pick out. The half-naked mother stepped forward, snarling and hissing. Golden Boy galloped in, swinging his horse around so that his sword arm was on the right side, chopped down, aiming for the neck, but getting her across the face and cutting it diagonally. She hissed again and staggered sideways, and as Golden Boy pulled his horse around so that he didn't career into the tightly packed mob of bodies and lose momentum, it knocked into her and she went down.

The Bracknell girl with the lance was right behind him; she managed a direct hit on a young father, the head of the lance going right through him. The horse carried her on, but she wasn't able to pull the lance clear and, so rather than risk being unsaddled, she let go and left the lance there as the man flipped and flopped on the grass. She yanked out a sword and slashed at a pack of grown-ups who were crowding around her. Malik saw two fall down before the Bracknell girl was able to pull away. It was all happening fast. There were horses on both sides of him now. He had to thin the kids' numbers. He had to take some of them out of the game.

He chose the Sandhurst rider first. He wasn't confident in the saddle and was kicking wildly and swearing as he tried to get his horse to do what he wanted. And now the horse bolted, racing across the arena, and Malik picked his moment. He waited until the jittery animal came close, then he darted out of the pack and jumped in front of it, waving his arms in the air. The horse reared up, and the Sandhurst boy gave a disappointed cry as he went tumbling backward over the rear end and landed with a heavy thump on the blood-wet grass. In its mad scramble the horse trampled on the boy's legs, and he rolled clear before crawling toward the side of the arena to get away. Two Ascot guards scrambled over the barrier to help him.

Malik was still moving. He was out in the open and exposed. He was right behind the Bracknell horse, however. The girl was good, but her horse was panicking, spooked by the riderless Sandhurst mount that was whinnying as it dashed around the confined space, looking for a way out. Malik slapped the rump of the Bracknell horse as hard as he could, and it bolted, crashing into the Maidenhead horse. The two of them blundered into the barriers, where the Bracknell horse tripped, spilling the girl into the seats. Spectators shrieked as they jumped out of the way of the rider. The Maidenhead boy managed to stay in the saddle but had lost his lance, which had become tangled in the barrier.

That was two down, four left.

A shout.

Malik spun around.

Golden Boy had spotted him.

Ed was impressed with the grungy sicko. He was smaller and slighter than the others, probably the youngest one out there. He must be a teenager. His face was awful, like a doll that had been chewed by a dog. Knotted with scar tissue. Ed sometimes gave in to self-pity when he looked at himself in a mirror. Greg had cut him badly down the cheek and without proper surgery the wound hadn't healed well. Compared to the young sicko, though, he was a fashion model.

He was used to seeing sickos, used to the way the disease ate away at them, erupted from under the skin, making their faces a vile pizza of boils and lumps and sores, with other parts rotted and falling away. This sicko was one of the worst Ed had ever seen. He was also the best fighter he'd ever seen. He was fast and seemed clever.

It was chaos in the arena and a lot of the sickos were just wandering aimlessly; others, seemingly made bolder by the young sicko, were more dangerous and made murderous dashes at the riders. It was clear that Golden Boy and the others hadn't been expecting any real opposition from the sickos. This was meant to be kids showing off their horse-manship and their skills with sword and lance. This was meant to be a one-sided polo match, but the young sicko had turned it into something different. It was a competition now, and the spectators were enjoying it.

The place had held so many races over the years; so many bets had been won and lost. Ed had been struck, when Golden Boy had led the riders into the arena, that this was how it used to be. Riders coming in and parading around before a race.

Surely nothing quite like this had ever been seen here before.

"Look at him go, man," said Lewis, who was sitting next to Ed. "My money's on the sicko."

"Let's hope he makes that Windsor ass look stupid," said Kyle.

Golden Boy tried to run the grungy sicko down, but he darted back into the main pack and got lost among them.

Golden Boy viciously cut down an older father on the edge of the pack, slicing half his face off. The Maidenhead boy had gotten his lance free and was now charging at the pack himself. They parted, suddenly exposing the young sicko, and it looked like his game was surely up. There wasn't quite enough space in the arena for the boy's charge to gain speed, however, and the young sicko just had time to shunt the tip of the boy's lance down into the ground, where it stuck fast. The lance levered the boy up, lifting him out of the saddle and tipping him over to the side. He let go of his weapon and flung his arms around his horse's neck and somehow managed to cling on.

Both actions had gotten a massive cheer from the crowd, and Ed glanced over at Arno. This was supposed to be the triumph of good over evil, but one of the demons was winning the crowd.

One of the kids needed to kill him, and kill him quickly.

Ella was trying to push her way to the front of the grandstand, but all the kids were up and out of their seats, blocking the aisles, shoving each other this way and that for a better look, shouting and roaring. Someone barged into her and knocked her to the floor. She was in danger of being stepped on.

She couldn't see what was going on in the arena. From the reactions of the crowd it sounded like it was going crazy.

"Let me through," she screamed. "Let me through!"

They ignored her, or didn't hear her, didn't care.

"Let me through . . ."

It was hopeless. She'd have to find another way down.

The grown-ups were being thinned out. The shaved-head boy in the white hoodie was expertly riding through them, chopping left and right. Malik wanted to keep well clear of him. With his white hood hiding his face, he reminded Malik of the guy in *Assassin's Creed*. And that's what he was—an assassin. The Slough girl and the Maidenhead boy had stopped moving, they were too penned in by bodies. The Maidenhead boy didn't seem to have another weapon now that he'd lost his lance, and he was kicking the sickos who clawed at him.

The Slough girl sat there, her sword rising and falling, rising and falling rhythmically. Malik recognized her as one of Josa's gang that had tormented him back in the day when he'd been Tyler's bitch. He sneaked in closer, never taking his eye off that deadly, flashing steel, up and down, up and down, blood flying off the blade. He timed his move, leaped in, grabbed her forearm, and easily pulled her from the saddle. She really hadn't been expecting this and went stage-diving into the pack of adults. He left her there, floundering around on the ground as the adults pawed and groped at her.

The Maidenhead rider had seen what was happening and slid out of his saddle, elbowing his way toward the fallen girl. Well, that was brave at least, and Malik left him to it. The Ascot Assassin was also coming over to help, cutting a path through the sickos.

The three of them had their hands full and now was Malik's chance. He needed to get an advantage. He wanted a horse. He wriggled clear of the grown-ups and ran into the center of the arena, getting Golden Boy's attention. Golden Boy gave a happy whoop as he closed in for the kill.

Malik had observed how Golden Boy's skills had been getting sloppy as he'd grown more and more angry.

He was still armed, though, and on horseback. This was no time for Malik to get sloppy as well. He'd wanted to show these kids how to fight, not how to die.

Golden Boy was coming fast, his sword up, leaning forward slightly, his face red with fury, teeth bared like a grown-up. Malik stayed still, tensed, letting the boy pick his target and line of attack. As Golden Boy got close enough, he took a swing. Malik was ready. He quickly dodged around to the other side of the horse, and as it went past, he grabbed Golden Boy's boot and boosted it upward, spilling the already overbalanced boy, made heavy by his black-and-gold armor, out of his saddle. He tumbled to the ground in a tangle of limbs. Malik hurried to keep up with the horse, slowed it by pulling at the flapping reins, then easily swung up onto its back. Roy and Waggers and Tomasz and the other survivalists back on the farm all those months ago had taught him how to ride.

To ride and hunt.

And he'd discovered he was good at it. He felt comfortable being back in the saddle. This horse was well trained, a joy to ride. Malik cantered around the arena, getting the feel of it. Golden Boy was standing up, and Malik guided the horse toward him, nudging him over with the horse's flank, and as he tried to get up, knocking him down again. Some of the crowd were yelling abuse at him, but some were laughing and cheering. They hadn't expected this. A sicko on a horse.

The Maidenhead boy and the Ascot kid had rescued the fallen Slough girl and taken her to the side. Maidenhead was now running over to help Golden Boy. Malik left them to it. The Assassin was the real threat. Malik rode over to the center of the arena.

He wheeled his horse around and was close enough to look at the Ascot boy properly for the first time, even though most of the boy's face was shaded by the white hood. He was pale, with dead eyes that showed nothing. A memory stirred deep down in Malik's brain. There was something familiar about him.

Was it just that he looked so much like the *Assassin's Creed* killer, or was it something else?

Where did Malik know him from? *Think.*

· · ·

Ed didn't know what to think. His plans had been to try to win the races for Ascot and choose his prize. But Kyle had had to retire from the first gladiator event after Josa had attacked him. So there had been no points there. As far as he could tell, Ascot was just behind Windsor in the scoring. Whichever of the two teams won this event would be the outright winner. At the moment, however, he was rooting for the young sicko on the horse. The guy was going to be killed. There was no way of escaping from the arena alive.

Not for a sicko.

He was brave, though, and he'd won over half the crowd. He sat there on the white horse in the center of the arena, unarmed, daring the king's bodyguard to come for him.

And the Ascot boy was carrying a hefty sword. A great cleaver. He walked his horse toward the sicko, an unreadable expression on his face. If he killed him now, Ascot would have surely won.

Ed saw a movement in the crowd. Sophie and her archers were getting ready behind the barriers with their bows. Arno shouted a command, and a few of them loosed arrows point-blank at the last of the other sickos.

That left just the young guy on the horse, and Sophie's archers were all now aiming at him. Just to make sure there could be no mistakes, a small group of kids armed with swords and clubs climbed over the barrier and formed up behind the king's bodyguard.

They were taking no chances.

Golden Boy pulled away from the Maidenhead kid, who was helping him, strode across the arena toward the body-guard, and shouted as loudly as he could.

"Give me your horse."

The Ascot boy didn't react in any way. Golden Boy shouted again.

"I said, give me your horse. I order you."

Golden Boy stood there for a moment longer, frustrated. Then looked around the arena. Some of the crowd started chanting.

"Kill him—kill him—kill him . . ."

And the band piped up, blasting out a two-note fanfare in time with the chanting—*Blaa-bah . . . blaa-bah . . . blaa-bah . . .*

Other kids were trying to shout them down.

"Let him fight!"

"Give him a chance!"

The bodyguard raised a palm toward the archers, indicating that they should hold back, and then he walked his horse closer to Malik, making no effort to ready his sword. He didn't look like a boy about to kill someone, though Ed had no doubt that he could easily take the sicko down if he wanted. He'd watched him in action, slaying sickos with a well-rehearsed savagery.

The Ascot boy stopped his horse. Seemed to be studying Malik.

Golden Boy, meanwhile, had run across the grass, grabbed his sword where it had fallen, and mounted the Maidenhead horse. Now he came charging back toward Malik. But the Ascot boy shifted his horse slightly and Golden Boy had to veer off to one side.

"Get out of my way, you retard!" Golden Boy yelled, cantering at Ascot. Ascot casually punched him in the face, knocking him out of his saddle. For the second time that day Golden Boy hit the ground, this time much harder. He lay there, stunned and amazed, for a couple of seconds, then looked over to Arno and the king. Arno was as mystified as anyone. The king was enjoying the show, rolling his head and grinning.

"What the hell's going on?" Golden Boy shouted. "Are you going to let this happen? What is this?"

Arno shrugged.

Everyone waited to see how it was going to play out.

The hooded boy rode right up to Malik, held out his hand, and Malik gripped it.

And then he remembered.

"Henry?" he said quietly. And he laughed. He'd never expected to see Henry again. Henry, the damaged kid who'd disappeared in Slough after Andy died. Henry, who'd never been quite all there. Looked like he'd finally found his place in the world, here in Ascot.

Maybe there was a place for everybody after all. Maybe there was a place for Malik? If Henry was one of them, maybe *he* could be too.

"You're okay?" he said.

Henry nodded, still blank-faced.

Malik laughed again, dug his heels into his horse's flanks, and began a circuit of the arena. Jumping over fallen bodies, waving to the crowd, taunting them.

Would they dare kill him now?

67

Ella was crying. Whether she was happy or sad she didn't
know. All she knew was that there were tears pouring down her face. She watched as Golden Boy ran over to
Arno and the king and started waving his arms and shouting. Other kids came down and joined them. Arno talked to
them for a while as Malik rode around and around. Ella was
so proud of him. He was the champion of the races. He was
her hero.

Arno lifted up his staff and the crowd quieted down, the
band ceased making a noise. Malik stopped in the center of
the arena, next to the Ascot boy.

"There are some rules at the races," Arno shouted. "And
there is one rule in life, and that rule is that all grown-ups
must be killed. It's no different here. Okay, so this one has
shown he's smarter than most, but we can't let him go. Henry,
if you don't want to do it, you have to come away and leave
it to someone else."

The Ascot boy, Henry, shook his head.

"Henry, your king commands it. That thing must die."

Ella realized she was running around the barrier to the king. She grabbed Arno's sleeve and pulled it, bringing his staff down. He looked a little bit surprised and a little bit angry.

Ella turned to face the kids in the seats.

"He's not a thing!" she shouted. "And he's not a grown-up. He's my friend. He's a boy like you. You just never bothered to find out. He's one of us. You have to believe me. He's just a boy. Just a boy."

Arno leaned over and talked quietly to her.

"Go back to your seat, little girl," he said. "I'm in charge here. I have to do this, okay?"

"No . . . no . . . you don't . . ." Ella was crying again. She thought she was going to choke on her tears.

"Holy crap," said Lewis, rising from his seat. He shook Ed's shoulder. "It's her, Ed. It's Ella."

"What? You're joking."

"Straight up. That little girl down there is Ella. We've found her, man."

Ed stood now and made his way down to Arno with Lewis and Ebenezer. Arno raised his staff again just as they got there.

"Wait!" Ed shouted. "I think we should listen to what the girl's got to say."

Ella was staring at him with her mouth open. Lewis and Ebenezer went to her. Ed left them to it. They crouched down by the startled girl, jabbering away, trying to explain what was going on. She threw her arms around Ebenezer's neck and hugged him tight. Ed was aware of everything slipping into chaos. Kids were getting out of their seats. Guards were stepping over the barrier and moving in on the grungy guy. Ella was babbling on about him being her friend. It seemed really important to her.

"With me," Ed commanded, and Lewis came over to him. Ebenezer scooped Ella up and followed. As Ed entered the arena, he spotted Sophie with her archers, ready to shoot.

"Put your weapons down!" he shouted.

She looked confused. Nobody knew what to do.

"You remember Ella?" Lewis called over to her. "This is her, right? This is who we been searching for."

"Oh my God." Sophie now climbed the barrier with some of her archers, and they joined Ed in the middle of the arena. Ella was still rattling on, and Ebenezer and Lewis were trying to make sense of it. Ed saw Arno look really furious for the first time, as control was slipping through his fingers. He had to find a way to fix this without Arno losing face. The races were important.

The grungy guy on the horse was the key. Ed started walking toward him. Could he really be only a boy as Ella was claiming? Up close he looked even worse. His face had been torn apart; one eye was red and blind. The other eye seemed to be weeping but was staring at Ed with a look of intense intelligence. And Ed felt like it was looking at him from out of his past. As Ed got to the horse, the guy suddenly slipped out of his saddle and grabbed him. For a second Ed thought he was attacking him, and then he realized the guy was sobbing. Ed relaxed. The guy whispered one word in his ear.

"Ed . . ."

Ed was more astonished than ever. It was a voice from a million years ago. Cracked and croaky, but unmistakably the same voice. The voice of a dead person.

And then the dead person let him go and got back on his horse and rode over to Arno and the king.

"My name is Malik," he said, loud enough so that all could hear, and then he went on, his voice growing in strength and clarity as it got louder and louder. "I am fifteen years old. I went to Rowhurst School in Kent, and I grew up in Slough. I am a boy. I am one of you. This is how I look, and you are all just going to have to get used to it."

He rode back into the middle of the arena, raised his arms, and yelled at the watching kids.

"I am a boy, all right? And I am never going to forget it again."

There was silence for a moment; everyone was still. And then a girl threw down a doll, someone else threw a teddy, then a baseball cap came spinning down, and the air was filled with toys and clothes.

Ed was surprised to find tears running down his face. He was doing something he hadn't done for almost a year.

He was crying.

He pulled his baggy white Ascot T-shirt off.

"Put this on," he said to Malik, and Malik understood. He slipped the T-shirt over his head. He dismounted, and Ed and Kyle hoisted Malik up on to their shoulders.

"Ascot!" Ed yelled. "Ascot wins!"

CLOSING

There were thirteen children gathered in Arno's meeting room inside the stadium: Ed, Kyle, Malik, the Golden Twins, Josa and Kenton, the leaders from Sandhurst, Maidenhead, and Bracknell, plus Arno Fletcher, the Mad King, and his bodyguard, Henry.

On the way in, Arno had taken Ed aside.

"I'm letting you do this because we have a weird situation on our hands," he'd said. "You've seen what the races do. You've seen how important they are. If they fall apart we go back to the bad times. You turned it all upside down. The kids are still arguing out there."

"They'll be talking about what happened here today for months," Ed protested. "For years. That's a good thing, Arno. Your races will be legendary."

"I have rules, though, Ed. First among them was that Ascot was never, *ever* going to win. That way I could never be accused of cheating or fixing anything. If the king and I lose our authority, the races won't work."

"Let me say my piece," Ed had pleaded. "If I can pull this

off, nobody's gonna worry about any of this. All the attention will be on me. The heat'll be off you. Okay? You trust me?"

"Not really, no. Not after today."

"Christ's sake, Arno. I had no idea any of that was going to happen."

"Whatever. We've got to clear the air. So I'll let you say your piece. But it better be good."

Ed waited for the other kids to settle down around a large conference table. He was reminded of the last time he'd tried to make a rousing speech, back at the museum. He just hoped this wasn't going to be a repeat of that embarrassment.

"So what's this all about?" Golden Boy asked, his voice cold and businesslike.

Ed took a deep breath. "Ascot won the races," he said.

"That's debatable," said Golden Boy.

"So we get to choose our prize."

"Go on, then," said the Sandhurst leader, Dara. He at least knew Ed a little from their crazy get-together the other night. "Let's hear it."

"It's simple." Ed smiled at them. "I want you all."

"What are you talking about?" said Golden Girl.

"Why don't you all shut up and let Funny Face finish?" said Josa. "Then we can get to the party."

"It's like this." Ed looked around at their faces. He had their attention, which was a start. "You all saw the sickos the other night," he said. "The night of the bloodred moon, a wave of them passing through."

There were mumbled yeses from around the table.

"They were headed for London," Ed went on.

"How do you know that?" asked Dara.

"I just do, okay?"

"We're from London," said Kyle. "We've seen what's going on. There's a massive army of sickos building up there."

"So what?" said the Bracknell boy. "That's not really our problem, is it?"

"It is, though," Ed insisted. "If we allow them to get strong, to build an army, they'll wipe us out. All of us. This is our one chance to end it for all time. If we got our own army together we could slaughter every last one of them. I've seen what you lot are capable of. I saw your best fighters in action today, and it was awesome. All I want from you—my prize as the winner—is that you bring your best fighters with me into London, your horses, your vehicles, your weapons, and we take the fight to the enemy. We'll make the races real. We'll defeat the sickos for real. We will win this!"

Ed stopped. Held his breath. The faces around the table were giving nothing away.

There was a long silence.

And then Josa stood up.

"I'm in," she said.

Dara shook his head. "I'm not letting you have all the fun," he said, and he too stood up.

Ed let out his breath.

Perhaps his plan had worked.

The journey back to the Beeches seemed to take no time at all, and, no matter how much he told himself not to worry until he got there, Ed had to admit he was nervous about what they'd find. When the sickos had gone on their stampede the other night, had they gotten inside? The place was pretty well protected, so it was possible that if they'd come through this way they would have just gone around the walls.

Maybe this was going to be one of those days when everything went well.

Wouldn't that be nice?

It had certainly started well. A convoy of vehicles and horses had left Ascot. Kids from Slough and Sandhurst, Bracknell and Windsor. Sophie and her archers from Ascot. Only Maidenhead had turned Ed down.

The sun was shining and they hadn't spotted a single living sicko since they'd left Ascot. Not even a sentinel. You could almost imagine it was over and the sickos had all left or died.

Now that *would* be a good day. If all went well, if there were enough of them, then maybe that day would come.

Ed had spent a lot of the previous night catching up with Malik. Still couldn't quite believe that he was alive and they'd met up again after all this time. At first Ed had been scared that Malik would hate him for abandoning him back at Rowhurst, but there had been none of that. Malik had said he understood; that as far as Ed knew, Malik had been killed. So Malik had told his story, and Ed in turn had told him what had happened to all their friends, the sad list of death and horror and madness. There was still a lot of catching up to do. But there would be time. Ed really hoped there would be time.

The one thing Ed was still finding hard was his old school friend's voice coming out of that face. One more thing he was just going to have to get used to. His own injuries seemed trivial compared to Malik's. The two of them were sitting in the back of the Chrysler with Ella, who seemed to have an incredibly strong bond with Malik. Kyle and Lewis were up front. Brooke and Ebenezer in the middle seats. Everyone talking. Excited. Nervous.

When they got to the Beeches' driveway, Ed told Lewis to stop, and he got out. The rest of the convoy stopped behind them, spread out all down the road. Ed walked over to the lead Sandhurst vehicle, a battered old pickup truck with about fifteen kids crammed in the back.

Ed indicated for the driver to wind his window down. "You all stay out here, and we'll go on in. We won't be long. But if we all rock up together, they'll be seriously freaked out."

"No worries," said Dara. "I'll tell the others. See you soon."

Ed got back in the Chrysler, and they turned into the driveway. Everything looked fine. There were some signs of disruption, what you might find after a storm, leaves and branches strewn about the place. So it was possible that the sickos had come through.

Wait and see, Ed. Wait and see. Could just be the wind.

They pulled up on the parking area in front of the house and Ed cautiously got out, remembering the last time they'd arrived here with an unwelcome hitchhiker on the roof. He superstitiously checked the roof rack, although he knew that was stupid. There was nothing up there.

"Well?" Lewis had gotten out and was staring at the house, checking the windows. There didn't seem to be any signs of damage. No broken glass, or splintered wood. Ed looked at the garden wall. It was surely too high for any sickos to climb.

"Let's not stand around here all day, yeah?" said Brooke. "We need to keep moving. Let's knock."

Lewis shuffled over, pants hanging down, scratching his head. He swung the big door knocker three, four times.

They waited.

Lewis knocked again.

"What if they've gone?" said Ebenezer. "Tried to excape the grown-ups or something?"

"Where would they go?" Ed asked. "A bunch of old people. Half of them demented."

He went back over to the car. Leaned in the door. Malik and Ella were the only two who hadn't gotten out.

"You want to stay there or come inside?" he asked. Malik looked to Ella, the two of them inseparable.

"As long as they're not mean to Malik," said Ella.

"They won't be. They're good people." Ed could hear Lewis and the others banging on the door and calling up at the windows. "If they can accept Trinity without a blink, they'll accept Malik."

"I just want to get back to the museum and see Sam," said Ella.

"We will. We have to pick up Trinity, then we'll go. The cars, the faster vehicles, can go on ahead. The rest of the kids can catch up. We'll be an hour on the road at the most."

"We'll get out," said Ella, undoing her seat belt.

Brooke came back over from the house, smiled at Ella. Her face changed when she smiled, which wasn't that often. The scar on her forehead almost disappeared, and she looked younger and more carefree.

She put an arm round Ella and squeezed her.

"You looking forward to seeing your brother again?"

Ella nodded but said nothing, too emotional to speak. She'd been completely hysterical when she'd realized that Sam wasn't dead. That he was waiting for her back in London. Since then she'd hardly slept and had a perpetually anxious look on her thin little face. She was scared that something would happen to him before she got back there.

Kyle called over to Ed.

"You want me to kick the door in?"

"No, Kyle. I don't."

Ed strode up to the door. He was going to try himself. As if his knocking would be any different from Lewis's. Just before he grabbed hold of the knocker, however, the door opened a crack.

And there was Trey. His face broke into the biggest, happiest smile Ed had ever seen, and as the crack in the doorway widened, it revealed Trio, also grinning like an idiot. They came running out and started hugging everyone, even Ella.

"Don't say it!" shrieked Trio. "Don't say it! I don't believe it. Are you the famous Ella?"

Ella nodded, a little overwhelmed.

"Too much," said Trio, and they turned to Malik.

"Is he with you?" Trey asked. "Or should I be scared right now?"

"Malik's with me," said Ed. "He's an old friend."

Malik managed to somehow form his damaged face into something like a smile.

"Any friend of Ed's is a friend of ours," said Trio, and they hugged him too.

"Welcome to the club, dude," said Trey. "Always good to have another Twisted Kid around."

"That's enough huggy-kissy crap," said Brooke. "This is turning into the end of a bad American sitcom."

"You've got no heart, Brooke," said Trio.

"I've got a heart, all right," said Brooke. "But I've also got a Yuckometer. What took you so long to answer the door?"

"We were in the back is all," said Trey. "The oldsters are having lunch. We weren't listening out for anyone. We don't exactly get many visitors. Maybe the occasional package from Amazon, but that's about it."

"We are just so relieved to see you," said Trio. "I was,

like, we're never going to see them again. A whole, like, army of the fallen went past."

"Tell us about it," said Kyle. "We nearly got trampled into mincemeat."

Ed smiled. "Today is a good day," he said. "And we're gonna make sure tomorrow is even better. I feel it in the air. The tide has turned. We're gonna roll the sickos out of here. We're gonna win, Trinity. We are going to *win*."

Dr. Norman appeared in the doorway, wobbling on his sticks, beaming and jovial. He shook everyone's hand as they went in, pleased to see them all safe and sound.

As they walked toward the dayroom, Trey had a quiet word with Ed.

"What did I tell you?" he said. "Rule of three."

"How do you mean?"

"Three scarred faces. It's significant. You and Brooke and your friend Malik. It was always going to be."

70

The light was washing in through the long windows down the side of the dayroom, falling on the old people, who were enjoying the warmth and the brightness, outlining their faces with silver. Some were sleeping, some were talking, some were reading, some just sat there lost in thought. It was a scene of peacefulness and calm.

Ed spotted Amelia's sister, Dot, sitting all alone, staring out of the window and talking quietly to herself, her fingers picking distractedly at the arms of her chair.

A thought struck him. There was someone missing.

"Where's Amelia?" he asked. "I don't see her."

"Ah . . ." Dr. Norman sat down at an empty table, seemingly too tired to stand any longer. Ed and the others joined him. The doctor's skin looked pale and transparent with the sun on it, his skull showing clearly, laced with blue veins, his hair so fine, his eyes like clouded glass.

"She caught a cold. It went down into her lungs. Got pneumonia. I did what I could. I tried antibiotics. It wasn't enough. It's never enough. I'm sorry. She liked you all very much. She asked about you just before . . ."

Ed sighed and rested his head in his hands. All good things came with bad things.

"Her sister?" he asked. "Dot?"

"She's fading fast. We all are."

Trio put a hand on Ed.

"We learned so much before she died. She taught us everything she knew. And Dr. Norman as well." She smiled at him and he blushed like a teenager. "He pretends not to remember. But he's still got it."

"We passed our knowledge on to a new generation," said the doctor. "We're the last of the old world. We'll all be gone soon. This place will be empty, except for ghosts. All most of us want now is to be able to sit in the sun one more time. It's a ghastly world out there, beyond these walls. It seems that every generation leaves behind a mess for the next one to clean up."

"We'd better go," said Ed.

"Won't you at least stay for some lunch?"

"Sorry." Ed shook his head. "We've got to get back to London."

"We'll need some time," said Trey. "We've got to get our stuff together, and there's some useful equipment that Amelia said we could take. I mean, there's a few last things I want to . . . I need to . . . there's a spider on the wall . . ."

"What?" Ed looked at Trey. His eyes were twitching, darting about.

"Blue, Bluetooth, Blu tack . . . Blu-Tack Bill can count

them all . . . my helicopter . . . my hovercraft . . . there are three . . . bright eyes . . . they've taken bright eyes . . . I won't fight . . ."

"Are you okay?" said Brooke, although it was clear that Trey wasn't. And Trio had closed her eyes now, her head lolling.

Trey's eyes began to slowly roll back in his head, and then he flopped forward. The doctor gently helped him down so that Trinity was lying on the tabletop.

"It's been happening more and more lately," he said. "Mr. Three's been getting worked up all the time. He's very agitated. I do wish we could understand more of what he says, though."

Sure enough, Mr. Three was uncurling from where he nestled on Trinity's back. His bulgy eyes opened and he shuddered, shook himself, like a dog having a bad dream.

And then suddenly he was screaming.

"You've got to go! Before it's too late!" He was waving his tiny arms frantically, looking around the faces of the kids with a deranged expression. "You've got to go fast and you've got to help the others in London the others they're in terrible danger you have to help get there as soon as you can they're being massacred killed . . . Sam! Sam! They're after Sam! Help him help the boy they've killed the boy you have to help us! They've killed the boy . . ."

His voice got louder and more demented, growing to a shrill, piercing shriek.

"Go now! Go now! Go now!"

ABOUT THE AUTHOR

Charlie Higson is an acclaimed writer of screenplays and novels, and is also a performer and the co-creator of the British television shows *The Fast Show* and *Bellamy's People*. He is the author of the internationally best-selling Young Bond series: *SilverFin*, *Blood Fever*, *Double or Die*, *Hurricane Gold*, and *By Royal Command*, and *SilverFin: The Graphic Novel*; and six books in the Enemy series. Charlie, a big fan of horror movies, is hoping to give readers many sleepless nights with this series.